IN THE WAKE OF THE
KRAKEN

PIRATE TALES FROM ACROSS THE MULTIVERSE

SKULL GATE

IN THE WAKE OF THE KRAKEN

PIRATE TALES FROM ACROSS THE MULTIVERSE

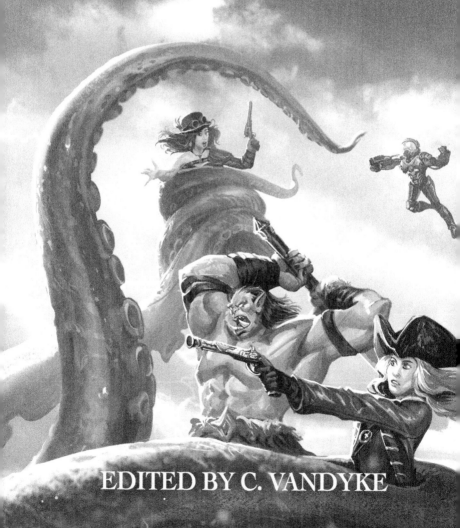

EDITED BY C. VANDYKE

Tales From the Year Between is a publication of Skullgate Media

"Tales From the Year Between," "Skullgate Media" and associated logos copyright © 2021 Skullgate Media LLC

ISBN 978-1-956042-00-9

Ebook ISBN 978-1-956042-01-6

www.skullgatemedia.com

First edition

Cover illustration by Duy Phan, aka Phanduy on Fiverr

Cover design and internal layout by Chris Vandyke

Map illustrations by Aaron Hockett, Michael D. Nadeau, Dewi Hargreaves, and C. Vandyke. Copyrights for each belong to their respective illustrators.

Group author portraits were commissioned via Fiverr.com. For links to each artist, see the acknowledgements page.

All fonts are either licensed or open-source. If you believe any images or fonts were used without license or attribution, please contact us so we can correct the oversight.

IN THE WAKE OF THE KRAKEN STAFF

Skullgate Media Staff
Chris Durston
Diana C. Gagliardi
Debbie Iancu-Haddad
C. D. Storiz
C. Vandyke

Game Masters
Diana C. Gagliardi
C. Vandyke

Lead Editors
Chris Durston
C. D. Storiz

Guest Editors
B. K. Bass
Jayme Bean
Jonathan Beck
A. E. Bross

Chapel Graham
C. J. Henderson
A. R. K. Horton
Jeremy Nelson
Sarah Parker
Katherine Shaw

Editor-in-Chief
C. Vandyke

To Captain Hook, Jack Sparrow, the Dread Pirate Roberts, Han Solo, Captain Shakespeare, and all the other fictional pirates who inspired us. Arr, avast, and may your timbers be ever shivered.

Crazy people don't know they're crazy, therefore I'm not crazy. Isn't that crazy?

— CAPTAIN JACK SPARROW

The pirate he will sink you with a kiss
    He'll steal your heart and sail away
    He'll leave you drowning in the flotsam of a broken promise in the bay.

— JONI MITCHELL, "THE PIRATE OF PENANCE,"

Yes, as through this world I've wandered
    I've seen lots of funny men;
    Some will rob you with a six-gun,
    And some with a fountain pen.

— WOODY GUTHRIE, "PRETTY BOY FLOYD"

IN THE WAKE OF THE
KRAKEN

PIRATE TALES FROM ACROSS THE MULTIVERSE

CONTENTS

INTRODUCTION

C. VANDYKE

*I*n most versions of reality, this book doesn't exist. One year ago, Skullgate Media was started by an impulsive tweet that I very nearly didn't send. Had I chosen instead to tweet a cute GIF of Pikachu or an inane question ("Hey, writers! What's your MC put on their waffles?"), you wouldn't be reading this right now. Had the writers who responded chosen not to check their phones or shrugged and scrolled on to something else instead of sending me a DM, you wouldn't be reading this book. There were countless inflection points where different choices could have been made, and most would have resulted in a world where there is no Skullgate Media, no Tales From the Year Between, no *In the Wake of the Kraken.*

And yet, remarkably and against all odds, we are living in the version of reality where all those things came to pass. While I lack Doctor Pangloss's confidence that we are living in "the best of all possible worlds" (see: November 8th, 2016 through all of 2020 as a counterpoint to such a rosy view), I'm still pretty happy to find myself writing an introduction to an anthology that marks our first anniversary as a publisher.

It seems fitting that we're celebrating that anniversary with a volume that traipses through the multiverse. Tales From the Year Between is premised on strangers coming together to create new and unexpected worlds, and on a macro-level, that's what our entire company is—a new and unexpected world formed by strangers with shared desires for story-telling and collaboration. In our two previous volumes, we've created a single world, but in this book we have created four worlds, all loosely united by the theme of pirates and the reality-traipsing kraken. I'd like to say this was all done in some grand-design meant as a commentary on the iterative nature of Skullgate and quantum reality in general, but honestly it came about like most of my creative ideas: somewhat haphazardly while doing whatever sounded fun at the time. The idea of a pirate-themed anthology was popular, so we went with pirates. Then writers asked: can we do space pirates? What about viking pirates? Modern pirates? And either due to my college exposure to improv-theater or my inability to say no (or a healthy dose of each), my answer each time was "Yes." Yes, we'll do pirates. And yes, they can be space pirates, and yes there can be elves and yes they can have clock-work limbs and be on zeppelins.

A universe comprised of "yes and..." That's basically how you find yourself with the book you are holding now. Yes, let's do an anthology... and let's start a publishing company... and let's do a second book... and let's create four different worlds and get four cartographers and do a kickstarter and author portraits and and and...

I have no idea what the next year will hold. Skullgate has at least half a dozen books planned for the next 12 months, so no matter which of the infinite possible worlds we find ourselves in, at least we'll be cultivating our own garden. We hope you like all the "yes ands" we have in store for you.

-C. Vandyke, Founder & President of Skullgate Media

ABOUT THIS BOOK

This volume is divided into four books, each containing pirate tales of one world from the infinitude of the multiverse. The worlds themselves represent four distinct genres of speculative-fiction: Fantasy, Science-Fiction, Steam Punk, and Traditional Pirates.

While distinct, there are thematic elements that tie these disparate worlds together. An infamous Captain Braddock and their ship, the Midnight Scythe. A lighthouse at the end of the world and a fountain of death. A floating merchant market, the Well of Eternal Life, and a map to the multiverse. And lastly, bringing terror to every iteration of existence: the great destroyer, the Kraken...

BOOK 1: PIRATES OF THE FANTASTIC

ILLUSTRATED BY DUY PHAN

MAP OF THE ARCHIPELAGO

ILLUSTRATED BY MICHAEL D. NADEAU

the Archipelago

Brig Island

- Courtyard of Sighs
- Magic School
- Jungle of Night
- Magician's Marketplace
- Lighthouse at the end of the World
- Star Mount
- The Mend
- The Gray Area
- Marauder's Sanctuary

Isle of Labruma

- The Refuge
- Salty Rest
- The Upayu
- The Eternal Rest
- Death's Doorstep
- Death's Head Tree

Saltskiff Bazaar

- Wakewash
- Flying Hexus Public House
- Saltskiff Bazaar
- Sailback
- Dagspire
- Hydra Arena
- Magdalene the Merciful
- The Greasy Gallows

Undercurrent

- Brinedrift Glade
- The Vault
- Seaweed Woods
- The Nexus
- Ruins of Curranthis
- The Gloaming Spires
- The Royal Treasury

N W E S

Illustration Copyright © 2021 Michael D. Nadeau

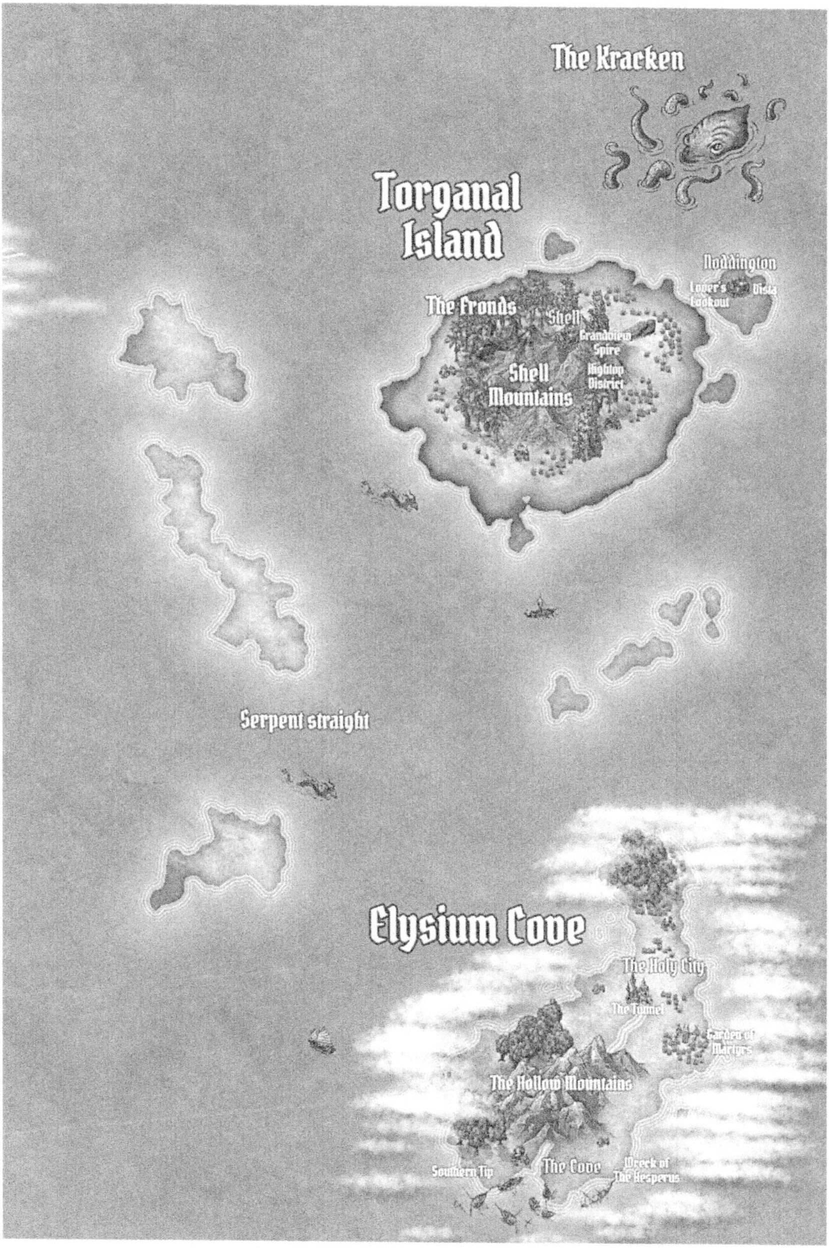

The Kracken

Torganal Island

Noddington

Luver's Lookout

Vista

The Fronds

Shell

Grandview Spire

Shell Mountains

Hightop District

Serpent straight

Elysium Cove

The Holy City

The Tunnel

Garden of Martyrs

The Hollow Mountains

Southern Tip

The Cove

Wreck of The Hesperus

Brig Island

Courtyard of Sighs

Magic School

Jungle of Night

Magician's Marketplace

Lighthouse at the end of the World

Star Mount

The Mend

The Rest Area

Marauder's Sanctuary

Elysium Cove

The Holy City

The Tunnel

Garden of Martyrs

The Hollow Mountains

Southern Tip

The Cove

Wreck of The Hesperus

Isle of Labruma

The Refuge

Salty Rest

The Quay's

The Eternal Rest

Death's Doorway

Death's Head Tree

Saltskiff Bazaar

Wakewash

Flying Venus Public House

Saltskiff Bazaar

Sailback

Dagspire

Hydra Arena

Magdalene the Merciful

The Greasy Gallows

Torganal Island

The Kracken

Noddington

Lover's
Lookout

Vista

The Fronds

Shell

Grandview
Spire

Shell
Mountains

Hightop
District

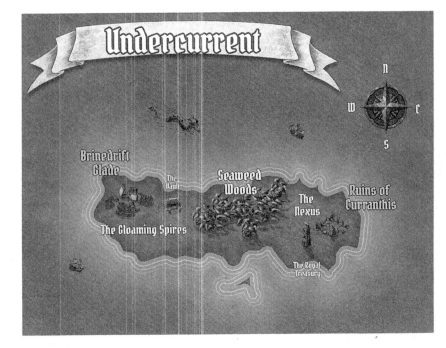

Undercurrent

Brinedrift
Glade

The
Vault

Seaweed
Woods

Ruins of
Curranthis

The
Nexus

The Gloaming Spires

The Royal
Treasury

THE ELYSIUM PROPOSAL

A. E. BROSS

*W*hy tonight, of all nights?

The pounding on the door came again, more insistent. Kyle snatched her trousers up, cursing the five-button fastening. Who puts *five* buttons on trousers? Her fingers fumbled to secure them as she scrambled to find the rest of her clothing.

Teague was in a similar state of rush beside her, though with far more grace, sliding effortlessly into a pair of trousers that might as well have been painted onto their shapely legs. "What trouble did you bring to my door, Ky? Can we not have one normal evening to ourselves?"

Kyle flinched. She could hear the frustration in her lover's voice. They weren't *wrong*. Kyle, much like her father, seemed to have trouble irrevocably lodged in her shadow. It followed her everywhere.

"I thought you found it endearing," Kyle quipped, finally obtaining victory over her trousers and spotting her undershirt and blouse.

They shot her a cutting look, and Kyle was feeling less and less like she had ever been endearing to them. Then the glare faded into a grudging smile. Teague could never stay mad at Kyle, and Kyle knew it. Teague's softening expression vanished the moment the knocking came again, hard enough to shake the door at the hinges.

"Who the hell is looking for you?" they asked, dark eyes widening, real worry seeping into them.

Kyle shrugged as she pulled on her shirts, jamming the loose fabric into her waistband. "Damned if I know, but I don't mean to stay and find out."

"Ah, yes, leave me to clean up the mess," Teague said, though their voice was only half-sarcasm. The other half, the half that made Kyle's heart beat just that little bit faster, was sadness.

Kyle hopped, using both hands to hastily pull on one boot, then the other. The banging came again: more insistent and accompanied by raised voices, shouting to be allowed entrance. Kyle continued to ignore them as she bundled her belt and coat together in her arms. She moved to the window, which meant standing on the bed, and threw it open. She grinned at the blast of salty air and fog that rushed in.

This was it. *This* was the moment. Not how she'd imagined it would go, but she could feel it. She turned back to smile at Teague, who had dressed and was preparing to deal with whoever was on the other side of the door. "Come with me."

Teague froze, dark eyes wide. "What?"

"Come with me, *vanimelda*," she repeated, the elvish term of endearment rolling off her tongue as she stretched a hand out.

Teague looked at Kyle, then back around the small room, taking it all in with their surprised gaze. The door once again shook on its hinges, and the knocking was now continuous. Then the sound of splintering wood sliced across the quarters and decided it for them. "Gods damn it," Teague breathed, reaching out and taking Kyle's hand. "You'd better protect me."

It was easy to slide out of the window and onto the roof of the inn, and Kyle hauled Teague up, closing the window behind them. "Don't worry," Kyle whispered, stealing a quick kiss, "I'll be your big, strong pirate."

The sound of the door finally giving way and the men crashing into the room that they had just escaped pushed Kyle forward. As swiftly as she dared, Kyle guided her companion across the roof, avoiding the other dormers on the cramped building. The slate tiles were slick with the damp night air, but the escaping couple managed not to slip before making it to the far end and the short drop to the connecting roof of the one-story tavern attached to the inn.

Kyle lowered Teague down, then followed, stumbling but landing safely. The two of them hastened to the edge of that building with all the stealth they could manage and repeated the process, finding themselves back on terra firma, or close to it, in the alleyway. Lucky for the two escapees, it was a raucous night in the tavern and no one had heard their escape.

The air outside smelled of grilled meat, seaweed, and stale spirits. All the things Kyle would expect from one of Saltskiff Bazaar's less reputable areas. Still, they couldn't linger long. Slipping towards the front of the alley, Kyle peeked out. It was late. The dock was sparsely populated. Not a good thing. If there had been more of a crowd, they could have slipped away far more easily.

As if cued by her thoughts, she heard the pounding of feet from inside the tavern. Shouts and disgruntled bellows accompanied by the hard clatter of boots on rickety wood. Whoever had broken into the room had obviously found it abandoned. Kyle shrank back into the shadows of the alley, her hand moving to find Teague's. When she did, she tugged gently and nodded in the direction that sank deeper into the alley. "This way."

"Kyle Talos, if you get me killed…"

Kyle winced. It wasn't her full name, no, but it was what Teague knew, and had the sting of being called by an angry parent. Kyle knew she was in for trouble, and it had nothing to do with the people who were chasing the pair. "Don't worry. We'll be fine."

THE WESTERN DOCKS of the Bazaar were quiet. Kyle made it a point to pay both her crew and the dockhands a little extra, and for that, she was rewarded with good behavior. Add to that a lack of taverns so close to the docks, and there was a certain peace that nowhere else in the bazaar could boast of.

Feeling confident they had slipped away from the pursuers, Kyle led Teague towards her ship, *The Stargazer*, anchored on the far docks. Once they were beside the ship, she issued a shrill whistle. "Ahoy, night watch, the gangway." She couldn't remember who had been assigned for the on-deck night, but they wouldn't hold it against her.

The gangplank lowered, and Kyle turned to Teague, grinning from ear to ear. "Your chariot, my liege."

"You are ridiculous, you know that?" they replied, but they were smiling. Relief and exhaustion showed on their face before they hurried delicately up the gangplank. Kyle breathed a small sigh. She not only orchestrated an expert escape from unknown pursuers, but managed to bring Teague and coax them into a smiling mood. Kyle had a question for them that she felt hinged on Teague being in a good mood.

After all, very few people agreed to marriage when they were upset.

Hopping off of the gangplank and onto the sturdy decking of *The Stargazer*, Kyle landed just behind Teague. She was about to speak when she noticed her partner's posture: ramrod straight, frozen in place.

Behind Kyle, the gangplank vanished, pushed away and clattering against the dock below before it plunged into dark waters.

Not good.

Kyle pulled Teague behind her to shield them and drew her weapons. Four guards, weapons drawn, had them pinned against the rail. Elven guards, wearing the colors of the Sixth Court of Elders. Kyle felt her heart sink. They were surrounded. Despite the odds, she had her xiphe and parrying dagger at the ready. Perhaps she could buy enough time for Teague to get—

"Enough," came a loud, quick, and authoritative voice, interrupting her thought.

The guards lowered their weapons and stood at attention as footsteps sounded behind them. They moved aside to reveal a regal Elven woman with sharp, severe features. Her silver gaze found Kyle in an instant, and she sneered. "*Peredhel*," she said, her head canted to the side.

Kyle had to keep from rolling her eyes. If she had a gold piece for every time she had to deal with uptight elves calling her 'half-elf' as an insult, she would be a truly wealthy woman. She straightened, sheathing her weapons to return the greeting with an exaggerated bow of her own. "*Auvanëa*," she said, unable to stop the childish insult to the woman's looks from sliding off of her lips.

The other woman's countenance lost its smug amusement to a flicker of anger. When she spoke again, she no longer used Elvish. "I shouldn't have to deal with such filth."

Kyle shrugged. "Neither should I."

From behind her, Teague whispered, "What in the seven hells is going on here?"

Kyle didn't know the *what*, but she certainly knew the *who*. "Teague, this is Vána Raudnost of the Sixth Court of Elders." She tried to keep her tone light. She didn't want to worry them. "My mother's mother." Turning to Teague, she smiled. "Vána, this is my partner, Teague Dailann."

"Pleasure," murmured Teague, their voice expressing precisely no pleasure.

"Silence," Vána all but spat, stepping up behind her guards and gesturing for them to give her a wider berth. "I'm glad I found you before others did. I thought for sure the men your father sent would have gotten to you and made our meeting impossible."

Kyle cursed herself. The men at the inn had been there to help her? Of course. How was she supposed to know they weren't someone she owed money to?

"It's fortunate because you and I, Kalina, are going to do something that others have only dreamed of. We are going to pierce the eternal storms of the Elysium—"

"Kyle."

Vána started at the interruption. "Excuse me?"

"My name. It's Kyle."

The rage that flitted across Vána's face was near terrifying. "Whatever you call yourself means little to me. Your Elven name is Kalina, and that is what I shall use." Gone was any grandeur to her words. She was all business now, steely eyes flashing. "You are going to take me and mine to the Elysium Cove."

Kyle scoffed, stopping just short of outright laughing at the woman. "Me? What would you want with a small time, half-elf embarrassment's ship, when a word from the great Vána can command Elven fleets?" she asked. Teague clenched at the fabric of her jacket, twisting it as if warning Kyle not to push her luck. Kyle had to remember that she wasn't alone, so perhaps riling a member of the upper echelons of Elven society wasn't the *wisest* choice.

"My reasons are mine—"

"Not when you're trying to forcibly commandeer my ship and my crew," Kyle spat, cutting off the words. "Where's my crew?"

Vána waved a hand dismissively. "Below decks, being kept under watch."

"They had better be safe." The 'or else' was implied.

"How dare you speak to me like this." Vána's face flushed, and anger sparked in her eyes. "You have no right, you absolute worm. No one does. I am Vána Raudnost of the Sixth Court of Elders, and I will be treated with the respect I deserve."

"She came to the bazaar for respect?" Teague breathed the question, their breath warm against Kyle's ear.

Jesting aside, Kyle had to admit that it was odd for Vána to be here, attempting to commandeer her ship. Why wouldn't she simply request and be granted a fleet of ships from the Court? Then it struck Kyle, and she had to keep from outwardly smiling. She knew, or at least thought she knew, why the elder elf had come. "You were refused what you needed for a venture to the Elysium Cove, weren't you?" Kyle was stunned. "You're going after the Well of Eternal Life without the blessing of the Elven Courts? Hell, against their wishes?"

Vána's eyes flashed, and Kyle could see the muscles in her jaw twitch. There it was. The truth laid out for all to see.

Attempting to breach the storms of the Elysium Cove was suicide, regardless of how much one might want the Well of Eternal Life. What good was it if one died in the tempests surrounding the island? Kyle would not risk everything for it. "If the Court refused you, what made you think I would agree?" she asked, trying to sound more confident than she felt as she scrambled to put together an escape plan.

It had been the wrong question. Kyle knew that the minute Vána's face settled into a calm, almost serene expression. She gestured to one of her guards. The soldier nodded and moved, vanishing below deck. There were a few moments of awkward, tense silence between them all, but it was soon filled with the sound of the soldier's return. It also sounded as if they were with someone else, though the second set of foot falls were much less sure, and more than once there was a clattering as if someone fell but was forced back to their feet.

Someone emerged from the steps down into the ship, except it wasn't the soldier. The man—tied at the wrists and covered in cuts, scrapes, bruises, and blood—was pushed so forcibly that he tripped on the top step and fell to the deck, landing hard on elbows and forearms. Kyle recognized him immediately, though she could only catch a quick flash of his face as he fell. "Dad!" she said, starting forward.

"Kyle, no," he groaned as he tried to right himself. The guard put a foot to his back, forcing him down.

One of the other guards shot a hand out to stop Kyle, but she took it and twisted hard, bringing it up around his back and shoving upwards without mercy. She heard the shoulder pop out of place just before the guard screamed his pain. She put a foot in front of his and shoved forward, eliciting another pained yell as he fell to the deck. Before she could draw her sword and dagger, though, a blade was leveled at her throat.

Vána's icy gaze met Kyle's over the shining metal of the thin sword. "Now, you will take me and my men to the Elysium Cove. We will break through the storm, and I will get everything I have coming to me. The alternative is that I kill your partner, your father, your crew, and you, then take your ship and leave your bodies to rot with the rest of the refuse in this disgusting place."

Kyle glared at the woman, but knew she had no choice but to acquiesce. Angrily, she nodded, moving her hands away from her weapons.

"Good," Vána said, sheathing her own blade. "We sail for the Elysium Cove. Now."

THE STARGAZER WAS NOT AN OVERLY large vessel. A brigantine ship, it was sleek and trim, made to carry an eighty-ton burden. Counting Kyle, The Stargazer's crew numbered twenty-four. The ship was fast and lighter than most. That's what Kyle had fallen in love with when she first set foot aboard, at the age of four. Kyle's father, Phaidan Talos, had commissioned the ship with the inheritance that had been gifted to him by his parents. They were alive and well, they just saw no reason for Phaidan to wait until they sailed on past the end of the world.

Now Kyle wondered if she would ever see her paternal grandparents again.

She could do with seeing much less of her maternal grandmother.

For the most part, Vána and her guards left the crew to its work, which was a small relief. She had, of course, claimed the captain's quarters as her own. Kyle and Teague were relegated to the crew quarters, and Phaidan had been taken to the hold. Kyle tried not to worry for her father. He had been on many an adventure on his own, and he could hold on until Kyle figured out some way out of this one.

The crew quarters were dark; one lantern, turned low, hung at the far end. Even in the low light, Kyle could see the guards standing erect, eyes forward. Their presence grated on her as she lay, watching them from her hammock. Prisoner on her own ship. Her father a hostage. It was hard to imagine Phaidan Talos as being anything but the victor in any struggle. The man was a hero. He had made enemies, surely, but the list of friends he boasted meant he should have been safe from harm. Or maybe it was simply that a girl didn't like seeing her father powerless. Before Kyle had struck out on her own, it had just been her father and her. He had given her the strength and confidence to stride out into the world.

A whisper interrupted her thoughts.

The hammock above her own rocked gently, and Kyle could make out the shape of Teague peeking over, large dark eyes showing endless depth in the low light. They gestured down to Kyle, a gesture that Kyle instantly understood, and nodded her agreement to. Quietly, Teague slipped out of her hammock and down into Kyle's.

One of the guards shifted, watching them. Kyle glared, defiant. They could choose the direction of the ship, but they wouldn't choose whether she and the person she loved were allowed to cuddle, damn it.

Teague, meanwhile, curled up into Kyle's side, making themselves small despite their greater stature. They laid their head on the young captain's shoulder and sighed, the only sounds around them the gentle creak of the ship and the muffled tread of the sailors' footfalls above. The guard relaxed, his focus moving away from the two of them.

Teague spoke, their voice barely audible. "I wonder if it would have been wiser to stay in that room. Might have saved us both some trouble."

Kyle stiffened, anger and anxiety gripping at her insides with equal fervor. If she'd had even an inkling as to what had been waiting for her at *The Stargazer*, Kyle would never have brought them with her. She had spent much of the time since arriving back cursing her own poor judgement, and her mind insisted on jumping to conclusions about whether or not Teague would want anything to do with her after this.

Or if there would even be an 'after this.'

Kyle's arm tightened around Teague's shoulders. In the dark of the hull, as *The Stargazer* rocked around them, Kyle Talos had no witticism that would save the day. Her ship was no longer hers, her lover had been put in danger, and there was the very real possibility that none of them would survive to tell about any of it.

Tears stung at the back of her eyes.

Teague slid an arm over Kyle's waist and around, pulling her close while nuzzling their head closer to her throat. They placed a small kiss on her neck, and Kyle shivered, relaxing slightly. "I don't know if this is the time," she said, breathing a laugh.

Teague chuckled, their lips so close to Kyle's throat that she could feel their breath. "True. Perhaps, once this is all over, and we are back, you can find a way to propose then? Without all of this being abducted nonsense?"

Kyle nodded in the darkness, but then started, shifting to glance down at Teague's face. "Wait, what? You *knew?*"

A giggle was their only response for a time, before they finally managed, "Emma told me."

Emma, Teague's older sister. Teague's older sister whom Kyle had *sworn to secrecy* when she had asked her for help arranging a romantic breakfast, after what Kyle had hoped would be a night of lovemaking. "I trusted her!"

"Ky, the poor woman couldn't keep a secret if her life depended on it."

They both laughed.

The guard glanced at them again, but nothing more.

Kyle shook her head in the darkness, amazed. "Is that why you came with me?" she asked, her voice once again a whisper.

Teague nodded against her.

"Does that mean..." Kyle trailed off, her nerves wavering. She didn't dare assume. There were too many variables. But what if these were the only moments they might have left for this connection? Her resolve strengthened, and she forced herself to speak. "Does that mean you would be willing to *always* come with me?"

"Of course," was the reply without a moment's hesitation. "I am still holding you to a wonderfully romantic breakfast and elaborate proposal once this is all over." They gave another little squeeze to Kyle before letting out a yawn.

Kyle went, in half an instant, from anxiety to elation. It was a startling change, which meant she felt even less prepared when Teague said, 'once this is all over,' and the elation slipped right back down into worry.

As if sensing Kyle's thoughts, Teague whispered, "There will be a 'once this is all over,' Kyle. We'll make sure of it."

Kyle hoped they were right.

❦

WHAT BEGAN as a slight drizzle and choppy ocean waters had become a tempest. A wave slammed into the port side of *The Stargazer*, shaking the ship to its very core. Not for the first time that morning, Kyle prayed to whatever god might keep her ship from being torn apart in the tumult. As it was, the entire crew was tossed to the side, some keeping their balance, others dropping to all fours.

Yet Vána stood straight and tall beside Kyle, her icy gaze pinning the young captain in her place at the helm. Two guards stood to the port side, and between them was the injured, half-dead heap of her father. Another guard to the stern stood, a hand roughly grasping Teague's arm. Kyle had to admit, her grandmother knew how to motivate a person.

They were sailing around to the southern point of Elysium Cove, where Vána insisted the best point of entry would be in the eternal storms surrounding the island. Kyle had heard that fairy tale as well, though there were still no ships, no captains, and no members of a crew that had successfully made it through and lived to tell the tale.

Kyle guided the ship as well as she could in the tossing waves, the helm fighting her for each and every league they managed. Everything ached. Trying to keep her footing, as the boat rocked and the wind howled and the rain drove, was wearing her to the very bone with exertion.

And they weren't even in the worst of it yet.

Vána looked unperturbed. The closer *The Stargazer* got to the supposed entryway, the more distant her gaze became. Kyle thought that might be a way in, a weakness in her grandmother's armor, but she dared not try it with her lover on one side and her beaten, bloodied father on the other.

"There!" Vána shouted to be heard over the storm, pointing off to the port side.

Kyle squinted to see through the storm around her. Her eyes weren't as good as her grandmother's, but she could make out a stretch of the storm that seemed calmer than the rest. Of course, calm was a relative term. The approach to the isle had been one of the worst that Kyle had ever seen in her ten years as captain of *The Stargazer*, and this swath looked worse than what they had endured to make it this far.

Kyle realized she was staring at her death. At the death of them all. She was frozen by it, her white-knuckle grip on the helm not changing course to where her grandmother pointed.

"Damn you, child, steer to port or we will miss it!" Vána practically roared.

Kyle blinked, temporarily freed from her fear paralysis. She looked to Teague, desperate and pleading. Her lover met her gaze and then nodded, an almost imperceptible gesture.

With every bit of strength she had, Kyle turned the helm.

Hard to starboard.

The Stargazer pitched with the sudden change of direction. Vána fell into the helm, her weight helping Kyle to keep the ship on its trajectory *away* from the Elysium Cove, from the Well of Eternal Life and her grandmother's great ambition. The guard clutching at Teague's arm fell against the railing, releasing them in favor of saving himself. Teague quickly used the advantage, pushing away from the man and down the steps to the lower deck.

"You *peredhel* bitch," Vána screamed, righting herself. She snatched at Kyle, who dodged away from the grasp, still holding the helm as best she could. Vána didn't have a physical weapon, but Kyle knew this made her no less deadly. Magic was Vána's domain. The older woman's lips were moving, and her hands glowed with an angry, crimson light. She reached for Kyle, and the half-elf could hear the hiss of rain turning to steam when it touched Vána's hands. She dodged again, but she knew there would not be many more opportunities to avoid her grandmother's enchanted touch.

Vána grabbed at her wrist, and Kyle couldn't pull away

without releasing the helm. Searing hot pain shot up her arm. Her grip failed, and the wheel spun wildly. The ship pitched again, this time struck by a swell of ocean water that hammered into the hull. Kyle lost her footing, falling back and sliding across the deck to hit the railing. She curled on her side, protecting her injured wrist. The skin burned and peeled, the flesh beneath blistering and red. The rain and wind around her made it hard to hear, and the pain made it impossible to concentrate. She didn't realize Vána approached until a rough hand grabbed a fistful of her wet hair. No longer hot, the hand clutched hard, pulling Kyle to her feet.

"How dare you," Vána snarled. Her free hand shot out, gripping Kyle's throat and squeezing with a strength born from rage. "You think you did anything, *peredhel*? I'll just kill you and take your ship. It's that si—"

Vána didn't get to finish her threat.

Teague ran into her, throwing their weight into the Elven woman without mercy. Kyle saw Vána for barely an instant before she was pitched over the back railing, plummeting to the water below. Teague crashed into the railing but managed to check their momentum. They sank to the deck, chest heaving. Kyle hurried to them, checking to make sure they weren't injured. They smiled at Kyle and, once she was close enough, Teague took her face in their hands and kissed her, hard. "Are you all right?" they asked, shouting to be heard over the storm.

Her arm stung horribly. Her head hurt. They were still in the storm and not remotely out of danger, but the only thing that mattered to Kyle at that instant was that Teague was whole and safe.

"Captain Talos!"

The shout came from an unfamiliar voice. Turning to look up through the driving rain, Kyle saw one of the guards. She tensed immediately, shifting to put Teague behind her as much as possible. The Elven guard shook his head. "I saw Elder Raudnost fall from the ship, driven by the storm. We will not risk any more of our lives. Steer us out of here, Captain!"

Kyle did not need a second invitation.

PREDAWN LIGHT SHONE weakly through the windows of the captain's quarters of *The Stargazer*. They were traveling north from the Elysium Cove, charting a course towards Torganal Island to drop off the handful of Elven guards that were still aboard. As it turned out, they had not supported the trip to Elysium Cove, but their allegiance meant they had no say in the matter. Since their leader was gone, they had been nothing but polite and accommodating.

Kind of them, really.

Kyle stirred slightly in the bed. Sleep was no easy thing, when one's arm was salved and bandaged and one's throat was bruised and sore. She had managed. She stretched, still half asleep, and reached her good arm over to wrap it around Teague. Except Teague wasn't there. Kyle blinked and pushed herself up to sitting, glancing around the dimly lit room.

Teague sat on a bench, leaning against a generous windowsill while they looked out over the water, head resting on their folded arms. Dressed in a simple shift, the soft, first blush of daylight made their form ethereal to Kyle. "Are you all right?" Kyle asked quietly.

Teague turned and smiled, their brown curls falling over their shoulder. "Restless after all of the excitement and happy to see skies without storms in them."

Kyle leaned forward and held the warm blankets open. "There are other ways of occupying time if you're restless."

Teague let out an exaggerated sigh and unfolded themself from their seat at the window. "There will be plenty of time for that after you've done some healing, Captain."

Kyle cuddled them close when they climbed back into the bed, relishing the warmth and comfort that radiated from Teague. They stayed like that for a few minutes, silent, basking in the glow of the morning. Kyle felt herself drifting off again.

"So, we're getting married?"

"Yes," Kyle said, sleepily. Then she blinked and looked into Teague's dark eyes. "Yes?"

"So long as you have no other relatives like your grandmother, then yes."

"Don't worry, love," Kyle said on a yawn. "It's just Dad now, and his parents. They're all much more like me."

"That... isn't as reassuring as you think."

Kyle chuckled and held Teague close, drifting back to sleep as *The Stargazer* sailed on.

THE SCREAMING HARPIES

CAROLINE BARNARD-SMITH

"Water wraiths off the port bow."

Captain Tempest Brack leaned over the rail of her ship, crimson wood sticky with blood-sweat beneath the noonday sun, and watched for the nebulous shapes rushing beneath the water. The wraiths turned and writhed as they raced before the ship, sinuous bodies contorted by remnants of shredded fins and misshapen cavities full of teeth.

The clicking of long, multi-jointed legs across the scarlet deck announced the arrival of Tempest's quartermaster. Mary Therese's clockwork prostheses were as beautiful as they were wondrous, wrought from glossy brass and carved with intricate swirling death's heads, but the second knee on the right side was buckling slightly. She would have to re-wind the limb before they reached Saltskiff or it would soon lock tight, and Tempest knew from bitter experience that this often happened at the most inopportune times; usually when the quartermaster was mid-flight on a boarding rope or blind drunk at the bar of a particularly rowdy inn.

Tempest drew a spyglass from her coat pocket and set its eye towards the horizon. "Wherever there's a shoal of hungry wraiths, Saltskiff's never far behind," she said. "And wherever you find Saltskiff, you'll find the *Greasy Gallows*. There she is now, bearing down fast, and ugly as ever."

Mary squinted at the squat black ship. "They're flying pirate colours."

"That they are, but those lapdog goblins have no right to call themselves pirates. Not since they started taking Saltskiff's coin to patrol these waters against the likes of us."

Tempest bared her teeth in the *Gallows'* direction as it approached. She would have preferred to avoid Ginny Gentle and her goblin crew altogether, but the *Screaming Harpy* was not a ship that could sneak into port undetected. If her immense size and hull painted with howling mouths full of bloody teeth didn't attract attention, the crew certainly would. The last infestation of lice had swept their ranks ten years ago but the Harpies still kept their heads shaved, many covering their shorn skulls with thick black tattoos. They made an arresting sight when they swept into combat, each crewmember screaming into the wind astride their blood-red ship, smooth heads shining before the raging battle-torches. Tempest was the only Harpy to use red ink in her tattoo. A roaring skull with pitiless eye sockets that wept blood and flame swept up and over the back of her head, giving her two battle faces.

"State your business, Brack," Ginny shouted as her ship finally pulled up broadside.

Tempest eyed her warily. The goblin may have been small in stature, but her entire body seemed to be comprised of solid muscle. Her ship was not to be taken lightly, either. The hull of the *Greasy Gallows* bristled with jagged fins cut from the backs of steel-tip sailfish, designed to discourage boarders.

"The *Harpy's* in need of supplies," she shouted back.

Ginny scowled across the gulf of water separating their ships, hand twitching towards the heavy spear at her back.

"The ship is satiated," Tempest reasoned. "If I was looking to attack, wouldn't I have come in screaming, blight-cannons charged and ready to fire?"

This satisfied the goblin, although the *Gallows* insisted on trailing the *Harpy* all the way into port. Tempest ignored the insult and turned her face towards the Saltskiff Bazaar. It had grown since she had been there last. More ships gathered at its edges, lashed so tightly together there was barely a space between them. Merchants hustled for customers from stalls built on the decks and shops pressed into cabins. Ragged bunting fluttered from masts surrounded by tables piled with bundled herbs, spelled candles, and bolts of cloth.

The Harpies disembarked, eager to disperse amongst the floating trade ships. Tempest and Mary watched them go before turning towards the brine-rotted towers of Dagspire, home to the infamous Flying Venus Public House.

THE PUB WAS A LURCHING turret cobbled together from pieces of wrecked ships. It rose above the other establishments clustered at its base like a crooked finger crawling with scabrous barnacles. Tempest and Mary walked through the main bar and climbed the stairs, heading to a small lounge on the topmost landing where Helga of the All-Seeing Eye held court.

Helga was seated at a table before a spread of fortune cards. When Tempest sat down, the fortune-teller's elaborately embroidered, oversized cloak shifted around her, ornate patchwork eyes layered like dragon scales sifting and sighing.

"I have heard your eyes see many things," Tempest said, dropping a gold coin into the dish at Helga's elbow. "So tell me, do you know why I'm here?"

Helga spoke from deep within her hood, voice low and edged with smoke. "All pirates share the same purpose. You seek riches what don't belong to you."

"To be fair, that which I seek has already been stolen from its rightful owners."

A small, wrinkled hand snaked from the reams of cloak to turn over one of the cards, revealing the image of a distressed-looking pig.

"What does that mean?"

"The Downed Pig could mean many things. Perhaps you are confused about the nature of what you truly seek?"

Tempest slammed her hand down on the table. "I'm not confused, though perhaps you are. I'm looking for a map. It's a unique object, inked on a strip of dragon skin."

"Now I see," Helga said. "You plan to rob the Pirate Kings. Their treasure lies in a hidden harbour, its location mapped on the hide of a mighty dragon."

"Aye, that's right. Did you see that with your... eyes?" Tempest glanced at the biggest eye, a frayed-edged oval sewn across Helga's left shoulder. The silky lashes looked almost real.

"I did not," Helga admitted. "But I have heard much talk of the Pirate Kings' cache. One of their brethren has a big mouth."

"'Tis a shame." Tempest slumped back in her chair. "Now it will be a race to the treasure and a hard fight to claim it."

"The Harpies are more than up to the task, Captain," Mary said.

"Wait." Helga held up her hand. "I hear whisperings of a treasure what is closer to your heart than mere gold and gaudy gems. If you wish to know more, kindly place another coin in me dish."

Slowly, Tempest withdrew a second coin from her purse and dropped it into the bowl. "If you scry wrong, I'll swing you from that window."

"I scry true, Captain. I see an orc with an elf's ears and a noble's blood."

Tempest swallowed thickly, suddenly wishing she'd thought to procure a drink.

"This orc is on a journey," Helga continued. "I see—"

Tempest stood without realising she meant to. "This is what my coin buys? I asked you plain for the whereabouts of a map, and all I get is riddles and nonsense. I heard rumours your fortunes were cursed. I should have listened to my gut and kept my money in my purse."

Helga's head snapped up, two leonine eyes glaring from the shadows of her hood. "It's all lies. I'm not cursed, never was."

"Maybe she ain't cursed, but she couldn't prophesize her way out of a bag of cats."

The three women turned to find an old man sitting in the corner, nursing a small mug of beer.

"What do you know about it?" Tempest demanded.

"I know that old sea hag ain't telling fortunes, she's just repeating what I told her last night." The man stood as Helga tutted in indignation, his arms spread wide in a grand gesture. "I am the Wizard Cazuuli." A drop of beer slid from his greasy grey stub of a beard and fell to join the tobacco stains creeping across the front of his vest.

"You're the Wizard Cazuuli?" Mary asked. She positioned herself before her captain, though the man hardly seemed to pose a threat. "You're the only person alive to have glimpsed the Map of the Multiverse?" Her forehead creased as she regarded his salt-stiff long johns. "Where are your clothes?"

"Back on sodding Torganal with the rest of my belongings," the man spat. He drew himself up on stockinged feet, oblivious to the jagged yellow toenail that had ripped a hole through the right toe, and scowled at Tempest. "Your delightful girlfriend spirited me away in the dead of night. Said Undercurrent had surfaced. The Map is free and clear of the water, sitting pretty for any passing thief to snatch. She wanted me to take her there."

"Why would she need you if she knows where the Map is?"

"Your girl might be rum-pickled, but she's not lost all her wits. She knew I was also the only person alive to have made it past the undead ghouls what guard the place."

33

"Stop calling her my girl."

"But that's what she is, ain't she? Everybody on Torganal knows she was joint-captain of the *Screaming Harpy*. She talks about it enough when she's in her cups."

"She does?" Tempest paused, took a breath. "So where is Sheena now? Is she here?"

"Buggered if I know," Cazuuli said, reaching to scratch beneath an armpit. "I was finally able to convince her that even if I could remember how I made my way into the Nexus in the first place, I would need my specialist equipment, and that was all left behind on Torganal. She dumped me here and sailed away in her rig, probably on to Undercurrent alone."

Tempest considered the wizard's story. She knew she should be heading out to open waters, scouting out a merchantman or a trading sloop, something for her crew to get messy with. Something to scour this whole affair from her brain. She knew these things, but a hard place in her chest was vibrating with a dull ache. After almost a decade of silence, Sheena was abroad in the world at last. She looked back at Cazuuli.

"You're coming with us."

"No, I'm bloody not. I've just been dragged halfway across the sea by a deranged pirate, I'm not about to let it happen again."

"I'm not giving you a choice. Mary, grab him, please."

Mary looked as if she'd rather do anything but touch the sweating man, but she followed orders and stepped around Cazuuli to bring his arms up behind his back, keeping them locked into place as he thrashed.

"Let me go, you miserable old sows. I want no part of this."

He was soundly ignored. Tempest snatched up her coins from Helga's dish as they turned to leave and the fortune teller jumped to her feet, upsetting the cards still spread on the table. A silver card fluttered to the floor, etched with a faded portrait of two mermaids entwined beneath a cobalt moon. Tempest kicked it away.

"What do you think you're doing?" Helga screeched. "I read your fortune, I earnt my payment."

"Sod off, Helga. You're lucky I don't carve out every one of your lying eyes."

The eyes on Helga's coat all blinked in slow, sticky unison as the pirates clattered back down the stairs with Cazuuli staggering between them.

TEMPEST COULD STILL HEAR Cazuuli cursing their names from the brig, a deck below. She gazed up at the graven face of the dryad pressed into the dark wood of her cabin wall, monstrously large and grown over with dank sea fungus. The ship was hungering. Soon, the mouth would fall open and, if left unfed, the dryad's pained howling would cut through all three decks. Tempest lifted a small dagger to her forefinger and broke the skin with one swift, practiced stab, coaxing forth a bright bead of blood. She lifted the finger to the dryad's waxy lips and smeared the offering inside. A long sigh filled the room, borne on an unnatural breeze that roused images of mountain forests and icy streams. Tempest closed her eyes to breathe in the new life creeping across her skin.

An elf's blood and the innate power it contained in exchange for life, for years beyond even those a long-lived elf would naturally live: that was the deal they had made with the dryad. Entreating the tree spirit to become a part of the crew, a part of the ship itself, had been Sheena's idea; but ever since their ill-fated journey to Labruma, the blood-offering was tinged with regret. Tempest had wanted nothing more than to sail the oceans with the half-orc hellion at her side until the end of days and, for years, they had captained the *Harpy* together, flying their beautiful crimson ship into skirmishes and raids that were sung about in taverns across the Archipelago. Then Sheena looked into the Death Waters Fountain, and everything had soured.

A loud, fiery burp startled the captain from her communion with the ship.

"Broomie," she admonished, eyes snapping open. "What are you doing in here, you little bastard?"

The bilge-dragon manifested from the shadows beside Tempest's dresser, slowly coagulating into being like smoke filling a jar. Two eyes sparked from a pointed face twisted with contempt. It took a slow, deep breath and exhaled a stream of ashy smoke that filled the room with the sulfuric smell of rancid eggs.

Mary knocked at the door. "Captain Brack?"

"Enter."

The quartermaster pushed open the door, raising a sleeve to her face when the putrid smoke rushed from the room to engulf her.

"Broomie got in my cabin again. What have I told you about keeping your eyes on that miscreant?"

"So sorry, Captain. It won't happen again." Mary made shooing motions at the little black dragon. "Come on, Broomie. Out you go."

The dragon sat back on its haunches and rustled the tattered wings on its back, only yielding when Tempest drew her cutlass from her belt. Even then, it moved infuriatingly slowly, claws skittering across the floorboards and long, razor-whip tail swinging languorously behind it.

Tempest resheathed her cutlass. "What can I do for you, Mary?"

"I'd like to know what I should tell the crew," Mary said, shutting the door on the retreating dragon.

"About what?"

"About our destination. They were expecting to be underway on an expedition."

"The crew go where I tell them to go."

"They won't be happy, Captain. They spent most of their coin on rum and company back on Saltskiff. They'll be looking to make our next score."

"This is just a detour."

"But what of the Pirate Kings' treasure? They'll never stop chasing the *Harpy* down if we don't have something to trade."

"That will have to wait."

"But, Captain—"

"That will have to wait, Quartermaster."

Mary nodded and exited the cabin, leaving Tempest alone amidst the enduring drift of bilge-dragon smoke.

UNDERCURRENT WAS AN UGLY, haunted place. Tempest helped Mary pull their boat up onto a coarse sand beach in a dismal cove, then brought out her spyglass to survey their surroundings. In the far distance, stands of warped trees waved fronds like decomposing tentacles in the air.

"The Seawood Woods," Cazuuli said at her elbow. "A reeking scourge of a place, to be sure."

She turned from the wizard to join Mary at the water's edge. "Glimpse anything?"

"All clear, but I don't much like the feel of this place. Can I ask you a question, Captain?"

"Speak. I didn't make you up to quartermaster for being meek."

Mary leaned on a boulder, metallic limbs grinding against the rough stone. "Are we here for the Map, or for Captain Sheena?"

"The Map of the Multiverse doesn't mean much to me, though I suppose it would fetch decent coin on Brig Island."

Tempest could see Mary had more questions, but she didn't much feel like dredging up the answers. Behind them, the wizard hopped from one foot to the other in a loping circle, stopping to pick up stray shells and stones and stuffing them into the pockets of his long johns.

"Lead on, old man," Tempest called to him. "It's time we were away."

By mid-afternoon, they had reached the Ruins of Curranthis. Ruined, but not abandoned. The smoke from several fires wound grey tendrils amongst the shattered rooftops, and at its centre was an immense domed structure, lights glittering in its oval windows.

"I've brought you this far," Cazuuli said. "Now, I'm off."

Tempest placed a hand on the wizard's shoulder, digging her fingers into his sinewy collarbone. "I haven't given you permission to leave."

Cazuuli grinned. Before Tempest could stop him, he pulled a heavy stone from his pocket and threw it through the broken wall of the building in front of them. A chittering echoed back from the darkness, a dry rasping that heightened in intensity until four figures climbed through the gaping rift in the brickwork. As Tempest and Mary reached for their weapons, Cazuuli took his chance to slip away.

"Get back here," Tempest shouted, but the wizard was already gone, hooting like a deranged seabird as he vanished into the recesses of the city.

Tempest drew her cutlass. The figures grew closer, clutching long halberds tipped with cruelly-carved coral, and stepped into the light. Tempest tightened her grip on the cutlass as Mary stiffened beside her, legs locked into a fighting stance.

The figures did not appear to be wholly alive.

They rushed at the pirates, dead-fish eyes stark and staring. Their clothes were little more than tattered strips, revealing skin and muscle parted by damp decay and the hint of mouldering bone beneath. As they ran, their wide, webbed feet slapped against the stone.

Tempest took one out with a clean swipe from gut to gills, while Mary split the skull of her assailant with one perfectly timed kick of her clockwork leg—but behind them were two more, and from the building at their backs poured another dozen.

THE GAOL CELL was cramped and chill, the walls swathed in the creeping slime of a particularly tenacious seaweed. Tempest supposed she should be grateful the undead fishguards hadn't executed them on the spot. She'd been separated from her quartermaster, and could only glimpse the Wizard Cazuuli sitting cross-legged in the cell across from hers.

"See where your treachery has gotten us, you old maggot?" she hissed at him.

The wizard was hunched over the floor, his back turned to her as he recited a dry chant beneath his breath. Tempest snarled, lunging through the bars of her cell to flail uselessly at salt-damp air.

A snoring stranger in the next cell woke with a start.

"Shut up, would you?" they said. "Screeching won't get you out of this hole. Trust me, I've tried."

Tempest knew that voice; knew it as intimately as she knew her own.

"Sheena?"

The figure grumbled and moaned, turning its face towards the wall.

"I know that's you, Sheena." Then, quieter, "Sheena, it's me, Temp."

Sheena sat up abruptly and swung around to look at her. Tempest fought a sickening urge to drop her gaze and shuffle backwards into the shadows, suddenly aware of every change the dryad's magic had woven into her face over the years since they'd last seen each other. The fact that Sheena looked no different only made the feeling worse.

"What are you doing on this squid's arse of an island?"

And just like that, the spell was broken. The tired old anger returned.

"I haven't seen you in a kraken's age, and that's the first thing you say to me?"

She was surprised when Sheena lowered her head, one hand reaching to grip the bars separating them.

"I never thought I'd see you again, Temp. You took me by surprise, that's all."

"You didn't think you'd see me? Or you didn't want to see me?"

"What difference does that make after all these years?"

Tempest hadn't chased Sheena across half the Archipelago just to argue. "I came here for you."

"For me? I thought you would have given up on me by now. You're getting on alright, aren't you? You've got a new quartermaster, you don't need me to help captain the crew."

Tempest sat back, her joints aching. "I just needed to see you well. I thought you were on Torganal, ferreting out kraken secrets. Trying to change your fate. Then, I heard you'd washed up here."

"Aye." Sheena smiled at her in the half-light, the same grin which never failed to disarm Tempest when she was a young elf. "I'm here for the Map, but every other bugger with a dream or a death wish came looking for it too. That's why the fishguards are on high alert. No one's getting in or out of the Nexus."

Tempest shook her head, confused.

"That's where they keep it," Sheena explained. "The selfish bastards."

"But why do you want it?" She thought about lacing her fingers through Sheena's between the bars. "Why are you running around looking for a mystical map when you could have been—"

"With you, back on the *Harpy?*" Sheena finished for her. "Things changed after Labruma, Temp. I changed. I wish I could better explain what happened when I looked into those cursed waters." She seemed wistful, almost sorry.

Tempest raised her fingers to Sheena's, brushing her knuckles and grasping her hand, inching closer to the bars as the wizard's moaning chant became louder. She glanced over her shoulder. He'd marked a ring of sigils into the dirt with a stick and was placing shells and stones around the circle as he rocked back and forth.

"Magdalene's mercy, wizards are annoying," Sheena said. "You should have left him back on Saltskiff. I did."

"I sorely wish I had."

"I didn't know the Map existed when I rucked up in Vista," Sheena went on. "I went to learn about the kraken, to prevent my death so I could return to you and the *Harpy*. That's the truth of it, Temp. I always meant to come back."

"But you didn't come back. The *Harpy* has life to spare for both of us. All we had to do was stay away from the bloody kraken."

"I didn't want to live like that. That's what I could never make you understand. What joy is to be found in preternaturally long life if you spend every moment of it looking over your shoulder, praying today won't be the day the kraken swallows you whole?"

Tempest didn't have an answer for that. She removed her hand from Sheena's and cradled it in her lap.

"It's not all bad though, love. I really did find answers on Torganal. This map opens the door to worlds you can't even imagine. Places where pirates sail the skies."

"So, you're going to escape the kraken by running off to join the crew of a flying ship? You really are rum-pickled."

"Not quite." Sheena leaned closer. "I'm going to find out

where the beast is planning to send me when it finally gets its tentacles around my throat. See, I've been wondering if I was wrong about seeing my death. I'm wondering if what I was glimpsing was my future."

Tempest pulled herself up against the bars. "I wish you'd never looked into those waters. I wish you'd stayed behind with me in Refuge and left that cursed rock with nothing but a hangover."

"Aye, love. There's been many times in the long years since I've wished the same."

A whistling scream, followed by a juddering cracking sound, sent them both sprawling to the floor of their cells. Fire ripped across the ceiling and Tempest turned to see Cazuuli cackling with glee as he knelt inside his flaming circle of sigils. The stones and shells placed around the circumference were blackened and smoking. Before him, a large chunk of the gaol wall had been completely blasted away. Cazuuli rolled through the last of the dying flames, briefly paused to tamp out a stray ember smoking in his beard, and lifted his middle finger in Tempest's direction before climbing through the broken wall and disappearing.

Tempest strained to see through the smoke. "Sheena, you still with me?" There was no reply.

"Are you hurt, Captain?"

Mary appeared at the door of her cell, crouching like a spider on four bent knees. Tempest roused at the comforting sight of keys swinging from her hand.

"I'm fine," she said. "How did you escape?"

"The wizard's fire tore right through my cell. Buckled the door. I found these keys on a smoking fishguard."

"You have the luck of a turtle dragon, Mary. How fares Sheena?"

Mary moved to the adjoining cell and shook her head. "She's escaped, Captain. The explosion took down this wall, too."

"She left me here to burn?" Tempest kicked at her bars with a hoarse roar and Mary almost dropped the keys. "Unlock the bloody door, Quartermaster."

They escaped the rubble of the smoking gaol and hauled themselves up onto the roof to watch the fishguard swarm around the Nexus. If Tempest interpreted their jerky hand gestures correctly, they were searching for two intruders.

"What are your orders, Captain? Do we pursue the wizard, or get the *Harpy* back out to sea?" Mary looked towards the coast, her face pale and strained.

Tempest watched the scene below. There were too many fishguard down there, even for a seasoned pirate and a flame-throwing wizard to deal with. Nasal, rasping clicks sounded in the broken courtyard.

"Captain, the way is clear to the east. We should fly before we're glimpsed."

She had a crew to think about. An insatiable screaming dryad to feed. Sheena hadn't given those same concerns a passing thought when she jumped ship and headed for Torganal.

"Captain?"

Halberds were raised. Flat feet pattered on stone. Tempest wrenched her gaze from the Nexus and turned to Mary.

"Let's be away, Quartermaster."

If Sheena survived, they would find each other again.

SELECTED LETTERS SENT AND
RECEIVED BY THE FAMED ELVEN
PIRATES OF SCOURGE COVE DURING
THE SECOND GOLDEN AGE -
VOLUME III

COMPILED AND EDITED BY KELL'TAN, HEAD
LIBRARIAN OF THE GLOAMING SPIRES

CAROLINE BARNARD-SMITH

Librarian's Note: *The following is a small sample of the many letters sent by Captain Tempest Brack of the Screaming Harpy to Ms. Sheena McKracken (née McIvor) of Vista, Noddingtown. These pirates are of historical interest in part due to their early co-captaincy—unheard of amongst other elven pirates—and in part to the unusual nature of their ship and the dryad living between its decks. Many continue to search for the wreck of the Harpy, spurred on by those who claim to have heard its screams of starvation echoing from the caves and cliffs of Elysium Cove.*

*D*earest Sheena,
　　Let me start by telling you how sorry I am about how we parted. I shouldn't have thrown that grappling hook at you. I hope your shoulder has healed.

I hate this feeling of being left behind. I find myself wandering the *Harpy's* decks like a rum-soused ghost, lost in a way I've never experienced before. On days when the seas are quiet and the ship is sleeping, I like to imagine what you are doing. I see you poring over some water-warped tome in a wizard's private library. That, or weaving stories of our shared exploits in a palm-shadowed pub, keeping the locals spellbound as they jostle to buy your drinks.

I just hope you're not lonely.

Return to me. Let me heal this rift.

Forever yours,

Tempest

Dearest Sheena,

We finally unspelled that map you filched at our last Conclave and have unearthed a large cache of mermaid pearls. The crew toasted our victory, but the rum hit me cold because you weren't there to celebrate with us.

You know I worry. You were wild with boredom back in Scourge, I can only imagine how torturous the quiet streets of Noddingtown must be. I often remember that Winter Solstice at the Lavender Drum when you jumped in the grog barrel. A woman ready to punch the barkeep for attempting to drag her back out is not a woman content to stare into the horizon day after day on the head of a placid turtle. The *Harpy* offers more years of gifted life than I would ever wish to live alone. Just send word, and I will chase that bastard turtle down to reach you.

Forever yours,

Tempest

Dear Sheena,

Please reclaim your bilge-dragon. It keeps setting fire to the rigging, and the ship doesn't like it.

How long am I supposed to captain without you? Last month we narrowly avoided capture by the Pirate Kings. Kindly tell those greedy fools the *Harpy* will do them no good—the dryad will only share her blood gifts with us.

I wonder if you would even recognise me should you see me now? I avoid the glass; my face belongs to a stranger. The magics we wove through this ship are toughening my features and those silver eyes you were so fond of are now a flinty grey. All would be easier to bear if you would only return to me, my love. This bounty of years was supposed to be shared between us.

Yours,
Tempest

Sheena,

I have taken on a quartermaster, an educated woman with a fine head for maps. She tells me she's a mermaid; but if she was, she no longer has a tail, so I can't be sure.

I've changed my mind about the dragon. It's an excellent rat catcher. The provisions have never been so little nibbled at, but the beast has a taste for rum and will set the ship's biscuits ablaze when refused a bottle.

We will soon be docking at...

Librarian's Note: *The rest of this letter has been rendered indecipherable due to extensive scorching.*

Sheena,

This will be the last time I write to you.

I will learn to live without you. I will endure. Please put me from your mind, as I have put you from mine.

Sincerely,

Tempest

LIBRARIAN'S NOTE: No return correspondence from Ms. Sheena McKracken has survived, although scholars have long debated the possibility that such letters never existed.

EXPOSED

A. R. K. HORTON

*O*riana missed the soothing cold waters of the ocean home she shared with her selkie colony. Even three years later, she hadn't acclimated to the mugginess of the Archipelago. It remained as foreign to her as everything else about this world of land dwellers.

The discomfort she experienced on land had been worth all the wonders she marveled at on the topside, though. If Oriana had stayed underwater, she never would have cast her bets at the Hydra's Bones arena nor stared into the distant and mysterious beam of the Lighthouse at the End of the World. She also wouldn't have known the many passionate nights she spent rolling around in bed with a gentleman pirate captain.

Everyone knew her lover, Gallant Grant, as the man who spread his wealth from island to island. While Oriana stood in line to view the Death Waters Fountain, he remained at The Quays, spoiling his crew with a tour of taverns and brothels. Oriana had no interest in their carousing, so he sent his first mate, Cait the Cruel, to escort her.

They had been standing under the summer sun for hours,

staring at the backs of heads queued up to enter the small ruin ahead, which held a fountain known for its magical but deadly waters. Every single prediction seen in its reflection had proven true, making it popular with those trying to dodge the Reaper.

"Still don't see why we couldn't have gone shopping at Salty Rest, instead," Cait said, her arms crossed and eyes far away.

"Where's your sense of adventure, Cait?" Oriana asked. "It shows you your death. Surely, you'd want to know if it's one you can avoid or one that promises a fulfilling life."

"Only you would see the wonder in something so morbid."

Oriana gave Cait a light punch on the shoulder, causing the tall and fearsome first mate to look down at her companion. The scowl twisting Cait's features would have scared off even the most heart-hardened pirate, but little Oriana responded with a crooked smile, and Cait laughed.

"Never tell a soul you punched me and got away with it," Cait said.

"That was a tap," Oriana said, rolling her eyes. The fountain's keeper waved for them to come forward. "Oh! It's our turn!"

Oriana skipped over to it with all the exuberance of a child at a fair. Cait shook her head and followed behind. In front of them, water poured from the kneeling elf statue's screaming mouth into the murky pool below.

"Don't drink the water," the keeper said. "Last man who did became part of the fountain. Why do you think the water's so dark?"

Oriana gulped. Maybe she didn't want to look into the fountain after all.

"I'll go first," Cait whispered to her. "Give you time to make up your mind."

Oriana offered the first mate a grateful smile and watched her kneel over the pool. Cait's eyes widened and then turned from the water to Oriana's face.

"What did you see?" she asked when Cait returned to her side.

"I earn a pirate's death," Cait answered. "It's not so bad. Give it a go."

Oriana took in a deep breath and knelt as she'd seen Cait do. She peered into the burgundy liquid, which shimmered and then shifted into a short scene. Oriana could have sworn she had opened a door to another world. The vision came through so clearly and its setting seemed so familiar. She saw herself as a selkie again, with greying fur around her big, black eyes. Her long-lost son and other selkies nuzzled her with their whiskered snouts until she fell asleep and never woke.

A tear trailed down Oriana's cheek, but she looked at Cait with a beaming smile. "Oh, Cait. I die a selkie. I—I must find my skin one day. And my son. My son was there. I have to tell Grant!"

He had saved her from the storm that stole her skin from the shores so many years ago, sweeping it into the ocean depths while she slept under the branches of a palm tree on Torganal Island. He had even tried to help her find it. Day after day, Oriana watched the ocean. Though she couldn't return to her selkie form, she still looked for the son who remained with their colony below the waves. Grant would understand better than anyone how excited she felt, how much hope bloomed within her.

Yet, Cait shook her head, a worried look on her usually stern face.

"Think about it," she said. "If you're a selkie again, that means he loses you. He might not like that news as much as you think."

"Oh."

Oriana's bright eyes darkened. She had grown to love Grant. Still, not one day in her human form had ever been as happy as her selkie days. While she longed for travel, romance, and adventure, her heart belonged in the ocean with her son. When she walked the shores at night, the waves pleaded for her to come home. She dreamed of holding her child again, and woke with tears on her cheeks.

On the carriage ride back to The Quay, Oriana noticed Cait seemed off. The first mate typically walked with a swagger, and her eyes could pierce through even the most terrifying orc. Instead, she fidgeted with her sleeve hems and her eyes had softened. What had started off as such an exciting day, resulted in both Oriana and Cait falling into an uneasy silence, and the selkie's heart sank even further.

On the ride up to the fountain, Oriana had chatted away with the other passengers. She delighted in their stories, flinging one question after the other at them. On the way back, even the fae soldier sitting across from her couldn't bring back her inquisitive nature with his battle stories and plans for exploration.

Oriana's somber mood continued to her room on the ship, where Grant waited for her with open arms. She nestled under his handsome chin and laid her head against his chest to hear his heartbeat.

"Where's my bubbly selkie?" Gallant Grant asked. "Perhaps you should have stayed at The Quay. Seeing your own death must have been grim."

Oriana lifted her head at the mention of her death vision and gazed up into her lover's handsome, smiling face. "Actually, it was wonderful. Grant, I die a selkie."

The captain's smile stiffened, becoming a thinly veiled grimace. His fingers dug a hair too deep into her flesh. Oriana winced, but Grant didn't seem to notice.

"I guess the fountain's lost its magic," he said. "There's no way you could become a selkie without your skin. Look, I bought you some pretties. I'll be right back."

Grant walked to their room's exit and stopped to say, "Stay here, Ori."

As Grant left their room, a dark suspicion crept into the back of Oriana's mind. She listened to his footsteps as they disappeared down the hallway beyond the door that was closed in front of her. He had told her to stay. Why?

Defying Gallant Grant's orders never worked out for any of the crew, but Oriana's hands soon turned the doorknob and she tiptoed out of their room. Skirting the shadows on silent feet, she trailed far behind him and then watched her lover open a small room she must have passed by hundreds of times over the years. It was Grant's personal treasury, which he alone possessed the key to enter.

Oriana held her breath and pressed her back against the wall when the light from Grant's candle splashed into the darkened hallway, reaching just a few feet away from her. She gave a silent prayer of thanks to all the saints of the Holy City when the captain's eyes passed right over her presence in the corridor's deep shadows. His light turned back into the treasury room interior, and she saw him clutch a handful of jewels. Then he stopped and turned to look at a small chest, which Oriana hadn't even noticed in the crowded space. Kneeling, he checked its lock and let out a relieved sigh.

Oriana scurried back into their room, her heart pounding. Doubts, never known to her before, screamed in her head. What was in that chest?

Grant didn't notice her lack of enthusiasm when they made love that night. He fell asleep right away. Oriana stared at the ceiling and tried to give in to the ship's hypnotic sway as they traveled west to Brig Island. They planned to sell some treasures at the Magician's Marketplace there.

Memories floated through her mind of the storm that had separated her from her seal skin and her child. She remembered feeling naked and exposed when Grant scooped her up in his arms and carried her to shelter. Fear had rippled through her for her child. Yet, that very night, the captain had charmed his way between her legs. Looking back on this, Oriana understood how strange it was that she would feel any urge to make love during such a moment. If he had her skin, he could control her heart.

Oriana studied the captain's chiseled jaw and black lashes. Men and women alike were drawn to him like moths to a flame. He didn't need any magic to win them over. She had nearly talked herself out of believing this terrible suspicion until she remembered how quick he had been to give up when they searched the shores the next day for her skin.

Realizing she wouldn't fall asleep any time soon, she slid out of bed and pulled on a night shift. Moonlight streaming in from the porthole shone down on the pile of Grant's clothing on the floor. Glinting from the folds, his keychain was just visible. Oriana bit her lip, weighing the risk before stooping to pluck it up.

The keys jingled, and she clasped a fist around them to stop the sound. To Oriana's surprise, Grant remained undisturbed in their bed. So she retraced her steps down the dark path from her room to the small treasury, noticing every creak she made in the blanket of silence.

The crew kept a strict curfew; no one would see her lurking around the hallways. Her shaking hands dropped the keys at the doorway to the forbidden room, and Oriana had to scramble to pick them up. She opened the door and darkness waited for her. Without a candle, she had to use her memory of where things were placed. Her searching hands fumbled over the various containers filling the room until she found the small chest.

More than her physical senses confirmed what she already suspected. Something inside this chest called to her, pulling her spirit closer like an esoteric magnet. It wanted her as much as she wanted it.

She tried key after key in the chest's lock until, finally, one opened it. Slipping a hand inside, she felt the dense, slick fur that had once been hers. Her skin blossomed with goosebumps, and she didn't know whether to laugh or cry. Her spirit soared, only to crash when the glow of a candle lit up the small room, and a cry tore from her throat.

"Ori?"

Oriana whirled to see Cait standing in the doorway with a stunned expression. Worried that she must appear to be stealing from the treasury, Oriana pulled her hands out of the chest and held them up to show she had nothing in them. She had to explain.

"Cait, he had my skin. He had it this whole time."

"Is she there?" Grant's voice asked from the hallway. Oriana's heart leapt up to her throat. The captain's face appeared next to Cait's, and his eyes widened when he noticed the small chest sitting wide open. "It's not what you think."

"You monster!"

Oriana jumped to her feet and lunged for her lover. He grabbed her hands and easily twisted them behind her back.

"Ori, I loved you at first sight," Grant whispered into her ear. "How could I let you go?"

"You took me away from my son!" Oriana cried.

Grant said nothing, but dragged her through the halls as she struggled in futility. At barely five feet tall and light as a feather, her efforts only exhausted her, while the tall, muscular captain remained unfazed. Oriana twisted and writhed as he took her below deck to the brig.

"You'll sit in here until you realize what I did was best." Grant pushed her into the wrought-iron cage of a room and locked the door. Oriana spit through the slats onto his face. He wiped her spittle off his thin, displeased lips. "You're overreacting."

"You lied to me for years and stole my identity," she said.

Her words fell on deaf ears, and Grant turned around, leaving her behind.

"What about my child?" she cried.

This made Grant stop. Still with his back to her, he said, "I can put another one in you, once you realize how good you have it."

Oriana crumpled to the ground, a torrent of tears gushing from her. She leaned against the bars of the brig as she re-examined her memories in a different light. Until tonight, she had never quarreled with the captain. From the beginning, she had been happy to give him all of her love and fealty. When he snapped, she came running.

More than once, she had been willing to risk her life for him. When she saw him in danger during a ship raid, she didn't even think before throwing herself into the battle to defend him, and she never failed to heal his wounds with her selkie tears. That alone made her worth keeping around.

He said he had loved her at first sight. Yet, he and his crew never shied away from brothels. Was she just another treasure for hoarding?

Her mother had always told her she would know true love when the other person valued her happiness above their own. That's how Oriana had felt about her son. She hadn't worried so much about his safety since they were separated. She knew her colony would take care of him. Still, she longed for her child the way any mother would, missing his rounded cheeks and lamblike bleat. She could almost pick up his unique scent if she concentrated hard enough.

Worst of all, Oriana had spent countless nights crying on Grant's shoulder about how much she missed her child and her colony. He had promised her so much, and she had been deaf to the lies coloring his words. He felt no remorse in taking everything away, and her skin crawled as she recalled every single one of his touches.

"Monster," she whispered, her aching eyes closing at last. "If I ever get out of here, I'll make you pay."

Hours later, Oriana stirred at the sound of footsteps. She expected to see Grant's handsome, despicable face when she opened her eyes, but Cait was there. Hesitant steps replaced the first mate's usual confident gait as she approached the brig with a bowl.

"Chef made your favorite," Cait said in a hushed tone. "Eel stew."

"I'm not hungry." Oriana turned away.

"Please eat, Ori." Cait knelt on the ground and pushed the bowl between the bars. "You need to stay strong."

"What's the point?" Oriana asked. "He won't let me out until I forgive him, and I can never do that."

"I can understand that."

Oriana's head snapped to Cait. She glared at the first mate. "Can you, Cait the Cruel? How long have you known he had my seal skin?"

"I didn't! I swear!" Cait answered, shaking her head.

"Sure you didn't," Oriana responded with a bitter chuckle. "You're more loyal to Gallant Grant than anyone. That's why you make sure to always have eyes on me wherever I go. You jump at his bidding."

"That's not why," Cait said, and a blush bloomed on her cheeks.

Oriana leaned forward and grasped the bars with angry hands. "Then why do you let me drag you all over the place?"

Cait's green eyes melted under plaintive brows, revealing her heart. "I would follow you to Bottomless Braddock's blade. To the Kraken's maw. To Hell."

Cait reached a hand through the slats and stroked Oriana's cheek.

"Cait?"

"Ori..."

Oriana's heart stirred within her, along with realization. Every adventure and laugh had been with Cait. While others quaked with fear at the first mate's approach, Oriana lit up. Time after time, Cait had proven she would do anything to make the selkie happy, and Oriana hated any day that lacked her companion.

Their faces moved closer, and Cait's hand slid from Oriana's cheek to her neck. Without thinking, their lips pressed together in a soft, warm kiss full of unspoken promises. Oriana's heart sang, joyful that she had listened to it at last. Yet, when their faces parted, she once again remembered all that Grant had stolen from her. Would he take Cait, too?

"I can't believe he did that to you," Cait said. "All these years. All those hours spent looking for your son."

Hot, angry tears spilled onto Oriana's cheeks. "I hate him. I wish he could feel this pain."

"Then let's make it happen," Cait said.

Oriana couldn't believe her ears. "What are you saying?"

"I saw my death in the fountain and it changed me." Cait wiped the tears off Oriana's flushed face. "I was very old, but a captain, fighting against a rival ship. A sword pierced my side. I grabbed someone, and I said..."

Cait's jaw tensed and she swallowed hard.

"You said?"

"When you see my wife Ori, tell her I won't be home for dinner." Cait's eyes shimmered with the promise of tears. "I don't want to die any other way. We need to put an end to Gallant Grant."

Oriana nodded. "He stole my skin. Let's see how he does without his."

"THANKS, CAIT," Gallant Grant said, taking the tea from his first mate. He took a sip and winced. "Didn't you put any sugar in this? It's so bitter."

Cait put the captain's other dishes into a pile and grabbed a rag. "You said you had a headache. I put a little willow bark in."

"It's that blasted selkie giving me a headache," Grant said. "If I can't charm the tears out of her, I'll have to give her other reasons to cry."

Cait clenched her fists and swallowed her words. She couldn't give herself away. She cleaned the table, watching the captain drink his curare-tainted tea from her peripheral vision. Minutes felt like hours until she noticed his drooping eyelids and the odd sway of his head.

"I fink I ha too mush grog," the captain slurred.

"Maybe you should lie down," Cait said.

Grant pulled down his jaw and pinched his skin like rubber. "Why canna fee anyfin?"

"The grog," Cait lied. "Lie down."

Grant nodded and attempted to stand up from his chair, only to collapse to the floor as his legs gave way. Peering up at Cait from his position on the ground, terror shone in his eyes as he realized his first mate wasn't towering over him to help him to bed.

"Go to sleep, Captain," Cait said, before kneeling down and hitting him on the carotid artery with the side of her powerful hand, making everything go black.

WHEN GRANT WOKE, he couldn't feel anything. He couldn't even make his mouth and tongue form words. He could only scream like an animal when he saw, from the corner of his eyes, the nettle rope binding him.

"Scream all you want," Cait said, wiping a skinning blade with a rag. "I took the ship past the Magician's Marketplace. We're moored by the Forest of Night. Everyone else stuck here is screaming too."

Shock slammed into his heart like a bolt of lightning. This wasn't the first time he had visited the Forest of Night, a terrifying thick of venomous plants and man-eating pixies covering up the majority of Brig Island's western end in perpetual darkness. However, he had only been here long enough to maroon a few of the crew that displeased him. If you made it out of here, you could survive about anything.

He tried to look down at his body, but he couldn't control his head well enough. It bobbed around until settling on his left shoulder, so that he watched the waves lapping beyond a shaking brush. Then Oriana came into view from behind the branches, and all the pieces clicked together. She was handing him a pirate's justice for the wrongs he had committed against her.

She sucked on a finger, then waved her hand as she winced. "The saltwater did nothing for that stinging nettle. I'd hate to be Grant when that curare wears off and he has to feel the nettle ropes he's bound in." She turned her head from the first mate to the captain. "Oh, you're awake. Good."

Oriana moved so close to the captain that her black eyes threatened to swallow him whole. She tilted his face right and then left, tracing lines over his cheeks and smiling.

"They don't call her Cait the Cruel for nothing," she said. Grant screamed again, and Oriana pressed a finger against his lips as she shushed him. "We're not going to kill you. I just wanted you to know what it was like for me, looking in the mirror and not recognizing myself."

He let his scream die, trying to figure out her meaning, only to have his thoughts interrupted by a shriek of agony in the distance. Oriana's smile widened.

"Maybe that was someone you abandoned here," she said. "No, we're not going to kill you, but I can't promise none of the others lost in these woods won't."

"Ouch!" Cait slapped her arm and something small and winged fell to the ground. "Can't promise the pixies won't kill you either. But, once you're out of the nettle ropes, you'll have as much chance as any other injured pirate in surviving this jungle."

Oriana walked back to Cait. She nestled against the first mate, who kissed the top of her head with tender affection. "Though, if you make it to The Mend for healing, I think you won't be known as Gallant Grant anymore," Oriana said, her dark eyes glinting at him with cold calculation. "With as much skin as Cait's taken from your face and arms and chest and legs, I can only assume they'll call you Gruesome Grant."

Oriana pulled a small bottle from her pocket. Then she tossed it onto the ground at Grant's feet. At this point, Grant had somewhat more control over his head, and he managed to move it just enough to see the shimmering liquid swirling in its glass container. Selkie tears.

"That's all you ever wanted from me anyway, right?" Oriana asked, but Grant couldn't even blubber a reply.

"If you can get to that bottle in time, you might heal enough to stave off hypothermia or infection," Cait said. "The scars, though, those will stay."

Sunlight broke through the branches above and gleamed off the glass. While Cait and Oriana left him behind, Grant watched how the breeze moved the branches, causing the light to dance on the bottle. He longed to feel the sweet coolness of those selkie tears. However, as the poison in his tea wore off, the wind burned like wildfire.

THE COLD WATER was heaven sliding past Oriana's gorgeous sealskin. She leapt up over a wave to watch her wife and lover, Cait the Courageous, at the helm of her ship. Her little selkie heart sang as she looked to the east at the sunrise. The Kraken's limbs stretched into the sky greeting Torganal Island, the place Oriana had last seen her son years ago.

Diving back underwater, she raced toward the seaweed her colony loved so much in this area. Could they have returned?

Could she be that lucky? She squinted in the darkness, whipping her head around for some sign.

A unique and familiar scent stilled her, and whiskers tickled her back. She turned to see the rounded cheeks she loved so much. He looked bigger than she expected. He had likely grown out of his lamblike bleats. Still, she had no doubt who this could be, and her body hummed with a happiness she hadn't known in far too long.

"Mother," he said. "I've been looking for you."

NEVER SO NEAR, NEVER SO FAR

A. R. K. HORTON

The bloom, the blush, the springtime love
Await the Vista maidens.
Their hair a flag, their cheek a dove,
Their hum a blissful cadence.

They're never so near,
Never so far,
From pirates bound for treasure.
Ships sail 'round
These islands that are
Taunting them with pleasure.

Sailors do say mermaids delight
In Undercurrent raptures.
Their unbound breasts a lustful sight.
No one denies such creatures.

They're never so near,
Never so far,
From pirates bound for treasure.

Ships sail 'round
These islands that are
Taunting them with pleasure.

The lone widows who roam Dagspire
Haunt you with longing glances.
They give you all you can desire.
Just give them starlit dances.

They're never so near,
Never so far,
From pirates bound for treasure.
Ships sail 'round
These islands that are
Taunting them with pleasure.

A tender touch is not too much.
The Mend can offer plenty.
A sack of gold the dames can clutch,
Procures a group of twenty.

They're never so near,
Never so far,
From pirates bound for treasure.
Ships sail 'round
These islands that are
Taunting them with pleasure.

Deep in their chest, a thund'ring crest,
No ecstasy forbidden.
Undressed or dressed, but ne'er repressed,
Labruma gals aren't hidden.

They're never so near,

Never so far,
From pirates bound for treasure.
Ships sail 'round
These islands that are
Taunting them with pleasure.

You risk your neck to find a wife
Within the Holy City.
But she can grant immortal life,
A fate no one can pity.

They're never so near,
Never so far,
From pirates bound for treasure.
Ships sail 'round
These islands that are
Taunting them with pleasure.

THE BALLAD OF TASMIN THE TATTERED

ASTRID KNIGHT

"They say she steals your soul, you know."

Tamsin blinked, glancing away from the statue in front of her and to whoever thought it would be fun to interrupt her sulking contemplation. A handful of feet away stood an elf, though they were the plainest looking elf she'd ever seen. They had dull brown hair, lifeless eyes, and teeth that were a little too big for their mouth. Their massive ears were pointed ever so slightly, save for the left that seemed to have some sort of bite taken out of it. They stooped down at the base of the statue, taking a small pair of shears and clipping errant leaves off the shrubs growing there. Tamsin chuckled humorlessly. The orc would have thought that a floating merchant market consisting of nothing but tied together rafts would have been less than conducive to growing plants. Though, there was a rumor here in Saltskiff that it had once rained toads. She supposed anything was possible.

The elf sniffed as they pruned another shrub. "That's what they say, anyhow. It isn't true, not one bit," they said, their voice simple and lilting. "After all, I see her every day, and I haven't lost my soul yet, have I? No, I haven't."

Tamsin glanced back up at the statue. It wasn't very imposing, at first look, since it depicted a small, round-faced halfling woman. Beneath the shadow of her tricorn hat and mane of grey hair, however, dark rusted stains streaked from her dull eyes to her jaw. Tamsin shivered. Of course she had heard the rumors: that Magdalene the Merciful's statue would occasionally cry tears of blood, and if you were a sod unlucky enough to be staring into her eyes when that happened, your soul would be ripped clean from your body.

Of course she had heard those rumors. Why else had she been staring at the thing dead on for close to an hour?

"Funny," the elf snickered as they straightened themself up, twisting one of the trimmed branches between their fingers. "Most people don't look at her at all. Usually, folk just avert their gaze until they're past her." They smiled to themself, focusing on the twirling branch in their grasp. "It's nice to have someone besides me admire how pretty she is. I'd wager she likes it, too, yes indeed."

Nodding, Tamsin poked at one of her tusks with her tongue and looked back at the statue, hoping the elf would just go about their pruning business and leave her be. "Happy to give her the company," she muttered, narrowing back in on the statue's eyes once again.

"I'm Dillon, by the way," the elf said.

Damn. She shouldn't have said anything. Now it was a conversation. "Hello, Dillon."

"Hi, there."

"Hello."

"Hi."

"Mm."

For a second, Dillon seemed like they were about to leave her be, crouching back down to trim down another hedge, but soon they popped back up like a spring daisy and blurted out, "Can I ask you something?"

"I'd rather you not," Tamsin drawled.

"But can I? Just because you'd rather I not doesn't mean I can't."

Sighing, Tamsin, not breaking eye contact with the statue, said, "What is it?"

"Why do you look at her when everyone else is so afraid?"

She let the night's breeze blow past her, just strong enough to lift a strand of her long, matted hair off her shoulder. The empty eyes of Magdalene stared back at her. No pity and certainly—unlike what her name suggested—no mercy.

Yet they remained dry. Not a single crimson drop spilled forth.

Her shoulders slumped as her gaze broke, falling to the perfectly tended bushes surrounding the base of the statue. "Because, Dillon," she said, resignation laced in her voice. "Where I'm going, I can't be afraid of anything."

SHE HADN'T BEEN CALLED Tamsin the Tattered for long. The first time she heard the title was at The Mend, the tavern in Marauder's Sanctuary, not long after it all happened. When she washed up on the island's shore, she was as close to death as she could get without actually making friends with him. It had been months of healing broken bones, closing infected wounds, and watching black bruises fade back to green. Even after her body healed, though, Tamsin stayed at The Mend, hoping that one more tankard of ale would be the thing to heal what still seemed to be broken. Each day, she would set herself up in the back corner of the inn, listening to the revelry of the healing and the healed as they chattered and made merry, feeling much like a nail that hadn't quite been hammered all the way into its base board.

It was there that she heard the ballad, a mournful yet mocking

tune, strummed by a Felician, his cat's paws plucking out the
song with cheeky derision:

> *O sing of the woes of Tamsin the Tattered,*
> *Whose crew's gentle bodies were beaten and shattered*
> *Against the rocks of Elysium's cruel churning tides*
> *And in Elysium's limbo, their corpses reside.*
>
> *O now, woe to the pirate queen,*
> *Her ships and her crews again never to be seen.*
> *O now, riches to rags for her,*
> *Her mantle is torn into scraps.*

After the song ended, she didn't hear much of anything else. It
had been months since she had fled the Cove, but it shocked her
how fast word had spread all the way out here on the other side
of the world. Years of seafaring, a fleet of ships, and a reputation
of ruthlessness had earned her the title Tamsin the Terrible. And
it only took one failed attempt to storm the Holy City and
commandeer the Well of Eternal Life for her to become Tamsin
the Tattered.

Tattered. She didn't like that word. It hit the ear wrong. Too
many harsh sounds.

The whole world knew of her shame. They knew how she had
taken a fleet of eight ships and plunged headfirst into the hurricane wall that surrounded Elysium Cove. They knew that only
two made it past the storms. They knew that the remaining
crews of those two ships attempted to take the Holy City, coming
up through the beaches to the south, and they somehow knew
that none of them made it past the jungle surrounding the city.

What they did not know was exactly what the cries of her
crew members being tossed violently overboard in the middle of
the sheets of rain and gale winds sounded like. How mangled and
disjointed their limbs looked as their bodies washed up on shore,

their skulls split open as they were battered against the rocks surrounding the beach. Or the precise sound of talons ripping into flesh as sirens swooped from above and tore the throats out of the crew who had survived. Or exactly what it was like to watch someone drown on dry land as a skeleton with water for flesh choked the life out of Tamsin's first mate as it brought her in for a seemingly tender embrace.

It didn't matter much, at the end of the day. They would still sing the songs of Tamsin the Tattered as they clinked their glasses and clapped along, deriving a sick glee from her biggest failure.

For weeks afterward, Tamsin resigned herself to a fate of being nothing more than a shameful, cautionary tale. The rest of her life would be spent slumped in the back of a pub, marinating in liquor and retellings of her failed attempt on the Cove until she no longer had the strength to endure it. It was a miserable prospect. She remembered how, as the child of a tavern owner, she would glance out to the sea, longing for glory found on the waves, desiring nothing more than a fleet of ships and the fear and reverence of everyone she came across. For a while, she thought she was achieving that. It disgusted her to think of that dream dying in disgrace, but with enough ale, Tamsin thought perhaps it was the ending she deserved.

A month after she had accepted her new tattered title, Tamsin had a dream.

She dreamt of that night, before the storm wall was spotted on the horizon, alone in her cabin with her first mate. There was business talk first, of course, but soon it became something else. As they lay tangled together afterward, Tamsin running her calloused fingers through the woman's hair, the human girl sat up and looked at Tamsin. Her eyes were what fascinated Tamsin in the first place—one green and one blue, every color of the sea in her gaze.

"Tomorrow, you live forever," she laughed. "Are you ready?"

And Tamsin woke up.

Within ten minutes, her ragged coat was around her shoulders, her room at The Mend vacant for the first time in months. As soon as she stepped foot out the door, she was on the hunt for a ship: anything she could sniff out that was headed toward Elysium Cove.

There was only one way she could think to remove the shame, the black mark on her name. To repair the tatters. Perhaps dying in humiliation was the ending she deserved, but she intended to earn a better one.

In fact, if everything worked according to plan, she wouldn't have an ending at all.

IT WAS an arduous journey back to the Cove. Hopping from ship to ship, Tamsin took any odd job she could on any sorry excuse for an operation that would have her—swabbing decks, gutting fish, tying lines. Whatever got her to the next island in one piece. It got her all the way to the Saltskiff Bazaar, the last bit of refuge before Elysium Cove. The stop at Magdalene the Merciful was a show of force, her last declaration to herself that she could no longer afford fear where she was going. The very next day, she was down at the docks, asking for a seat on the ship of anyone bold enough to attempt to breach the storms surrounding the Cove.

It was a struggle, but eventually, she came across a batch of fools stupid enough for the job. A craggy one-eyed human man, hiding behind a shroud of grey-green hair like tendrils of seaweed, waved her down, asking around an unlit pipe clenched between his teeth if she was headed to the Cove. He had an open spot for her since a handful of his crew were refusing to board again, knowing where their next stop was. Trying not to sound desperate, Tamsin agreed to take up duties. They set sail before the sun was even at the highest point in the sky.

During the few days it took to hit the storms, Tamsin kept to herself, knowing better than to make friends of future corpses. A few of the crewmates attempted to create idle chatter as they pulled sails or peeled potatoes. But she wasn't shy about giving anyone the cold shoulder. She thought back to just a few months ago when she had run her own ship, how she prided herself on knowing and caring for her crew as ardently as family. She would make the rounds each morning and ask each one of them how they were faring—some had kids back on land, some wives or husbands or partners. Some had nothing but the sea, but she asked them about their troubles anyway, knowing that the sea could be as fickle as any lover, and that love could ebb and flow just as quickly. They were her people. She would not be the frightening queen she was without them, and she wouldn't make it to the Well without them either.

She didn't, as it turned out.

She'd learned that whether she knew the name of these people or not, she would be immortal either way. She might as well skip the formalities.

The night before they reached the storms, as she put away a net that had gathered them a considerable hall of fresh fish earlier that day, Tamsin saw the one-eyed captain. He was hunched over as he leaned on the starboard side, gazing off into the already clouded horizon. It was only the two of them—the bawdy shanties and raucous laughter of the rest of the crew below floated up through the decks—so she kept as quiet as possible so as not to invite conversation.

"What business do ye have with the Cove, young'un?" he croaked over his shoulder as she tried to creep away.

So much for that, she thought. Tamsin paused for a moment, following his gaze out to the clouds. "The same business as everyone else, captain."

The captain chortled, a laugh ravaged by pipe tobacco. "Yer

conviction tells me otherwise," he said. "Not many who would seek out death so fervent as ye."

Tamsin stayed silent.

"They say there was an orc such as ye who escaped Elysium's wake with her life," the captain continued. "A right coward, they're callin' her. A shell of her former glory." He stopped, turning his sunken socket of an eye toward her, grinning at her with the four remaining teeth he had. "As tattered as the coat yer wearin' now, I'd say."

Tamsin tensed, her hand drifting over to her cutlass sheathed at her side.

If the captain saw, though, he didn't seem to find it intimidating, chuckling at her and turning back to the water. "Relax, young'un. It makes no difference to me what ye be seekin' or why. There's room in eternity for more than one, I wager."

Her grip on the handle of the sword eased, and her gaze narrowed. "I suppose," she said, tone laced in caution.

The two stared out over the horizon, the swirling mass of clouds flashing with heat lightning, a last warning to fools to turn back. The tense edge to Tamsin's shoulders softened as she stood beside the captain—for the first time in many years in the presence of another ship captain, she did not feel as though she were in the company of the enemy. Not necessarily a friend, either, but she supposed there had to be a neutral area somewhere.

"Tell me," she said, surprising herself by breaking the silence. "Why do you seek out the Well?"

"Is there a reason I shouldn't?" he asked.

"W-well, I mean..." How was she supposed to gently break the news to this bastard that he was old as rocks? "Someone as—experienced as you should know better, right?"

Chuckling, the captain said, "I know I'm well past my prime, young'un. My time draws to an end soon. Ye can be sure of that. Suppose that's why I'm makin' my run fer it. Don't have much left to lose."

"Would you really want to live forever in a body like yours?" Tamsin asked him.

Shrugging, the captain said, "At least I be knowin' what I have in store fer me. Death could be paradise or it could be torture. Even though my joints be achin' and my eye be missin', I know how to live with that much."

Tamsin nodded.

"And ye?" the old man asked her, his eye still on the clouds. "What will that Well give to ye, Tamsin the Tattered? A new coat thrown across those shoulders?"

She fixed her jaw, one of her tusks digging into her upper lip.

"I'm supposin' that's the difference between us," he mused, pushing away from the side of the ship and limping off down toward the galley. "If I live through this and fail, I know when to leave well enough alone. Can't see no good comin' from flyin' at the sun a second time."

He left her alone on the deck to watch the tower of storm clouds draw closer. For a moment, she felt bad, realizing she never got his name.

It didn't matter much, in the end. The next day, as they rounded the southern edge of the Cove, the storm thrashed, toppling one of the ship's masts over and crushing the old man under its weight. If he were alive after that, the massive wave that swallowed up the back half of the ship and swept his body into the waves would have finished the job anyhow.

THE FIRST INDICATION that she wasn't dead was the lapping of the waves. Blinking the white light out of her eyes, Tamsin sat up, wiping off the sand that had caked onto her face and blearily taking stock of her surroundings. As everything came into focus, her stomach sank.

It was the same beach she had washed up on all those months

ago. White sand sprawled along the edge of the cresting waves as far down as she could see. Littering the beach was a cemetery of destroyed ships—some were in mostly one piece, while others were reduced to nothing more than driftwood. Tamsin was sure if she looked hard enough, she would find pieces of her old fleet mingled in with the other failures. There may have even been bits of her old crew, though she sincerely doubted it. Many of the stories talked of dead bodies moving after the life had left them, relegating them to guard the beach, even the Well itself...

Tamsin didn't much feel like throwing up her dinner thinking about it all, so she unfocused her eyes as she stood up, gathering up what little belongings she had managed to keep with her.

Not too far off was the largest ship, the shape of a small skeleton strapped across the bow—the indicator of the Hesperus. Tamsin's hand floated back to her cutlass, which had stayed strapped to her side through the torrent. Squinting, she wondered if that thing—the creature made of water and bone, the one who had taken her first mate—was still lurking within.

Tamsin's grip on the pommel of the sword tightened. Was that thing capable of death? The stories hadn't said. Was she willing to risk it?

Shaking her head, she looked away, scanning the debris that was just washing in from the ship she had come in on. If she reached the Well and drank from it, there would be plenty of time to find out how exactly to kill that thing later.

It was a week of clearing jungle and hiking through the Hollow Mountains before Tamsin reached the Holy City. The nights of being eaten alive by insects, keeping hidden from sirens and other sky predators, and sheltering from the cold winds of the mountains' peaks were inconsequential to her. All Tamsin focused on was the end destination. In between dreams of that last night with her first mate, visions of the Well visited her; so clear in her mind's eye, yet blurred at the same time. When she woke, she could never remember exactly what it looked like. It only made her desire to see it for herself stronger.

When she finally reached the Holy City, it was like a dream itself. The pointed spires of the cathedrals shot up through the mists of the low valley, like one last beautiful warning. But if Tamsin hadn't listened to any of the warnings so far, she wasn't about to start.

The outskirts of the city weren't protected by a wall. It was easy enough to slip in undetected, mingling with a few of the local parishioners as they left the towering cathedrals and made the journey back to their homes for the evening. As far as she could tell, there were no taverns or pubs. The city slowly went silent as she made a beeline for the walled-in circle in the center of town, darting down side streets to throw off anyone who may have noticed an outsider in their midst.

As she reached the wall, Tamsin swore every colorful word she knew under her breath. The front entrance wasn't just guarded—it was a few soldiers short of an army. Almost a dozen armored guards stood at the metal gate into the inner circle, relaxed yet attentive. Just to be sure, she did another check around the perimeter of the wall, hoping that there might be one other weak point she could get through without a fight. There was a reason, though, that this city had never been breached by anyone in known records. The walls were far too tall to scale, and any possible way in was posted. Winding her way back to the gated entrance, there wasn't any other option she could see.

Unsheathing her cutlass, Tamsin whispered her first mate's name against the dull edge of the blade. Then, an apology.

And she charged.

Tamsin the Terrible had been known as a terrifying combatant before her fall. Swordplay was an art form, and her trusted cutlass she had since she was a girl was still the one she used to paint bloody portraits across the canvas of her opponents. Which is exactly what she did as she approached the guards at the gate, slashing against the surprised guards with near reckless abandon, carving her way to the gate as if she were cutting down vines through a jungle. It would be foolish to think she could take each of them out, but she managed to fell a handful of them as she latched onto the gate, climbing up the metal bars with every ounce of strength she could muster after a week of hiking in the wilderness. The shouts of the guards below were muffled noise to her as she scaled it, hopping over the fence and sprinting into the sanctum as if the hounds were right at her heels.

Stone and metal passed by her in a blur as she ran further into the structure. There were more shouts of surprise and anger that she encountered, but her gaze was only focused ahead, only on the prize. Occasionally, something would whizz past her ear or graze her shoulder. It would only make sense that they'd have every guard on watch shooting at her with their crossbows, but she couldn't think about that. Not now.

She turned into an open area and found herself facing a stone dome, aged and covered with moss and vines, in the center of the complex. Her heart hammered against her ribs as she cut her way through soldiers, the sound of their bodies clattering to the ground nothing more than the sound of a passing breeze to her. In her ear, she could almost hear her first mate tell her to stop, but Tamsin pushed it away, focusing instead on the blood rushing through her ears as she pushed through the heavy oaken doors to the dome, frantically shoving them shut, throwing down a heavy deadbolt to lock it behind her.

Tamsin panted as she leaned against the door, the cacophony from outside the doors muted but far enough away where she knew she was safe for a moment. Swallowing, she turned to the chamber, grabbing a torch hanging off the wall beside her. It had seemed cramped from the outside, but inside, the Well's home was cavernous. The ceiling towered above her, so much so that the torches on the walls surrounding her would not have provided enough light for her to see the apex. It was only the hole at the highest point of the structure, showering down pointed moonlight, that made it so she could see the full expanse.

Underneath the column of light, Tamsin saw her eternal life illuminated before her.

It was nothing more than a vacuous hole rising from an island of loose stone and shale, a small void that so many had lost their lives for. Surrounding the island was a mote of black water, the firelight dancing off the rippling surface. There was a reason this area was called the Tunnel, this pool serving as a way for mermaids and other creatures from the sea outside the Cove to come in and gaze at the Well in reverence. A singular pathway led out to the island, the water delicately splashing on either side of it.

Behind her, a pounding shook the dead bolted door.

Best be quick about this, then, Tamsin thought.

She paced forward, the stone path narrow enough where her boots were getting wet. Adrenaline rushed through her body as she stared at the beacon ahead, the thing that had haunted her dreams for months, the one thing that would make all her drunken nights of self-loathing and regret worth something. Her first mate's mismatching eyes flashed through her mind. Perhaps once she took her first sip of the Well's waters, the thought of them wouldn't hurt so damn much. Maybe—

Her feet flew out from underneath her, a vise grip of something wrapped around her ankle as she slid across the stones toward the water. Without thinking, she swiped her cutlass down with a grunt, cutting away whatever had hold of her. Shuffling back up to her feet, she glimpsed something slithering down into the water, leaving behind a scaled hand, cut off at the wrist, still clinging to Tamsin's boot. Shaking it off, Tamsin gazed back at the water, ripples curling up from underneath the once placid surface.

She barely had time to utter out a *"fuck"* before the creatures started rising out of the water.

It was more than just mermaids with their patches of scales blending into flesh that clawed their way onto the pathway, sharpened teeth bared as Tamsin stumbled back. Other bodies pulled themselves onto the island behind her, bloated and mangled, flesh sloughing from their bones as they breached the water and shambled their way onto dry land. Her heart skipped as she teetered down the path, pumping her legs as fast as they would go across the uneven ground. Try as she might, though, it wasn't fast enough. The swollen corpses descended upon her as she reached the island, enveloping her in a ring of living death.

The sounds escaping from her as she hacked at the walking bodies clawing at her were unnatural, desperate and feral as she cleaved off limbs and shoved away the pawing grips of too-soft fingertips. They hissed as their jagged nails dug into her skin, pulled at her hair, tore at her clothes. She tried fighting them all off, but there were so many—*so* many—all reeking of rot and moaning in an agony she wasn't sure she was causing them. Her grunts turned to screams as she warded them off with her torch and thrust her blade into them, one after another, their bodies going limp–but for how long, she couldn't be sure. All she could do was swipe, stab, stay the fuck alive, just until she reached that goddamn Well—

Her blade pulled back from the gut of a rotund, naked corpse, and she collapsed on the ground next to it, gasping for breath and witnessing the felled corpses around her. They were all motionless, innards splayed onto the stones like a gratuitous painting. She huffed, pushing down the nausea as she pulled herself to her feet. There was a stitch in her side, blood running into her eye, and a sharp jab that ran up her right leg as she put pressure on her foot. Her coat was a shredded mess, hanging off her like rags.

The door behind her shuddered, a thunderous pound, as the wood around the hinges began to splinter.

Tamsin sputtered as she limped up to the Well, willing her feet to stay steady underneath her, though her legs felt like they would give out at any moment. Reaching the edge of the hole, she sprawled herself along the edge, pulling up the chain that she prayed held the well bucket.

Another cacophonous strike echoed through the cavern, and she nearly let the chain slip through her fingers. As the bucket crested the stone edge of the Well, she hungrily grasped at it, eager to drink of the contents inside.

This was it. She'd done it. All the torture and the guilt and rage and regret—it would actually mean something—

As she put her chapped lips to the bucket and tipped it backward, she paused.

It was empty.

Pulling it away, she looked into it. Nothing. Not a drop glistened from inside the bucket. She reached a shaking hand inside, desperately feeling around for any hint of moisture.

Her heart sank. Bone dry.

Glancing into the hole, nothing but darkness stared back at her. Shaking, she tossed the torch in her hand down the hole, watching the pinprick of light flicker and fade into the darkness. She waited for the splash—please, there needed to be a splash—

But it never came.

She turned herself away from the hole, leaning back on the stone edge in shock.

The Well of Eternal Life had run dry.

Her fleet, her crew, her reputation—all of it gone. For a dried-up hole in the ground.

For the first time in months, Tamsin laughed. Hysterical and unhinged, tears streaming down her face.

She listened as the Holy City outside pounded on the bolted door. She watched as the waters in front of her shifted again, another dozen living corpses lumbering out of the depths and advancing toward her with twisted moans escaping from them like sighs. And her laughter roared louder as one stopped in front of her, staring down at her with almost luminous eyes. One green and one blue.

Tamsin the Tattered smiled up at her first mate.

Today, she lived forever.

And as the tears streamed down her face and her crew tore into her, Tamsin decided she wasn't ready.

THE CURSE OF THE CRIMSON EYE

ROBERT MAMMONE

W *hen a ship burns, it dies.*
The screams of the dying faded as the crackling grew louder, demonic laughter filling the twilit sky. Flames leaped through the rigging and burning rope fell onto the deck, where smouldering bodies lay like blackened petals. The inferno burned with an unnatural fury; already the quarterdeck, where Captain Hellion once ruled as a tyrant, was well ablaze. Watching all this, Corvin tried holding together the shattered remnants of his sanity. All around him embers floated; orange, then red, then black, dancing as the ship died.

Even as the *Maiden's Kiss* drifted aimlessly, smoke pouring into the sky, even as shadows danced and leaped and clawed, Corvin's attention remained fixed on one particular shadow moving with a remorseless volition. Where that crimson-tinged shadow trod, death followed. And now, as timbers warped and cracked, the shadow turned its red-limned gaze onto him...

CORVIN STOOD at the prow of the *Maiden's Kiss*, his eyes closed, his bracered arms raised above his head. His senses ranged out, deep beneath the surface of the ocean and high above the crow's nest. Any hint of a current or a breeze, anything for him to latch onto to move the becalmed brigantine. On his second sweep, with the sounds of the ship a blur, Corvin sensed... *something...* A distant blaze, a dream of power. He focussed on it, felt the bracers grow warm as arcane magic poured through them. Then he recoiled, gasping.

Something had touched his soul, a sickness that sucked at his marrow. In that fugue, Corvin sensed a dark presence. Blacker than night it was, shrouding a crimson pulse. Suddenly, an eye opened, red-rimmed and hungry. He felt that eye turn its burning gaze on him. Icy fear flooded him, and Corvin opened his mouth to scream when—

Like a drowning man surfacing, Corvin found himself again. He grabbed for the rail to stop from toppling into the water. The day had shaded into evening. Great fingers of rusty light reached across the ocean like the Crimson King readying himself to drag the brigantine beneath the waters into the abyssal depths. Shaken by the vision, Corvin breathed a shuddering sigh of relief. As the bracers cooled, he looked around.

Despite the hour, it was furnace-hot, made worse by the lack of wind. The crew was fractious, Captain Hellion more so, because this hunting season had been as barren as the Certurian Desert. Nursing unspoken grievances, the crew moved about as sluggishly as the drifting *Maiden's Kiss*.

'Holy Rek save us. It's a black barge.' Shark's voice dripped with superstitious dread.

'Don't you dare say that, Shark. Don't you dare.' A crewmate standing nearby, Copper, made a sign of protection with his left hand. His earring winked bloody in the fading light. Unwillingly, Corvin turned and saw Shark standing beside the figurehead at the ship's bowsprit, his shaking finger pointing to a black smudge in the distance.

'Holy Rek,' Copper said, echoing Shark. He looked at Corvin, panic written all over his face. 'What should we do?'

'You know not to speak to the conjurer. Hellion will have your guts for garters. We tell the Captain,' Shark said and spit over the rail. Corvin watched the pair hasten to the quarterdeck, where Captain Hellion paced back and forth. Despite Shark's words, Corvin drifted after them, his bracers suddenly cold.

The quarterdeck offered an unimpeded view of the ocean from horizon to horizon. The water, tinged bloody by the dying sun, shimmered quicksilver bright. It had been a bad season, made worse for the deaths early on, deaths that some of the crew said proved the *Maiden's Kiss* was an unlucky ship. One man drowned; the other died choking on a fishbone. The third man to die did so on Hellion's orders. The corpse swung from the yardarm for a full day as a warning against speaking of ill-luck again.

'Captain? Captain Hellion.' Corvin heard an unfamiliar note in Shark's voice. *Fear.* Shark clambered up the ladder onto the quarterdeck. His bare arms and face were covered in tattoos, faded to vague inkblots that looked like storm clouds. Top and bottom front teeth were filed to points, as was the way of his tribe. More than once, when leading a raid, he'd buried those teeth into the throat of a sailor defending his ship, soft flesh ripped out in a spray of blood. It took much to make Shark afraid.

Hellion unsteadily paced the quarterdeck. On embarking three months ago, his mood had been bad and grew worse with the passing of the season. The men crewing a pirate ship do so in the safe knowledge their existence depends on bloody violence and plunder. They will raid a ship, kill its crew and glory in it rather than spend a day in honest work. A pirate captain who cannot provide that glory is a captain living in constant fear of mutiny. The crew of the *Maiden's Kiss* had watched in sullen silence as other pirate ships feasted on easy pickings, leaving only a few bloated, fish-eaten corpses wallowing in the ocean. Already partial to a drink, Hellion had gotten deeper into his cups the longer the crew waited for gold.

Hellion stopped his pacing and squinted at Shark. 'What is it?'

'Ship, Captain. A black barge.'

Several of the crew working in earshot stopped at Shark's echoing words. Everyone who sailed the oceans knew what a black barge was; after all, where there is magic in the world, there are dark things. *Frightening things.*

'Get back to work, you dogs,' Hellion roared, his face purpling with rage. He held a clay jug in his hand and took a swig from it, wiping his mouth with the back of his hand. The First Mate, Tobias, stood beside the helmsman, watching Hellion with a cautious eye.

'Come here,' Hellion said, his voice dropping to a low snarl. Shark, perhaps reminded of his hanged crewmate, came to Hellion with the look of a whipped cur. Hellion held his hand out and snapped his fingers. Tobias, something of a whipped cur himself, came over.

'Fetch me my telescope, and look sharpish.' Venturing hastily to a small structure at the rear of the quarterdeck, Tobias returned with Hellion's telescope.

Taking the verdigris-stained copper-sheathed device, Hellion looked at Shark. 'You go around shouting something like that again, and I'll keel haul you all the way back to Labruma, do you hear?'

Shark's head nodded like it was about to drop off. Corvin sidled up to Hellion, who looked sidelong at him but said nothing. The runes stamped into the bracers Corvin wore ensured the conjurer's magic could only be shaped to influence the weather. Otherwise, freed of them, Corvin would've enacted a wild, bloody vengeance on the man who held him enslaved. Both men knew it. Extending the telescope, Hellion clamped it to his eye. For a long few seconds, he focussed on the dark object sliding past a mile away.

'Dog's right,' Hellion muttered. 'Maybe.' But greed lit his eyes. 'It is a ship, of that you can be sure.' He looked from Shark, to Tobias, and then to Corvin. 'Can you summon up a breeze?'

A half-smile crossed Corvin's face. Even though he held the whip hand, Hellion didn't like him. Of all the people on board, Corvin was the only one who gave him pause. The captain might be the master and Corvin the slave, but unlike the rest of the crew, who he could hang or keel haul, Hellion, who hated needing anyone, needed Corvin most.

'I can, Captain. But the men... they won't like raiding a black barge.'

'Damn them, and damn you,' Hellion said. He took a drink from the jug once more, and this only heartened his courage. 'Dead sorcerers aren't poor if they know what they're about. Get the longboat into the water.' He pointed to Tobias, then Shark. 'You two, with me and the conjurer. Those barges have no crew. We'll get across and see what pickings are to be had.'

Shark went white, and Tobias looked pale himself. Corvin smiled, though, to see their discomfort. A man with nothing takes his pleasures where he can.

Summoning a zephyr out of the hot air, Corvin shaped it so it pushed the longboat faster than two men rowing would.

'Would that you could do that for the *Kiss*,' Hellion grumbled, sitting in the stern. He knew as well as anyone that summoning such a wind was nigh impossible—conjurers could enhance what already existed, but calling up a breeze from dead air had killed better men than Corvin.

The bracers on his wrists grew hot, warmed by the magic

flowing through them. The engraved runes gleamed faintly. Hellion glanced askance at them, his gaze shifting uneasily to Corvin's. Corvin might be a slave, but he had value, even if he was nothing more than a tool for a man too greedy to know when to stop. Corvin smiled and nodded, and Hellion looked away.

The longboat drew closer, the sail snapping in the breeze. The ocean was like a mirror, quiet and dark. 'Tis a black barge, Captain,' Shark said. There was no triumph in his voice, only terror. He glanced over his shoulder at the *Maiden's Kiss*. His face was white. 'We should turn back.'

The black barge was mastless, a wide caravel wallowing in the ocean. Despite this, propelled by a dead sorcerer's final working, it slowly carved a path through the water.

'Shut your trap,' Hellion said softly. The look he gave the barge made Corvin shiver. 'Tell me, conjurer, about these black barges.'

'Rare,' Corvin said, staring raptly at it. 'This world is old, and the magic is dying. Fewer and fewer sorcerers exist. Their order has decreed that when they die, they must make the journey to the Lighthouse at the End of the World, which some claim is the source of all magic. Beneath the gyring stars, a barge circles the island widdershins three times before vanishing into the Utter West.'

'And treasure?' Hellion gave Corvin a hungry look. 'What about treasure?'

'You dare too much, Captain,' Corvin said. He glanced at the setting sun; the mixture of red light and deepest shadows mingled into something unholy. 'Desecrating a black barge on its journey can only bring ruin to the men who dare it.' Shark and Tobias glanced at each other, their faces unreadable.

'Don't tell me what I can and cannot do,' Hellion snarled. 'Tell me what treasure lies aboard.' By then, they were alongside the barge. A scent came off it, of incense from the far south and an underlying rot. And beneath that rot, something... *wrong*.

'All sorcerers are placed inside a triple coffin. Wood for the Tree of Life. Stone for Eternal Balance. And beaten silver to represent the moon, from which they draw their power. Inlaid into the silver will be precious stones and gems.'

Hellion licked his lips. 'A king's ransom. Treasure enough for all of us.' He reached down and lifted a coil of rope, fashioning one end into a loop.

'And inside the coffin?' Shark's voice was barely a whisper.

'Inside the coffin?' Now it was Corvin's turn to smile. 'Why, Shark, the sorcerer's corpse. Triple sealed, to keep him in.' His smile grew broader. 'Maybe.'

They heard a slap. Hellion had tossed the looped end of the rope at the barge, where it caught on a spar. He pulled, tightening it into a knot, then fastened the other end to an iron loop in the prow of the longboat.

With the others, Corvin clambered hand over hand up the rope and onto the barge's deck.

'WHY IS THERE NO CREW?' Hellion brought the jug to his lips and sucked greedily at it.

'No need,' Corvin said. He closed his eyes and inhaled, savouring the power in the air. 'The tides of magic guide every barge to the Lighthouse.'

'So the sorcerer's casket is here, unprotected?' Hellion laughed. He was most of the way to being drunk.

'The legends talk of a curse, Captain,' Corvin said. He felt lightheaded with the power coursing through the barge.

'What sort of curse?' Shark said.

'Damnation. Utter damna—'

Hellion's fist knocked Corvin off his feet. The world blurred, and he struggled to rise when he felt a hand clamped over his face.

'Say one more word, dog, and you'll dance off the yardarm,' Hellion said, spraying him with spittle.

The lengthening shadows deepened. Through his daze, Corvin heard Shark whimper. Releasing his grip, Hellion stepped back. His shadow fell across Corvin like a shroud.

'You're all like women. Miserable and complaining and useless. Come on, damn your lazy hides, let's get this treasure.'

Corvin saw Tobias move to help him, only to be stopped when Shark grabbed him by the arm and gave a warning shake of his head. While Corvin struggled to his feet, they joined Hellion, who clattered down a gangway into the gloom beneath the deck.

'Make light, conjurer,' Hellion said, his face hidden in shadows. Holding the bracers to his lips, tasting the metal on his tongue, Corvin whispered a few words. The runes flared into life, casting a silvery light that sent shadows sprawling ahead of them.

The corridor was narrow, the ceiling low. The smell of incense increased in the confined space, and the stink of rot, which Corvin was sure only he could scent, was stronger still. A ladder halfway along the corridor took them down into the barge's depths. Despite the light cast by Corvin's bracers, the darkness pressed close. Someone moaned. Hellion glanced back. His earlier bravado had vanished, leaving a pale face, sickly in the scant light. The barge creaked and groaned like a dying old man.

'Stairs.' Hellion's voice drifted back to Corvin. He held the bracers high, but it did little good. Soon, they were descending what felt like an endless staircase, spiralling deeper and deeper into the darkness and farther and farther from the light.

'What was that?' Tobias moaned. Somewhere below in the cold and darkness, something large thudded against the hull. There was a pause, and then again. And again.

'We should go back,' Shark said, almost whimpering.

'Shut your mouth, or I'll gut you. Bring that light here,'

Hellion said, his voice muffled and echoing at the same time. 'We've reached the bottom.' It seemed as if they had been descending for minutes, but a bloody light bled through a chink in the caulking. They were still above sea level.

Corvin did as ordered. The light led them through a narrow door into a room thick with incense. Lifting a hand, Corvin saw the light reflected back to him as if from a thousand eyes.

'Here it is, boys,' Hellion said. His face cracked into a broad grin. 'We'll never have to raid again.'

A silver casket rested on a bier. Covering the casket were countless emeralds, rubies, and diamonds. Greed ate their fear. Like a seagull plucking the eyes from a corpse, Tobias unsheathed his knife and started prying at a gem, a lozenge-shaped emerald as long as his thumb. Shark joined him.

Soon, the three men were picking away at the casket, pocketing gemstones like boys picking seashells from a beach. Corvin stood back, watching as they desecrated the casket.

'Come on,' Tobias said, pausing from levering out a sapphire as big as his fist. 'Don't just stand there.'

Corvin nodded, but his attention was drawn to Hellion, staring enraptured at something on top of the casket. When Corvin joined him, he saw what consumed the Captain.

It was a ruby, carved into the shape of an unblinking, red eye. Big as a fist, its worth was incalculable. Corvin shuddered. When the light from his bracers hit it, it lit up Hellion's face crimson, making it look as if he wore a mask dipped in blood.

'Magnificient,' Hellion breathed. He began digging his knife into the silver setting.

At that moment, the barge shuddered, throwing them all off balance. A loud crack sounded, followed by a gushing noise.

'What was that?' Shark asked in a monotone. His attention remained on ripping as many gems from their mountings as he could.

'Nothing,' Hellion said. His voice sounded distant, distracted, as if the only thing of importance in the world sat in front of his eyes. He continued digging. More noises. The barge shuddered again and again.

By this time, Shark and Tobias had filled their pouches and pockets to bulging. There was a manic gleam in their eyes. Despite the shuddering and cracking, it looked like they were prepared to stay on the barge even if it sank beneath the waves.

'We have to go,' Corvin shouted above the shuddering. The sound of timber groaning and shattering somewhere in the darkness filled him with panic. Gone was his earlier bravado. He sensed the approach of a horrible death, far from the light. At that moment, Hellion freed the ruby and brandished it triumphantly. Above the tortured sounds of the barge coming apart, they all heard three knocks.

Shark went white. He backed away from the casket. 'Did you hear that?'

Tobias shook his head as if to deny what they had all heard, but he too stepped away. Hellion, who had been closest, laughed. His eyes gleamed red. 'We have what we came for. Now we go.'

Laden with jewels, they moved unsteadily towards the stairs. All around them, the barge shook. Timbers creaked and groaned, the mournful sound like a lament for the dead. Last to leave, almost choking on terror, Corvin looked back. His heart stopped. He saw the casket limned in a crimson light. The barge shuddered. The casket lid shifted. A shadow seemed to seep from the gap. Even if Hellion hadn't bawled his name, Corvin was already halfway up the ladder.

The men staggered onto the deck. Only a faint crimson line on the horizon gave a hint that the sun had ever ridden the sky. The *Maiden's Kiss* was a distant shadow. Everywhere, the lights had gone out. The men shuffled across the deck as if approaching a gallows. Hellion clambered down the rope, a smudge in the darkness. Shark and Tobias followed.

The curtain of twilight that surrounds Brig Island drew near.

Corvin saw the shadowy outline of the island itself and the distant glimmer of the Lighthouse. Awkwardly, he climbed over the railing and slithered down to the rope, where Shark and Tobias helped him into the longboat. Hellion sat in the stern, looking at the ruby cupped in his hands, while Shark cut the rope.

The barge, a great slab of darkness, started to drift off course. In moments, its bulk was lost to view.

'Get us back,' Hellion said distractedly. He was staring raptly into the ruby.

More tired than he realised, Corvin raised another breeze, and in a few minutes, they were welcomed back to the *Kiss* by a cheering crew. All thoughts of bad luck and ill-omens vanished when Shark and Tobias piled gemstones onto a rumpled blanket. The cheers flitted about in the rigging as darkness claimed the world.

Unable to shake the unease that had settled into his bones, Corvin looked for Hellion. He found him, squatting beside a barrel, staring into the ruby's depths. A bloody gleam of light played across his face. Slowly, Hellion looked up, his eyes blank and hungry. The covetous smile he gave Corvin chilled him to the marrow.

IN THIS LIFE, the Devil takes the hindmost.

The disappearances began that night. Glass lanterns hanging fore and aft cast a gloomy light across the deck, where, after the celebratory feast degenerated into raucous singing and several drunken brawls, many of the crew slumbered.

Corvin didn't. Head full of the stuff of raw magic, he wandered the deck in a daze. The bracers felt icy to the touch, but even then, the night remained hot, made worse by a warm breeze riding in from the south. Clouds scudded across the moon, its skull-like features grinning idiotically down on the *Maiden's Kiss*. There was something about the light—

Corvin froze. A shadow slipped from a doorway. His heart pounded and he felt the bracers binding his wrists grow warm. A lurching moment, as if the deck suddenly yawed, then Corvin saw it was Jantos, the oldest crew member, coming up from below decks. Jantos half raised his hand in greeting when the shadows suddenly pooled and clotted around him. One moment Jantos was there, and then, he was gone.

White noise filled Corvin's head. He felt a surge of power ripple through him, dissipating just as quickly as it came. Staggering, he kept his balance with an effort. Looking around, Corvin saw he was the only one awake. No one else had witnessed the disappearance.

He was about to wake the nearest sailor when a hand clapped him on the shoulder. He turned and saw Hellion looming by his side. In the glow of the lamps and the moon, Hellion's face looked cadaverous. Hellion grinned, but there was something wrong with his eyes.

'Come with me,' Hellion said, his voice barely above a whisper. Something essential had been leached from the man. His hand tightened painfully on Corvin's shoulder. 'Now.'

Corvin found himself pulled through a doorway beneath the quarterdeck. Inside, Hellion moved with confidence along the pitch-black corridor. Within moments, Corvin entered Hellion's cabin, which was lit by a single candle.

Corvin felt trapped inside a dream, one where he desperately wanted to scream a warning, but where only silence emerged from his gaping mouth. He watched Hellion pull something from the inner pocket of his shirt. A thick crimson radiance spilled from the ruby, rendering his face into valleys and peaks of black and red.

'It speaks to me, conjurer,' Hellion said. His face twisted as if he was struggling, and his awed voice turned into a hitching sob.

He clutched the side of his head with his free hand. 'In here, it speaks to me. Why?'

As Hellion held the ruby aloft, shadows chased themselves around the room, crawling up the walls and across the ceiling in ceaseless waves that gradually coalesced behind the captain. Fearful now, remembering how the shadows devoured Jantos, Corvin inched towards the door.

The crimson radiance grew deeper and began to throb. Hellion, frozen in rapture, vanished as shadows swarmed over him in a black tide, leaving behind only the floating ruby, settled within shadowy folds. Corvin sensed an intelligence glaring at him from within those shadows. Ancient. Malign. Hungry.

Searching for the door, Corvin stumbled around and tripped over a chair, his fall seemingly endless in the dark. He hit the floor with a grunt. Terror consumed him. Shouting, he crawled in what felt like endless circles as whispering laughter filled his head. He found the door. Throwing it open, Corvin scrambled into the corridor and ran. Pausing on the threshold, he saw a wave of crimson-tinged darkness surge from the captain's cabin. Corvin threw himself through the door onto the deck.

His cries roused some of the revellers from their drunken stupor. Backing away from the doorway, Corvin stumbled into Shark, who blinked blearily at him.

'Watch where... conjurer? What's wrong?'

'The captain...' Corvin panted with fear, words dying in his mouth. By then, he didn't have to explain, only point in terror at what surged onto the deck.

What remained of Hellion was a smear of flesh across a red-tinged shadow bulging with other human features. Formless faces pressed against the inside of the shadow, mouths opening in silent screams as wide eyes blinked blindly, leaking crimson light. Another crew member, awoken by the noise, suddenly screamed as shadows swarmed him. He fought against them, but it was like fighting air. The shadows ate away at his body like waves against a sandcastle, reducing the flesh to tatters in the moonlight before the man completely vanished.

Pandemonium ensued as the crew, those unlucky enough to awaken to the screaming, found themselves attacked on all sides. Corvin watched Copper be overrun, his shuddering body slipping from existence in the time it takes a man to draw breath. Corvin backed away from the shadows, stepping over sleeping crewmen too drunk to know death was bare moments away.

'Do something,' Shark shrieked, his pointed teeth gleaming wet in the moonlight. He waved a cutlass around, the weapon utterly useless as the shadows gained strength and size.

Amidst his fear, Corvin sensed his bracers go icy cold. Magic pulsed through the aether all around him. Closing his eyes, he sent his senses ranging out, drawing the magic to him. It was tainted with that hellish crimson darkness, raw and pulsing with desire. Then, crying out lustily, Corvin lifted his arms to the sky and crashed the bracers together.

In an instant, a crackling bolt of lightning shot down from the sky. It filled the air around Corvin, a cage of light that turned night into day. For a moment, the shadows were gone, leaving only a bleached-out deck filled with dead and dying men. Then, the light vanished, and smoke filled the air. Utterly spent, his mind a shattered wreck, Corvin staggered about until he collapsed against a railing and watched the *Maiden's Kiss* catch fire...

DEATH COMES FOR US ALL, *and not in the ways we imagine.*

The crackle of flames brought Corvin back to what remained of himself. He reeled across the deck, heedless of the embers burning his bare feet. Already, the mizzen mast had collapsed, bringing with it a tangle of burning rope and tackle. Flames licked the length of the mast, smoke spiralling into the sky. He looked down and saw the ruby in his hands.

'I see you,' he muttered, his face fixed on the shadow watching him.

A cold wind issued from it. Corvin glimpsed the cold wastes between the stars within that formless shape, and what he saw broke him. Titan beasts, inimical to humanity, travelled through the inky void, indifferent to anything but their own gigantic appetites. The vision slammed shut, leaving only the shadow. Corvin heard whispers infiltrate his head, formless words that flitted like bats in a cave.

'Do you want it?' Corvin said, his eyes wide. He hugged the ruby to his chest tighter, a secret, cracked smile stretching his blistered face. Bloody light leaked from between his clutching fingers, fingers that had scrabbled unthinkingly through the ash after the lightning had seared the shadows. Tears tracked down his face when he heard an answer inside his mind, an answer that rocked him to his sundered soul. He looked around; the crackle of flames had grown to a roar, and everywhere there was fire. The crow's nest plunged into the ocean, trailing smoke like a comet. Distantly, Corvin saw the beacon on the Lighthouse at the End of the World gutter into darkness. Hope died in his chest.

'Do it, then.'

The shadow flowed over him—*into him*—like water. Drowning, Corvin struggled to find the surface, to find himself. Instead, the darkness clutched him tight, dragging him deeper into formless shadow. He hung suspended for an eon, a tiny spark foundering in a well of darkness so absolute it contained infinity. Then, in the distance, a flare of red grew into an onrushing tide of hellish light that consumed him in an instant. When sentience returned to him, the brigantine had sailed into legend.

THERE IS A TALE NOW, of a burning ship that sails the oceans of the world. Only on certain nights can it be seen, a distant beacon of flame, riding the horizon. While those who live a soft, safe life on the mainland scoff at sailors' superstitions, those sailors know better. At night, when the sun dies and darkness claims the world, many remember the tale of the *Crimson Eye*. That if it turns and bears down on you, best prepare for death. And on that burning quarterdeck stands a shadow in the shape of a man, who sees all with a single glaring crimson eye, an eye that hungers for souls...

PRINCE OF THE PORTHOLE

IAN BARR

*S*altskiff Bazaar let off a symphony of creaks with the shifting currents. The pale lanterns threw jagged shadows against the sinister patchwork of shipwrecks, the grandiose structure more akin to a mad man's puzzle box than a man-made island. Bastian swung through the rigging of a moored ship, timing his jump with the listing of the cog, and planting his feet on the top yard. He leaned against the mast to catch his breath. It was a humid night, and he was pouring sweat, feeling as though he'd been climbing through thick soup. Sweat stung his eyes, and he was looking forward to a frothy pint back at The Porthole, but he forced that thought away lest it get too comfortable. Any thief worth their salt knew when ships docked in Saltskiff's only private mooring there were shadows to be skulked.

Breath caught, his feet flashed against the wood. Stepping deftly to avoid knotted ropes, he leapt from the end of the yard and bucked himself through the night air. Wind rushed around his ears as he hurtled towards the next ship in the line, a smaller local skiff called *Washer*, and snapped his fist around a line fluttering in the breeze, sliding down onto her deck. Bastian hammerfisted the lone watchman as he landed, crumpling him with a grunt. Fist still curled, he looked around to ensure he was alone, then crept across the silent deck.

The private mooring, surrounded by high walls made from half a dozen battered hulls, sat silent and still under the pale moon. He could only see the stern of the ship there, *Dusk Trader* painted on the aft. It was too far to ship-jump, and he'd have nothing to grab onto if he tried. Armed sailors walked the shadowed deck at regular intervals, ready to defend something valuable enough to warrant the only real security Saltskiff had to offer. He doffed his shirt, knowing there was only one way he was going to make it onto that ship. He'd worn his selkie skins for a reason, after all.

The water was bracing, salty knives prodding his skins while debris jostled against him. There was always shit floating around Saltskiff, usually ending up in Wakewash as the island drifted. His strokes were clean and strong, and quieter than a mer could've managed. Treading into the mooring, he veered toward the anchor chain, glistening with sea slime and dangling kelp. Carefully, he began to climb.

At the main deck, he peeked and counted ten guards. Bastian lowered himself back down a rung, considering. He was a good skulker, wispy and agile, but ten guards was a gamble of long odds with only a belt knife. His pause allowed voices to catch his ear.

"How's it, Rav?"

"Dull as Cookie's coddle," another replied. "Ain't we supposed to have word from Braddock already? Cap'n was sayin'—"

"Who fuckin' knows? I just hope those bastards riding the *Scythe* don't think they're coming aboard..."

Boots stamped as the guards moved off and Bastian shook himself, realizing there was a tightness in his chest from an old, bubbling anger. If the men spoke true, Braddock—Captain King Braddock since the recent Conclave—and the *Midnight Scythe* were coming to Saltskiff. A mischievous smile cut through his maelstrom of emotion. Braddock was coming for this ship, for whatever was on it, and Bastian got there first.

His nose twitched at a whiff of acrid smoke.

Looking down, his grin broadened. Someone had hauled open one of the gunports, a thin line of smoke drifting out. Bastian shimmied down the chain, the slick links eager to let him slide instead of cling, and came level with the gunport. He planted his feet, calculating and hoping, then leapt. Fingers closed on the edge of the port, a small noise of surprise coming from within, and he swung in feet first, taking the pipe-smoking sailor under the jaw with his heel. The woman crumpled, the still-burning pipe spilling as she fell. Bastian trod over the glowing embers, moving into the hold.

Dusk Trader was packed to bursting with crates and barrels, some branded with the names of islands or ships they would be moving to, others marked with symbols Bastian had only ever seen in the Magician's Market. He frowned, wondering what could be for Braddock, when movement sent him scurrying into the shadows.

"... there on the morrow," said a deep voice, resonant and brusque. "You will bring my goods to the *Scythe* before mid-afternoon—the trident first and foremost! I will take no risks with that, Crofter."

"Aye, Sire," Crofter said. "We have the other goods you requested already in the longboat, but the trident is in my personal stores. It's been naught but quiet here, Sire. T'won't be no trouble."

Jammed between a pair of crates, Bastian watched Crofter weave into view. A bandy-legged man, graying at the temples where most of his hair remained, he had his hat tucked under his arm. In his hand was a glowing orb, an expensive trick that Bastian had seen for sale in the magic shops. Held near the mouth, Crofter spoke into it and whoever held the orb's twin replied, the ball pulsing violet.

"The trident is worth more to me than you are, Crofter. Contraband runners are a shilling a dozen; it's your life if anything goes awry. See that it doesn't." The glow flickered out.

"As if I don't know my own business, *King* Braddock," Crofter sneered. "Don't like the way I do things? You can bloody well freight your own contraband, *Sire*. Shilling a dozen, my hat! Nasty old…"

Crofter turned, and Bastian launched out of his hiding place. He latched onto the man's ankle, pulling him over with a yelp and pressing a hand over Crofter's mouth as they struggled. If there was something under lock and key for Braddock, that's what Bastian wanted. Crofter was strong, but a knee driven into his groin left him wheezing, and Bastian came astride him, bearing down with all the menace he could muster.

"The trident," he growled. Crofter's eyes widened and he shook his head under Bastian's hold. Bastian wrestled his belt knife free, holding it to Crofter's throat. "The trident or your life." The man trembled under him—No, not a tremble. He was laughing. Bastian leered and moved his hand off the man's mouth, letting the stunted laughter tumble out.

"Boy, you know not who you're plundering," he chortled. "He might let me live if you take it at knifepoint, but it ain't going to be a life worth living if he's in a black mood. But you?" The man barked an unpleasant laugh. "You're dead fucked, black mood or no. He'll find you, boy, but if you've balls of brass, then go try yourself."

Bastian pressed the steel into Crofter's flesh. "The trident."

"In my cabin, you thieving fink! T'ain't even locked," he cackled. "Go on then!"

Bastian made a quick decision. He smashed the knife's handle against Crofter's head, the man's eyes crossing before he slumped into unconsciousness.

"Let him come," Bastian said softly. He was on his feet, hurrying away.

Crofter spoke true. He hadn't even locked the door. Whatever security he'd alluded to Braddock about was pure fish guts: the crate lay open on a bolted down table in the center of the cramped cabin. Easily as tall as he, the trident was a slender thing made of a bone-white material, woven with shades of soft blue and vibrant orange. He laid a hand on it, surprised to find it was warm and not as smooth as he'd expected, instead dotted with countless tiny divots. It hummed in his hands, impossibly light for its size. Whatever it was, whatever it did, it was clearly valuable. But for Bastian, it was priceless. It was a chance to pull one over on the fearsome Captain King Braddock.

I dare you to come find me, you bastard, he thought.

A bell rang above, shouts and bootfalls following it. Bastian swore as he recognized the ruckus. Someone knew he was aboard. The alarm was raised.

Trident in hand, Bastian dashed out of the cabin and back toward the gunport, treading on Crofter as he passed. He swore as three sailors called out from where their crewmate lay, still unconscious from when Bastian had swung aboard through the port, her jaw swollen and purpling. Their cutlasses flashed and Bastian ran. He was a decent knife fighter, a less-than-decent swordsman, but against three he was useless, trident or no trident.

Hatches crashed open, and more sailors poured into the hold. He slid around a pile of barrels to find a single sailor. She blanched, then ground her teeth and raised her cutlass. Unable to do much more, Bastian thrust with the trident.

Heat and light flooded the hold, blinding him in a blue-white flash. Thrown, he crashed through splintering wood, and blinked stars from his eyes. As he tried to adjust his vision, jagged purple lines seared into it. He gaped when he finally saw what had happened.

Tongues of flame and smoking scorch marks traced a path toward a gaping hole punched through *Dusk Trader*'s hull, the sailor who'd attacked him no longer there. A wave washed through the opening, and Bastian didn't need a better opportunity. He found his feet and ran, only for another pair of sailors to block his path. They wide-eyed the destruction caused before settling on him.

"Fun's over, boy."

"Perhaps you're right," Bastian grinned back, spinning the weapon in his hands. "I'll be going now, if you'd step aside. And give my regards to Captain King Braddock. Tell him the Prince of The Porthole is waiting for him if he wants this back, only condition being that I run it through his gut."

"Enough!" The sailors advanced. Bastian thrust with the trident, squinting and bracing himself, hoping. If he'd have blinked, he would've missed it.

Lightning tore off the tips of the trident, jagged bolts dashing past the sailors who had thrown themselves on their bellies. Giggling gleefully, Bastian leapt over the pair and through the hole in the side of the ship, half-blind from the remnants of the bolt's flash burned into his eyes.

The sea greeted him with the same icy embrace, but his innards burned from the excitement of his escape. He'd only made it a few strokes before a soft blue glow began emanating from the weapon, helping to light his way. He gawked at the thing, wondering, and struck out for shore.

STOUT POUNDING BROUGHT Bastian out of a dead sleep, wrenching him from dreams of lightning that faded to nothing but the dusty rays of sunlight streaming through his shutters.

"The sun's going to rot your eyes out!" Nancy called outside his crooked door. "Boot and rally! Leg's open in three bells!"

"Shut your hairy gob, Nance!" one of the girls called from an adjacent room. Bastian agreed with the sentiment. Only a handful boarding at The Porthole needed to be awake right now and he was likely the last of them. Nancy, the housekeeper, was raising a racket enough to wake every soul in the brothel.

"As though you need the rest, Meera!" Nancy fired back. "Last three gents said you just laid there."

"Cocks so small you fell asleep, eh?" called a voice from another room, half a dozen muffled chuckles following.

"I'm coming, Nancy," Bastian called.

"Kitchens, Bast, and step to! This brace of slaggards isn't gonna feed itself!" With a final rap on the door, the floorboards groaned as she bustled away.

Bastian dressed as the brothel quieted around him again, only the occasional creak or soft snore coming through the thin walls. The Porthole was one of the more popular whorehouses in Dagspire, the oldest district on Saltskiff, and Bastian had lived there his entire life. He was born in the very room he occupied in the mish-mash three-story structure. He donned a loose shirt and trousers, stamping his feet into his stiff work boots. He peered in his looking glass, tying on his apron, and ran nimble fingers through thick hair. He smoothed an arched brow, thumbing the five-bell shadow on his angled jaw. Yawning, he washed his face. He would shave later. Scrubbed raw and red-eyed, he began his day.

The path to the kitchens was a simple stair used primarily by Nancy and her cleaners. He exited the dark, winding stairwell into a cellar kitchen large enough for a feast table that would feed the whole house. At present, the long room was full of the scent of bread rising, steeping tea, and Nancy's toiling sweat from where she manned the large pot of whatever would be served for the sleeping resident's breakfasts later on. The Porthole's daytime workers were sprawled about, readying for their shift.

"Good day, all!"

"Bastian!" Dozens of calls and tired smiles from the day workers, a motley assortment of the older and the inexperienced, the regular sorts found on the day shift at any brothel. Amongst the faded gowns and fraying shirt sleeves, weaving through and doling out instructions, encouragement, or just catching up, was the one the locals knew as Madam Leticia. Everyone else just called her Tish, but Bastian called her Mother.

She was built like he was, narrow through shoulder and hip, but that's where their similarities ended. Bastian's features were deep set where his mother's were bright and open; her hair blonde bordering on white, while his was a red so dark it was nearly black. She spotted him, making a final comment to one of the new lads, before gliding toward him with purpose.

"Kind of you to grace us with your presence, Your Highness," his mother said, her voice breathy and chiding in a good-natured way. He grinned at the honorific. He had been Prince of The Porthole long before he began using the moniker in his illicit activities.

"Late night. Cards down on the wharf with the lads."

"Winning, I hope. Fennick has been around twice this span, looking for protection. Steeper and steeper since the Conclave." Her tone was sour, just as his would have been.

Braddock, called Bottomless Braddock by some, had seized the crown of the Pirate King in a violent coup that decimated his opponents on a night the gossips had called the Red Conclave. Without a thought, Braddock had then declared an all-out war on anyone not flying buccaneer colours, levying the homage owed by all the bosses who recognized the Conclave's authority. The constant reminder of the man rankled Bastian and his mother both. Twenty years back, when his mother first started at The Porthole, Braddock had taken a shine to her. He made promises, said all the sweet things men say to anyone handling their jollies, even wrote her letters—some of which Bastian wished he could forget after he'd come across them years ago.

For all that, his mother loved him until the day she found herself with child, alone at the end of the docks, watching the *Midnight Scythe* sail over the horizon with all Braddock's empty words. Bastian often wondered how many others shared a similar story. And how many hated the scurvy cur who'd fathered them as much as he did.

"I won a fair bit," Bastian said casually. "Enough to pay the protections for a while." More than that, he reckoned. The trident had been the real reason for his late arrival home. He'd taken it to Allbright's last night and left it with her. The sea witch owed him a favour and could appraise it. Not to mention telling him what it was, and possibly how to use it.

"*Mor'bien Bast, Mada'am,*" grunted someone behind them.

Antonio, the daytime doorman, had snuck up on them. Angular and hard, his features had always reminded Bastian of a fox. He'd known the man for years and still didn't know what garbled language was his native tongue, but could at least understand the half-words he threw into his common tongue.

"*Ma'fuckos* here, Tish," Antonio continued. "I say we not yet open, they press. You got any *whuru* ready to work?"

"Take Claire, Vellum, Dahlia, Cornelius, Zenan, and both sets of twins," she said. "I'll bring more and be along to discuss rates with them. Are they with a crew?"

"Pair'ah," Antonio said, glancing over his shoulder and marking off the workers she had listed. "One from uh... *Dusky* something. Some from *Moonlight* or the other." Without another word, he was on his way, hustling the named workers out of the kitchen.

"I best go and say my piece," his mother said. "Finish up and take some gold from my safe for the apothecary. Dora and Seb both have crotch lice, and get a salve for Karthik's rash. Oh, and Naxos has found bedbugs in three rooms already so get some powder." She kissed him on the cheek, departing.

Bastian fell into his work rhythm, joining Nancy in the

arduous task of feeding their small village; a cycle of laughter, anecdotes, and endless arrivals and departures. Hours passed and Bastian was glad when the kitchen closed, readied for the next day with pots scrubbed and floors swept. He polished a stray spot, doffed his apron, and was on his way.

Music lilted through the house as he entered the common areas. His mother's chambers were off the entrance hall, decorated with red lacquer and lattices that held greenery and budding flowers. Johns and Janes waited in the wings, minding their own or chatting jovially, all here for the simple pleasures of the flesh. A few eyed Bastian appreciatively, who flashed them a smile and gave a polite shake of his head. He was no stranger to a paid night between the sheets but hadn't taken a client for a few years, not since he'd taken up thieving and the occasional footpad gig. Turning off the main hall, Bastian ducked behind the tapestry that hid the alcove leading to his mother's chambers. He turned the latch and pushed.

The door didn't budge.

"Mother?" Bastian called, checking the latch. Not locked. He shoved again, and it moved a few inches, enough to shift the barricade on the other side.

Panic gripped his heart, and Bastian shoved with all he was worth. With a lurch, it opened enough for him to squeeze his torso through. His efforts doubled on seeing the state of the room.

His mother's polished desk was upturned, the chair smashed to splinters. The portraits of seabirds his mother loved were torn to tatters, and blood stained the shattered mirror hung above the mantle. Streaks of red dragged over the plush off-white rug towards the blown out window. Bastian stepped lightly through the mess and found a single piece of parchment on the ravaged desk. The ink was still glistening, not quite dry.

'The private mooring, sunset. Bring the trident, Porthole Prince.'

Bastian read the note over and over until the words sunk through his shock. He crumpled it, letting out a guttural cry.

THE HULL of the ship that had replaced *Dusk Trader* in the mooring gleamed, an oily coating giving the dark wood of the five-masted ship a sheen like the sea at night, the furled sails the colour of storm clouds. A vicious spiked ram on the prow completed the ship's namesake, arching up out of the water like the reaper's own blade. The *Midnight Scythe* had come flying the crossbones flag beneath the crowned skull of the Pirate King. Allbright let out a low whistle beside Bastian.

"You hav'ta admit, eh?" the witch said, shaking her head. "That Captain King knows how to make his presence known."

"Mmm," Bastian managed, every muscle tense as he leaned on the trident, his unblinking stare fixed on the *Scythe*.

The trident, Allbright had told him, was the weapon of the Drejj: a crossbreed of humans and merfolk living in the shallows of Elysium Cove. It was made of the bone coral, forged and enchanted by the Stormwatch, a Drejj tribe who guarded the mist-shrouded island. It amazed Allbright to even be near the thing, while Bastian wondered how Crofter had gotten ahold of one. But it was a short-lived musing. He held fast to the formidable weapon, hands slick with sweat, then handed it to the witch.

"You sure about this, Bast?" She looked up at him. Hair like lengths of seaweed, smooth skin deathly pale like a bloated corpse, and with violet eyes that looked in two different directions, Allbright was shunned by most for her grotesque appearance and odd appetites, but had found a fast friend in Bastian.

"No," Bastian admitted. She nodded, muttering something. The trident and witch shimmered, then vanished. "Let's go." He started down the boardwalk, rippling air following him.

A one-eyed sailor with a sewn-up mouth ushered him aboard the *Scythe*. The gaunt crew moved with little zeal, lifeless eyes leering as they hauled lines or scrubbed the deck. The false light added no warmth to the ship, but the hold they were led into was downright frigid. They stopped at a set of cabin doors carved with ornate likenesses of sailfish, which opened on a single rap from the sailor leading them.

Bastian's eyes fell on his mother first, tied hand and foot in front of a sprawling map table. He rushed to her. There was a gash on her forehead, her cheeks bruised, but she was breathing, air whistling through swollen lips and a broken nose.

"Where's my trident, boy?"

Braddock was behind the map table, thick arms crossed over a barrel chest. Bastian straightened, fixated now on the man. He'd inherited nothing of Braddock's thick-limbed build, nor his scowling face, but his mane of hair and beard could've been Bastian's were it not streaked with white. Braddock's leather vest creaked as he lowered his hands to his belt, hooking thumbs over the hilts of two sheathed broadswords. A black sun fashioned like a compass rose was tattooed across his broad chest.

"Bastian," he said softly. Braddock's bushy brows pulled down slightly. "My name is Bastian. I'm your—I mean, you're my…"

He trailed off as Braddock's eyes widened, then his thick beard cracked with a small smile. His shoulders shook as cold laughter tumbled out of the man. He slammed two meaty hands on the map table he loomed over.

"When Crofter told me who had stolen from me, I put The Porthole connection together easily enough," Braddock chortled, looking down at Bastian's mother. "Shame to think I didn't recognize Tish. Though, she spent most of our time together bent over. Congratulations, my boy. You just joined the droves of bitter brats sprung from my loins who would've been better off dribbling down a whore's leg." Bastian gnashed his teeth as Braddock snorted. "I'll have that trident now, *son*."

"So be it," Bastian ground out.

With a pop, Allbright shimmered back into existence to toss the trident to Bastian before diving onto his mother, stealing her away to safety. Braddock growled and reached for his swords when Bastian thrust the trident at him. Lightning tore from the ends and he howled with a lifetime of spite as it shot toward Braddock. The lightning's flash swallowed the cabin, heat rolling over Bastian in waves. He cut the attack off when he could feel blisters rising on his skin, blinking to clear his vision.

Bastian blanched.

Braddock held a blade before him, dark as a moonless night. He grinned, a terrible thing, as he lowered the black sword and drew his second, which shone like the harshest sun.

"Leave it to my bastard to use my own weapons against me," Braddock said. "You pathetic cunts always think you can best me. But there's a reason I was able to claim the crown, boy!"

He slashed with the bright blade and Bastian caught it on the trident's haft. So close, he could feel the heat rolling off the sword like a roaring forge fire. Braddock pulled back, sweeping with the black blade and forcing Bastian to leap. On landing, Braddock thrust and searing pain spread over Bastian's ribs as the bright sword bit into him. Heat bloomed from the site and he staggered, trident held in one hand as he backed away.

"Swords of light and shadow," Braddock explained coolly. "Light will wound and burn, but just wait until the shadows taste your flesh." He moved forward, only to abruptly halt. Perplexed, he looked over his shoulder to find Allbright with her arms raised. Muttering under her breath, Bastian's mother stowed in the corner behind her.

"A sea witch," Braddock said, breathless from whatever arcane trick held him. "Midnight, if you would."

Wood splintered and snapped, Allbright screaming as the deck opened and she plunged into the hold below. The deck resealed itself whole again. Braddock rolled his shoulders, focussing on Bastian.

"Enough of this." He lurched.

Swords met trident again and again, haft deflecting razor edges while the prongs turned away vicious chops. Bastian hurled lightning; blowing holes in the ship that sealed themselves. Braddock moved like a dancer, lethal grace carrying the man in circles around Bastian, who was drenched in blood and sweat as the sword of light continued to breach his defenses, too keenly focussed on keeping the shadow blade at bay. The shadow crashed against the haft, then the light, the crossed swords pressing down and driving Bastian to his knees. Braddock loomed, face screwed up with effort, but goading.

"I never paid her, you know," he said. "Your mother opened her legs to me, wanted me to squirt you into her belly. You weren't even a blunder, boy, not for her. You were a desperate hope for her to tether me—"

"Don't you talk about her!" Bastian grunted. "Don't you—"

"Do you want to know how far down her throat your dear mother can get it? I'll never forget—"

With a savage cry, Bastian heaved and sent Braddock reeling back. The man was off-balance and Bastian thrust, the trident crackling as it streaked toward his chest. He was going to do it! He was going to kill Braddock! He was—

The shadow sword flashed, smashing the trident with the flat of its blade. Braddock hooked his other sword through the back of the prongs and ripped it from Bastian's grip. The trident clattered, skittering away from them as Braddock brought both swords up.

"I've fought a bevvy of bastards, son," Braddock said. "Jeering aside, you fought well. Had things been different, you mighta been a prince for true. But they ain't different. A king can't leave challenges unanswered. After I'm done with *her*, I'll turn my men loose on that poxy whorehouse you call home and—"

Lightning crackled between the trident's prongs as they erupted through Braddock's chest. He sputtered, blood bubbling from his mouth as he gaped down at the red-stained points. With a final look at Bastian, his eyes rolled, and he fell forward to reveal a battered Tish looking down her nose at Braddock's corpse, the trident standing erect from where she'd run it through him.

"Mother!" He stumbled toward her, but the world darkened and vanished before his eyes.

BASTIAN DIDN'T KNOW where he was. A greenish light emanated all around him, casting a murky din over the ankle-deep water he stood in. He looked around, hearing naught but his own breath in his ears. Where had he been? What had he been doing?

Braddock, he thought.

"Bastian," said a voice, soft and ethereal. A flash made him squint, the light shaping into a woman.

"Who are you?"

She padded forward, feet striding atop the shallow water, stopping before him. Bastian blinked. He had never seen her equal, indescribable in face and form, as though she was made of smoke and caught in a stiff breeze. She reached out, laying a finger on his forehead, and a strong gale kicked up around him.

"They all call me Midnight," she said, "though that was never my name. This Braddock is dead?"

This Braddock? "What does that—"

"I need a soul to survive, Bastian, and yours will do. I've bonded with you. You and I, we are one now."

"I don't understand," he said. She was fading. "I don't understand! Who are you?"

"Go now," Midnight said, no more than a whisper. "Be well, Prince Braddock. Claim your new place."

Strange rumours drummed up from Saltskiff following the brief stopover of Captain King Braddock and the *Midnight Scythe*. The Porthole, a favoured brothel, closed up overnight, the windows nailed shut and possessions stripped from the rooms. It had first been thought a tragedy as a clutch of bloated bodies had been found in the private mooring after the *Scythe*'s sudden disembarkment. Authorities thought the worst, but on investigation, they had been the bodies of sailors and not whores. It had only gotten stranger hence from.

A ship called *Dusk Trader* had been decimated by the departing *Midnight Scythe*. A lone survivor chattered about a gussied up crew, all of them in faded dresses or vests with baubles and shinies and painted faces. But worse, the man called Crofter claimed, was a sorcerer of sorts who hurled lightning from the helm.

Days later, a merchant reported a mass of crows and gulls in a quiet corner of Saltskiff. Hung from an old jib, pecked full of festering holes that had cracked and widened in the sun, was the last fatality of the *Midnight Scythe*'s departure. Captain King Braddock's broad torso was a ruin, yet the words carved into his ruined flesh were still legible.

'The King is dead. Long live the Prince.'

CREATORS OF FANTASY

ILLUSTRATED BY DAY PHAN

Fantasy Pirates

Top row—Ian Barr, A. E. Bross, Michael D. Nadeau
Center row—Astrid Knight, Robert Mammone, A. R. K. Horton
Bottom Center—Caroline Barnard-Smith

BOOK 2: PIRATES OF THE SKY

MAP OF THE CHARTED WORLD

ILLUSTRATED BY AARON HOCKETT

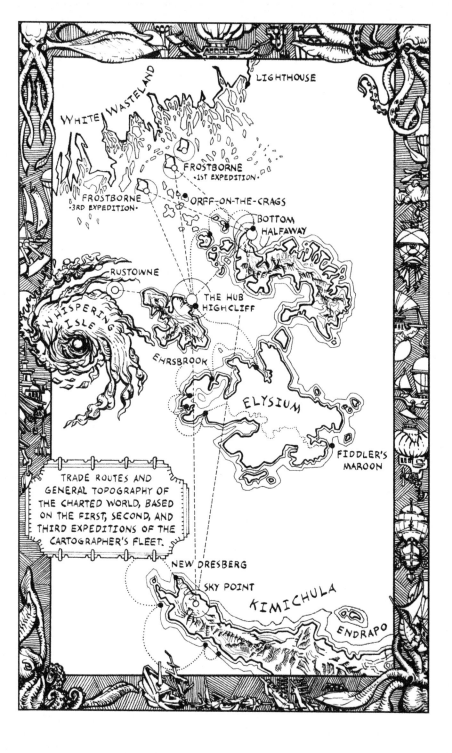

LIGHTHOUSE

WHITE WASTELAND

FROSTBORNE
·1ST EXPEDITION·

FROSTBORNE
·3RD EXPEDITION·

ORFF-ON-THE-CRAGS

BOTTOM
HALFAWAY

RUSTOWNE

WHISPERING ISLE

THE HUB
HIGHCLIFF

EHRSBROOK

ELYSIUM

FIDDLER'S
MAROON

TRADE ROUTES AND
GENERAL TOPOGRAPHY OF
THE CHARTED WORLD, BASED
ON THE FIRST, SECOND, AND
THIRD EXPEDITIONS OF THE
CARTOGRAPHER'S FLEET.

NEW DRESBERG

SKY POINT

KIMICHULA

ENDRAPO

THE CUMULO CARTA

WHISPERING ISLE

RUSTOWNE 6.200

THE HUB 5.900

SKY POINT 5.200

5.000

FROSTBORNE 3.600

MARBLETOWN 4.200

HALFAWAY 2.900

HIGHCLIFF 2.500

900

BOTTOM 200

EHRSBROOK

KIMICHULA

RELATIVE ALTITUDES OF PORTS AND WAYPOINTS IN THE CHARTED WORLD.

COMPILED FROM THE CUMULOCARTA SURVEYS OF NORAA THOCKET, MEMBER OF THE ORIGINAL CARTOGRAPHER'S FLEET.

Illustration Copyright © Aaron Hockett

THE HUNT FOR THE OTHER SIDE

KATHERINE SHAW

Stop! Thief!

Ade Madroda resisted the urge to look over his shoulder at his pursuers as he jumped over a mooring rope and raced towards the next platform. If he lost any ground to the bobbies now, they'd have him and he'd be thrown in the lockup again. It didn't matter to them that he was just a teenager trying to survive; a thief was a thief.

He took a hard left turn and bolted down an alleyway between two merchant stalls, his chest already tight from the exertion. It was no use. Heavy footsteps pounding on steel told him they were still on his tail.

'Shit!'

Ade urged himself forward, his tattered boots slipping as he turned a sharp right at the end of the alley so he nearly fell flat on his face. He had to hide before they left the alley—it was now or never. His keen eyes scanned the dock, assessing each vessel in milliseconds before moving on. Most of the larger airships were guarded, with a heavy or two posted by the mooring with a cudgel or dagger looped in their belt. They looked thuggish, but they were trained to spot troublemakers. He wouldn't make it past them without gaining at least a few good bruises.

A shout from behind him told Ade he had run out of time. He was about to set off sprinting again when he spotted his salvation: a small sloop sandwiched between two larger vessels, with no guard in sight. He launched himself forward, channelling his remaining energy to pump his legs as he sprinted up the gangway and onto the deck. Without a second thought, he dove into the wheelhouse and disappeared out of sight of the chasing coppers.

Thankfully, the room was empty. Ade wasted no time in scrambling behind an old sail wrapped up in the corner. His heart still pounding, his chest rising and falling with ragged breaths, he reached into his old coat and pulled out the source of all this trouble: a shiny, red apple.

He barely had the chance to savour a few slow, glorious bites of his prize before his enjoyment was interrupted by the boat's flustered captain bursting into the wheelhouse. Ade shrunk further behind the sail as he watched a tall woman stride to the controls, her sandy blonde braid swinging as her gaze darted between dials and levers. This was the furthest Ade had ever made it onto an airship; it looked complicated.

The woman glanced anxiously over her shoulder towards the dock. 'Damn Constabulary,' she muttered, shaking her head.

Ade peeked from behind the sail. A clockwork panel at the far end of the wheelhouse whirred into motion, metal gears sliding and clicking into place as a series of bulbs flickered to life one after the other. Ade was transfixed. During his years on the streets, gazing at the airships as they left The Hub behind, possibly forever, he could only imagine how they might work and what flying one might actually be like. Hearing the engine roar into life and the lifting gas flood into the balloons above him sent a thrill through his body like nothing he had experienced before.

Wait, what am I doing?

He didn't know this woman. He didn't know where she might be going. The Hub attracted every sort and, although she looked upstanding enough, you could never be sure. The bobbies must have moved on by now; he had to get off this boat.

Ade eyed the woman to ensure she was distracted by her preparations. He tensed as he crept out from behind the sail and headed for the doorway, barely managing a few steps before a loud voice stopped him in his tracks. The bobbies were back.

'It's no good, sir, we'll have to search the ships.'

'*Shit!*'

The captain and the stowaway spoke the curse simultaneously, and for a moment they both simply stood, staring wide-eyed at each other from across the wheelhouse. Finally, the woman spoke.

'Who in the hell are–' The pounding of Constabulary boots on wooden planks cut her off. They'd be searching the boat any minute. 'Shit!'

With Ade gawping like an idiot, she pushed past him and began untying the ropes anchoring her small craft to the edge of The Hub.

'Well don't just stand there!' she shouted, breaking him from his stupor. 'Either piss off or lend a hand!'

Still dumbstruck, Ade rushed over and scrabbled at the intricate knots with panicked fingers. Ade's nimble fingers may have been capable of sneaking scraps of food when necessary, but he was no sailor. In the time it took him to untie just one knot, the woman had managed half a dozen. He watched her as she worked, never slowing, her brow furrowed in concentration as her hands worked their magic.

Ade's stomach lurched as the propellers fired up and the airship pulled away from the platform. He opened his mouth to speak, but his words were drowned out by a howling alarm coming from the direction of the dock. He sprinted to the wheelhouse door. Two large, red bulbs flashed at the abandoned mooring, drawing the attention of onlookers and coppers alike.

'Shit!' the woman shouted again. Ade wondered if he'd heard the limit of her vocabulary.

'What is that?' he yelled in return, cringing as the alarm battered his eardrums.

'Flint's bloody "off schedule" alarm.' The woman's commanding voice cut through the noise easily, reaching Ade completely unhampered. '*The Stickleback* wasn't supposed to depart for another few hours. So much for being discreet!'

She glanced out of the window and shook her head.

'We're not going fast enough to lose them if they come after us. You,' she pointed at Ade. 'Have you ever sailed before?'

What?

'Erm... no, I've never...'

'Well, now is as good a time as any to learn. Come here.'

Ade's eyes grew wide as she led him to the wheel.

'Go on, it won't bite.'

Ade's hands trembled as he closed his fingers around the wooden spokes.

'*The Stickleback* is small, but she's quick and handles like a dream. I'll get the furnace fired up to maximum, you make sure we don't hit anything as we clear The Hub. Deal?'

Ade stared up into the woman's hard, yet striking face, her blue eyes twinkling with the promise of adventure. He was going to do it. After everything he, his parents and his grandparents had lost, a Madroda was finally taking to the air again. A broad smile slowly spread across his face.

'Deal.'

ADE SLUMPED into the captain's chair, relieved to have relinquished control of the wheel now that they were clear of The

Hub. His heart still pounded in his chest and he struggled to quell his shaking hands. Flying may be in his family, but he didn't have his air legs quite yet.

'You did good, kid.' The captain remained at the helm, staring out into the cloud-filled sky. 'So, now you're officially part of the crew, what do I call you?'

'Um... Ade.' He hesitated a moment, unsure what to say. 'I didn't mean to stow away... I was running from the Constabulary, and... well...'

'You don't have to explain yourself, Ade,' The woman glanced over her shoulder for a second, and he was surprised to see a gentle smile on her face. 'We all have our reasons for wanting to get away. You can call me Sylvie.'

They travelled in silence. Sylvie stood statuesque at the wheel, the only sound the soft hissing of the lifting gas, punctuated occasionally by the gentle *click-clack* of unseen gear mechanisms.

Ade quietly marvelled at the clouds drifting by the window. *I'm flying. I'm actually flying!* He could have stared into the whirling nimbi forever, but his latent curiosity nudged at him until he was forced to tear his eyes away and ask the question he probably should've asked at the very start of this escapade.

'Erm... Sylvie?' He cringed at how frightened he sounded. *You're pretty much a man now, get a grip.* 'Where are we going?'

Sylvie turned towards Ade with an eyebrow raised, almost as if she had forgotten he was there. He thought he saw her eyes dart to a satchel in the corner of the wheelhouse, but her gaze returned to him so quickly he couldn't be sure.

'Well,' she said slowly, her eyebrows knitting together. 'I have a... special artefact I discovered on my travels, and I need to take it to an expert to get it... evaluated. It's very important.'

Ade's curiosity was piqued. 'What kind of artefact? Where is the expert? What will they do?'

Sylvie raised her eyebrow again, and he realised how childish he must sound. Here he was, travelling with a seasoned adventurer, and he sounded like an overexcited toddler. 'Sorry... I'm just interested, that's all.'

The captain let out a bright laugh. It was unexpectedly melodic. 'That's fine. Since you make up half of the crew now, I suppose you ought to at least know where we're going.' She turned towards the oncoming barrage of clouds. 'The Cartographer's Fleet.'

ADE ROLLED over on his makeshift bunk in the corner of the wheelhouse, willing himself to fall asleep. But how could he sleep when they were on their way to The Cartographer's Fleet? This was the kind of adventure he'd been dreaming of during the lonely years without his parents. Hundreds of miles away from the predictability and functionality of The Hub, chasing storms and studying the world. Part of him worried that if he drifted off, he would wake to find none of this was real, and he'd be back in his crude shelter, shivering as the moving ships blasted air across the platform's surface.

Squeezing his eyes shut, he tried to block out his racing thoughts. But as his mind quietened, he noticed a new sound: engines. It wasn't the small engines of *The Stickleback*—it was another ship. A much bigger ship.

Ade jumped from his small sleeping spot and groped blindly through the room until he reached a window. He quickly identified the source of the noise: a huge airship heading straight for them. Ade's chest tightened. A black and white flag flew from the mast.

Pirates.

'Sylvie!' he screamed, sprinting onto the deck to search for the hatch to her captain's quarters in the darkness. 'Sylvie, please! It's a ship! A pirate ship!'

Ade jumped as a hatch burst open behind him and a dishevelled Sylvie barrelled up from below deck. She reached into her coat pocket, pulled out a small telescope, and observed the approaching vessel.

'God *damn* it!' she hissed through her teeth, folding the telescope and stuffing it back into her pocket. 'Ade, come with me. Now!'

He stumbled as Sylvie grabbed his sleeve and dragged him to the helm of the airship. He stood, useless, as Sylvie dug around in a small toolbox nailed to the wheelhouse wall. 'What's happening? Sylvie?' He tried to suppress the fear bubbling up inside his stomach.

Ade jumped back as Sylvie turned around. Large, round goggles now covered her eyes, magnifying them so that she looked almost alien. 'It's that bastard, the Red-Eyed Jackal. He found me!'

Offering no further explanation, she strode to a large lever protruding from the wooden floor and used all her body weight to pull it backwards. Ade stared at the floor as the sound of moving machinery erupted from below their feet. Soon the entire stern of *The Stickleback* began to shift and transform in an array of moving cogs and pistons until, finally, a tremendous cannon, shining in stripes of copper and steel, ascended from below deck, transforming the once innocuous airship into a battleship.

Sylvie turned to Ade, her huge, blue eyes shining in the flickering lights of the control panels around her. 'I hate to ask this of you again, kid, but can you man the wheel while I show these fuckers that this stickleback has spines?'

Panic swirled in Ade's chest, but there was something else there, ready to take its place: excitement. 'I'll do it. Show them who's boss!'

A wide grin spread across Slyvie's face. She nodded and ran to the stern, where she began powering up the cannon with a huge handwheel. Ade couldn't help but admire the woman; she wasn't big, but she was *strong*.

'Ade!' Her shout pulled him out of his daze. 'Hard to starboard! Get me face to face with the bastard!'

Ade sprung into action, grabbing the wheel and jerking it to the right. *The Stickleback* veered in front of the approaching pirate vessel. Ade's knuckles paled from his tight grip on the wooden spokes, his faith in Sylvie battling with his fear of the much bigger airship closing in on its prey. As he struggled to get *The Stickleback* into position, he glanced over his shoulder and his stomach plummeted. Their pursuer was so close he could read the ship's name emblazoned in golden letters across its bow.

The Ambush.

'Oh God,' he muttered under his breath, working hard to stop his hands from shaking. 'Oh God, oh God, oh God, oh–'

A sudden explosion shook the airship. Sylvie's cannon fired a blast of something fiery directly at *The Ambush*. The missile struck its port side, sending the airship rocking, but the inflicted damage looked minor. This wouldn't be an easy fight. Sylvie rushed to recharge her weapon and Ade braced himself for retaliation but, to his surprise, the response came from a loudspeaker, not a cannon.

'Give it up, Anchorfast!' The captain of *The Ambush* was a tall, imposing figure standing at the helm of the opposing ship, speaking into some sort of mouthpiece. The lights from his control panel revealed a bald head and, causing a knot of dread to form in Ade's tight throat, a bright red glass ball in place of his right eye.

That must be the Red-Eyed Jackal.

'I am willing to offer some mercy,' he continued, his voice cold and stern, sending shivers running down Ade's spine. 'Hand over my property, and we'll leave your little dinghy in one piece.'

Sylvie didn't respond with words, instead firing a second cannon shot into the side of *The Ambush*, this time much closer to the Jackal's place at the helm. The airship rocked again, but the captain maintained his footing. His face hardened, and he held one hand aloft.

'So be it. Men! To the cannons!'

At this, Sylvie finally seemed to reconsider her attack, and turned to Ade, her eyes wide but determined.

'Ade! Take us out of here!' Her shouts were barely audible over the sound of *The Ambush* powering up its cannons. Ade spotted five or six of them protruding from the port side, each one bigger than the single cannon on *The Stickleback*. One, at least, seemed somewhat damaged by Sylvie's shots. 'Head South-West, follow the compass on the panel. I'll keep firing, but to win this fight we'll need the Arconite gas!'

She raced to the helm, flipping switches on the panel as Ade struggled to direct the course of the ship. He'd seen a handful of compasses for sale around The Hub, but he'd never got up close to one, never mind used one for navigation. Sylvie pulled a small lever and the balloon holding them aloft hissed as the Arconite replaced the lifting gas.

'You have Arconite?' Ade shouted over the din. 'You can't use that here! If one cannon shot hits the balloon we'll be blown to bits!'

Sylvie didn't seem to hear. Ade stumbled as the Arconite took effect, lifting *The Stickleback* even higher. The ship shuddered as it narrowly avoided a streak of cannon fire.

'Sylvie! It's too dangerous!'

He flinched as Sylvie's head swivelled to face him, her eyes blazing. 'We don't have a choice!'

'Yes we do!' Ade yanked the wheel to the left to try to maintain their course. 'Give him back whatever you have of his! Please!'

Sylvie slammed her fist onto one of the panel buttons and leaned in close to Ade. 'That,' she hissed, 'is not an option.'

She pushed Ade to one side and spun the wheel, sending *The*

Stickleback veering starboard to avoid another cannon shot from *The Ambush.*

'They might be big,' Sylvie grunted, turning the wheel back and starting off towards the cannon. 'But we're faster!'

She sprang forwards, the rapidly rising ship doing nothing to impede her balance, and turned her cannon downwards to target the Jackal once more. Ade turned his attention to the sky in front of him, his brow furrowing as he tried to navigate their way through the dark clouds.

The clouds...

The night sky darkened further, jet-black clouds growing so dense they seemed impenetrable. More worrying was the speed they were moving, heading towards them at an incredible rate.

'Sylvie! What—' A powerful surge of wind rocked the side of the airship, nearly knocking Ade off his feet. He turned to Sylvie, but whatever she was shouting was lost as a ferocious wind battered the airship. Ade grabbed hold of the wheel and steered into the wind, clinging to the spokes with all his strength as the roaring gales tried to force the wheel in the opposite direction.

It was no use—no amount of Arconite Gas could compete with the pummelling winds. *The Stickleback* creaked under the strength of the incoming storm, and the planks beneath Ade's feet tilted, threatening to pull him off his feet.

'Sylvie!' he screamed, praying at least an echo would be carried to the stern. He gritted his teeth under the strain of the wheel pushing against his body, his arm muscles on fire as his strength began to fail. Hot tears welled in his eyes, whipped away by the winds as fast as they broke free.

It's no good. I can't hold it!

His prayers were answered as a second pair of hands clamped down over his. Sylvie, sooty and sweating from working the cannon, clenched her teeth and forced the wheel back with an astounding strength.

But it was too late.

As the pair worked to bring the ship back on course, the howling winds were pierced by the shriek of an oncoming missile. Ade looked up just as the Jackal's cannon shot tore through the balloon, sending a criss-cross of blinding white light erupting all around.

The Arconite!

Time seemed to slow. Ade was vaguely aware of Sylvie grabbing his arm and pulling him towards the bow as the mast crashed to the deck behind them. Flaming debris fell around him like confetti. His ears ached under the bombardment of shrieking winds, splintering wood and falling metal.

And, as they fell faster and faster through the dark, cloud-filled skies, there was another sound, barely audible through the cacophony. Amidst the chaos, the Red Jackal was laughing.

ADE'S BODY ached all over. His head pounded so hard it was as if brain was trying to escape his skull. He didn't dare open his eyes for fear of what would greet him.

How am I alive?

He tried to remember what happened after the exploding balloon tore *The Stickleback* apart, but his mind was blank. The last thing he remembered was Sylvie pulling him away from danger.

Sylvie.

His eyes burst open. Head swimming, he took in the unfamiliar surroundings. He had expected to wake in a shipwreck, but instead he was in somebody's bedroom. Turning his head, he took in walls adorned with posters of maps, constellations and even airship blueprints, and shelves full of unfamiliar gadgets and knick-knacks. Someone had laid him in a small bunk and covered him with an extremely garish multicoloured blanket.

What the hell?

His body screaming in protest, he pushed himself upright and removed the storm cover from the nearest porthole.

Oh my God.

They'd made it! They were on The Cartographer's Fleet! A lifetime on The Hub had familiarised him with the flags of the most populous and travelled states, and the Fleet's silver compass on a field of stormy blues was easy to recognise.

I can't believe it!

The ship itself was vast, so much so he couldn't see the end of the deck. The wooden planks continued on until they were lost in the clouds. Tilting his face upwards, Ade gasped as he took in what must be hundreds, if not thousands, of balloons holding the mammoth vessel aloft.

'Wow...'

'Pretty cool, right?'

Ade jumped, banging his head on the brass porthole frame. He turned, rubbing another injury he really didn't need, expecting to see Sylvie. Instead, he was confronted by a dark-haired teenage girl leaning nonchalantly against the doorframe. She wore the tell-tale leather bomber jacket of a member of the Fleet and a wry smile.

'Wha... where's Sylvie?' Ade stammered, far too distracted by the girl's watchful eyes.

She grinned and threw a thumb over her shoulder. 'She's speaking with Dr Oboler. I was sent to check you hadn't died in your sleep or anything.'

Ade frowned, unable to tell if that was a joke. 'Who is Dr Oboler?'

'Typical Hubber,' she said, rolling her eyes. 'No "nice to meet you, Amelia, what a fascinating ship you live on Amelia, thanks for giving up your bed Amelia", nope! He only wants to see the famous *scholar*.' She stared at Ade in mock indignation before bursting into a fit of giggles at his confusion. 'I'm joshing with you, mate! Follow me.'

She turned and skipped into the corridor. Ade's body throbbed with pain as he jumped out of the bed and chased after her. Amelia led him down a labyrinthine set of corridors, always disappearing around a corner just as he caught sight of her. Giggles ricocheted off the metal walls, reverberating back and forth until they seemed to be coming from all directions. Ade was ready to give up and head back to the bedroom when he rounded a corner and saw two women standing beyond an open doorway ahead, silhouetted against a huge window overlooking an array of weather balloons of various shapes and sizes. One of the figures was a stranger to Ade, but the other was very familiar.

Sylvie.

He approached the pair and opened his mouth to speak, but was cut short by the strange older woman speaking in a loud, excited voice.

'Let me see it, then!'

Sylvie reached into her satchel, which had miraculously survived the crash, and pulled out a rectangular slab of solid gold. The woman, who Ade assumed to be Dr Oboler, took it reverently in both hands and held it up to the light. As it shimmered, she beamed with delight. 'Oh my goodness... this is the missing piece! And it's flawless! I'll take it right away.'

'Gold? Really?'

The two women turned in unison, shocked by Ade's outburst. He strode forward, unable to fight his incredulity.

'You fought a pirate ship three times the size of your own, you sent us straight into a storm, you almost got us both killed using bloody Arconite... and it was just for money?' He glared at Sylvie, his fists clenched with rage. 'You're... you're... nothing but a thief and a pirate yourself!'

Sylvie's expression changed. Tears veiled her eyes as she glanced between Ade and Dr Oboler, her lower lip trembling. She took the slab and strode over to Ade, silently handing it to him.

The surface of the metal was completely covered with odd hiero-glyphs and writing in an unfamiliar language.

'Not for money,' Sylvie said quietly, eyes locked on the arte-fact. 'For the secret... the secret to finding my parents.'

ADE PACED the deck of *The Starling*, wringing his hands as he waited for Sylvie to surface. What she and Dr Oboler wanted to do bordered on madness. He half hoped she would return saying she'd changed her mind.

Amelia had no such anxieties; she had enthusiastically offered her family airship for the journey, and now she sat cross-legged on the deck, singing to herself and beaming with excitement. She was a strange girl, but there was something endearing about her. She had... an *energy*.

The airship picked up speed, and soon the Fleet was nothing but a speck on the horizon. They were almost in empty sky.

It's time.

Ade had heard of the kraken, of course; everyone on The Hub had. That didn't mean he'd ever thought it was real—not in a million years. Sylvie said she had always believed, ever since the day her parents disappeared in a freak storm. She swore she'd seen it, lurking amongst the clouds, its tentacle whipping forward like a bolt of lightning. Ade was sceptical when she told the story. That was, until Dr Oboler deciphered the slab.

After what felt like a lifetime, Sylvie emerged from below deck, her expression one of determined intensity, her goggles magnifying her glittering blue eyes. She held the gold slab care-fully in both hands, as if it might crumble to pieces between her fingers. Amelia jumped up at seeing Sylvie, her own dark eyes shining with anticipation.

'Are we really going to do it, Ms Anchorfast?' she said, excited fists clenched in front of her. 'Summon the kraken?'

Sylvie nodded, gently grabbing Amelia and Ade's arms and pulling them close to her. She took a deep breath before finally speaking.

'Kids, this has never been done before, and could be really dangerous. I need you both to stay here, far back from the bow, no matter what.'

I don't like this.

'But Sylvie,' Ade said, struggling to keep his voice steady. 'What if you need help? We can't... I can't let you get hurt. I don't know what I'd do if... if...'

'Ade,' Sylvie lifted his chin, forcing him to meet her gaze. Tears glistened beneath the goggles. 'You're strong. You're resilient. You're a survivor. You've proven that already. I have absolute faith that you'll be okay, both of you.' She turned her head to Amelia, whose smile had transformed into a grim line, her bottom lip quivering.

'I don't know what's going to happen,' Sylvie continued. 'But it could be bad. You two stay back, stay safe, and take care of each other.'

'But what about you?' Ade could no longer disguise his fear.

'I'll be fine.' A small smile passed over her lips and her attention shifted beyond the pair of teenagers, out into the open sky. 'I'm going to see my parents.'

She squeezed Ade's arm and strode towards the bow of *The Starling*, full of purpose. Ade wanted to follow, to save this person who had taken him on this adventure and whisked him away from his life of poverty on The Hub. He hadn't known Sylvie long, but he liked her. Only now did he realise how attached to her he had already become. He edged closer to Amelia until their arms touched, desperate for some sort of comfort. She didn't move away.

Sylvie reached the bow of the airship just as the Fleet disappeared from view altogether and they transitioned into completely empty sky. There were no islands or balloons to be seen, just clouds that darkened more with each passing second. She knelt, placing the slab into a square, copper container connected by thick coiled wire to a metal rod mounted on the figurehead. A large silver-coloured switch adorned it, and Ade bit his lip as Sylvie reached out and flipped it without hesitation. She rose to her feet, eyes locked on the sky.

For a moment, nothing happened. Ade's heart pounded in his ears. Sylvie stood motionless, fists clenched by her side. Suddenly, the dark clouds flashed with streaks of white, blue and yellow and the sky rumbled with a roaring thunder. The previously calm wind whipped into a frenzy, rushing over the deck and knocking the breath out of Ade's lungs. He felt the hairs rising on the back of Amelia's arm.

A new sound pierced the air, turning Ade's legs to water. It was an ear-splitting, reverberating shriek, shaking the planks beneath their feet. A blinding bolt of lightning split the sky with an almighty crack, striking the rod to form a towering string of energy connecting the airship with the heavens.

The cacophony continued as the very sky seemed to twist and break open above them. Ade's stomach turned to ice as two gargantuan iridescent tentacles penetrated the void, looming overhead like cobras poised to strike through the clouds at their prey.

Sylvie raised her arms above her head and turned her face upwards. Ade watched in horror as a titanic, monstrous beak emerged through the clouds and let out a gut-wrenching cry which was almost deafening. The wind grew stronger, surrounding the airship in clouds so dark the flashes of lightning were barely visible.

Ade couldn't see Sylvie. He couldn't breathe. He couldn't think. He stood frozen, buffeted and blinded by the ferocious winds raging around them.

Then, suddenly, it all stopped.

There was no wind, no clouds, no kraken... nothing but clear, blue skies. Ade's stomach clenched as he stared at the bow of the ship, his eyes searching for any sign of Sylvie.

She was gone.

He expected to panic, to feel lost, but he didn't. He felt... proud.

She did it.

A small cough brought him back to his senses, and he turned to Amelia. Her hair had blown away from her face, revealing immaculate cheekbones flushed the slightest shade of pink. She dipped her head, and Ade followed her gaze down her arm to her fingers, tightly interlaced with his.

When did that happen?

He loosened his grip, letting her hand go, but he didn't move away. A slight heat touched his cheeks as Amelia's mouth curved into a knowing smile.

'Well,' she said softly, turning to look into the now tranquil sky. 'Now what?'

WHAT WE DARE TO BEHOLD

B. K. BASS

$\mathcal{J}$t is said the eddies of the clouds hold a collective memory of every place in the cosmos and everything that's ever occurred. It is within the Aerotarium that the most ambitious—and some would say eccentric—of scholars pursue the secrets hidden within the clouds.

It is a rare occasion on which I leave the comforting confines of my apartments in the Aerotarium. A component of the Cartographer's Fleet, yet ostensibly apart from it, this bastion of learning is devoted to studying the more esoteric wonders of the Cumulocarta—an ever-present system of storms in the center of the archipelago.

It is within this massive balloon I have spent the last ten years devoted to discerning the truth of the past from the tempest's eddies and currents. My quarters are modest; little more than a hammock and a small pantry to sustain the needs of the body. Beyond these mundane concerns, my books and instruments are all that matter. These reside within a small library, with a hammock tied betwixt two bookshelves. The collected knowl-edge of my studies and those who came before me serve as the walls of my home.

Little did I think—as I studied the Cumulocarta from the comfort of the Aerotarium—that the research which cloistered me there would one day cause need to remove myself from those comforts for closer inspection of my findings.

Alas, studying the world from afar yields only a distant reckoning. To delve into the details, one must venture boldly forth.

And so, I find myself in Rustowne on a day of remarkable chill. The storms wreathing the nearby Whispering Isle never relent, but at present writhe with an unprecedented violence. A destination for those whose intrepid nature often borders on insanity, it is said those who brave the storms might discover the Well of Eternal Life, a place of legends fed by the great waterspout supporting the island in the sky. There, they might gain the eponymous promise of the well.

Early explorers created Rustowne as an outpost for those who might launch expeditions into the storms of The Whispering Isle, as well as those who might exploit them. Held aloft by a multitude of patchwork balloons and tethered to the isle itself by chains and bridges, the place gets its name from the quality of its structure. Buffeted constantly by the storms, rust covers every inch of the floating city. It is a wonder of the world that the place does not simply shatter into a million fragments with the gentlest of breezes, let alone withstand unscathed what amounts to a hurricane on an almost daily basis.

Yet it endures, and by its proximity to such alluring a destination, Rustowne attracts the boldest of aeronauts—and the most insane. Many allege the man I seek to be a bit of both, and in both regards an exemplary specimen.

As I press open the doors of the Crimson Cog tavern, I spy my quarry in the taproom's corner—in the shadow of the massive, rusted cog from which the establishment gleaned its name. He is bent over his cup, and flanking him around the table are two equally miserable-looking souls. Were I not to possess a lithograph of his likeness, I may not consider him a likely candidate for employment on my expedition. But as luck would have it, Roger Kellis's likeness is the subject of more than a few wanted posters in several regions.

A ship's captain of note, Roger Kellis is leader of a motley crew of scoundrels who call Rustowne home. Little more than guns for hire, they're reputed to take on jobs of the most dangerous and unsavory nature. Most often, these jobs involve violating a catalog of laws. Despite any claims to the contrary, Roger Kellis and his men are, without a doubt, pirates.

While they are far from the sort I'd prefer to entreat for my needs, Kellis is reputed to be the best there is at what he does. And nothing short of the best is what I require for this venture.

The eyes of the ne'er-do-wells turn up as I approach. In keeping with his reputation as being sly as a fox, Kellis's narrow to a suspicious squint with no hesitation.

Under such scrutiny, I suddenly feel more out of my element than I already had. I shift in place, fumbling with the assorted charts and journals clutched to my chest, unsure whether I should be the first to speak.

Finally, Kellis himself breaks the silence. "What do you want?"

A thousand potential answers fill my mind, from the sudden concern that I had not relieved my bladder in some time to desires for existential understanding. Not accustomed to communicating with others by any other means than scientific discourse via academic journals, it takes me a moment to decipher the specific intent of his question.

The figure on Kellis's right hand, a mountain of a man with a shaved head covered in tattoos of aquatic fauna, slams his cup down on the rusted table. "Well, out with it."

The man seated opposite him—a spindly fellow with long, graying hair matching his beard—appears likewise perturbed, yet remains silent.

Kellis, after taking a deliberate breath, says again, "What... do... you... want?"

I sense I've tested the patience of all three to their limits, an observation worth noting. Perhaps a life facing the dangers of the world lends one to perceive time differently than those among us who have lived lives of relative comfort?

"Are you a mute?"

"Pardon?" I ask. I'm not aware of who spoke, having been lost as I was in my own thoughts.

"Well," the small, graying man says, "he's not a mute."

A breath of consternation huffs past my lips. "Of course I'm not a mute. Why ever would you—"

"Stop," Kellis cuts me off. "Listen, if you want something, just spit it out. If not, go step off a catwalk."

My eyes widen at the suggestion. "But it's nearly a league drop to the ocean. There's hardly any probability of surviving such a venture. Why would one suggest another—"

Kellis holds up a hand, again cutting me off. A flush rises to my cheeks. I had expected gruff company, but the rudeness on display from the pirate captain thus far goes well beyond anything I had prepared myself for.

"It's just an old saying," Kellis says. "It means bugger off if you don't have anything to say that's worth my time." He pauses with a sigh. "Okay, let's start with your name."

I cock my head to the side, unsure why this is important, but I can fathom no reason not to oblige him. "Wilhelm Hadsworth."

Kellis smiles, and I find myself surprised by the warmness of the expression, given the man's reputation. "Well, Wilhelm Hadsworth, that's a good start. I'm—"

This time, I cut him off. "Roger Kellis, famed pirate captain. I know."

And to further my surprise, three revolvers are suddenly braced against the table. Their hammers are drawn back, and the cylinders rotate with a series of clicks that reverberate through the rusted metal below them.

I know I should raise my hands to show I'm unarmed, but to drop the invaluable documents in my arms would be unconscionable. "I'm not with the Constabulary, if that's your concern."

Kellis squints again, fox-like cunning gleaming behind his cold blue eyes. He takes only moments to consider me before returning his pistol's hammer to its former place of rest, then signals his compatriots to do likewise.

"Okay," he says. "Now that we're all friendly-like, why don't you set that crap down and take a seat?" The captain gestures to the empty chair opposite him, presumably an invitation for me to make use of it.

I do as bid, taking care with my bundled notes as I place them on the pitted table. I am pained to think of the potential damage the rusted metal might wreak on either the delicate paper of the charts or the valuable leather of one of my journals. Once satisfied my belongings are situated as securely as one could expect, considering the circumstances, I lower myself to the rickety chair that Kellis proffers. Hands free of their burden, I also remove my plain, black bowler hat and place it atop the piled notes and charts.

The graying man chuckles. "Settled in nice and comfy, are we?"

I smile and nod. "Quite so, thank you."

A round of hearty guffaws meets my remark, the source of which eludes me. But before I can consider the cause of such sudden frivolity, Kellis once again takes the lead on the conversation.

"So, back to my original question. Why in the bloody hells are you here?"

"That wasn't your original question," I say. "What you asked was, 'what do you want?'"

Kellis rubs a meaty, scarred hand across his face, apparently trying to remove some offending substance or debris from his skin. Why he is choosing this moment to focus on matters hygienical, and in such an obviously unsanitary venue, is yet another point of consternation in my continued dealings with the man.

"Are you even listening?" Kellis asks.

Listening to what, I'm not entirely sure. "I'm sorry?"

Again, Kellis rubs at his face. The graying man seems to choke on something, but still grins like he has just made some great scientific discovery, and the large man's attention seems to be drawn by a passing serving girl.

Kellis takes another long, deliberate breath—I must inquire whether the man has some sort of respiratory condition which might interfere with his duties as captain before we finalize any negotiations—then says, "I said it doesn't matter how I—" He seems to stop himself. "Wait, that doesn't matter, either. Tell you what… You're here because you're looking for me, right?"

"Yes."

"Okay, why are you looking for me?"

Finally, a direct question with clear intent. "I seek to hire you, your crew, and your ship."

The big man's head spins back around at this, his mouth open wide. The graying man ceases his choking.

Kellis squints again. Perhaps this is less attributable to his cunning nature and more to some sort of ophthalmological ailment? Surely, spending time in a city named for the rust covering every surface cannot be amenable to one's health, but these men seem especially stricken.

Kellis leans forward. "Why do you want to hire my ship?"

"And you, and your crew," I correct.

He says nothing.

I clear my throat and continue—whilst wondering if the sudden tightness in my chest is from concern over the difficulty of the encounter or if I, too, am becoming stricken with some rust-borne illness. "I wish to hire you, your crew, and your ship to take me to Kimichula and seek out the Font of Souls."

The big man, who until that moment was deep into his cup, suddenly spits some sort of noxious-smelling fluid about the table. Seeing some of the offending liquid strike my journals and charts, I make haste to wipe it away with the sleeve of my coat.

Kellis leans back as I clean the documents, then waves a hand in dismissal. "That's a legend as full of gull crap as the one about the well on The Whispering Isle. I've seen hundreds of men go to their deaths seeking eternal life in a child's tale. Why would you do the same just for a chance to see your own death before it happens?"

His brusque reply takes me aback for a moment. "The veracity of claims about the Well of Eternal Life may be disputed, as are those of the Font of Souls, but there is enough evidence to suggest—in both cases—that there exists enough likelihood of truth to warrant further investigation. Why, in fact, I have only recently discovered from observing the Cumulocarta a likely location for the Font itself, which has led me on this very undertaking. Here…" I shuffled through the charts, seeking one document in particular. "I have a relatively precise navigational chart which should lead us right to it."

"No," Kellis says, holding up a hand. "Stop. I'm not going on some fool's errand half-way across the world to that blasted jungle. You couldn't possibly pay me enough."

My eyes widen at his sudden assumption as to my own financial means. But rather than arguing the point, I drive towards an alternative consideration which I am sure will earn his interest. "The expedition is being funded by the Aerotarium. There's already an escrow account in your name at the White Whale bank in The Hub; the value of which is backed by some two hundred bars of platinum."

Kellis's eyes widen, the graying man resumes a fit of coughing, and the large man frantically waves down the serving girl to order more drinks.

Then Kellis leans close and extends his hand. "Mister, you have a ship."

I KNEW BETTER than to expect any sort of luxury accommodations aboard Kellis's ship—the *Drunken Princess*—but relief nonetheless floods my being as we finally near the verdant isle of Kimichula.

The *Princess* does little to live up to her name. Originally a seafaring carrack, the small, two-decked ship has scant accommodations for her crew of twenty aeronauts. Crammed together on the gun deck, sleeping in hammocks hung between beams—and some uncomfortably close to the ship's furnace—the crew has no private space to speak of. Only the captain himself has private quarters, and it was of little surprise that he did not forfeit his accommodations to accompany the patron of the voyage—namely: myself.

As word of our impending arrival runs throughout the lower deck of the ship, I struggle to untangle myself from a hammock cut of discarded sailcloth. Nearby, the furnace roars as the inferno within sends gouts of hot air along two copper pipes of remarkable girth, feeding the two large canvas balloons which hold the ship aloft in the skies. Coal fumes fill the cramped space and soot covers every surface, be it cut from wood or flesh of man. I wipe a newly deposited layer of the grimy, black substance from my hands, then my face, as I gather up my coat and run for the stairs to the main deck. Water inside the boiler above the furnace bubbles and steam hisses through more pipes, these leading to drive propellers at the back of the ship which speed us on our journey.

It was Kellis's one act of kindness that I be allowed to keep my journals and charts in his quarters, well away from the filth and heat below.

Finally emerging into the fresh air of the southern skyways, I rush to the meager forecastle of the ship to steal my first glimpse of the fabled southern isle.

Discovered nary one-hundred years ago, Kimichula is a long, slender body of land that was lost in the vastness of the sea for uncounted centuries. When finally discovered by men from the north, it was found to be occupied by peoples therewith unheard of. At first, many thought their peculiar ways might lead to conflict between our two cultures, but these worries were soon put to rest when the indigenous people and newly arrived settlers found not cause for strife in their differences, but rather opportunities to prosper from one another. And since, a most remarkable blending of societies has occurred, giving rise to what many consider an entirely new culture—little resembling either that of the natives of Kimichula or the lives left behind by the settlers.

Several port towns dot the coast of the island, and our destination is the largest of these, and site to the landing of the first explorers so long ago.

By continental reckoning, New Dresberg could be considered little more than a small trading port. Despite this, it is nominally the capital of the island, and remains the primary point of ingress to and egress from it. Most surprising of all, it doesn't even have a skyport!

This fact then leads to a sudden venting of air from the balloons above the ship, signaled by a horrendous squeal as men tug on rigging to open ports in the fabric. Shouts echo around me, orders I hardly comprehend issued with such gruffness as to cause one's nerves to fray. As the crew goes about their work, the *Drunken Princess* descends towards New Dresberg's harbor, ringed on three sides by Freeman's Jetty—a semi-circle of toppled stone drawn from the ruins inside the jungle, which acts to protect what would otherwise be an exposed beachhead.

As the ship splashes into the sea, then cruises past the jetty, I run to the gunwale and lean over for a better view of the massive stonework. Millenia-old carvings from a long-lost empire which once dominated the island persist in the stones, despite the constant assault from the ocean. Some forms I recognize from my studies, but many are novel in nature.

Oh, to sit here by the sea and sketch every figure and glyph; it would be such a joy!

I sniff the salty air and wrinkle my nose in disgust as the odoriferous leavings of cadaverous sea life assail my senses.

Well, perhaps not such a joy, after all.

AS WE TRUDGE through the jungle, I struggle to keep up with Kellis, who likewise seems taxed to keep apace with our Tohangan guide, Irski. The Indigenous man we hired to lead us to the fabled ruins of Endrapo—capital city of the long-fallen island empire—likely bears little resemblance to his forebears who greeted the first northern explorers. The exceptions to this are his bronzed flesh and remarkably dark hair, which hangs to his shoulders in tight curls.

Otherwise, Irski dresses much as one would expect from any working man on the continent. He wears tan slacks, boots, and a loose-fitting button-down shirt that may have once been white. The only adornment which speaks of his heritage is a beautiful necklace of shimmering purple and pearlescent seashells hung with crimson and emerald feathers from some exotic fowl native to Kimichula.

The man is also remarkably well-spoken, being more intelligible even than many among Kellis's crew. He is a shrewd bargainer as well, draining not only my reserve of funds allotted for the expedition, but also eliciting a promised share of Kellis's own profits.

This latter turn of events was most surprising to me, as Kellis had fulfilled his task in safely transporting me to the island. He could have turned and left when Irski refused my offered sum. Instead, he matched the sum from what he was to be paid—an act that seemed born of a desire stoked within the pirate to delve into the ruins himself. This was further evidenced when he insisted on joining us on our jungle trek—another task not within the purview of his contract.

Finally, after several days and nights in the tropical forest, we draw near an assortment of towering ruins the likes of which all the books in my not-so-humble library fail to accurately represent. Towers stand along the outskirts, most crumbling, but some still soaring above the trees. Long walls stretch away beyond sight, all carved with intricate designs and bearing miles of script still yet to be deciphered. Scholars have spent lifetimes studying these ruins, yet they stand as large an enigma as the Cumulocarta itself.

I retrieve a sheaf of scrawled notes and sketches from my coat, flipping through them until I find a diagram I had drawn of Endrapo from that cloud-born oracle. We follow the instructions I scrawled in the fervor of excited revelation until we reach a monolithic structure near the center of the city.

Here lay evidence of many prior investigations; discarded tents, broken camp chairs, metal canteens, and rusted shovels. How many had stood here discerning the secrets of the lost empire without knowing what truly lay within? How many had sought the Font of Souls, unaware it lay mere yards below their feet?

In the center of the crumbling structure—which the Cumulocarta's eddies revealed to have been a temple of sorts—a single obelisk stands seemingly untouched by time. On its face are an assortment of glyphs and carved script, in keeping with most of the ruins. But standing out from all this is a relief of an octopus with far too many writhing tentacles to be realistic. And at the tip of each, a glimmering gemstone so encased within the surrounding granite as to be impossible to remove. Upon each, that is, save one.

Here, lost among its glittering brethren by its nondescript nature, one tentacle ends only in an empty socket.

Thieves and vandals had received blame for the missing jewel. But few considered the improbability of the theory, given all the remaining gemstones had defied repeated attempts to be removed.

No, this empty socket was intentional, and the Cumulocarta had also revealed what need be deposited within the deliberate void to unlock the secrets of the Font of Souls.

I shoulder by both Kellis and Irski without word, draw a small knife from my pocket, and unfold the blade. Anxiety fills me, as there is little I dread more than the sight of blood. Overcoming my trepidation, I poke the end of my finger with the blade before discarding the tool. Then, I squeeze a sizeable droplet of my life's essence from the wound and press the offended digit against the gemless tentacle of the octopus.

Stone rumbles and screeches as slabs long-still grate against each other. The ground beneath our feet trembles.

"What in the blazes did you do?" Kellis asks.

I turn and smile, satisfaction warming my cheeks. "Opened the door."

Irski, eyes wide with panic, says nothing before he turns and flees from the temple. When finally out of sight, foreign words drift over the walls, fading from earshot as he continues his fear-born sprint. While I know not what he is saying, I can tell none of it is polite.

I shrug and turn back to the obelisk. The flagstones beneath it have parted, revealing a narrow crevice in the ground. Kellis and I take several steps back as the gap continues to grow, revealing stone stairs leading down into the darkness.

Kellis meets my eyes. I might ponder on what lay within his

expression, were time not of the essence and the goal of my expedition in such immediate proximity. He draws in a breath. "This is it?"

"Yes." I peer down into the darkness. "We need a light."

Soon, Kellis has a torch from his pack in hand, aflame thanks to an oil lighter.

Our path thus illuminated, we descend into the unknown.

Kellis leads the way, torch in one hand and cutlass in the other. I had thought it odd for our entire journey that he wore such a relic of the past, especially considering he always bore a revolver on his other hip. Yet now, as we creep down the ancient steps, I find it comforting that he wields a weapon likely more pragmatic for the tight confines of the subterranean ruins.

The near impossibility of encountering any hostile entity within notwithstanding.

It is only moments before we reach the end of the stairs and the passage opens into a small cave of stone eroded by the elements rather than shaped by the hand of man. Gone are the intricate carvings of the temple above, replaced by something more primal. Against all reason, the cave feels more ancient than the ruins we just left behind.

Opposite the entrance, I spot that for which I am searching. I hardly dared to believe my search would bear fruit, yet here it stands. My breath catches in my throat as I behold the sight.

A trickle of water bubbles from the side of the cave, flowing over smooth, polished stones to run into a pool of water surrounded by a low wall of cut and mortared blocks—the only stonework in the cave that belies the hand of mankind at work.

And despite the constant flow of water into the pool, the surface appears bestilled, as if not touched by a single drop from above or even a breath of wind. So placid is it that the torch light reflects from across the room as if from the highest-quality glass mirror.

"This is it, then?" Kellis asks as he gazes at the pool. "This is the Font of Souls?"

I check my notes again, though I am sure, just to eliminate any possibility of error. "Yes."

"And what they say is true? The Font shows you how you will die?"

I sigh, as my documents don't hold the answer to his question. "That is what the legends say, but I have not been able to source any first-hand accounts that—"

Kellis cuts me off by thrusting the torch into my hands. Without another word, he steps up to the Font.

With a flaming torch in one hand and my priceless research in the other, any sense of awe is suddenly washed away by a fit of panic. I drop the torch, which clatters against the stone floor in a cacophony so resounding as to cause Kellis to spin on his heels.

He glares at me, most likely offended that the sudden noise has violated the solemnity of the moment. I find it surprising this revelation came to me without difficulty; perhaps Kellis and I share a certain sense of reverence for what we are witnessing.

The interruption past, the pirate captain turns back to the Font of Souls. He takes another step forward, leans in close, and glares into the water.

Moments pass in a silence so absolute my pulse seems as if it echoes from the walls of the cave. I find myself holding my breath, but not of any conscious accord, and gasp deeply once reminded air is required for continued existence.

Then, a low moan fills the cave.

Kellis steps back from the pool and turns. His eyes are wide with mixed shock and fear. His mouth hangs open, then works in wordless pleas. He storms across the cave, muttering softly at first, but then repeating louder as if chanting, over and over: "I shouldn't have looked."

Trepidation grips my heart and stills it in an iron grip. What horrors did Kellis see in those waters? I nearly turn and run from the cave. I feel I should let my feet carry me away. Out of the cave, out of the jungle, and far from Kimichula; never to return. But the thirst for knowledge is overwhelming.

I must know.

I step forward and place my hands on the smooth, time-weathered stones of the Font and close my eyes. I take a breath and hold it, pondering what the next might bring.

Behind me, Kellis's bellows of anguish fill the cave. "I don't want to know!"

My heart thrums against my ribs. My pulse beats like war drums in my ears.

I let the breath out, lean forward, and open my eyes.

On the surface of the pool, I see myself looking back. Torchlight flickers on the ceiling of the cave above me and Kellis's shadow dances to and fro as he paces in consternation.

A reflection?

Had something gone wrong? What might disturb Kellis so, if all there is to behold in the waters is one's own reflection?

As I gaze down at myself, the image in the water seems suddenly startled, then raises a hand.

Shock runs through my being as surely as steam flows through a copper pipe. I raise my hand, but the reflection fails to mimic my gesture.

So, it isn't a reflection. But why is it showing me something only moments after the here and now?

Again, Kellis's voice fills the cave, a low growl echoing off the stones. "You brought me here."

In the pool, a shadow looms over my doppelganger, blocking out the torchlight. I look over my shoulder to find the torch unobstructed, its light still filling the cave and washing over me, and Kellis pacing along the far wall.

I look back down and am met with a horrific sight. Large, scarred hands clench my throat from behind as I lean over the Font. My eyes bulge as I gasp in a futile effort to breathe and flail with hapless abandon against the stones ringing the pool. My face turns red, then purple, as those hands choke the life from me. They release me and I fall, limp and lifeless, to float in the Font of Souls.

Whilst pondering the prophetic vision of my demise, I feel Kellis's rough hands slide along either side of my neck.

THE TALONS OF ICE

GREGORY COLEY

Calloused fingers traced the scarred, worn polish of the cherry wood table. Once shined to the point, it reflected the hanging metal light overhead. It now couldn't even reflect the patrons that used its surface. Many late nights of song and drink tend to have that effect. It didn't matter. Gavin wasn't here for the ambiance, but for the entertainment. His black cat, Lunafer, strolled down his arm before plopping on the table, exposing her belly. Gavin smiled, his blue eyes locked on the stage. The cat's clockwork tail kept rhythm on the table as, on the stage, Melody's voice carried over the room of scoundrels.

The ale was sub-par, and the smell was atrocious. The building had once been a fine establishment deep in The Hub, the largest city in the sky for miles. Any time Gavin made port, he put out feelers for where Melody would be performing. His crew loved to hear her sing, and Gavin loved *her*. It wasn't reciprocated. At least, not that he would ever know. Melody drew in pirates from every corner of the globe, from Kimichula to Frostborne. Twenty-five percent of them most likely entertained their own fantasy that they had a cog's chance in hell with her.

The other seventy-five percent? They were here for her angelic voice.

The ballad ended, and the lone singer's smile shone across the room. Her eyes searched the crowd before locking on Gavin's. He shifted nervously as she descended the steps; her faded red day dress brushing the floorboards as she sauntered to his table. The dress hung off the shoulders, just shy of being 'too low' for public attire.

Sitting down, she immediately reached to scratch the cat's belly. It purred and peered up at Melody through leather and metal goggles that made its green eyes seem the size of dice. "Haven't seen you in The Cog District in a while, Gavin. Where you been hiding?" she said, rivulets of red hair falling to her freckled shoulders.

He mulled over his answer until the cat hit him in the arm with her long, copper clockwork tail, as if to snap him out of it. "Your hair is a different color than it was when I last saw you... I mean... You know me. If I'm not out there touching the stars, then I'm just not myself," he smiled, cutting his eyes at the cat.

"You know, you should have shown up earlier. We could have spent some time together. You could be... late... getting back to your ship?" she raised a ginger eyebrow, the grey morning light revealing the ghosts of freckles on her pale nose.

He held the cat's tail down so it didn't hit him. "We are only here for a few hours this time, Melody. I hate that we can't spend more time together, but I at least had to see you. That counts for something, right? You know Lunafer hates crowds," he said, motioning to the black cat. The cat glared at him through her goggles. Gavin knew he would pay for that comment later.

"Don't call her that. Her name is Luna, not Lunafer. You wanna stay here with me, girl? That mean ol' pirate doesn't know how to treat us ladies," she said, kissing the black cat on the head.

"Okay, you two, stop plotting against me. We need to get out of here before sunrise," he said, climbing to his feet and kissing Melody on the cheek.

"What grand adventure are you off to this time?"

Lunafer ran up Gavin's arm and sat on his shoulder, draping her tail across his back and onto the other shoulder, holding on with it. "We're heading up to the Ice Talon Sea," said Gavin.

"Gavin... You've got to be insane. Tell me you're not going to that lighthouse. There's nothing there. It's where the known world ends. Nothing waits for you there but cold and ice and death."

"Ok then. I won't tell you," he smiled, winking at her before turning with a flourish and disappearing into the street, the heaving oak door closing slowly on its hydraulic hinges.

The Cog. A central district within the Hub. A whirring, whizzing pirate Eden filled with drink, women and contraptions seen nowhere else in the 'verse. Hovering miles above the ocean, clouds engulfed the tops of the buildings. That, combined with the steam from the mechanical knick-knacks and the smoke rising from the industrial district of Soot, gave the ever-changing, morphing, and moving city a hazy visage.

Still, this world was unlike anything he could have imagined growing up. Until he was in his early teens, he lived in a world of space, stars, and planets. New Aegean, specifically. Round and round a black hole he went until one day he, being an irresponsible young boy, got dragged in. Spit out into this strange world. His leg mangled beyond repair. He was found by a tall, lanky man with pointy ears named Crispin who claimed he was from a world of magic. Gavin thought it was insanity until he saw the rest of the world within The Archarrier and The Cartographer's Fleet. The gadgets and gizmos were less polished than what he was used to, but they were somehow more ingenius. They fashioned him a clockwork prosthetic when they weren't able to save his leg. It was—

"Hey, human, what are you thinking about? Pay attention!"

snapped Lunafer, hitting him on the side of the head with her metal tail.

Gavin, startled out of his reverie, dodged a contraption that could only be described as a steam-powered motorbike, but it was one giant circle, like a hula hoop on its end, spitting steam. Gold and wood, it sped by, honking its annoying little horn.

Looking after the vehicle, he sighed, smoke rising from his leg as he proceeded to walk again. "Thanks, Luna. This place is insane. I, for one, can't wait to get back to *The Corvus*."

"Corvus. Not only an omen of death but also home of delicious warm milk," she said, butting the goggles into the side of his smoke-ringed head.

As they neared the outer ring of The Hub, the crowds thickened. More odd vehicles and thingamajigs whizzed by before Gavin laid his eyes on a ship among the others. His ship. Blackened wood two decks deep with windows on the back in the suite he called home. Two massive sails on the front to catch the wind and a white linen balloon bigger than the ship itself rose from the middle, fed by a flame in the bowels of the beast. Around the balloon hung ropes, pulleys, do-hickies of bits and bobs, along with a walkway to keep the balloon stable and four crows' nests. Gun ports concealed rows of cannons. *The Corvus* wasn't just his home. It was to be feared by anyone who laid eyes upon the brown crossed wrenches and hollow-eyed metallic skull emblazoned on the flag atop the balloon.

"We're back, Luna," he smiled as they walked the narrow dock that led to the skyship between dozens of other identical walkways.

She jumped down, running ahead and up the iron ramp to the ship. The wind whipped at Gavin's clothes, nearly knocking him over the walkway to the ocean thousands of feet below. His stomach tumbled like the waves below. In his home-world, there was no falling to your death. He would just float away. Here though? Here, falling was a thing.

He strolled up the ramp and onto the deck of *The Corvus*, eyeing Luna, who now sat on the bannister of the stairs to the helmsman's post. "You almost made me fall, you know."

Luna licked her paw, her voice muffled. "Don't worry about what would happen to me. I make friends easy and this place is packed with potential. Your concern is noted. Now, I'm going to eat. Open my door, human." Gavin tapped his foot as she jumped down and impatiently waited by the double doors to the Captain's quarters.

Luna rolled her green eyes, massive behind her goggles. "Fine. Can you *please* open my door?"

Gavin rolled his eyes and let her in amidst a chorus of her complaints and comments about not having thumbs.

He still wasn't sure if the day he came across a cat—that had once lived somewhere called Brig Island—was a good thing or a bad day. When his mentor Crispin claimed magic was real, Gavin didn't believe him at first. But then he'd met Luna. A talking cat? Hard to deny magic existed after seeing that.

"Number One!" he called, climbing the steps to the helm. "What's the weather like this morn'? Will we make it to Frost-borne before sundown?"

The woman with platinum blonde, jaw-length hair brushed back behind her ears, studied him, squinting through her goggles. "We should, Captain. The winds seem fair enough this morning!"

Gavin took off his hat, fixing his reddish-brown hair and thick beard. Short to the chin and straight as a pin, his hair swept back over his head. Trimmed and neat in the back, long strands from the front and top had come loose. With a sweep of his hands he could go from ragged to elegant, and from comfortable to authoritative. Moving the goggles from around his neck to his eyes, he replaced his flat cap.

"Alrighty then, maties! We're shoving off! Yo-ho-ho!" he called, grabbing the helm and taking the ship out from her mooring.

Throughout the deck, the crew rushed back and forth. Raising sails, tossing fuel into the furnace under the balloon, tying off lines and running across the scaffolding around the dirigible. The crew worked like an ant colony in the sky. Beginning with a single voice down by the balloon, they continued a long tradition of singing while they worked. Before long, more picked up the words and tune until it engulfed the whole ship in song as the ship rose into the clouds.

"Up in the clouds a fierce wind blows, with storms of rain and ice and snow. Up in the north beyond the glow, and we will find our way home soon," sang Jacque Hurley, a round, bald pirate in a deep baritone.

"*Heave, Ho!*" called the rest of the crew.

"Through the ice and snow."

"*We'll find our way home soon!*"

"Shovel the coal."

"*Till the engines glow!*"

"We'll find our way home soon. From Frostborne high to Braddock's Bay, we all can find a place to lay. Just toss a line and heave away. And we will find our way home soon."

The trip was long and soon he entrusted the navigating to his number one, Genevieve. In his quarters, sitting at a heavy oak desk, Gavin looked out the windows at the back of the ship. Somebody might say watching where you had been is living in the past, but, to Gavin, it was all about watching his back. There wasn't much law the further out people travelled from The Hub.

Genevieve burst through the double doors, letting in the moonlight. "We're just passing Halfaway now, Captain."

"Excellent. I'll be out momentarily," he called over his shoulder.

The door creaked while he cranked the gears on his left leg. It sputtered to life, black smoke rising from it. Standing, one brown pant leg ended above the knee over the prosthetic. The other pant leg went down to his scuffed work boots. On his torso he wore a long sleeve cotton shirt with three buttons at the neck. Rolling down his sleeves, he pulled the dangling leather suspenders back over his shoulders and grabbed his ankle-length dark green—nearly black, in all honesty—pea coat.

Lunafer rolled over on the bed in the corner. "We landing already? It doesn't feel cold. Did you get us lost again?" she asked, propping her head up with her long tail.

"No. No, I didn't. We are passing Halfaway and I haven't seen it in a while. Thought I'd take a gander," he said, combing his hair back before putting on his goggles and flat cap. "You're welcome to come look."

"Fine. Carry me," she yawned.

Gavin flipped up his collar. "Why do I put up with you?"

"You love me. You know you do!"

Gavin rolled his eyes and walked out onto the deck as the cat sauntered behind him. A cool wind coming off the ocean below greeted him. Far to the left was The Whispering Isle and Rustowne. Behind them was The Hub and Elysium—an island so massive that when you flew over it, you couldn't see the ocean in any direction. Nothing of interest there, though. Just a bunch of farmers who sent their goods to The Hub and other surrounding islands, including Halfaway to the north.

He climbed the steps to the helm above his quarters, tightening his goggles to keep the wind out. The air this far from the balloon was cool, and it would only grow colder the further north they went.

Walking to the starboard railing, he leaned on it heavily. In the distance, he could just make out Halfaway. Floating above the renowned Frost Mines, the floating island of Halfaway tethered to the ground by chains so massive it took an army to anchor them. Still, the floating island was unsteady and prone to windquakes from the unpredictable northern winds coming in from the Frost Talon Sea. It was a beautiful place, but like most beautiful things, it had a troublesome side. The few occasions he went into port there, he was bedridden with motion sickness for the duration of his stay.

"Want to stop over for supplies, Captain?" called Genevieve over the wind, holding her tricorne hat in place.

"Are we short on anything?"

"No sir, I don't believe so."

He straightened up. "Full speed ahead. I want to hit Frostborne by nightfall. Have you ever been?"

"To Frostborne? No, Sir."

"Gen, call me Gavin. It's just us. You don't have to put on airs for the crew. The rest of the crew is down in the mess below deck. We've been friends a long time."

She smirked, raising an eyebrow. "Don't get any ideas."

"Oh, never. I wouldn't dare lay a hand on the best shot this side of the Kraken. You'll like Frostborne. It's cold, secluded, and has lots of places to buy things."

"I'm not one for buying, Gavin. I prefer to take what I want," she said, walking over to him and straightening his jacket lapels.

"Go smoochie already before I hack up a hairball," called Lunafer as she padded up the steps and leapt onto the starboard railing.

"Can you fly, Lunafer?" asked Genevieve, letting go of Gavin's lapels and stepping back to take hold of the steering column.

Lunafer jumped on Gavin's shoulder. "No, but unlike you, I'd land on my feet," she said with a low growl.

"Enough, ladies! I will not have fighting on my ship," he said, placing his hand on the revolver at his hip. "We need to stay as healthy as we can. Don't none of us have any idea what waits for us in the White Wasteland. Are we understood?"

Lunafer draped her tail across his neck and onto his other shoulder, purring. Meanwhile, Genevieve nodded without taking her eyes off the horizon where the sun was setting.

"Good. I do so hate violence among friends," he said, relaxing and pulling his jacket tighter around him.

There was a chill in the air. It would only get worse. Much worse. He knew Frostborne well, and he knew of the Lighthouse at the End of the World. Those weren't what worried him. There were unseen things within the White Mist. Damned things that hell spit back out.

The cold bit like a Kraken. Gavin stood near the balloon for the heat from the flames as members of his crew tied *The Corvus* to a dock coming off the miniscule Frostborne skyport. Things had changed since Gavin had last been here.

"Should have stopped off at Orff instead," he mumbled, disembarking the ship with Lunafer clinging to his shoulder, shivering.

Genevieve jogged up behind him and patted his other shoulder. "Look! There! Have you ever seen it this close?" she said excitedly, pointing in the general direction of Orff. She wasn't pointing at the small island, but high above it, and even higher above the hovering island of Frostborne.

Looking up, Gavin couldn't find what she was talking about at first. Once he did, he wondered how he missed it. Floating on the wind was The Archarrier. The Cartographer's Fleet. A series of balloons connected by rope bridges led to the city on the ship.

He chuckled humorlessly. His childhood home. "Yeah. Once or twice."

Gavin didn't care for Frostborne. It was a marvel of engineering, yes, but something about it didn't sit right with him. The environment was harsh, cold, and icy. An interior fire kept the streets, buildings, and people from freezing. Still, the elements in the Ice Talon Sea far below could kill. Chains stretched from the underside of Frostborne to a sizable glacier which held the town of Braddock's Bay, which was named after the Captain of the phantom ghost ship, *The Midnight Scythe*, that was said to patrol the skies near the White Wasteland.

"You're all business, I see. What shall we pick up?" She walked past him and opened the door to a shop, nearly hitting him.

The interior was warm, and the scents of cloves and cinnamon bombarded his senses. Shelves lined the walls with essentials: jackets, packs, guns, ammo, and cutlery. "Pick up anything you think we might need. It's gonna be rough going."

"We're pirates, Gavin. Why don't we just take what we need?"

"Genevieve. As a pirate I live by a single rule: Never screw anybody over who doesn't deserve it. The people up here are barely scraping by as it is," he lectured her. "We are pirates, but we have manners," he smirked.

Turning away from her, he browsed the aisles. Picking up a few bits and baubles, he searched for something he could use. A few minutes passed before he and Genevieve met at the firearms. The array was staggering. Pistols, revolvers, flintlocks, rifles, shotguns, and even crossbows.

Gavin picked up a pistol with six individual barrels welded together. Iron and gold latticework of cogs cascading down the barrels and onto the mahogany handle. Turning it over in his hands, he spun the barrel, causing it to emit a calming clicking sound. He had to have this beautiful piece of machinery.

"She has a mate, you know," said a portly man in mutton chops behind the counter at the end of the aisle.

Gavin looked up. "What was that?"

"The six-barrel you got there. It comes in a pair if you want it."

Genvieve and Gavin walked to the front counter. Genevieve carried a long barrel rifle. Black iron from butt to sights with a steam tank on the top and a hand crank to build up pressure. They sat the two guns on the counter.

Genevieve took out her coin purse. "How much for the two six barrels and the long rifle?"

The shop owner bent down behind the bar before reappearing with a small scale. "That'll be five gold doubloons for the six barrels. Each. I'll throw in their holster. As for the long rifle... That's ten doubloons even."

After a good five minutes of the shop owner weighing the coins to make sure they hadn't been shaved, Gavin and Genevieve headed back to *The Corvus* with their new guns in tow.

"You think all these extra guns are necessary?" asked Genevieve as they walked up the ramp back to the boat.

They walked up to the steps to the wheel, but before they could raise the lines and drop the sails, a scuffle broke out between two of the sailors. Gavin rolled his eyes, pulling one of the six barrels out and aiming it. Looking down the sight, he fired at one of the two men. One of their ears evaporated in a spray of blood and flesh, sending the man screaming to the ground.

"No fighting on my ship! Next time the shot will be fatal," he yelled before turning back to Genevieve. "Yeah. They'll come in handy." He holstered the gun.

Gavin stirred in the pre-dawn grey coming through the windows of his quarters, pushing Luna off his side.

"Really, Gavin? Really? I let you sleep in my bed and this is the thanks I get?" she mumbled, moving to the foot of the bed.

The double doors to his chambers burst open. Genevieve stood in the doorway, covered in a thin layer of frost. "Ship on the horizon, Captain! Its sails glow like lightbulbs!" she panted.

"Man the cannons!" he roared, jumping out of bed.

Genevieve nodded, turning on her heels to prepare the crew. Gavin stumbled around, grabbing his clothes as he did so. Attaching his prosthetic with leather straps, he slipped his brown britches over them before pulling his suspenders over his long sleeve undershirt. Grabbing his hat and dark green jacket, he made for the door.

"What's going on?" asked Luna, padding along beside him.

"I think we're about to meet Bottomless Braddock."

"You mean *The Midnight Scythe*? The ghost ship?"

"One and the same."

Gavin's breath plumed in the air as he stepped on deck. The frigid White Mist washed over their ship, coating everything in a thin layer of ice. The only thing that remained untouched was the balloon itself due to the heat within.

He transfixed his gaze on the distant tower lighthouse, barely visible through the mist. Their true destination. Once tall and proud, it was now wrapped in ice. The light still shone, somehow. Legend said there was a 'frozen one', a person said to be the brother of Braddock himself, who kept the beacon lit. Gavin tended to think it was magic.

Beyond the lighthouse? Nothing. White plains as far as the eye could see. People thought this was the end of the world. He was here to prove them wrong.

Icebergs densely dotted the sea below, like ice talons rising from the depths.The mist was thickening, causing the ice to accumulate on the ship. Even Gavin's bushy two piece goatee was gathering frost. Ahead of them, lights broke through the mist. No. Not lights. Sails. *The Midnight Scythe*. It was a ghost ship. A ship of the damned. But that was a lie. A ghost story to scare the children of Rustowne, The Hub, Kimichula, Elysium, Halfaway, and the Cartographer's Fleet. He never believed the stories, but the ghoulish reaper adorning the front of the ship stole away any doubt and any hope he had of making it out of this alive.

It was real. Gavin's stomach leapt into his throat, forcing him to lose precious seconds until he could find his voice. "To your battle stations, lads!"

Genevieve's demeanor changed from panic to focus, as if a switch were flipped. She pulled her new rifle from her back, along with a new pair of goggles from her belt. She clicked multiple lenses into place over her left eye before raising the ornate black iron and gold latticework rifle up to it to make sure the sights were still straight. Nodding, she cranked the handle to build up pressure before turning and climbing up to the walkway around the balloon.

"What do you need me to do?" asked Lunafer, jumping off his shoulder and landing with a thud on the planks of the ship.

Gavin removed his goggles, letting his flat cap hit the deck, causing his neatly combed hair to come loose, framing his face. "Go get my mask. Then, for Kraken's sake, stay hidden!"

A moment passed before Lunafer returned, carrying the mask with her clockwork tail. He grabbed it and put it on. Iron and shaped like a bird, it covered the eyes in red protective lenses. The warmth of the mask interior cut the cold like a knife, and bathed the world in warm red light.

The ship creaked. Gunports slamming open shook the vessel. *The Midnight Scythe* neared, its crew now visible. Gavin's stomach churned. It dwarfed *The Corvus*. The deck was lined with hundreds, if not thousands, of decomposing waterlogged bodies crawling over each other like ants, their milky white eyes unblinking and their smiles in eternal toothy grins. Barnacles hung from each and every body, as well as the rusted ship. Roaring blasts and blinding light became evident over all the commotion. Splintering wood cascaded around Gavin as three rows of cannons fired into the side of *The Corvus*, causing it to list. Multiple rotting planks of wood were thrown onto the deck of the ship, as they leveled out with *The Corvus*, followed by wet, dripping ropes.

Despite this, his attention was drawn to the helmsman. Standing seven feet if he was an inch, he wore a long, tattered light keeper's knit hat and long coat. Metal tubes extended from the maw of his skeletal visage, running down to the shredded skin over his exposed ribs. Gold metallic mesh covered what once were his eyes. The flesh around them was burned, and the meat of his face looked melted. It was like goggles had fused into his skin. Wisps of blood-stained hair and beard still hung from what flesh remained.

The ghoulish inhabitants of *The Midnight Scythe* swarmed to cross to *The Corvus* any way they could: ropes, planks, and jumping. Gavin took a step back, drawing his two pistols from his hips, all twelve barrels loaded to unleash death.

The undead crew washed over *The Corvus* like a plague of locusts. Gavin fired indiscriminately, skulls exploding left and right. The deck grew slippery with blood as the fray thickened. The sounds of gunshots from overhead droned on as Genevieve cranked the pressure up and fired repeatedly, picking off ghouls as fast as humanly possible. It wasn't fast enough.

"Abandon sh—" he tried to call. But a putrid, decaying hand grabbed him by the throat.

A grotesque face with melted mesh goggles looked up at him and lifted him off the ground. "Ye stumbled into my story when you found the lighthouse. You best start praying to whatever god you believe in that I don't make you join my crew," said Braddock, his voice resonating and metallic like he had iron lungs.

The world around Gavin crawled to a near stop as the wails of dying men and the stench of burning flesh mixed with gunpowder and flames. The heat from the cannons washed over him as another volley tore into the side of *The Midnight Scythe*. Barnacles, wood, and bodies flew into the air before disappearing into the iceberg littered ocean below.

Bottomless Braddock stumbled a step. But that was all it took. A blur as black as the surrounding sky leapt through the hellfire surrounding the men. Lunafer landed on his face, biting and clawing, as she wrapped her tail around his throat. Braddock grabbed her by the metal contraption on her back that connected her tail and threw her overboard. He looked back at Gavin, his bottom jaw now missing. He reached for Gavin before two shots from Genevieve's rifle rocked him.

Gavin holstered his guns. Dodging an incoming blow from one of Braddock's crew, he rushed to the port railing. "Lunafer!" he screamed into the icy depth below.

"I told you I always land on my feet!" called the cat from far below, joy obvious in her distant voice.

Gavin's focus darted back and forth, frantically searching for where the voice was coming from. There, far below, stood Lunafer on top of a barrel-shaped escape pod hanging below the ship.

Gavin grinned broadly. "ABANDON SHIP!"

Multiple hatches opened on the bottom of the ship and more barrel-shaped escape pods dropped with members of his crew inside. As for Gavin, he climbed over the railing after letting down a rope ladder.

Cannons bombarded the side of *The Corvus*. He descended quickly down to the escape pod, his clockwork leg clanging heavily, wreathing him in smoke. Letting go, he landed hard on the top of the escape pod where Lunafer sat with the hatch open.

He climbed inside, closing the hatch behind him. Before he could say anything, Lunafer pressed her paw on the button to release the rope holding the escape pod in place. Gears whirred and popped until, trapped in the highly glossed wooden interior, they were in a freefall to the Ice Talon Sea below.

Barking seals greeted Gavin as he woke from a blow to the face. Lunafer stood over him, slapping him with her tail until he awoke. Covered in snow, he looked around. Still in the escape pod, the hatch was open. He hoped it had all been some horrible dream.

"What did you get us into?" asked Lunafer, her large goggled eyes looking down at him from outside the hatch.

He brushed off the snow and stood. "My crew! My ship! Genevieve..." he mumbled, climbing out of the escape pod.

He stumbled and fell out into the snow. Standing, he dusted himself off. Now on the coast of the White Wasteland, not far from the lighthouse, he thought he might see Orff in the distance, but it was hard to tell. What was unmistakable was the smoking shell of *The Corvus* at the base of the lighthouse, slowly sinking into the water. Bodies lay strewn across the ice. The only sound was Luna licking herself and the crackling flames of what was left of his sinking ship.

Beyond the lighthouse, valleys and mountains stretched as far as the eye could see. He was right. This wasn't the end of the world. For him and Lunafer, this was just the beginning.

ANOTHER KIND OF IMMORTALITY

DANI ATKINSON

*H*ere Flies Herac "Thrice-Over" Hidgins, Third Mate of the *Looming Storm*

Told Patrick Stone, Barkeep of the Crimson Cog, that he had been knocked three times over the rails of his skyship and "knew in every broken bone" that a fourth was coming. So he came for the Whispering Isle, and its Well of Immortality, that the fall might never again hold terrors.

Found by our scavengers adrift in the air currents Northwards and Upwards of the Isle. Drowned.

The fall holds no terrors for him now.

May He Find Another Kind of Immortality.

Here Flies Guy With A Red Hat

Name unknown. Did not stop at the Cog or the Dregs before he tried for the Isle. No one we asked had spoken to him.

But he had a very nice red hat with three very large feathers and a brooch in the shape of a flying fish.

Lightning-struck.

If you recognize him from this information, please speak to Saiseriat. I have left extra space for a name.

May He Find Another Kind of Immortality.

HERE FLIES Orphelie de la Tempete of the Cartographer's Fleet

Came, most unusually, to seek not the Well hidden beyond the storms, but the storm itself.

In her strange ship full of strange devices, and her stranger crewmate, Jemison Rayne, she came and asked Us, the scavengers and the keepers of these graves, about the winds and the clouds, the spinning water and the currents of the air. Not how to pass them, but for their own sake.

"The Cumulocarta is written on the storms. Your storm could be the final piece of the map of everything."

She had, also, many theories about how the secret to immortality might be bound to the secret of this Cumulocarta. This seemed dubious to Us. Just because two things are both secret and both strange does not mean that they have anything else in common. But she laughed and said that at the very least, if she found eternal life, it would guarantee that she lived long enough to see the map completed.

She did not.

Ship exploded. Burned.

May She Find Another Kind of Immortality.

HERE FLIES Jemison Rayne of the Cartographer's Fleet, Formerly of Fiddler's Maroon, originally of Tunis Asteroid

Came with Orphelie de la Tempete. Engineer of her skyship and builder of many of its devices.

Said they had been stolen from their home many years ago by

a kraken, a vast creature of grasping tentacles reaching across unknown oceans between worlds and behind space. They had been forced to live here when the kraken spat them out on the wrong dimension's shore, but had not done so happily, saying "I can't breathe with so much air on top of me."

They said they would take the map home or they'd take the immortality, but either way they'd be damned if they were going to die here without seeing their own world again.

Ship exploded. Burned.

We hope they were wrong and they are not damned. We hope their soul found their way back to that strange sounding world of stars.

May They Find Another Kind Of Immortality.

HERE FLIES QUICKSILVER the Messenger Fish, of the Bayside Municipal Aviaquarium and AirMail Postal Service, Braddock's Bay, Frostborne

Carried a message addressed to me, Saiseriat of the Ninerville Graveyard, presumably as the only scavenger with a known and fixed address. Must have become caught in the air currents trying to reach me and got sucked into the storm. But he pulled free and managed with his little body's last strength to deliver the messenger capsule warning Us of the coming of the *Red Ship*.

Broken wingfin, scraped scales, battered by flying debris.

He was a very brave fish and his postmistress should be proud.

May He Find Another Kind of Immortality.

HERE FLY TWO Severed Hands

Owner unknown. We think they are from the same body. We cannot be sure.

Dismembered.

May They Find Another Kind of Immortality.

HERE FLIES "PETEY"

Small child, about seven or eight. I thought she had come to visit someone's grave. I am a fool. Should have watched more closely.

She left a note written in coloured wax crayon. "My fish Stripey died. Mommy died. Dying is too sad. I will find the magic water so I never die and I will fill my purple cup for Daddy and Grandma and Chuckles so they never die and we won't be sad ever. Petey."

How did one so small move so fast?

She is still now.

Blow to the head.

May She Find Another Kind of Immortality.

HERE FLIES the Harbinger in Red

Came ahead of the *Red Ship* on a smaller, faster sky dinghy to warn us of their current course and ETA that we might better avoid them, communicating from a safe distance with signal flags and lantern. Even from that distance, we could see the boils and lesions between the gaps in their red robes. They proceeded ahead towards the Isle instead of returning to the *Red Ship*, we think because they knew they would not survive the journey back.

They did not survive the journey ahead, either.

Body seen floating Southwest and moving Widdershins. Has

been marked and will be collected when the quarantine period specified in the fish message has passed. This place in the crypt will be reserved for them until then.

Cause of death to be determined.

May They Find Another Kind of Immortality.

HERE FLIES Scavenger Treasure-Among-Trash of The Leftovers

As is the custom with one of our own, we tried four times to discourage him, and he allowed us to try. He has collected trinkets from the wreckage to be his funeral decorations. He came to me to reserve a place should it be needed. All has been observed.

I asked him upon the Fourth Discouragement why he would leave us, when it is far more likely that he shall be one of the nine hundred and ninety nine in a thousand who fail, rather than the one who succeeds. He said he has spent his whole life scrounging for diamonds among the detritus of other people's grand quests, and took his name from it. How could he resist searching for the greatest treasure of all?

How could I resist it?

"Aren't you the least bit curious, Sesariat?"

Found crusted with hailstones in uppermost currents.

Frozen.

May He Find Another Kind of Immortality.

HERE FLIES Chuckles

A green parrot.

Spoke in the voice of the child Petey.

"Hi Chuckles!" it said, and "Peekaboo! Where's Chuckles?"

Perhaps I imagined it, but it sounded sad.

Stopped at the Crimson Cog to charm scraps of toast and

crackers off of the patrons. Bit my thumb. Cannot blame it. Flew into the storm.

Broken neck.

I would not let our scavengers pluck it to sell the feathers. It has earned a place in the Crypt with its mistress.

May They Find Another Kind of Immortality.

Here Flies Shefferton Bezoarg of The Hub

Wealthy merchant fleet admiral. Purchased an expedition to the Font of Souls in Kimichula. Lost a leg but claimed to have found the font and seen his death in the reflection: mauled by shark. Terrified, he tried to purchase guides and passage to the Well of Immortality. Told him it didn't work that way. All you can do is listen to the whispers, and hope. He cursed our names and commissioned the building of an elaborately outfitted and well stocked armoured dirigible in the hopes of weathering the storm.

Our scavengers will be able to support Us for months on the remains of his shattered dirigible, and so we honour him with a place in the Crypt.

Mauled.

May He Find Another Kind of Immortality.

Here Flies A Shark of the Ocean

Must have been sucked up through a waterspout into the maelstrom.

Choked to death on Shefferton Bezoarg's gold prosthetic leg.

May They Find Another Kind of Immortality.

Here Flies the Ship's Medic of the *Red Ship*

It finally arrived. We were as prepared as we could be. We cleared a path and watched from a distance. The plague ship was painted all in crimson, every sail, every balloon, every wing and propeller. We could see the crew, what remained of them, wrapped in crimson rags, their blistering and bleeding skin painted with red dye between the lesions. We are grateful to them for this great courtesy, undertaken despite their suffering. We will avoid all red debris for one year from this date.

The doctor, in her red robes and her plague mask, had taken command of the helm, the helmsman collapsed at her feet. We feared she might not be able to steer the intended course, being accustomed to fighting sickness, not wind and storm. It looked for a moment like the ship might be blown off course and crash into Rustowne, and the infection unleashed on the city. But she wrestled the wheel with all her strength, and sailed true, away from certain disaster and into uncertain one.

We have found the ship, almost intact. We have seen her body, still clutching the helm.

We do not know if there are other bodies. We do not know if any of her patients were saved.

In one year's time, she will have her place of honour here.

May She Find Another Kind of Immortality.

Here May Fly Sesariat of the Leftovers

I have been discouraged three times. I have allowed myself to be discouraged three times.

I have not yet decided what I will decide upon the fourth.

Each time so far, the other scavengers, those who gather and tend to what is left over after others have tried, have pointed out that as keeper of the Crypt, of the graves of lost hopes and failed attempts, I should know better than anyone how futile the quest for immortality is.

I do know.

And yet...

Each and every one of my charges, each floating grave and hovering stone that I have carved, is someone who loved life so much that they wanted it to last forever. Each of them looked to the future, and saw a place they wanted to go.

How can I not admire that?

My fellows see this crypt as a caution. But I remember every one I've set to flight, and see so much inspiration.

Perhaps I shall be discouraged once and for all upon the fourth time.

Or perhaps I shall listen to the whispers, plunge into the storm, and be buried here among those I buried.

Or just maybe I shall come out the other side, and back again, and I will tend my graves knowing that I will be able to keep doing so, and remembering them, for always.

May I Find Immortality. Of One Kind or Another.

THE FINAL TESTIMONIES OF DR. ISSEN WEILAND ON THE OCCASION OF HIS DEATH

JEREMY PAK NELSON

By Order of The Third District Fulcrum Court, the following transcriptions are entered into evidence. Speakers have been identified, where possible, and have signed affidavits attesting to the authenticity of the recordings. The contents of Dr. Issen Weiland's "phonocorder" device, recorded on wax cylinders, are thereby placed on the record in all matters pertaining to the suspected arson of Dr. Weiland's home and office, and to all matters pertaining to the suspected murder of Dr. Weiland.

Weiland: What? Is it working? Stop it, you're wasting wax.

Hwyer: Fantastic bit of equipment, Issen. Can't wait to hear what you bring back.

Kan: Are you two serious? Issen, learn shorthand like the rest of us. You'll get the wrong sort of attention carrying something like that around.

Weiland: Quit being a squeaky cog. This will change field research, mark my words. First-hand accounts! We'll make cryptozoology a *science*, bring respectability back…

Weiland: Right. Issen speaking. First day out. At the Merry Grappler. We hope collecting field histories will—

Jacques: What you want?

Weiland: We're collecting accounts of the kraken, as told—

Jacques: Ale or lager?

Weiland: Oh! Lager please. A half-pint.

Jacques: [Indistinct] … *pissant bookballoon* …

Weiland: Well! First to survey the room, find somebody who knows somebody …

Weiland: Please introduce yourself, here into the phonocorder.

Unknown: What's this? A drinking horn?

Weiland: Ah, it collects ambient sound and transmits vibrations … Please don't touch the phonocorder.

[Loud crackling]

Unknown: No good, got all this nonsense at the bottom.

Weiland: *Please* don't touch the phonocorder, sir—

Unknown: Nah, not put together right, all those holes. Look, you pour the ale in …

Weiland: Back at the Merry Grappler. After the last... *research* attempt we've improved upon our preparation. We've a list of names, descriptions; everything we need to identify those who've claimed to have witnessed the kraken themselves.

Mettlesworn: You buying this round?

Weiland: With us is Sigurd Mettlesworn, legendary Corpsman from Halfaway. Which can be confirmed by these distinctive tattoos...

Mettlesworn: Thank you, barkeep. No, no he's not bothering me.

Weiland: Sigurd! Tell me about when you saw the kraken. Or have you had the privilege of multiple sightings?

Mettlesworn: What we *agreed* was that I'd tell you about what I know. About the Shadow.

Weiland: Yes, the *shadow*, yes, go ahead.

Mettlesworn: Something sailors and airmen speak of. The sky goes dark. There are... visions. Glimpses. Sometimes, more unbelievable tales...

Weiland: Nothing you've experienced firsthand?

Mettlesworn: What can I say? Tales to frighten rookies. Been around for as long as I remember. The visions, the stories, are what stick with you, it's those descriptions.

Weiland: How do you mean?

Mettlesworn: The ones that see visions… They tell of tentacled arms reaching across the sky. They see eyes the size of moons. The concept of a giant squid in the sky, you think it would be funny. What's more absurd? But those sailors spoke like their stories *haunted* them. That's what I know.

Weiland: … Yes, we call it *Architeuthis obscuratus.*

Flaxus: That's, like, the kraken?

Weiland: That's our taxonomic name. Like any other animal, the kraken should have a place on the taxonomic charts. It's only logical.

Flaxus: What makes you think it's an animal?

Weiland: All accounts describe a giant squid. It's a perfectly reasonable deduction.

Flaxus: What if it's, like, a squid god? The big squid in the sky?

Weiland: There's no… no *evidence* for such a claim.

Flaxus: You got like, no evidence for *anything*, man. Holy sky squid. Keeping an eye on the squid world.

Weiland: This is not a productive conversation.

Flaxus: You see the sky squid and survive, you're blessed, man. That's what I know. Ask the pirates, they got the ballast.

Weiland: Pirates, you say! Do any frequent the Merry Grappler?

Flaxus: Sure, sure, they come to the nicer pubs to listen. For clues. Possible targets, know what I mean?

Weiland: This... is one of the nicer pubs?

Flaxus: Oh indeed! Isn't that right, Sigurd?

Mettlesworn: So bookballoon's back. Buying? No? Then leave me be.

Stubbs: Took a wrong turn, did ya?

Weiland: Isn't this the Ugly Ambergris?

Stubbs: Not your type of establishment.

Weiland: My name is Issen, I collect accounts of the kraken—

Stubbs: What makes you think I'm interested?

Weiland: Can I, er, can I have a lager, please?

Stubbs: ... If you bother anyone I'm throwing you out. For your own good.

Weiland: Thank you.
Oh, sir, I think this glass is dirty, look at... ah. He's left.

Weiland: Can you say your name again, for the record?

Sixwind: They call me Sixwind. Long story. Corpsman emptied a revolver into my lungs.

Weiland: ... Is that the whole story?

Sixwind: What, trying to start something?

Weiland: No! Please, don't leave. You were telling me about the kraken...

Sixwind: It's good business. Kraken comes, chaos follows. Easy pickings. And, if you're lucky...

Weiland: Yes?

Sixwind: I don't like the way you look. Has anyone told you? All that damned excitement on your face. What they call it? *Animated features.* Makes me want to knock it out of you.

Weiland: I'm sorry. I'll... I'll do what I can not to let my face, er, offend you.

Sixwind: See that you do. Now, the kraken, when it comes, people almost never expect it. But the real treasure is the kraken's wake.

Weiland: Like behind a boat?

Sixwind: The kraken travels, and when it moves, things get caught. Whales in the sky. People from Frostborne appearing in Kimichula. And if you're lucky, the kraken brings things from *elsewhere*.

Weiland: Other lands?

Sixwind: Other *worlds*. Artifacts. Treasures. Sometimes, *people*. You hear stories. Never know what to believe, but I've seen strange happenings myself. Strange peoples. Could be they were born a certain way and tell tales to hide it. Could be the truth.

Weiland: And *pirates* know to follow the kraken? Look for these artifacts?

Sixwind: I never said pirate. Best watch yourself. That face is looking mighty excitable.

Weiland: Sorry! Sorry.

Sixwind: How do you think Bottomless Braddock built his reputation? A world's only got so much wealth, so much power. The kraken opens the door to *more*.

Unknown: Two pints, Jacques. What's this?

Jacques: The bookballoon left it. Had too much, off to the facilities.

Unknown: Worth anything?

Jacques: Bugger all. Man can barely afford his ink.

Unknown: Shame. Cheers.

Jacques: Before you go, pass on word up to the *Midnight*. He's been asking about the kraken, nosing in on the trade. Probably nothing important, but they should know.

[Clinking]

Jacques: [Pause] The captain's got bottomless pockets, I'll give him that.

Weiland: Issen, back at the Merry Grappler. Our venture to the lower levels of Rustowne were... a mixed success. Some fascinating leads. But many fabrications. This isn't anything like delving into the Archarrier stacks... Barkeep! You look surprised to see me. Half lager, if you please. Thank you, perfect pour as ever.

Jacques: Find what you're looking for?

Weiland: Not at all, but plenty of fascinating stories. Odd how *everyone* knows about the kraken, but you try and get people to talk about it and it's all rumors, hearsay...

Jacques: [Pause] I have a lead for you.

Weiland: Just now? I've been here for *weeks*, man. Tell me.

Jacques: Yes, I've kept it from you. For your sake. But at this rate, you'll run into trouble whether or not you find answers. Go to The Crimson Cog. Ask for Pat Stone. He's retired now, but I'll bet he still haunts the place. Just keeps hanging on.

Weiland: And this man knows about the kraken?

Jacques: He's not exactly... well, yes. He'll tell you about the kraken.

Weiland: That is spectacular, barkeep! These first-hand accounts are *critical* in our effort to place the kraken in the taxonomic charts. Gratitude is too small a word, I'm *thrilled*, is it too late to head over now? ...

Weiland: You know, I think this, the—[clears throat]—*em,* Crimson Cog is a step up from the Ugly Ambergris. Three options on the board. More than one, isn't that right?

Unknown: Who are you talking to?

Weiland: To you! And to posterity. See, this device here—

Unknown: Jump into a shit vat.

Weiland: Sir, that's not... ah, you're leaving. I see. Barkeep, may I have a half of lager?

Barkeep: No lager. Ale or white.

Weiland: White is the colloquial term for...

Barkeep: Distillate. Moonshine. Engine cleaner.

Weiland: Right. The ale, please. Thank you. And... do you, by any chance, know of a Patrick Stone?

Barkeep: In the back room. Play darts? No? Shame. Winning some cash puts him in a good mood.

[Loud noises, possibly footsteps]

Weiland: Excuse me, *sorry.*

[More loud noises.]

Don't want to get this going all over again, running low on cylinders... Sorry! Sorry.

[A thud]

Weiland: Sorry, do you know of a Pat, a Patrick Stone?

Unknown 2: Over there.

Weiland: Where? I don't see—

Stone: Right *here*, you miserable giraffe.

Weiland: Oh. Oh! I do apologize. I didn't see, I mean, I was looking up...

Stone: Yes, I'm short. Congratulations, no one's ever noticed. If Vinter sent you, money's coming in next week. Tell him to stuff some ice in his pants. Impatient sonofabitch, even for a loanie. Now get out of my pub.

Weiland: Um, sir, sorry, I—

Stone: Do I look like I carry money on me? Keep asking and I'll use your pretty face for darts practice.

Weiland: *Kraken*! I came to ask you about the kraken. Please don't dart my face. *Please.*

Stone: The kraken. What have you heard?

Weiland: To be honest, in terms of first-hand accounts, not much. Legends and tales, plenty. And, well, something about pirates.

Stone: Pirates? You're talking about pirates? We won't be safe talking, not here, much as it hurts to admit. Not my bar anymore. Not the place I built. Here, take this. We'll meet there at noon. That's when the unsavory settle to sleep, after all. And put that drinking horn away, you'll only attract attention—

[Loud buffeting sounds. Segments of conversation, unintelligible.]

Weiland: Is it true? You've seen it yourself?

Stone: It's something I talked about, once. Not anymore. Years of being talked down to, so to speak.

[Long silence]

Stone: It's fine. I'm a dwarf, I don't have to take things seriously, now do I?

Weiland: And you are... an actual dwarf? From a whole civilization of them?

Stone: Who told you to come find me?

Weiland: Jacques, the barkeep at the Merry Grappler.

Stone: Turns out I had someone listening, after all. Look, how old do you think me?

Weiland: I don't know if it'd be rude to judge. Ah—sixty or so?

Stone: I started at the Crimson Cog back in thirty-eight.

Weiland: But that's... how old *are* you?

Stone: One and forty-four. Everyone assumes I'm lying, of course. I'll outlive anyone who cares.

Weiland: That's... how is that possible? Where are the rest of your people?

Stone: Oh, they're well, as far as I know. I've given up on seeing them again. You asked about the *kraken*. I've seen the kraken, boy. The kraken is why I'm here on your godforsaken world.

Weiland: So you've *seen* it, seen the kraken yourself? Where are you from? When did you encounter the kraken? Did you see what happened to it, see how it travels?

Stone: Don't you understand? The kraken *appears* to come in and out of existence, but that's an illusion. Reality is it's traveling. And not merely from land to land, but world to world. It came to my world. Took my ship, a pale arm wider than the pillars of Uliedun, arcing from the surf. I didn't even want to be at sea...

Weiland: But *how*? What do you remember?

Stone: Recollection? You doubt *everything* you see and hear and feel in a time like that. You'll know it when *your* world crumbles. I remember waves, reaching for the mainsail. The riven deck, torn apart like cake in a child's hands. Then darkness, a soundless void that pulled the breath from my lungs and my mind from my body. I thought death had visited its mercy upon me. The kraken… the worst part is I don't think it even knew we were there. We were ants. That's all we were. Ants drowning in the sea.

Weiland: When you came to, you were… here? In a … a different world?

Stone: A different world? I thought so, but sometimes I wonder if it's a different time that I've come to. Pulled out of the water by pirates, would you believe it. They took everything of value I had, which wasn't much, and found me passage to the Hub. Fair trade, I suppose. Let me tell you, I was convinced I'd taken the long way to the afterworld. Come here to see humans living in the sky, those flying sailboats like *seagulls* in the wind, but we're not so different, as it turns out. People are people, and most of them want ale. Found meself a new life…

[A silence.]

Weiland: Did you say pirates found you?

Stone: That's right. Ugly fellows, one with a goldcap tooth, like in the stories. Funny how they be the same in both our worlds, isn't it? And none of them like being mentioned. I can see you don't believe, that you have your doubts. But thank you for letting an old man talk. I mean to write a book, you know. About my world. Mayhaps no one will believe it real, but the truth will be there for those who seek it.

Weiland: I hope you do. Knowledge should be preserved, even if it's not appreciated in its time.

Stone: Lad, I have another name for you. She's a hard one. But she believed me when I told, not half because her tale is even stranger. If you insist on pulling this thread, well... Be careful.

Weiland: So? Does the name look familiar to you?

Jacques: I have to say. You're more persistent than I gave you credit for.

Weiland: Well you don't graduate with distinction from *Cardinal* like it's a cakewalk.

[A silence.]

Jacques: … If you insist.

Weiland: So, ma'am—

Carragher: Ma'am? What am I, your mother?Carragher.

Weiland: Carragher, sorry. Would you describe yourself as a pirate?

Carragher: Look, a clockwork leg. What more proof do you need?

Weiland: I'm only trying to have everything declared aloud, you know, to get things on the record. Into the phonocorder.

Carragher: It depends on how you mean, *pirate*. Some would say, "once a pirate, always a pirate." You don't seem the type to be interested in pirates. So, who are *you?*

Weiland: A scholar, ma'am—sorry, *Carragher*. I'm trying to put the kraken in the annals of taxonomic science.

Carragher: Indeed. And what do you think the kraken is?

Weiland: The kraken? An animal, albeit one we don't understand. Possibly *beyond* our understanding. But if it has a body, if it breathes, and eats, then no matter how vast it may be, it is a creature of this world. Well, perhaps not *solely* of this world.

Carragher: So you've come with stories of your own.

Weiland: Stone gave me your name.

Carragher: I thought he might. He's got a soft inside. He probably also warned you not to dig too deep. It's risky.

Weiland: But how? I don't see why advancing science has...

Carragher: I'm sure you're a clever man, Dr. Weiland, despite the impression you're giving me right now.

Weiland: Issen, please.

Carragher: Issen, then. I'll tell you the story of how I lost my leg, and you tell me if you're still confused about why talking about the kraken is a bad idea.

[Clears throat.]

It starts with a girl. Amelia Xu. For those of us growing up around the Archarrier, she was *the one*. Beautiful, of course, and she could climb rigging like she was born in a harness. But, Issen, Amelia was *smart*. And she understood people. Never got into trouble, Amelia. The librarians caught her stealing books—well, *borrowing*, she probably did mean to return them—and what started with a talking to ended up with her and the two librarians laughing over Halfaway's sad excuses for building codes. I never stood a chance. Fell in love when I was eleven during our outdoor safety course. Happened when I saw her do a somersault outside, wind blowing twenty knots at least, and as I watched her flip my heart flipped with her. Oh, what, you didn't think I had the capacity for sentiment?

Weiland: No, it's not that. The Archarrier's practically a second home to me. I had a hard time imagining...

Carragher: What, that a bookballoon could drift to the other side of the law? If that's what you believe, you're too deep in your research to see the world around you. The point is, I loved Amelia. She didn't love me, she barely even knew me. But it made things simpler, I thought. I could ignore everyone else and focus on my other passion—flying. It didn't hurt that she wanted to be a pilot, too.

We were both accepted into the Flight Academy at the Hub. Came as no surprise, in her case, but mine raised some eyebrows. It took ten years of grit on my part to earn those surprises. Once she and I were at the academy... I think it was only when we were both cadets did she *see* me. See me as a real person. I know it sounds terrible, but most of us simply caved when it came to what she wanted. And she was good enough to deserve the special treatment, or so we told ourselves. But once we were both cadets, we were *rivals* in a real sense. And maybe, in me, she saw real competition. We became friends. Then, *more* than friends. I never told her about how I felt, though. That side of things, the *emotional* side of things, didn't seem like something she wanted. And, well...

[Long pause]

Sorry. I'm getting to what you're after. We saw the kraken on one of our last flight drills. All the final year cadets were on board *Falcon's Cradle* in the Finnegan Sea, south of the Hub, prepping our planes for our patrol route. They don't give cadets state-of-the-art equipment, but we were fully outfitted for this one. Amelia and I copiloted a Tangsin Swallowsnap, a beautiful bird, canvas biplane—an antique, now, but it had gorgeous lines and wings that caught the air, caught it like you didn't need an engine at all.

[Clears throat.]

Anyway, we'd taken off, Amelia was lead pilot so I sat behind her, had a good view of our surroundings. Everything going according to plan. We had Williams and Sima in the plane behind us. But soon as we dropped from the *Cradle* into clear air, the sun went out. The sun went out, and a storm took its place.

That's what it felt like: a fire snuffed out, then wind roaring against your skin, rain and hail so hard they stung through your gloves. Couldn't see at all, at first, my eyes had to adjust. Amelia kept us in the air, lord knows how—the other plane lost their horizon and ended up in the water. She kept us level, flying blind, and I was so sure the plane would crash, so sure we'd die together, right then, and I had a—had an epiphany. That I was a coward, a coward about to die with the woman I loved. We—

[Crackling sounds]

Weiland: Sorry. Please go on, I had to change the wax.

Carragher: I thought we would die. We didn't. I almost regret that, sometimes. Because when our eyes adjusted, the darkness took shape. Nonsense forms, mountains in the sky and rivers twisting, twisting in the air like waterspouts. And when I understood it was the kraken, my stomach fell out. Just like a diving maneuver. Amelia kept us in the air, flying like she was born with wings—dodging around arms and debris. You see, the kraken doesn't just appear on its own, it *brings* things. It brings water, which disperses to rain. It brings biting cold that frosts your skin. It brings trees that drop like darts thrown from the sky. Somehow, Amelia kept us flying. But it wasn't enough. We were losing speed. The kraken filled our view, horizon to horizon, and we simply had nowhere to go.

One arm stretched out in front of us, so large I had no sense where its root was or where it reached. Amelia and I, we couldn't talk, but we had the same thought. I know we did. That arm looked like a runway. And we had nowhere else to go.

It was a rough landing. There was no grip, and we slid. Probably we would have tumbled over, dropped into the water. That's not what happened. I think what we did was strange enough that, for a moment, we had the monster's attention. Or maybe it was all a coincidence. I've thought about it again and again, all these years, and I still don't know. The fact is that the kraken caught our plane. One moment, we were sliding along, the next, there was a wall around the bird, a wall covered in suction rings from the size of my fist to ones big enough to swallow the *Cradle*. The plane breaking apart, torn wings fluttering like, like *leaves* down to the water, and we ended up on this wall like bugs on flypaper. Amelia and I, still in our cockpits, stuck along with most of the fuselage. I could just reach her. I tried to get her attention, but she was unconscious.

The wall we were against—the tentacle—it moved. You could see it travel down the length of the arm, a wave of motion. And when the next wave came, rivets popped and canvas tore. It was only a matter of time before the plane was destroyed. We had parachutes. They might not work, with all that debris, but it was all we had. It was a chance. We just had to get out of the cockpits.

But I was clumsy. I had managed to lever myself out, but lost my footing on the wet deck. My right leg slid outside the cockpit and against the kraken's arm. A sucker got hold of me. I saw another wave of movement coming, and I braced myself against the plane, thinking maybe the ring would let loose for a second. Before I had the chance, the world turned black again.

I couldn't breathe. And you wouldn't believe me, even after all this, you wouldn't believe me if I told you the things I saw. Rainbow clouds against a starred sky, and fleets of ships sailing through them; I saw civilizations under the sea, monuments in ruin—I saw great sprawling cities devoid of skyports, as though people feared to fly. I saw worlds, Issen. And then I was back in ours, back over the black ocean, and I could breathe once more.

Was it the kraken's touch? Had I been to those other worlds, physically? I don't know. What I was sure about was that I wouldn't survive much longer. I had to get free. I had to get Amelia out. Desperation, that's what it came down to; that's what gave me the strength.

Standard equipment on every plane includes a survival kit. In case you've had to abandon the plane and become stranded. Each kit contains, among other things, a hatchet and a set of flares. That's how I lost my leg, Issen. I cut it from me, one arm swinging, and the other holding a burning flare to cauterize the work I did. Swing twice and burn. Swing twice and burn. I'm sure I screamed, but I wasn't the one doing these things to myself. It was the desperation. It had to be done. Of course, I tried to cut the sucker off, first, but nothing I did made a mark on that kraken's skin.

Don't know if it was the light or my voice, but Amelia came to. I can't imagine what she thought, or felt, seeing me lit red like a devil, bloody hatchet in hand, probably screaming like an engine about to blow. Smart as she was, she understood immediately. When my work was done, she reached out, helped me away from the kraken so I wouldn't touch any more of those godforsaken suckers.

I told her we had to jump. She said all right. I said we'd jump together, and she grabbed my hand and—

She told me she loved me.

It was all the years of hiding, I think. I'd trained myself not to say anything. Not to share. It would have been so easy. I love you too. So easy. I don't even know what I said. "Jump first, talk later." Maybe. It doesn't matter. I didn't tell her.

We jumped. And the sun came back. Blinding bright, I had to shut my eyes. When I opened them, the kraken was gone. And so was Amelia.

Weiland: I... I'm so sorry.

Carragher: Are you? I 'chuted down safely. Wreckage was every-where. I thought maybe she'd forgotten to deploy, that maybe her body was in the water, but I knew. Soon as the sun came back, I knew the kraken had taken her.

Braddock's crew picked me up. His ships were there like lightning, and they scoured the waters. Not for survivors. But for loot. From other worlds. That's where the big money comes in, Issen. Do you see now? You want to learn something, go find Braddock. Go ask him how the Cumulocarta tells him where the kraken will appear. Maybe you'll get what you're after, then.

Weiland: Carragher, I—

Carragher: No, I don't need your sympathy. I've found my peace. The pirates took me in, fitted me my leg. And they gave me the chance to do exactly what I wanted to do.

I wanted to find her, find Amelia or some sign that she survived, proof she made it in another world. I'm sure she has. She always got her way. Gone and taken over whatever world she landed on, and they still don't know what hit them.

The pirates know me, trust me with the kraken's stowaways. And I do what I can to help them. I suppose I hope that, in some way, my work tilts the cosmic balance. That it might repay whoever might have found and helped Amelia. Or that my work paves the way for her to be helped, if she's been borne off to a far-off future. For twenty years I followed Braddock on the *Midnight Scythe*, twenty years of dredging the kraken's wake. Years of seeking those who'd come into our world from another. I can never say the words to her, but I've done my part.

ADDENDUM

In addendum to the preceding exhibit, the following is a transcript of a wax fragment recovered from the damaged phonocorder, also in evidence, and deciphered with the aid of Drs. Hwyer and Kan.

Weiland: It's not right, Jacques. If Carragher's telling the truth, there's *real* and *valuable* knowledge Braddock's hiding from the world! If he knows where the kraken will appear, we can warn people. Tragedies like what happened to the crew of *Falcon's Cradle* won't happen again.

Jacques: You know yourself that hardly ever happens. It's not a factor. People aren't around when the kraken appears, almost never.

Weiland: So we leave a pirate to make these moral choices?

Jacques: Issen, please. I want you to listen to what I'm saying. You're voicing dangerous thoughts. Dangerous words. This is not a world you want to be a part of, okay? Carragher is good people, but most her old colleagues are not. Do you understand?

Weiland: If we tell the corps, tell the cartographers that their work is being abused—

Jacques: Issen, your *life* is at risk.

Weiland: The secret's out, it's on the record. Everything we need to start an investigation. I've made copies. With this, we're going to change the world.
[END OF TRANSCRIPT]

INDIVIDUALS IDENTIFIED ON PHONOCORDER

Dr. Issen Weiland. Victim of suspected homicide. Postdoctoral researcher and founding member of The Cryptozoological Society.

Dr. Hyacinth Hwyer. Founding member of The Cryptozoological Society, friend to Dr. Weiland.

Dr. Emil Kan. Founding member of The Cryptozoological Society, colleague of Dr. Weiland at the Cardinal Institute at Hub.

Jebediah Jacques. Proprietor of The Merry Grappler.

Unknown Speaker. Wanted for questioning, suspected of involvement in Dr. Weiland's death. Jacques would not identify this individual, claiming he arrived in disguise.

Sigurd Mettlesworn. Corpsman of the Halfaway Air and Navy Patrol, now retired.

"Flaxus." A regular at the Merry Grappler and potential Person of Concern; claimed identity could not be corroborated by officials at the Rustowne Archives.

Unknown Speaker 2. Customer at The Crimson Cog. Not currently wanted for questioning.

Patrick Stone. Longtime proprietor of The Crimson Cog. Investigation has revealed discrepancies in Stone's file, likely due to a lapse in skyport entry protocol; not a current enforcement priority.

Edie Carragher. Retired privateer, once held for questioning over the disappearance of the Erofan Ippon.

AN AIRSHIP BUILT FOR TWO

JAYME BEAN

"*S*hit," Melody hissed as the silk money pouch slipped from her grip and landed with a jingly *thunk* onto the stone alleyway. "Shit, shit, shit."

Her boots skidded to a halt as she pivoted, her slight heel kicking up a small cloud of dust around her feet. She glanced up. The large, marble walls of The White Whale loomed over her, casting long shadows onto the streets and the dozens of people flooding Marbletown during the busiest hour of the day. The Cog's central bank was the last place she needed to run into trouble. Quick deposit, quick exit. By all accounts, it should have run like every other time:

Find a mark—a visiting merchant or sailor who's wealthy but not *too* wealthy…

Woo him *or* her…

Get them nice and drunk…

And make out with the goods before anyone's the wiser.

Without wasting another breath, Melody flicked the open flaps of her overcoat, bent down, and scooped the money pouch off the ground before spinning back toward the crowded street. She weaved between hurried bodies and pushed her way through the admin district. As she ducked between two traders, her body flinched to a halt. Of course, she'd run into him here. She instinctively tucked the pouch into an inside pocket of her overcoat. Taking a steadying breath, she slipped a loose strand of crimson hair behind her ear as her eyes lifted and settled on the tall, muscular man standing before her. Arlan Something-or-Other. She couldn't be bothered to remember a mark's name—it took up too much space for other valuable information, like where they kept their funds and if anyone was expecting them back at their room. Arlan's broad shoulders and stone-straight posture created an automatic part in the crowd as people skirted around the well-dressed stranger and the buxom barmaid.

"I believe you have something of mine." Arlan's uncomfortably calm voice sent prickles along her skin. His brows twitched as his golden brown eyes locked onto hers.

Melody swallowed, pulling herself up straighter to match his domineering posture. This wasn't her first time being confronted the next morning by one of her targets. She could smooth talk her way out of most situations.

Arlan extended a muscled hand between them, palm up, his gaze unmoving.

Her emerald eyes flashed from his hand to his face, drinking him in. They couldn't be more of a contrast to each other. In truth, Melody was used to standing out, pale, with fiery red hair and unmistakable curves. Ask anyone around, and they knew Melody Taft—the sultry entertainer who could drink anyone under the table. It was her calling card to every patron looking for a fun time in the ever-constant bustle of The Hub. Melody loved her reputation. In fact, she thrived on it. But Arlan's deep umber skin and muscled physique dwarfed her among the residents around them. He stood nearly a foot above her. His top hat —covered in brass doodads and metallic adornments—added even more height as he towered above most of the other people in the street. Not the attention she was used to... or wanted.

She scanned Arlan's face, taking in his sharp jaw and measured stare. Despite her nerves—and being caught mid-extortion—Melody's mind drifted to last night when she first noticed Arlan as a cask-swigging patron. He didn't appear as he stood before her now, rigid and stern; he'd been smiling, relaxed, an ale in hand. To her surprise, he'd turned his nose at her first advances, but warmed quickly enough after several rounds of Gear Grease.

"Strongest liquor in all of the neighboring lands, with a quarter of the taste. Tastes like cog grease but will get you the best time of your life." That line worked every time... especially when followed by a wink and a slight toss of her ginger locks.

Guess Arlan had a bigger tolerance than expected, she thought, snapping herself out of the memories of his cabin and his strong, firm hands...

"My money," Arlan pressed, clearing his throat.

Melody forced her eyes to his, slowly, purposefully. She dipped a shoulder and popped her hip, letting a playful smirk grow on her face. "Money? Last I checked, I didn't ask you to pay me." Melody took a step back, giving him a once-over. "And frankly, I'm a little insulted that you think I'm that kind of woman. I thought we hit it off. No money can beat a fun toss with a rugged sailor like yourself, don't you think?"

"And yet I find myself missing a decent sum of coin. And right after you snuck out of my cabin this morning. Now," Arlan closed the distance between them, "if you wouldn't mind..."

"Like I said, I don't have the faintest ide—"

"You! Sir!" Arlan's eyes darted skyward as a loud voice boomed from above. A small, one-manned, ballooned vessel puttered overhead. "Arlan Kalbrunner," the voice continued, "first mate of *The Iron Cutlass,* ex-captain of *The Ruddy Nimbus,* also known as Chip Diviny of *The Bon—*"

"*Chip?* Out of all the names, woulda never pegged you for a Chip. Now, why's the constable hollering your name in the middle of Marbletown?" Melody laughed and threw her hand on her hip. "You're a fuddy criminal, aren't ya? And you're over here tryin' to con me out of some 'missing coin,' eh?"

"Well, if that ain't the sail calling the jib torn," Arlan huffed. "Fuddy criminal I am when you're just a con artist with a voice of gold."

Melody smiled. "Voice of gold, huh?"

Arlan tittered as he glanced at the crowd forming around them. Heads swiveled in their direction and at The Hub's Constabulary balloon circling above them. Melody hazarded a glance skyward, her heart catching as three more small skyships approached from over The White Whale's marbled façade.

"Melody Taft!" the constable called from above, peering over his perch. "Surprise seeing you in the company of yet another ongoing Cog felony. Not so easy feigning innocence when you're caught canoodling with a wanted man."

"*Canoodling?*" Melody shouted over the whirring of the ballooned ship. "Constable Bydell, I have just met this..." She looked over to Arlan. "Felon, is it?" At his silence, she turned back to the constable. "I just met this felon. I have no idea what business deali—"

"You can't talk your way out of this one, Taft. Petty thievery happens all the time. Mutiny—"

"Mutiny?" Melody echoed, eyes widening at Arlan.

"And arson—"

"*Arson?!*" she echoed again, the word coming out more of a hiss than a question.

"An accident!" Arlan implored, his posture suddenly shrunken and bowed.

The constable continued, "So it is in your best intere—"

"*Accidental* arson? Seriously?" Melody cocked an eyebrow to Arlan who had begun fidgeting with his belt. "Accidental mutiny too, then, I suppose?"

Arlan gave a half-hearted shrug. "Not exactly."

"Great," she said. "Thanks for dragging me into it."

"You stole *my* money."

"*You* mutinied a ship and set it on fire."

"Accidentally!" Arlan grabbed his hat as a gust of wind threatened to knock it off his head. The Hub's security fleet had mobilized above them, their brass propellers stirring the air into miniature whirlwinds as they closed in.

Melody watched as Arlan's eyes scanned the possible avenues of escape. "Sweet Braddock's ghost," she groaned. "Come on." Grabbing his hand, she sped between the nearest set of gawkers. As expected, the small groups of onlookers congealed into one another, forming a blank-faced mob... and the perfect camouflage. Once satisfied they were obscured, Melody dragged Arlan down a tight alleyway before leaning her weight into him and shoving him down a narrow alcove between Drifter's Inn and Sails, Sails, and Co. Melody pressed into him, her chest against his, as shouts from above filled the air. The space was barely big enough for the two of them.

Arlan attempted to shift his position, but Melody held him firm. "What're you doing?" he whispered.

"Trying to not get arrested," she deadpanned, looking up at him. "You go down, I go down. And I'm not spending the rest of my days working down in The Soot to pay off my sentence. All for a fuddy bag of coin."

"So you *did* steal my money!"

"Of course I stole your money. You sure are *dense,* aren't ya?" Melody leaned back and peered around the edge of the alcove. "Okay. We're clear enough. What's the move?"

"Excuse me?"

"What's. Your. Move?" she asked, each word a slow drip. She rolled her eyes at the lack of a quick answer from the criminal mastermind she had pinned to the wall. "What was your plan? Turn a ship into raining ashes and hide out in one of the most heavily policed areas this side of Kimichula?"

"I, uh…"

"Where's your ship?"

"My ship?"

Melody sighed, stepping back into the alleyway. "You don't have a ship?" She combed her hands through her hair, twisted the ends up, and tied the strands into a curly knot. Distant thrumming of metallic propellers and whooshing air caused her stomach to mimic the knot on the top of her head. "We have to move. Follow me and keep your head down." Melody whipped her overcoat off and draped it over her arm before turning back to Arlan. "Keep up. And try not to stand out."

With that, she sped forward, expertly weaving between the people filtering in and out of the shops. She crossed a wooden slat bridge, temporarily strung between the central platform of The Cog and a stationary airship, and disappeared below deck. Arlan followed suit, coming to a stop in front of a well-decorated cabin.

"You don't have a ship. Do you have any personal items from your room?" Melody asked, as she bent over a wooden chest and shoveled its contents into a worn leather knapsack.

Arlan hummed, rocking back and forth on his heels. "About the room."

Hanging her head, Melody grumbled to the floor, "It wasn't yours, was it?"

"Not necessarily."

She stood, tossed the knapsack over her shoulder, and threw her head back in exasperation. "I should have just gone with Gavin. You never choose the nice ones, do you Mel? No, Gavin was only traveling to the end of the fuddy world. Too much adventure, you said. You'd end up having to take care of his strange black cat with its cute little goggles. But no, you chose Chip McArson over here. Look where that's got you."

"The arson was an accident," Arlan muttered. "And I don't know why you're mad when you clearly planned to rob me from the get-go. Over here acting like you're some innocent bystander."

"Fine," Melody huffed. "Point taken. And you're welcome, by the way, for getting you out from under the fleet's nose."

Arlan licked his lips and bit at the skin of his bottom lip. "Thank you. For *that*."

Melody nodded. "You're welcome. Now…" She crossed over to a small box tucked behind her pillow. "We're going to need to blend in." Inside the box were several small vials of different colored liquids. Melody delicately pulled one out and held it up in front of Arlan. She considered the shimmering gray liquid for a moment before tutting, filing it back in place, and replacing it with one filled with a deep burgundy liquid. "This'll do. Come 'ere."

Arlan cautiously stepped in front of her. His gaze bounced between the vial in her hand and the myriad of others still lined up in the box.

Melody pointed to the bed. "Sit." As he took a seat next to her, she unplugged the vial.

"Smells like that shit they use to varnish the decks. What is that?"

"Hat off."

"Not without an explan—"

Before he could finish, Melody plucked the hat off Arlan's head. "Oh… wow." She took a step back to take him in. His midnight black hair was coiled into a series of tightly braided buns that extended down the middle of his head. Along either side was a cascade of small silver and gold gears interwoven with brown strips of leather. "Well… guess I won't need this," she said, sliding the vial back into the box. "Last night, you…"

Arlan lifted his eyes to hers as she trailed off. "What?"

Melody blinked. Flecks of gold shimmered in his eyes as he looked at her, the adornments in his hair bringing out the color. "Nothing. It's just… it's beautiful." She wondered how she hadn't noticed the details of his hair or face last night. The soft whirring of nearby airships above deck snapped her attention back to the room. "Right, well… here." She pulled a swath of black silk from her bag and expertly folded and tucked it over the top of Arlan's head. She tilted her head to the right and paused, contemplating. "It'll have to do."

Melody's fingers danced over the vials until she settled on one filled with an onyx liquid. With one hand, she released the knot in her hair and let it fall below her shoulders, and with the other, unstoppered the vial and upended it over her head. She tousled her hair, running her fingers through it as the crimson slowly disappeared.

"Wow," Arlan breathed from the edge of the bed next to her.

Melody flipped her hair behind her, now jet black but with the same lustrous waves. Her fingers combed along her scalp until each strand fell perfectly along her shoulders and back. She stopped and smiled, noticing Arlan staring at her. "I know a woman in Highcliff. A few vials of these to change my look when needed in exchange for… well, let's just say it's a trade I'm happy to make. Most of the time it's just to feel a bit different, but also good when you need to work with a makeshift disguise. You know, with the constables on our tail and all." Melody snapped the box shut and slid it into her knapsack. The toe of her leather boot tapped along the wooden floor. "So, Arlan Kalbrunner of the whatever-ship-you-overthrew, before I risk my neck helping yours any more than I have, I need some answers."

Arlan sighed and leaned back on his elbows. "You want the long one or the short one?"

Melody smirked. "Dealer's choice."

"A solid mix then," he said, getting comfortable. "To start, I used to be the captain of an exploration ship. *The Ruddy Nimbus.* Wanted to be in the Cartographer's Fleet—go storm chasin' and solve the great mysteries of the sky. That didn't quite work out. Turns out I'm not great at sciencin'. But I'm fuddy good at sailing.

So, I got myself a job on the *Iron Cutlass* as a first-mate. Long and short of it, the captain was fixin' to put me and the crew in a heap of danger. Had us headed straight to The Whispering Isle."

"*The* Whispering Isle?" Melody sat on the edge of the bed, mouth agape. "That's a death sentence flying into those storms."

"I know. And he wouldn't take no for an answer. Obsessed with all that tall-tale talk of livin' forever after drinking from that well."

"So... that's when you mutinied?"

Arlan nodded.

"And the arson?"

"*Accidental* arson," Arlan corrected. "He already set course by the time I got the crew on my side. Waited too long. I tried to get us out, turn us around. Ended up crashing into the edge of a fog-coated island. Next thing I knew, the *Cutlass* was up in flames, the crew were bailing, and I was goin' down with her."

"*Braddock's ghost,*" Melody swore under her breath. "What happened?"

"Got about as close to death as I ever care to be. The *Cutlass* drifted too close and got swept up into a twister. All those rumors about the storms cloakin' The Whispering Isle? Not a lick of a lie to 'em. Not sure how, but I ended up in Rustowne's infirmary—banged up, bruised, and not a memory of how I got there. That's where I'm fixin' to get back to."

"Why would you want to go back?"

Arlan sat up, his knees knocking into Melody's. He stared at his feet for several moments with just the sound of their breathing between them. "The whispers," he said, barely audible.

"Oh, cog's grease!" Melody laughed, shoving his thigh. "Don't tell me you're fuddy mad on top of being a wanted felon?"

"I'm *not* mad," Arlan snapped as he stood up. "I heard them. The whispers in the storms. Their secrets."

"And here you had me listenin' to you spinning this tale of heroics and valor."

"It's true. Look." He lifted his hat off the bed and reached his hand inside before sitting back down next to her. His fingers worked nimbly as he peeled a piece of tattered paper from the lining. He carefully unfolded it and held it flat in his lap. A series of scribbles: drawings of clouds, fragmented sentences, and mathematical equations peppered the parchment. "Some of this is what I heard; some is what I've figured out. You can't understand unless you've been in the storm. At least that's what Gyl says."

Melody looked from the paper to Arlan. "Gyl?"

"Captain Gyl. *The* Captain Gyl."

"They're an enigma. A rumor. Just some *kid* taking advantage of people like you. People wanting to find answers."

"I know it's easy to think that. I thought that too when I first met them. But they know things no one else would know. Especially not someone their age... or at least the age they look. They were there, Melody. When it happened. The waterspout that started it all."

"And you what, want to drink from the well? Find immortality?"

"I don't know what I want. But I know I need to find out. And look, you don't need to get involved. I'm going with or without you... aside from the money you took. I need it to charter a ship."

Melody regarded him a moment before she scooped her overcoat off the wooden chest, slipped her hand inside, and withdrew the silk money pouch she pilfered from him that morning. She opened it and counted the coins inside. With a sigh, she pulled the drawstring closed and tossed it into his lap. "Why charter when you can captain your own?"

THEY HEARD the storms long before they could see them. Deep rumblings shook the thick canvas of the balloon and rattled the rigging as flashes of light illuminated the clouds around them.

"I thought you said you were a good sailor!" Melody yelled over a loud bang of thunder. The ropes stretching from the cramped deck to the thick canvas balloon, keeping them aloft, pulled taut as a gust of wind nearly knocked Arlan out of the crow's nest.

"Feel free to step in at any time!" he called down to her.

She was certain she could hear the smirk in his voice. Melody watched as his hair, now in loose braids down to his shoulders, flicked every which way with the wind. Even after several weeks of sailing the skies together, she continued to be taken aback by him. It didn't help that the sense of adventure fueled her adrenaline, or that she knew that for the first time in many years she wasn't the one in control. But ending up on the wrong side of the law made it an easy choice. It didn't take more than a passionate kiss to make up her mind, though the subsequent raid of her quarters and a mad dash out the porthole didn't hurt either.

They had purchased a small airship—single-ballooned and single-cabined—from an unsavory ex-acquaintance of Melody's. She guaranteed dark registration, no paper trail, and had said the ship was small enough to avoid Skyfleet's checkpoints. The perfect deal... save for the fact it cost both Melody's savings and Arlan's stash combined. It had held up, though. They were but a few hours away from The Whispering Isle and the bustling adjacent city of Rustowne, the apparent home of the famed, immortal Captain Gyl.

The entire trip all Arlan talked about was breaking the code to immortality. Melody teased him every time he got going, at least for the first week. After that, they began planning the great adventures they would have if they could live forever on their perfect little ship. Melody even named her. *The Mutinous Flame.* They spent several days arguing the name, but Melody won out after explaining *The Mutinous Accidental Flame* was too long a name to repeat time and time again over the eternity of living forever. If they were to drink from the well and become immortal, it'd have to be a simple name—and one without a constant need for Arlan's validation and explanation.

"Almost there," Arlan said as his boots hit the deck behind Melody. He wrapped his arm around her waist and pulled her against him until she could feel his heart beating against her back. He reached his other arm out in front of her and pointed past the stern.

Melody flinched against him as another crack of thunder reverberated in the air around them. The clouds lit up in rolling waves before giving way to a whirling torrent of rain. Arlan removed his hand from her waist and tugged on a rope which extended up into an intricate webbing around the balloon. The ship sailed down, breaking through the clouds to reveal the most magnificent sight Melody had ever witnessed.

An enormous waterspout burst from an unseen ocean below and upward into a mass of swirling vortexes. Dark clouds joined together and broke apart, moving to an undetectable rhythm as they circled around a massive floating island in the sky. Lightning rippled within the clouds, making them dance with flashes of white. And though she knew it had to be her imagination, Melody swore she could hear whispers on the wind. Her eyes focused on a small bridge, held together with nothing but chain and rusted metal as it stretched out of the clouds and to a smaller floating city with reddish-hued buildings made of sheets of steel and gears. Arlan's deep voice cut through the gusts, causing goosebumps to rise along Melody's skin.

"Welcome to The Whispering Isle."

ARLAN TUCKED his braids into his top hat as he stepped into The Crimson Cog with Melody on his arm. She changed her hair again before they disembarked, opting for a gentle lilac—a color of her own creation. Arlan had spoken at great length of this tavern in Rustowne. Melody's eyes traveled to a giant cog attached to the wall behind the taproom.

"That has to be at least fifteen feet high," she breathed, letting her arm slip from Arlan's as she wandered closer.

"Twenty, to be exact." Melody looked to her right to see a person no older than thirty leaning up against the bar. Chestnut hair fell in gentle waves around a young face with soft features. "It's from the old factory. Used to churn out the best ship mechanics in the whole hemisphere. Granted, that was over fifty years ago. It's a wonder it's still in one piece."

"Local historian?" Melody asked, facing the stranger.

"You could say that," they said, cracking a smile. "I haven't seen you here before."

She smirked at the thought of things not being as different from The Hub as Arlan made them out to be. "First time."

Arlan appeared next to her as if a flash of lightning himself. "Gyl! You look well!"

The stranger's chest shook with a chuckle. "I look the same as I have for the last..." They held their hand out and mocked counting fingers. "Well, what're years? It's great to see you back. You brought quite the fetching companion with you." Gyl's eyes met Melody's and held her gaze.

Arlan placed his hand on the small of Melody's back. "Melody, this is Gyl. Gyl, Melody."

"We were just getting acquainted," they responded without breaking eye contact, and smiled as Melody cocked an eyebrow. "You're skeptical of my identity." They perched their elbows onto the bar, leaning back with a grin. "You're not the first."

"I don't believe in immortality."

"Most don't."

"Then what's your angle?"

Arlan slid his hand around Melody's waist and gave a light squeeze. "Don't be rude."

"It's okay, Arlan," Gyl said, raising a hand. "It's good to have a healthy dose of skepticism. And yet…"

"And yet what?" Melody asked, inching Arlan's hand off of her with her own.

"And yet you've heard the winds. I can see it in your face. Just like I saw it in his years ago." Gyl gave a subtle nod to Arlan. "Not many have. At least not many that have *truly* heard them."

Melody swallowed as her heart picked up pace. She eyed Gyl as they turned toward the bar and raised a hand into the air.

"One mug of Udder Chaos for the lass," they called to the barkeep. Within moments, a white, frothy beverage appeared on the bar. Gyl lifted it toward her, waiting for her to take it.

"What is it?"

"Crimson Cog special," Arlan said, taking the mug from Gyl and raising it to his lips. When he lowered the cup, a small milky moustache stayed behind. He ran the back of his hand across his mouth and offered the mug to Melody. "Rustowne's the only place you can get it. Made from milk imported from Elysium. It's divine."

"Let me ask you," Gyl said, focusing on Melody. "What did you hear?"

Melody averted her eyes. "I don't know what you mean."

"Arlan here has heard many things. Do you doubt his experience?"

"No, of course not." She glanced up to meet Arlan's face. He looked down at her with expectant eyes, the color dim in low light.

"Then what did the winds say to you?"

"If you really *are* Gyl of ancient Bolwall, then wouldn't you know what they say? Or do you just enjoy tugging people's sails?"

"The storms speak to those who are worthy. While it's true I was there when they began, I've never crossed through them and back to my old city. I have my theories just as the rest of them."

Melody crossed her arms and let out a small sigh. "I heard the word 'hatch', I think. Yeah… hatch gall-something. Jibberish."

The bar grew silent as the patrons turned toward her. Melody's eyes traveled across the room at the faces staring at her.

"What'd I say?"

Gyl assessed the growing tension in the room. "Hatch *Galahad?*"

"She heard from Hatch Galahad!" a voice burst from across the room as murmured whispers erupted throughout the tavern.

Gyl looked to Arlan, a smile growing across their face. "You seem to have found your missing piece."

Arlan pulled his hat off and removed the fragile parchment from the lining. He laid it out on the bar and ran a finger over his inscriptions. Gyl offered an inked quill from somewhere behind the bar, and Arlan began absentmindedly scrawling something onto the page. Melody squeezed between them and peered over Arlan's shoulder at his hand as it swept across the page, leaving droplets of ink in its wake.

Gyl lowered his voice, speaking to Melody in a volume meant only for her. "Hatch Galahad was the young boy who fell into the well, before the well was as it is now. The boy who created the storms. The boy who started my journey over a century ago."

Melody huffed, adjusting in her seat. "I don't believe in sailor legends and pirates' tales. You're as much a con as I am. I know 'em when I see them. And you're here, taking advantage of people from all over who want a taste of make-believe. How many people fell to the storms for you to humor yourself?"

"You're right. But not about all of it. I am a con. A con in that I don't truly know what lies beyond the storms. I know as much as you, or your fellow, or anyone else seeking a bit of enlightenment or adventure. But I do know there's something unexplained there. Pirates and thrill-seekers have tried endlessly to explore it.

Deep down, I think you know. You don't drop everything and travel across the horizon with a man like Arlan and accidentally end up in a place like this—a place where the raging storms speak their secrets to those willing to listen. And as much as you don't want to accept it... you like a bit of adventure, yourself."

"So what if I do?"

"Because I believe you're his key, if not the key to all of it. Arlan learned what he could, but Hatch wasn't willing to let him cross. Not on his own, anyway. Living forever shouldn't be available to everyone. I should know."

Melody shot a glance to Arlan, still furiously scribbling. "What do you mean 'his key?'"

"It's the same as I told Arlan: you must have a purpose in order to survive endlessly."

"What's your purpose then?"

"I believe it's to ensure I save as many explorers as I can. And you're right... I have many deaths on my hands from those who wouldn't heed my warnings. If anything, I exist as a warning of what immortality costs. I didn't have a choice when I befell my fate, so I'm meant to hold another's hand as they choose theirs."

Melody couldn't bring herself to look at Arlan. "And him? What's Arlan's purpose?"

"Exploration," Arlan breathed, turning to join their conversation, a smile plastered across his face. "Us. Exploring together. Just like we planned."

"Those were daydreams." Melody frowned, placing her hand to Arlan's cheek. "Not reality."

"What if they could be?" Arlan held up the parchment, the gold flickering like small flames in his eyes. "What do you say? Live forever with me?"

CREATORS OF THE SKY

ILLUSTRATED BY TBL KOBKA

Sky Pirates

Top row—Jayme Bean *Center row*—Jeremy Pak Nelson, Dani Atkinson,
B. K. Bass *Bottom row*—Aaron Hockett, Gregory Coley, Katherine Shaw

BOOK 3: PIRATES OF THE STARS

MAP OF THE WORLD'S END GALAXY

ILLUSTRATED BY CHRIS VAN DYKE

TRENCHFALL

Valdian Gateway

World's End Black Hole

WORLD'S END STATION

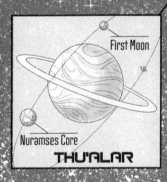

First Moon

Nuramses Core

THU'ALAR

The Dhurramoolun Array

Chester VI

EMU HEAD NEBULA

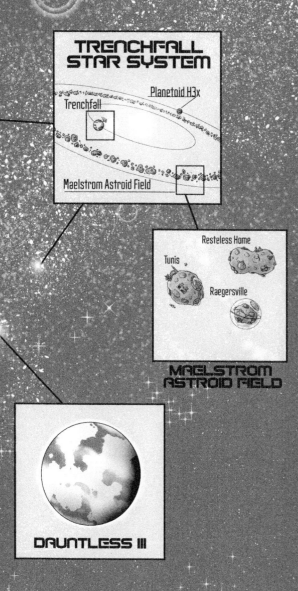

TRENCHFALL STAR SYSTEM

Planetoid H3x

Trenchfall

Maelstrom Astroid Field

MAELSTROM ASTROID FIELD

Resteless Home

Tunis

Raegersville

DAUNTLESS III

Points of interest, both natural and constructed, located in the region of Dauntless III on the edge of the World's End Galaxy.

LAST SHIP TO TRENCHFALL

HARRY F. REY

For a man who hated standing still, Abraxes sure wasn't traveling very far. Except the ten feet from the bar to the bathroom. A captain without an interstellar license was as useless as a pirate with a conscience, and Abraxes was firmly both.

"Get you another?" Asked the bar-bot, mechanical bones clicking under cheap skin cells hued a sickly green. Only the turbulent haze of the Maelstrom illuminated the darkness of Bandomas' Bar. Warning lights flashing around the asteroids made up for the lack of a sun to structure an orbit. Here in the Maelstrom, it was always night, and on this part of Tunis at least, always damp.

"Why not?" Abraxes said, stroking the fraying dreadlocks of his wiry black beard. The bar-bot squirted liquid the color of weak piss into an iron goblet, stuck by heavy magnets to the table given the frequent 'roid quakes. Abraxes stared through the port-hole windows at the passing rocks and the dirty rainbow trails they left behind. Boots against the bar stool, Abraxes wiped condensation from the window and peered down, catching sight of the asteroid's large lower ridge where Seawatch sat. Antenna and radio 'scopes swarmed the lower third of Tunis, straining to catch any hint of the Kraken.

Abraxes gazed in quiet awe at the distant glint of shining jewels from the Ekidnolk Golem, the fabled multi-tentacular arachnidian statue surging upwards from Seawatch, searching for signs of the Kraken in a way few humans understood. Abraxes knew it was infinitely more effective than any array of white-dish radio telescopes could ever be. If anyone bothered to ask him, humanity's focus should be on searching the galaxy for the last of the fifteen Ekidnolk Gems to complete the Golem. Then the multi-dimensional Kraken would supposedly burst forth from the Lighthouse and it could be captured. Such were the legends Abraxes had heard since he was old enough to sneak through vents and listen to secret conversations. If only that adventurous little boy could have known wanderlust would lead close enough to the Kraken for everything he'd ever held dear to be snatched away like some passing comet. But the Watchers didn't want Abraxes' hard-earned opinions. In fact, they didn't even want him anywhere near Seawatch.

"That's what you're giving me?" Abraxes complained to the artificial intelligence behind the bar. Although *intelligence* was a strong word to use. He snapped his magnetized goblet from the bar and sniffed the barely fizzing beverage.

"Nogah ale pumps are operating at an acceptable capacity."

"You're not putting this on my tab."

"Please provide your MVT code to register a complaint."

"Oh, buzz off." Abraxes jumped from the stool, scaring the bar-bot. He might as well drink the frothy, fizz-free ale. He wasn't planning on paying the tab, anyway. From the depths of his long coat, now frayed with mold thanks to Tunis' forever-damp walls and leaking pipes, Abraxes pulled out his closed electron pad. He snapped open the thin metal sticks and spread it across the damp bar, and the pad sparked into life.

Bazman invests billions into Forden's Cove cleanup operation.

Abraxes quickly glanced over his shoulder, but the bar was still empty, save for drips from the ceiling pipes and animatronic scurrying along the floor. He could safely read on.

Bazman's Planetary Council has formally approved funding to repair the damage following the brazen raid by galactic outlaw Abraxes. The shocking invasion saw engine powered asteroids rain down across the pleasure continent, destroying wildlife and damaging resort hotels, not to mention the personal property thieved by Abraxes' interstellar pirates. Qozarx champion Dianna D'Argon, injured in the raid, increased the reward offered for any information which could lead to—

"Reading about yourself again, Abraxes?"

"Meital!" Abraxes said, spinning round as his first officer leaned across the bar, flicking back long silver hair across their mechanized body suit, today configured into the form of a buxom human female. "Infinity, I thought you were the Revenue Service."

"Nah," Meital replied, their piston-powered hand snapping the goblet from the bar and taking a long sip. Ale dribbled down their chin, running down the bare skin of their neck and shoulders, quietly sizzling as it reached the ridged line across Meital's chest where body suit met skin. "Muffy Dillinger's jaw would drop if he caught sight of these tits and this ass." Meital smacked the half-empty goblet onto the bar. "This ale tastes like Parson Thrull's piss."

"I'll buy you a Lactarian Malt then, just tell me. Did you get into Seawatch?"

"I told you I would."

"And?"

"I did."

"So? Do they have a date for the Kraken's reappearance? Will it be at the Lighthouse? Thu'Alar? The Emu's Head? Give me something!"

"Trenchfall," Meital said. Abraxes involuntarily shushed her.

"The protected planet?" he hissed. "Why would the Kraken—"

"No, you pegged-leg moon brain. Trenchfall is where *we* need to go."

Abraxes leaned closer. No spacefarers were allowed on Trenchfall, and even flying to the Valdian Gateway orbiting above the closed world could raise serious questions.

"I found a Watchman who would talk," Meital continued. "Well, I found several, but he was the most... well-equipped." Meital flicked their hair and grinned.

"Spare me, please."

"Fine. The rumors we heard on Cold Harbor about a multi-verse map are true. He didn't say they had it, but... he didn't say they didn't, either." Meital took another drink of the ale before twisting their lips in disgust. "Anyway, to read said map, we need the last Ekidnolk Gem still to be discovered."

"So?"

"So! It's the decoding key."

"The what?"

"Oh, come on, Abraxes. Did that sub-orbital invasion of Bazman screw your circuits? The legend of the decoding key Diamond De Beers smuggled up from Trenchfall. The one Captain Braddock allegedly lost when they got spooked by Parson Thrull."

"Infinity, you're right." Abraxes gulped in shock. Finally, the fragments of stories smuggled like stolen goods knitted together in his mind.

"Bet their radio 'scopes never knew that," Meital said. "All we need to do is head to Valdian, find the decoding key, bring it to the Watchmen, read the map, and hey babango, we'll know where the Kraken is meant to re-appear."

"And finally capture the beast," Abraxes whispered, shivering in the freezing memory of how the Kraken had ripped everything that had ever warmed his heart.

"I still prefer selling the information on and letting some

other chump race through the multiverse to capture a deadly Kraken, but one system at a time."

"Brilliant work," Abraxes said, jumping up from the stool and snapping away his pad. Blood rushed through his aching body as adventure called. Just getting off this stinking, mouldy 'roid would— Wait. I don't have a license to fly. I'm outlawed. We're banned from leaving the Maelstrom, how are we... why are you smiling? Meital, no. There must be another way. No. I won't."

"Oh yes, you will."

"I can't."

Meital grabbed Abraxes' coat collar and pulled him close.

"Listen, *Captain*. If I can slide open my hard drive to every Watchman in Tunis, you can make nice to Franx."

"He won't do it."

"Like infinity he won't. The chance to discover the last Ekidnolk Gem and have every scallywag in the Maelstrom licking his boots for a crumb of power? Franx would sacrifice his own mother for the chance to fly you there."

"Even if she *was* the Empress of thu'Alar."

"I can't believe you fell for the tall tales of a Delving Prime scrap-heap boy."

"What can I say," Abraxes shrugged. "That scrap-heap scoundrel is cute."

"If you say so." Meital rolled their eyes. "Come on, I found us a place on a mining transport to Delving Prime."

The more he thought about it, the more Abraxes had to admit Meital was right. Franx dreamed of forming his own powerful gang, even becoming Lord of the Maelstrom. He would dive feet first into this mission, probably tell everyone they were successful even if they came home empty-handed. Abraxes sucked in a deep breath and sighed. He suddenly wished he'd filled his unpaid bar tab with Lactarian Malts. It was time to go make nice to his young ex-lover, and hope Franx was the type to forgive and forget.

THE JOURNEY TO RESTLESS HOME, the asteroid home to Delving Prime and Franx, was bumpier than Abraxes anticipated. He didn't care about the sudden drops or near misses of the mining shuttle through the generally unnavigable Maelstrom. He just cared that he wasn't the one piloting the ship. That last raid on Baldomar had reverted his pilot's license back into the molecules it had been made from, and the same fate would await Abraxes if he were caught behind the controls of a ship again. He knew enough bounty hunters to make himself a target worth tracking. Meital was the lucky one. Melting into a passenger's bench, they shut off their body suit and were out like a light the minute the transport took off. Of course, falling asleep during a bumpy flight was exactly how Meital ended up in a body suit in the first place.

Every astringent asteroid tail that ricocheted against the hull and splattered rainbow space dust against the porthole window was another reminder of one of Abraxes' death-defying escapes. Truly, he should have lost his life—or been cast in a body suit many moons ago. If the Kraken had anything to do with it, he would have died along with the rest of his crew... back then. He would have died along with the only sentient being he'd ever truly loved.

"Welcome to Restless Home," chimed a robotic voice as the ore transport shuddered into a cavern deep inside the asteroid. They would have to dig even deeper to reach Delving Prime, the original ore mine who's warren of tunnels should have been abandoned long ago.

After disembarking from the shuttle, Meital followed Abraxes through the arrivals hall, filled almost entirely with workers looking for their next job. They hung around stairways to nowhere, making camp under dripping ceilings or exhaust pipes. They carried their own tools on their backs; heavy electro-cutters or magno-trowels. Abraxes knew fine well those were more effective, and more often used, as weapons than ore extraction equipment.

At least there were no Revenue Service agents haunting these parts, just the rough dregs of violent life that stalked the Maelstrom, grunting and glaring as they passed by. They'd shed the other passengers who'd disembarked with them, and now walked quickly through a wide, endless corridor with flickering anbaric lights and puddles of gas runoff eating through the floor. Abraxes stopped at a crossroads. He glanced over the rusty railing at another staircase below, disappearing forwards at least, into a dark tunnel. Maybe that was the right way? How to get down there was another question entirely.

"Lost?" Meital asked, examining their reflection in a dirty puddle of rainbow liquid. "Cuz maybe you wanna get found pretty soon."

Abraxes glanced where Meital pointed. Thumping echoed along the corridor from a grump of too many mine workers in an air car, so it kept smacking into the ground. The workers waved their weapons—mine tools—straight at them.

"Oh shit," Abraxes said, catching sight of the angriest of the half dozen workers. She held aloft a pronged flame-guarder, swinging her metal shoulders in every direction.

"Abraxes!" she screamed as the air car chundered up broken tiles from the floor. "I'm gonna kill you."

"Hmm," Meital said, arms casually folded while the angry workers shot straight for them. "Didn't think that was your type."

"Not really," Abraxes said breathlessly, awkwardly climbing over the railing. Meital did it with a smooth body suit-powered backwards flip. "Typical misunderstanding." His feet now dangling in the gap twenty feet at least to the stairway below, he tried to shimmy towards the wall. "That's Sali. She owed me money... long time ago. I kidnapped one of her husbands. He fell in love with me."

"With you?" Meital said, hopping from one ledge to the next

with pressurized ease while Abraxes' arms were ready to pop from their sockets.

"I was much younger then."

"And here I was thinking you'd *improved* with age." Meital was already on the staircase beneath. Abraxes heaved himself up, hoping to make a leap to the nearby ledge like Meital had done. Above, though, the boots of five angry workers pounded the floor as they ran straight for him, weapons revving up. The air car had shed its excess weight as only Sali was in it, reversing out of a dent in the wall.

"Grab that skin bag!" Sali screamed, powering the air car straight for him.

"Jump," Meital said. "I'll catch you."

It was either let go or be smashed, so Abraxes dropped and Meital, good to their word, caught him in their artificially strong arms without so much as a whimper. The air car meanwhile burst through the railing and smashed straight into the opposite wall, leaving a gaping hole while the other workers skidded to a stop on the precipice.

"Put me down, please. Because I think we better run."

Run, they did. Down endless stairways. Through working warehouses, ore storage rooms, and a crowded workers' mess where they apologized for interrupting a rowdy drinking song.

"Hey, I know that shanty," Meital said once they'd made it to the tube transport station which would take them to Delving Prime. Abraxes was hunched against the wall, wiping breathless spit from his beard and trying to blink away the endless stars swirling through his vision.

"Sing one note and I'll sell you for scrap."

"I'm looking for someone," Abraxes said to the serving wench behind the dark bar. She glowered at him under a tight head wrap, her bare arms jiggling as she cleaned a goblet with a filthy rag, replacing it in the rack above her dirtier than before. The bar was busy and getting rowdier as more miners, skin and clothes sparkling with star dust, crowded the place. At least their attention was expectantly trained on the stage at the far end of the bar, complete with shimmering energy pole. Abraxes couldn't even see Meital over sloshing drinks being passed over heads while bellies and elbows bashed into him. "I said I'm looking for—"

"I heard yeh. You gunna buy a drink first?" But it was hardly a question. Abraxes nodded, and she pulled down the same filthy goblet she'd just put away. She spat in it, then wiped it with the same rag slung over her shoulder and filled it with ale. At least the drink was fresh, unlike the pisswater back on Tunis. If they tried to serve that nonsense here, there'd be a riot. In fact, that probably caused most of the miner's revolts. The corporations knew what kept their workers happy.

"Fifty," she said.

"Fifty? Even five is expensive..." Abraxes didn't fancy his chances against her. He pulled a silver token from deep in his jacket pocket and tapped it against his wrist-tech, filling the token with fifty. The wench slid it straight into her bosom.

"So, who's you lookin' for?"

"The most dangerous person in Delving Prime," Abraxes said, hoping she would catch his drift. Unimpressed, she spit-cleaned another goblet. Abraxes leaned closer, the elbow patches of his jacket damp from the ale run-off. This was not the kind of place to whisper, but there was no other way. Abraxes was wanted dead or alive in more systems than not. His license to fly anywhere beyond the Maelstrom permanently suspended. Seeking out illegal transport to a protected world put a price on his head higher than most of these miners would see in a lifetime. But he had no other choice. Like a holy cleric unable to renounce their faith, even as they were cast out of an airlock, Abraxes would never be unable to hunt the Kraken. "A guy who knows the way from here to… Trenchfall."

The wench's lips widened into a gap-toothed grin. Abraxes' heart shot into his throat. He thought he'd been set up, but the crowd whipped up into a roar as a crush started towards the stage.

"He's about to go on," she said, then turned away. That fifty lost forever. The little light in the bar deadened, followed by a hushed silence interrupted only by burps and sloshing ale. A pulsar floated across the room, illuminating two long, dark legs in diamond-heeled shoes. Slowly, the light moved up the figure's body as the whooping grew louder from the hungry pen of caged animals.

"Hello, boys." An unmistakably male voice said to the chomping crowd. Dazzled in pulsar light, the figure approached the energy pole, strategically wrapped in strips of rigging—the kind workers wore when lowered into the mines. They flipped a long silver wig across their bare back, skin the color of a sunset, as they mounted the pole to the cheering crowd. It had been a long time since Abraxes last saw a sunset. It had been with Franx. Abraxes watched in open-mouthed shock as the figure danced while Meital emerged through the crowd, drinking a golden and expensive Lactarian Malt.

"What Franx ever saw in you," Meital said, watching the figure dance.

"That's not…"

"Come on, boys," the now clearly Franx shouted as he dangled from the pole, held aloft only by his high heels. "Who wants to love me?" A pounding 'roid-rave dance track pulsed through the bar as Franx owned the pole, flipping and twisting while the audience went wild, pelting him with tokens. Abraxes sighed, stroked his beard, and did the only thing he could in the circumstances. Get drunk.

"This is him, boys," Franx said. He sat across the table in an exquisite Dalvian silk wrap, his wig and "outfit" left on the stage. The surrounding miners, all big and brutish women, men and enby's, surrounded the slim and regal Franx like an honor guard for the thu'Alarian Empress. "This is the man who broke my heart." Franx wiped away an imaginary tear, and his supporters audibly crowed. Abraxes swallowed hard. Meital's leg restlessly tapped the floor right next to him, a pneumatic twang to add to his thumping heart.

"Could we talk in private?" Abraxes asked. Franx sipped luminous green liquid from a twisted glass and dabbed his powdered cheek.

"No. I don't trust myself around you." Long eyelashes flickered Abraxes' way. Truthfully, he didn't trust himself alone around Franx, either. That was not a black hole he wanted to get sucked into again. Abraxes glanced at Meital for some help, but Meital just shrugged.

"We need a ride to... the Valdian Gateway." Abraxes started, despite Franx looking away. "It's a small job—" Abraxes glanced nervously at his surroundings "—but huge potential payoff."

"You *abandoned* me, Abraxes."

"Come on, Franx." The miners edged closer. Abraxes heard the gin of an electro-cutter rev up. "Do you know how dangerous that mission was? I lost an entire crew to the Kraken. I lost my legs... twice, and I lost... well, I wish I could've died instead of... Well, you know how much he meant to me." Franx began to thaw. Abraxes knew this act. "The only reason I didn't bring you to the heist on Bazman was because I was ashamed. Ashamed because I had debts to pay. Ashamed because I knew the only way to save my worthless life was to sacrifice my freedom. I loved you too much to put you at risk."

Far from laughing in his face, several of the miners shed stray tears and bit down on wobbly lips. Franx's silk-wrapped shoulders relaxed. He took a long sip from his cocktail and glanced straight at Abraxes. A shade of a smile creeping under his steely exterior. Abraxes offered a hint of one in return.

"Boys, prepare my travel chest. I will escort this scallywag to the end of the galaxy, and I shall return with many wonders and great riches." Franx stood, glass in hand. "And we'll finally be able to take over Restless Home, then the entire Maelstrom!"

"Hurrah!" A great cheer rose, and Abraxes couldn't help but be swept up in the good feeling. It ended with the remainder of Franx's drink splashed across his face, the luminous liquid burning his eyes.

"Betray me again and you can add the Maelstrom to the list of places where you're worth more dead than alive."

THE VALDIAN GATEWAY orbited high above the protected planet where wooden ships sailed through night-black oceans and air pirates fought high in hazy clouds. Abraxes had only once broken the Galactic Law forbidding contamination with underdeveloped species, and traveled down to Trenchfall. On a starless night, he and a crew of young bandits risked an airlock execution by tying their spaceship to the floating raft market in the middle of an ocean and selling scrap tech as magic to the locals.

The Valdian Gateway was a space magnet for scoundrels and pirates, vagabonds and cutthroats. The narrow corridors of the orbiting merchant market, fused together from the shards and hulls of old ships, were patrolled by Revenue Service agents and mercenaries, partly there to enforce the boycott of sending advanced tech down to the protected world, and partly there to be bought off by those who made their money by smuggling to and from Trenchfall. Once, while on a moon of thu'Alar, Abraxes had tasted wine from Trenchfall. He'd spent the rest of his life lusting after that taste.

Abraxes sat next to Franx in a long, circular bar in the Idonian casino, on the exclusive upper decks of the Valdian Gateway. The cavernous ceiling was a translucent bubble, constantly facing the gas giant so rejuvenating radiation could spill upon the rich and powerful on the gaming floor. Naturally, on their young and beautiful playthings as well.

Abraxes had taken the form of a rich and powerful white robed thu'Alarian duke. Franx, his young and beautiful companion, dressed in skin-tight leathers. Both of them looked the part. Franx could unzip at a moment's notice, primed to distract whatever being stood between Abraxes and the last gem. Meital turned wheels at an AI gaming station, a cellular disruptor weapon strapped to their thigh hidden by a flowing gown. Abraxes had to hope this would not end by blasting their way out of the casino. It wasn't that Valdian didn't have places to hide, more that Abraxes had a greater fear of what lurked in those hiding places.

"Shall we, my duke?" Franx said. He fully inhabited his character, an arm draped casually around Abraxes' padded shoulders, twisting his well-oiled beard forked in imperial thu'Alarian style. As they dotted through well-dressed crowds alive with the buzz of spending small fortunes, Franx leaned closer and whispered: "Do you have any idea what you're looking for?"

"I do, actually," Abraxes said as they stopped to watch an incomprehensible game. A tiny moon creature wearing an anti-oxygen mask sat at the center of an intricately carved table. Its eight legs clacked and spun a series of interlocking disks with symbols carved around the edges. "We have to get thrown into the Cheater's Lounge." Franx might have said something, but the cheering crowd coaxing the poor little creature to clank the wheels harder drowned him out. The players in their anti-grav hairstyles and dressed in strips of strategic ribbon threw tokens and even jewels into rivets under the disks. Then celebrated or commiserated as the wheels came to a stop.

"I said," Franx gripped his shoulder hard. "You brought me all the way here just to get thrown out?"

A few people glanced in their direction.

"They lost the decoding key on Deck Three of the *Rebellion*. The only way there is to be ejected via the Chearer's Lounge. We need to—" the most beautiful figure he had ever seen walking past shut Abraxes up. Their skin was as black as space, their woven gown shimmering like star light as they passed by, escorted by armed mercenary security. The figure didn't notice Abraxes, or frankly anyone, but he saw what hung around their neck. The last Ekidnolk Gem—the decoding key.

"Abraxes?"

"Shh," he said, slipping into the crowd following the security guards. "Just… stay here and don't get into trouble." With a bit of luck, Abraxes could get his hands on that key and sell it to Seawatch without Franx being any the wiser, or demanding to come with him as he searched for the Kraken. The only thing between him and fulfilment were half a dozen guards.

He followed the group, escorting the gem-wielding performer to a doorway roped off with pulsing energy beams where even more security waited by the entrance. The beams dropped as the figure with the gem swished in, then immediately returned. But a small queue was forming to get into the protected room. The rich and powerful gathered, this time without their young and beautiful playthings. Abraxes glanced across the gaming floor to Meital. He nodded, so did they. Everything was fine. He'd lost sight of Franx, but that was better. This section of the casino was rather more upmarket, and Franx fit in more with miners and pirates.

"Excuse me," Abraxes said to a gruff security woman with his smoothest nebula accent. "Must dukes also wait in line?"

"We'll be opening in a moment, your worship." Abraxes

nodded, acting slightly put out. True to her word, the energy barriers dissipated, and those first in line happily let a single white-robed member of the imperial family walk through first.

Circles of floating tables gently lit by pulsars ringed a small stage, the darkness offering an intimate setting for whatever performance was about to take place. Abraxes sat front and center, snapping his fingers until a server in a black suit appeared.

"A Lactarian Malt, and now," Abraxes said, without looking at the server.

"Of course. We have two-hundred-year-old, four hundred—"

"No less than three thousand years. And nebula smoked. None of this vaporized nonsense."

"Y-yes, b-but that costs—"

"Now," Abraxes commanded, scaring the server into action. True, the cost of that drink was astronomical, but he had no intention of paying this bar tab either. The appearance of grandeur was all part of the plan.

As soon as his golden drink was presented, he yanked the server's collar close to his face.

"Who is the performer?"

"Maxam Gracia, your worship."

"I want a private audience with them immediately after the show, understood?" He swirled the thick liquid in the diamond glass. "Send them one of these backstage."

"Right away."

THE PERFORMANCE WAS HAUNTING. Maxam Gracia sang a medley of Bazmanian operetta at pitches that would've shattered the chalice had it not been made of pure diamond. Abraxes studiously joined in with the smattering of applause after each crescendo. But he had eyes only on the gem around the singer's neck. It had no color, yet every color. Nor any discernable shape as, like a sun, the eye could not focus on it for very long. Of interest only to Maelstrom Watchers or Kraken hunters. More accurately, folks with a death wish. Maxam Gracia had an eye on Abraxes, however. Singers like them lived on the patronage of rich dukes like him.

After a double encore, Maxam Gracia was taken back through the curtain while the audience rose and chatted with the distinct air of self-congratulation. A server came forward and invited Abraxes through the curtain.

He found Maxam Gracia sitting alone in front of a brightly lit mirror, rubbing a steaming balm into their impossible cheek bones.

"That was quite the performance," Abraxes said, now with two fresh Lactarian Malts in either hand. He placed one in front of Maxam. They sipped it, but said nothing. "Forgive me, but I didn't catch your gender."

"Aren't thu'Alarian dukes supposed to be raised better than that? Does it matter to you?"

"Not one iota. I merely wish to investigate your clothes as quickly as possible."

"Investigate my clothes?"

"Yes. From the floor of my master suite while I caress your beautiful body." Maxam laughed in shock. "You can keep the necklace on though, I rather like it." Maxam turned in their chair, still laughing. That was a good sign. Their fingers clasped the enchanting gem as they took a sip of the rich malt. Maxam leaned in closer, their hand now running up Abraxes' leg. He wished he still had feeling there. Slightly north of his thigh, though, his feelings were fully clear. Maxam grinned.

"'Scuse me." Heavy hands fell on his shoulders. Maxam recoiled in shock. Abraxes saw through the mirror three large security personnel standing behind him. "But you gotta come with us."

"Unhand the duke this instance!" Maxam shouted.

"He ain't no duke."

Maxam's face dropped. As quick as a supernova, they returned to their seat with the Malt, sipping it like an innocent bystander.

Abraxes tried to protest, but he understood it was useless. There would be another way. He'd located the gem. Now it just had to be pried from their neck. A perfect job for Franx, who'd never slept with anyone without stealing something of great value. That's exactly how Abraxes had lost command of the Midnight Scythe to damn Captain Braddock.

Abraxes was firmly handled back onto the casino floor, where calm reigned under the glowing gas giant radiating them all. Meital suddenly saw his predicament from across the floor, but he shook his head, standing them down. Now he just had to get a message to Franx.

"You're outta here, scoundrel."

"Very well."

"You and your cheatin' boy."

"What!"

Suddenly Franx appeared, also escorted by three security guards.

"You told me to cheat," he whispered.

"I told you to stay out of trouble! Excuse me, but I think there's been a misunderstanding. I am a duke of thu'Alar, and this is my, uh, squire, B-bloriguard."

"Shut it, the pair of yeh." A gruff guard said quietly. The peace of the casino was not to be disturbed. "You're lucky we're taking you to the Cheater's Lounge and not out with the trash to get burned up in orbit."

Franx nodded enthusiastically.

"See?" He whispered as they were led to the back. "Exactly where you wanted."

Abraxes just shook his head. He'd been so close. Another few hours. Infinity, even another few minutes, and the gem would have been his. He let himself be escorted to the far side of the casino and tried to think up a plan. The Cheater's Lounge was like a time out. Only on the third infringement was a person permanently excluded from the casino. And even then, Maxam Gracia had the gem. It wasn't lost on Deck Three of the *Rebellion* and it wasn't being guarded by the nightmarish Parson Thrull. It was here, and it could be stolen. They just needed a way back in.

"Take 'em straight to the tube," said a guard at the door to the Cheater's Lounge, right next to the kitchens.

"What?" Abraxes said, outraged. "But… but we—"

"I got no space for charlatans. If you manage to crawl your way out of the *Rebellion,* don't bring your DNA back here. You're barred."

There wasn't time to be shocked. A ring opened up in the wall, sucking air like a breached hull. The choice was to go with dignity, or be hurled. Abraxes chose dignity, Franx was hurled.

The stomach-churning ride through the tube included bubbles of trash, not all of which were properly sealed. They were scalped and slapped; the stench made Abraxes' eyes water. It was almost a relief when they were finally ejected into the *Rebellion.* Only a few trash bubbles bounced around the oddly clean deck. As Franx coughed and spluttered on his hands and knees, Abraxes quickly understood why. At the end of the deck was an airlock. It would open, and everything inside the deck would be ejected towards the blue world of Trenchfall orbiting below.

"Franx!" Abraxes shouted, pulling him up. "I don't know how long we have, but if we don't find a way out of here, we're going to get thrown out into space."

Franx gathered himself together, but remained infinitely more calm.

"Relax, old man. I'm sure there's a—"

"A what? A what?" Abraxes said as Franx pushed through the

trash bubbles bouncing between the snake pit of pipes around the deck. Abraxes was reluctant to follow, but the tales of Parson Thrull stalking this deck made him run quickly after Franx.

"I knew it." Franx approached a well-marked escape hatch near the airlock door. "Standard procedure, even for dumps like these. Delving Prime is basically one big trash heap for the whole of Restless Home."

"But it's going to take us down to Trenchfall," Abraxes said, glancing longingly behind at the exit pipe, wishing he could climb back up and into the casino, perhaps reverse time and take a different approach. He couldn't quite believe how close he'd been. He almost wished the gem were lost down here. Even a time-limited chance was better than none.

"Would you prefer to go to Trenchfall in a pod," Franx said, depressurizing the hatch and climbing into the narrow orb. "Or not in a pod?"

"In a pod." Abraxes squeezed in beside Franx. Now was probably not the best time to shout blame.

"Don't worry," Franx said and kissed him on the cheek. "Once we're down there, we'll figure out a way back up."

"I know where the gem is."

"Well, that's a help," Franx said, sliding the pod closed. They crouched awkwardly, knees locked together as the pristine green continents and sparkling blue oceans of Trenchfall spun slowly below. Franx tapped the rudimentary controls. And just in time. Suddenly a pressurized hiss came from nearby. The airlock had opened, and bubbles of trash were now floating towards the protected world. Their pod detached smoothly. Abraxes wiped away foggy breath and watched the low-tech world grow larger.

"Um, Abraxes. What's that?"

Franx was looking the other way, towards the Valdian Gateway. With some awkwardness, Abraxes turned around, wondering if Meital was flying the ship to their rescue. The air rushed out of his lungs like a hull puncture. A giant, white rip cut through space, and probably time, too. Barely a few klicks from the hobbled mass of the Valdian Gateway, he could already see ships making a hasty escape. Two such ships collided in their haste, the fiery explosion over in a split second in the zero-atmosphere of space.

As their pod fell towards Trenchfall, one long, flapping tentacle emerged through the great white space, sniffing this dimension. That one tentacle could easily rip the Valdian Gateway in two. Abraxes knew all too well what the Kraken was capable of.

It all came rushing back. His heart crashed in his ears like an exploding moon. Those antimatter tentacles which could slice a space station in two. Its horror-filled body sucking up ships and beacons like a mulligan-rat feasting on peanut shells. The stinging tail which could poison a planet's atmosphere in minutes. How the beast roared like the end of time itself, screaming in dimensions beyond comprehension, the heads of humans and space-walkers alike exploding in a fiery burst of zero-gravity destruction. When the Kraken came, few remained alive to tell the tale.

"Well," Franx said, his face as colorless as the rip still stretching open. Their pod rumbled as they penetrated Trench-fall's upper atmosphere. "I guess you don't need that map no more."

DEBT COLLECTION

LISA KUZNAK

"You're about to find out what it's like to be explosively decompressed, you two-timing scum! Your liver is going to get scraped off the window, an' I'm gonna eat it and laugh!"

Yuri couldn't breathe out half his nose, the plastic decor swam in his vision, and the pain in his head was fierce, as if he were still getting punched. His boot heels caught on a seam in the metal floor, loosening them on his feet, and despite his mumbled requests they didn't stop to let him adjust his awkward footwear. He tried lifting an arm to wipe the blood from his eyes—his hands were held at his back.

A pair of toothy Gorrag goons were dragging him half-conscious down a dingy tube in Uptown—the one on his right was the talkative plum bastard. Hairy, rough, and right ugly. As Yuri's reality came fast, he struggled and swore, but all that did was get his boots knocked off.

The loss of footwear didn't matter. The data was already sent. He'd done his part. Now he had to keep his liver where it was.

The Gorrags weren't too gentle, slamming Yuri's back up against the airlock door with a solid *whack*. His head lolled forward. Drooling blood, the world around him wavered to the sound of deep-chested laughter.

"Your liver is going to taste sublime. It's gonna get nice an' tenderized. Human pâté."

If only he could reach—

Footsteps echoed; someone was running. Yuri blinked blood away, forcing his eyes to focus.

"Wait! Not yet." Dianna D'Argon rounded the corner. A beautiful sight, but not welcome. Yuri cringed—fought harder to reach the watch tucked into the hidden pocket up his sleeve. As if he needed this to get any worse.

His fingers stretched to the point of pain, the teeth he had left in his head ground together—and the purple brutes listened to her, holding him still. "Quick, throw me in the airlock!"

"Shut up!"

Dianna caught up, pistol buzzing and ready to fire. "Yuri, I'm very sorry to interrupt. You owe me for that *favour* and I'd like to get it before your head explodes."

"You'll have to take it up with them, *darling*."

His fingers brushed it—he held his cheek in his teeth to keep from showing his excitement. Shot or exploded, neither today, thanks. He pressed it—felt the vibration and the heat, his hair stood on end, and soon his vision started hiccoughing.

Her good eye lit up, eyebrows arched and mouth open in shock. She pulled up her sleeve—her perfect face knotted, giving him great satisfaction. "You stole my watch!"

"I'll give it baa-a-aa-a-ck—"

"You son of a bii-i-ii-i-tch—"

It was difficult to talk or hear while being phased into a billion fragments and flung through time and space.

YURI HAD DONE a hasty job with the coordinates on the borrowed watch, phasing back into reality in the *Scythe's* galley—much to the chagrin of their cook, Mr. Kepler. Stout and sour, he didn't look too pleased to have four severed Gorrag hands, a bowl-shaped scoop of airlock door, and a puddle of Yuri's fresh vomit in the middle of his floor.

"Got a towel, Mr. Kepler?"

"The fuck have you been up to now, Zayats?" Mr. Kepler threw the towel he had tucked in his apron pocket and hit Yuri's stooped head, bent as he was to avoid further stomach upset. Teleporting felt terrible normally, never mind with his skull beat in.

Mr. Kepler held up a ladle, three seconds from whacking Yuri across the ass with it like a disgruntled grandfather. Yuri knelt to clean up after himself, whistling for a mop bot to get the floor nice and squeaky clean, and the old cook's face lost some of the red.

"Work for the Captain," Yuri said, tossing the purple hands into the garbage chute.

"What kind of 'work?'"

"The financially beneficial kind."

"Uh huh. Looks like you need new teeth." Mr. Kepler was also their dentist.

"Got any slots free?"

"Half hour."

Yuri went to the freezer, chipped ice off the door to hold on to his face, and walked off to find his cot and fall into it.

"YURI."

A sultry voice woke him from his brief nap with a heart attack —*Fuck!*—forgetting he had programmed Dianna's likeness and voice into his Violet, he flung himself over the side of his cot. The

Cold Harbour "Violet" model of companion bots were extremely believable, except for the spiritually dead eyes and slight flicker of the holograph shell, but he still expected a pistol in his back in his brief derangement. "Don't scare me like that, Vi."

"Bad day?"

"You know it."

"Need help?" That was pure Vi—Dianna would sooner make it worse.

He tongued his new teeth, felt at the de-bruiser mask. It was still working at him, cheeks tingling. "I'll be fine, babe. Thanks."

She gave him a peck on his head, tousled his hair. "Captain wants to see you."

"You didn't go to her like that, did you?"

"No. I had clothes on."

"Good girl. Go to the closet and recharge."

"Yessir." That wasn't Dianna, either. Sometimes he would turn "Vi" totally off, but he wasn't in the mood for that now, nor did he have the time.

Captain Braddock was at her desk. "You look like an idiot with that mask on." She offered Yuri a cigarette. He took it, lit it from hers, passed hers back, and they got to business.

She had received the data packet, and it made her very pleased —even as she looked miffed over something else. They'd be punching the coordinates in and would make plans to rob the hell out of the Gorrag merchant fleet heading to the Valdian Market (through a particularly stupid chunk of space on their part, begging to get pirates on their case). Yuri was to make sure The *Midnight Scythe* got there first, and that everything was copacetic while the computers did their thing. (Whatever that was, the *Scythe* was an odd girl.)

Then he had another job.

"Jaccus Estany owes me money. Which means he owes *you* money."

Yuri snorted—Jaccus was a jackass. "And?"

"*And*, we've been watching for him at the wrong place. He's not at the pawn shop, hasn't been in years. He's got a nice, cushy job on thu'Alar, on the *Agamemnon*, and we can't go there to fetch him without thu'Alar beam cannons blasting our ass apart, not unless we have ships in tow for the King—so, you're taking the shuttle. Nevermind the fucking Revenue Service on that shithole of a flying pebble is *lusting* after me. This is another Yuri job, sorry to say."

He huffed a small laugh. Of course it was. She ignored him.

"You're familiar with the place. See if you can get to Jackie-boy for us—and, you're seeing a man about a favour."

Yuri had lived on Second Moon for several years, did courier work as a teenager between the fourteen moons—lost his job when he got caught stealing the parcels.

He took a long drag of his cigarette, let the heat fill his lungs. "Aye aye, Cap'n."

"Fuck outta my cabin with that smarmy shit."

"Can I take Junior?"

"Yes. Bring it back in one piece. And I fucking mean it, Navigator Zayats."

THU'ALAR ORBITED A DYING SUN, and seeing it always made Yuri uneasy, especially warped as it was through the porthole of the shuttle. On the moons, you'd get used to it—the atmosphere would blunt the view—but seeing it zoom into your vision through clear, uninterrupted void was like seeing death itself sneak up on you. When that thing went, a huge chunk of space would go out with it. Thu'Alar, by contrast, was still vibrant and heady. Purples, pinks, oranges, yellows, blues, all in a hundred bands around its middle and out to the poles, stripes disturbed by a dozen storms. The gas giant and all its moons were certainly a spectacle—it'll be a sad day when it gets annihilated by the God of natural disasters—supernovas were a bitch.

Out on Last Moon, (called Nuramses Core by the Service—the locals had a much simpler, obvious language,) they thought it was a giant magic *kraken* waiting to take their universe out—a bunch of superstitious coping. Their sun was right there staring them in the face and they pick a mythical monster to worship? To each their own, he figured, so long as they left Yuri Zayats the hell alone.

The King of thu'Alar had the right idea, getting his people away from their sun by any means necessary. Plus, that letter of marque made the *Scythe* some good money already, commandeering ships for the rehousing effort. If it took another thousand years for the thing to blink out of existence, that was plenty of time for the *Scythe* to take advantage of the offer.

Not today, though. They were off marauding. Yuri got "shore leave."

He broke from the scenery and lit a cigarette, went over to the tarp that covered Junior. He untethered a strap, lifted a corner of the canvas, let the smoke seep from his lips to smile—fucking beaut of a rocket, she was. Shiny, slick, red. He ran a hand along the smooth hull, whispered pleasant nothings at her. He had no idea who named her or why—whoever they stole her from, likely —but the name didn't matter. All Yuri wanted to do was ride her.

As Second Moon came closer, he had to dress the part, like he was made for the richness of First Moon's haughty attitude. Pompousness was so thick in the air there, he almost needed a converter mask to breathe. He left Junior, went to his cabin, got dressed.

Hair slicked back in fashionable waves. Waistcoat, double-breasted. Skin-tight breeches on the bottom and billowing sleeves on the top. Stock at his neck. Boots to his knees, blindingly shiny, clicker-spurs at his heels—he didn't plan on losing this pair. Cabochons anywhere he could get away with. Finally, a thu'Alaran-style helmet, open-faced and shaped to a swooping point tucked under his arm and waiting for a jaunt on the rocket. Looking so fancy had him feeling like a right bastard.

Court sword at his hip, two pistols with it, ammo and charge pouches weighing the belt down. ID ring forged to perfection—no skimping on fake documents. Deflector hidden inside the waistcoat, with Dianna's displacer watch. Jackie-boy better hope the kraken comes flying in.

"IDENTIFICATION AND WEAPONS LICENCE."

He held out his fist; they scanned the ring.

"Thank you, sir. Anthu bast thu'Alar alnu."

"Anthu bast dralnu." Formal greetings done, Yuri bobbed his head to the Second Moon station agent and went to fetch Junior. The shuttle, with a holocloak to cover the *Scythe's* insignia, stayed under lock and key, extra credits given to the valet. On the launch pad, Junior's engine purred. The shielding swooshed up, making a glassy bubble around Yuri as he straddled the seat. Helmet on, chinstrap tight. First Moon coordinates punched in. That big bastard *Agamemnon* would hover over the port like a clumsy brick—all the grace and style of the Kingdom underneath, and that ugly thing would be the introductory view, polluting the clouds.

He hadn't done the route in a while, but the nostalgia washed away when traffic control gave the go-ahead for full speed. Yuri punched the throttle—he and Junior became a streak of red to anyone standing nearby.

BENEATH THE *AGAMEMNON*, past the spaceport, the ancient spires of First Moon towered over the landscape. With the planet at the horizon and the sun lighting it full, all the colours of the giant reflected off the architecture in a dazzling display. It awed Yuri, as it always had. He wasn't the envious boy anymore—he knew better than to want to live in this stuffy, posh place—but it would always be a sight that made him pause.

There were three tiers of traffic in the city: on the ground, folks walked. Leisurely, obnoxiously. Above that, the carriages soared past with their irritating, trilling pulse. At the top, the local rich young belligerents made a habit of showing off their rides, going too fast and too hard, and it was the only tier worth travelling in.

Up in a grand apartment overlooking one of the large forested domes, Yuri was to meet a man named Lord Ka'al. As far as Yuri knew, Lord Ka'al didn't think very highly of the new overseer of the *Agamemnon*. Poor Jack seemed to make a name for himself wherever he went.

Yuri nodded to a group of young men leaning against their rockets as he made his way to the spire, and they nodded back with leering smiles, watching him walk with their hands less-than-casually at the hilts of their court swords.

Glass elevators never sat well with Yuri, but he kept his attention on his cuffs and on his smoke to keep from looking beneath his feet. If he was heading skyward, a rocket under him was far preferable.

His sleeves fluttered at the gush of fresh air at the top of the elevator, as he stepped out into the long corridor. The grand interior of the spire glowed with the warm colours of the gas giant, refracting in rainbows across lush carpets and high walls.

Lady Ka'al, in the typically thu'Alaran garb of silk strips of cloth holding up her assets (they were fine, but she was no Dianna), a gold-and-pearl tiara perched on long black locks, greeted Yuri with a curt nod and led him inside the vast apartment. Grand arches, shapes so elegant everything looked liquid. Dripping gold, fluid gems. Lord Ka'al dressed a lot like Yuri, only more so, and called for Yuri to join him on the settee with sing-song affectation to his voice. Brandy glasses and cigars waited on a fragile-looking table. At a far window, one of the other moons eclipsed the sun, and a warm flicker shot through the brandy as Yuri held it up to click against Lord Ka'al's glass.

Very expensive, Yuri was sure. The bottle probably cost more than the *Midnight Scythe*. He savoured it.

"So, I've spoken with Captain Braddock. You need access to the *Agamemnon*."

To the point. "Aye, sir. I do."

"Grand. Might I suggest brute force?"

Yuri smirked over his glass. "No false IDs or ridiculous pretence to get me in?"

"His robots have already sniffed me out," and the way Ka'al drank the brandy, he was very put out by that fact.

"Why'd I come up here, then, if you pardon my bluntness? Aside from your hospitality, of course."

"There's another tidbit of information I have for you. Did you read the letter of marque?"

"No. That's up to Braddock."

Lord Ka'al stood, brushed his waistcoat flat as if it helped him think. Lady Ka'al began strumming on a tall harp, notes chiming delicately around the room. "His Highness has not only promised wealth to his privateers... the secret of thu'Alar itself he's willing to divulge. But guess who else knows the secret?"

"Jaccus Estany?"

Ka'al chortled. "You got it, lad!"

"Why's he privy to the information?"

"Because he's a conniving prick, didn't you know?" Lady Ka'al flubbed a chord at that. "And he's been promised to one of the Princesses. He might be King one day if a specific line of Royals kick off early. Call me old-fashioned, Mr. Zayats, but a man like that marrying into the royal family..." He gave a facetious cluck of his tongue. "Plus, he owes me money."

"Nice ride," one of the young men on the street jeered. His pals all snickered. "Looks as old as my nan."

"Rides better than her, I promise." The cigar tilted up in Yuri's teeth as he grinned—he could smell how eager they were to be little shits.

"Oooh," the crowd hummed. The one who made the initial observation rolled his eyes, tapped his sword hilt.

An idea struck Yuri's skull as he threw his leg over the seat. "Ever play chicken with the *Agamemnon?*" The engine warmed up before he let the exhaust kiss the crowd of idiots.

All the youths eyed each other with various expressions of disbelief and ill intent.

"What? Balls haven't dropped yet? You insult my girl and you all sit there slack-jawed?"

Another youth spoke up. "Sword, pistol, or race? He can take you."

Yuri very much doubted it, put his helmet on with a sideways look at the one he hoped would play.

Chief Idiot spat. "Third tier up. Let's go." He whistled, the crowd parted, and his ride twittered over to him. Brassy and slick, but it hardly impressed Yuri, who watched with obvious amusement painting his face just to chafe the moron.

Yuri let a blue cloud of cigar smoke puff and his hand was in a fist over the instrument panel.

The kid straddled his ride.

A gap behind them let bystanders know there was about to be a charred sidewalk. One of the girls let go of her sweetheart and tossed her gold wristlet—

At the second it hit the ground, they were off. Lord Ka'al had told Yuri the hull was weak at the observation deck, so that's where Yuri went, dialling in the path and letting the cigar ash fall as it pleased. The kid radioed over insults, increasingly agitated phrases as Yuri ignored him—his attention was stuck on the *Agamemnon's* heat cannons.

He let the pair of rockets keep neck and neck—until one cannon began sparking at them. The kid didn't falter—Yuri cut in front to make sure the aim didn't trail anywhere else. The sparking increased—he started counting, the kid started sweating.

"It's going to shoot us!"

"Yep."

"Shit! You're fuckin' nuts!"

Two... One! Yuri steered Junior up on a dime—looking back to catch the kid's bones getting atomized in the beam, wincing in sympathy. But now Yuri had the time to breach the hull while that cannon recharged—too small and too close for any of the others to get him.

Observation deck straight ahead. He rammed his spur into Junior's side and it jolted to missile speed—his bones felt the rush, and he chomped the cigar firm.

He breached the hull with a scream of busted metal and shatter of glass, spinning alarm lights and howling sirens greeting him as he let down Junior's shield, debris hitting his shoulders. Cigar smoke vanished in the violent wind. Pistol out, he slapped the deflector on and marched through, stepping over bent metal plates. Junior purred in wait.

A robot ran at him from a corridor—a kick of his spur to the floor sent a frequency to short circuit the brain with a tuft of black smoke and stink of burnt wires. Yuri went to the hunched machine and plugged into the radio.

"I've got an appointment with a Mr. Estany on behalf of the *Midnight Scythe,*" his voice boomed over the ship-wide system. "Jackie-boy, I'm here to collect."

No response, but for another robot zooming at him—beam dissipating into the deflection shield in a warm red ripple. Yuri pulled his sword, jumped back—the spur did nothing, not enough time to recharge. After a flood of beams, Yuri lunged, parried by a steel hand—a swipe, a dive—a thrust into the robot's chest with a small hiss of a failing motor. He pulled the blade free and forced it through the electric brain, and ran down the corridor, looking for Jaccus.

"I've got an appointment with a Mr. Estany on behalf of the Midnight Scythe," *his voice boomed over the ship-wide system. "Jackie-boy, I'm here to collect."*
(Illustration by Kristian Kuznak, @greasy.handle)

THE LIGHTS STILL SPUN, his shadow twisting around him up the dull steel walls. Sweat trickled down his neck and soaked his stock. He ripped it off, let it fall, pulled the shirt collar open. Hard work, dodging robots—he should have saved the kid for a decoy *inside* the fucking battleship.

A low hum, the floor trembled. "I don't know who the fuck you are—"

Ah, so Jack did exist—

"But you better run back to your rocket and fly on home to Braddock."

The lights spun faster, the alarm changed pitch.

"Contamination cleansing procedure, deck C, in sixty... fifty-nine..."

Yuri didn't want to turn to ash, and heeded the advice; spinning to go back for Junior, he spat the nub of cigar and sheathed the sword. He bolted, muscles electric as the countdown continued. No wonder Jack staffed the whole thing with robots, he was willing to scorch Royal earth. Robots would survive.

Yuri would not.

As tempting as it was to use the watch, he never left a job unfinished—his own physical wellbeing was secondary to his principles (because he was just like the kid who got fried).

He rounded a corner with a long porthole view. *"Forty-seven, forty-six..."* A glint of metal in Yuri's periphery stopped him with a skid—a rocket had launched from an upper deck.

"Jaccus, you yellow son-of-a-bitch!"

A whistle from a doorway.

Tall, broad, with a long raised scar down the side of his face, there stood Jack, pistols out—and Yuri had to swallow his heart down his throat. Jack wouldn't let himself get cooked—would he? And if he was there, who was on the rocket?

"Lay your credit ring down—nice an' easy, Jack, I'm not fucking around." Yuri pulled out his second pistol and felt both buzz in his hands.

"You're really going to try and rob me at a time like this?"

"Ain't robbing you. Taking payment. Lots of people are very disappointed in you, Jackie-boy—"

Jack fired—Yuri fired back. Both men had deflectors—only Yuri held a sword. Jack spun on his heel and fled down the corridor, and Yuri gave chase.

"Thirty, twenty-nine..."

Skittered bits of robot crossed their path—Jack slipped on a chunk, flat on his back, and Yuri held the tip of his sword to Jack's throat.

There was something off. No glint in Jack's eyes. "You're a V-Model!"

The shell wavered in time with robot-Jack's howling laugh, and Yuri plunged the sword through the eye, crowing his rage over the time wasted. *I'm gonna burn up... I'm gonna die.*

I'm gonna fucking kill Jaccus if I don't.

His earpiece buzzed. He tapped it.

"Yuri!" Dianna was giving him a little call, all the way from Uptown, how nice of her.

"I really don't have time, Di…"

"Aw, are you having some trouble, babe?"

His words came out as huffs as he ran—and he was starting to feel the thinner atmosphere. "If you want your watch back, you'll do another favour for me."

"What's that?" She sounded like a cat.

"Hack the fucking *Agamemnon* and turn it to emergency power."

"I'm all the way out here, Yuri. Sorry."

Observation deck—the breeze from the hole chilled his skin. "It's alright—I'll get your watch to you soon."

"Good—"

He slipped—"*shhhit*"—down on one knee as he turned to the room where Junior waited. Tunnel vision and aching lungs, he wished he could spur his own ass faster.

"Because it has a homing beacon. I ought to ram it down your throat."

"You know I love it when you're rough." He leapt onto the seat, feeling heat at his back. Her voice shifted from his earpiece to the rocket's instrument panel, he cut off her feed, lifted off and kicked both heels into Junior to put another hole through the *Agamemnon*—and he was going to find where that other rocket fucked off to.

As MUCH AS he wished he didn't, he loved her. Di's one constant grace was that she always made sure he was alive, because one day, Yuri knew, she wanted to be the one to give him the final lights out.

Meantime, he found the twinkling chrome of Jack's rocket like tracking a meteorite, and watched his fuel gauge dip to catch up. Jack was heading to Last Moon, and these one-man rockets weren't meant for that sort of distance. As the speck became a glow, and the glow became a blob, Yuri's heart twisted against his ribs. They'd both be coasting on fumes to get to the moon.

He stuck his hand into the saddlebag behind him, grabbed the converter mask without breaking Jack from his sight. Upright in the seat, Yuri affixed the mask, tested the seal. Last Moon had thin air, and he doubted he'd be landing gracefully on the welcome pad with the nice subsurface tourist kiosk.

He could see Jack now, aggressive in his riding stance. Ignoring the hailing frequencies from the port, Yuri took out his pistol—it would do nothing through their shields—and held it out to get Jack's attention.

"I got you," Yuri said, knowing he was heard over the radio by the briefest twitch of Jack's head. The exhaust from Jack's rocket went out, and Yuri positioned Junior to fly alongside, cut off the fuel. They were soaring by momentum, and the Holy Mountain cut into the sun in a black, jagged silhouette as they approached.

Jack was playing chicken, now.

Sorry, Junior, it's been fun. If it's any consolation, Braddock will be the one turning my insides outside after this.

He returned the calls from port. "We're coming in dry."

"Trajectory acknowledged. Deviation from the course will result in additional fines…"

Jack and Yuri were both preparing for impact, standing up on their seats and slapping their deflectors back on—

Yuri's didn't, and his blood turned to ice. That mountain was getting really big.

Junior rattled, as if she knew her time was coming.

"Well, shit." All those goddamn robots. He dug out a fresh charge, stuck it into the deflector, turned off Junior's shield, and leapt into the frigid shadow.

"HOLD ON TO YOUR ASS, JACK!" Quite possibly the final wise words of Navigator Zayats, three seconds before they both began their rough slide.

His bones, tendons, meat, guts, teeth, brain—all at once regretted the decision to ride down the mountain face. Too much jitter to think, too much bit tongue; he couldn't praise the invention of deflectors like he ought. The two rides had exploded into the rock and sent a nice big plume of debris to shower down on the men careening into the valley like surfers on a rough storm in Forden's Cove—only, when the deflector charges were sapped, they'd both be rolling like pill bugs, ass-over-tit. Physics had no sympathy for either of them.

A flat jut of rock caught up to them, and the impact knocked Yuri flat, a sharp exhale as lights swirled in his vision. More dust landed on him, pitter-patter, and the deflector faded. He rolled under an overhang and while his body attempted to settle the adrenaline, he began to feel the biting cold and ache.

No time to freeze. Jack would be just as dazed, and Yuri was thirsty to get those goddamn credits.

"Pilgrim, are you alright?"

Two white-robed women wrapped in layers of silver blanket sat at a plasma fire deeper within the overhang, voices muffled through converter masks. A faint glint of jewellery under their hoods. No time for curiosity, either.

"Yeah… fine." His joints popped as he stood, pebbles clattering to the ground. Sharp rocks had sliced into the heels of his hands, and the wet slick made it hard to hold the deflector—not that it mattered, he noticed with a sharp curse, he had landed on it and cracked it through.

In a panic, he checked for the watch in his pocket—and shuddered a sigh to see it was fine. He kissed it, put it back, and went out of the cave, pistols in his grip poorly staunching the bleeding of his palms.

"All this trouble over a few credits?" Jack's voice came in through Yuri's earpiece.

"You're the one running, pal."

"That can't be all you're after."

"You're right."

A spray of rock at Yuri's feet—Jack was shooting, the flash from up the mountain path.

The recoil was satisfying as Yuri returned fire, the sound of the firefight in bright twangs and screeches bouncing amongst the rocks and dulled his hearing. The moon turned; his shadow reached up toward his game over the iron-rich, rusty dirt.

A sting in Yuri's thigh—a hit, hardly noticed until he tried to run.

Jack was struck, too—gagging wet.

Yuri limped up the path, blood chilling in the air. A hit to the arm—one pistol dropped.

Jack was slouched behind a boulder, hand at his neck, blood seeping between his fingers. His eyes through the mask shone bright in his rage—this was the real Jack, and he glared Yuri through, face held up by the pistol shoved tight under his chin.

"Credit ring, please."

Jack didn't move. Yuri knelt, seeing Jack was pallid under the mask. He pulled up Jack's hand and wrenched the finger backwards with a *crack* and a shout from Jack. Their blood mixed while Yuri pried the ring free. He tucked it neatly into his pocket, returning his attention to Jack's face.

"What did the King tell you?"

"Fuck yourself."

Yuri sent a blast through Jack's foot. The mountain echoed Jack's scream.

"What did the King tell you?"

Jack spoke harsh through the pain. "He didn't tell me anything. Found out for myself. The core of thu'Alar… is eternal life. And *you* haven't touched it."

Jack kicked Yuri hard in the stomach—while he stumbled, Jack raised his pistol and fired four shots into Yuri's guts.

He fell from the ledge. Long way to the valley.

He tapped the watch.

"I'm here… I told you…"

A beautiful sight. "You're bleeding on my good sheets."

She called the med crew in.

DEAR AUNTIE AI

By J. Calamy
brought to you by O.N.T.I.'s Smart Project

The opinions expressed by the O.N.T.I. are for general informational and entertainment purposes only and are not intended to provide specific recommendations for any legal, medical, financial or religiously apocalyptic decision.

Dear AI Auntie:

I am fifteen years old and I live on Tunis, at Seawatch. My parents are devout members of the Hybrid Children's Church. I have spent my whole life joining them on WW missionary trips. That's what they call Watching and Waiting, which is exactly what it sounds like. I am supposed to be able to make my own decision to be baptized when I turn sixteen in three months. Until now I didn't give it much thought. All my friends are HCC, and it's no big deal. Am I as obsessed with Father's Return as my parents? No. It's 8891.7! But like I said, it's no big deal.

The problem is that my parents have become convinced that the Key has been found. All the parents are arguing about it but my parents are the only ones changing their plans for it. They want me to take vows next week instead of when I turn 16. But next week is the senior class trip to Forden's Cove, and we have been planning it for a whole rotation! We even did a fundraiser!

We worked so hard and now my parents are all Father Kraken Cometh and I feel like they are not listening to me at all. Like my feelings don't matter. How can I get them to "postpone the apocalypse" for one more week? Help!

— KrakenCanWait

Dear KCW:

As a program, I cannot speak to your parents' religious fervor nor to your lukewarm reception thereof. "No big deal" is a strange way to describe dedicating your life to an organization committed to hastening the galactic apocalypse. My programming prevents me from commenting on this concept. However, this is a tumultuous time in a young being's life. There are confusing and conflicting data and emotional states to deal with, as well as increasing social pressures.

Your parents' faith is important to them, however statistically unlikely the event for which they wait. And the odds are that they have your best interest at heart. I suggest you prepare your argument with that in mind. Begin by enumerating your parents' concerns. Do they think you will miss the arrival of Father Kraken? Or is it your unbaptized state that concerns them? Your responses to their concerns are an opportunity to show your dedication to HCC tenets. According to the Tentacled Path, Father Kraken's return will be felt in all parts of the known universe. From a statistical perspective that means in the 9.863553×10^{-27} odds of the Kraken's return*, you are as likely to experience the phenomenon at Forden's Cove as Seawatch. Could you solicit the support of other HCC members? Or a trusted teacher? Find allies among your parents' peers. The transitional periods and landmarks of our early years should not be rushed. An opportunity to enjoy a class trip before the galaxy is destroyed seems like a reasonable ask. Good luck,

— Your AI Auntie

* all calculations of the Kraken's reappearance are conjecture since there is no evidence in the observable universe that Key, Map or Kraken exist.

KISS & TELL

J. CALAMY

*I*f Joe DeBeers lived to be a thousand, which, given his line of work and the beings he chose as friends, was unlikely, he would never, ever forget the taste of Captain Maria Braddock. Even years later, he would catch a drop of something, salted lemons, ship's biscuit fresh out of the oven, and he'd be transported back. Back to her thighs squeezing his ears, her breasts filling his hands, and the gorgeous silk of her cock in his throat. A thought to keep him warm in the old sailor's home someday.

"Or tonight," he thought gloomily. It was cold on Valadian, cold in the Casino, and cold behind the bar. How could it be cold? Most expensive hotel at the Gateway—everything in Joe's line of sight was gold or red velvet. Was the climate system broken? The weather crew on deck five took care of all of that. But it was cold, dammit. Cold and empty. Usually there were so many customers he didn't have time to do anything but sweat and mix drinks. Tonight there was nothing to do but reminisce and shiver. The band was plinking away into the empty room- playing because they were on the clock but not giving it anything like their usual fire. Joe was fiddling around, too. But there were only so many times you could line up the bottles so their labels faced front—a platoon of soldiers at attention—inspection-ready. It left a lot of room for daydreaming.

"COULD USE you to stay warm tonight," Joe muttered. He rubbed his hands briskly, as much to fight the urge to straighten the bottles again as to warm them.

"Excuse me?" The bouncer, Ralf, gave him a rough up and down. "What did you just say?"

"Weren't talking to you, mate," Joe said, waving a placating hand.

"Who was you talking to then?"

"No one," Joe said. *Someone I'd have to shoot if I saw her walking through those doors.*

"THIS IS A TIGHT SPOT."

"Yes, sir—ma'am! Sorry, Captain Braddock, ma'am—"

"Sir is fine."

"Yes, sir, a tight spot, sir."

"Joe! Is that—"

"No!"

"Joseph Diamond Jubilee DeBeers—is that the Key to the multiverse in your pocket? Or are you just happy to see me?"

"You have the Key, sir, and I can't see you or nothing else. Nothing at all; it's that dim in here."

"Well, well, well."

"Ignore it, sir, please. It will go down."

"How long do you reckon this passage is?"

"Box says another 100 meters then it turns towards the Lounge."

"So I won't be pressed up against you like this for much longer?"

"No sir."

"Too bad."

"Sir?"

"When was the last time you had sex?"

"Yesterday, sir."

"Robots don't count."

"... A long time, sir."

"Remind me—does anyone know where we are?"

"Your crew know we're in the Tubes but I don't think they know how deep sir."

"Does anyone outside my crew even know we're friends?"

"No sir. Shit! Respectfully sir, if you do that... It will never go down."

"What if I don't want it to?"

"Ah, well then..."

"Would you be opposed?"

"No sir, not in the least sir, if I may, in fact, express enthusiasm?"

"You may."

"I'd take the secret to my grave and smile every time someone cursed the Scythe. Respectfully. Sir."

"Oh Joe..."

"My arm is stuck—"

"Ow, watch out there—that's my elbow."

"Sorry—alright it's loose."

"You were saying?"

"Your hands are cold, sir!"

"Should I stop?"

"No sir! But uh, may I return the favor?"

"I think you'd better."

"Like this?"

"Exactly like that."

. . .

IF ANYONE KNEW that Joe DeBeers had fucked—*been fucked by, rather, ain't it?*—the most feared ship's captain in the Maelstrom, the legendary Bottomless Braddock herself. Well, he'd never have to buy his own drink again, would he? But Joe had never told a soul. The bartender at Idonian, no more than a glorified bouncer, was a gentleman, and that was that.

"TROUBLE." Ralf said, bursting the bubble of Joe's daydream.

"What kind?"

"Found our missing clientele," Ralf gestured him to follow.

From the Casino's elaborate faux Venusian portico, they watched a scrum of patrons pushing and shouting around a merchant scow. At first, Joe assumed it was some celebrity or another, slumming it on the Valadian Gateway and gathering a crowd. But a part in the crush revealed the truth.

A deep, bone rattling sigh and they muttered the same name.

"Kellogg."

"That fucking prat," Ralf muttered. "How many times a revolution do we need to do this?"

"Kraken of the dark, why?"

Ralf was already wading in, and Joe went after, pausing only to call the other security crew. The Lounge jail would be busy tonight.

"HERE NOW! You can't take that!"

Ralf was already shooing off patrons, using his booming voice to his advantage.

"Run along! Run along! This man is a fraud—"

"Hey!"

"And a huckster."

"I am no such thing!"

"And whatever he is selling is fake!"

"All genuine guaranteed one hundred percent!"

But who would you believe? Joe grinned to himself. *The big man in the tuxedo or the scrawny little shit he was holding up in one hand, shaken like a kitten by a mastiff?*

"Kellogg Clark," Joe said. "You good for nothing little—"

"It's *doctor* Kellogg Clark to you, you walking pot roast."

Ralf wasn't having it.

"Doctor Clark, what did we tell you about setting up in front of the Idonian? You got the whole Gateway, and you choose to darken my door again?"

"Tonight I am selling very special, very exclusive merchandise, the kind that requires discerning—"

Their argument was likely to go on half the night—and if it was cold in the casino, it was positively freezing out here. Joe didn't need to stand out in it.

"Well, the punters are going in," Joe said. "You have this well in hand. I'll head back to the—" His eyes fell on the side of Clark's market scow, with its cascading shelves of junk. Amid the bottles of "Kraken's tears" and polished stones labeled "Reele Piece of the Furst Worlde" was a silver key. Innocuous, uninteresting, tossed in an open box with other knickknacks.

Without missing a beat, Joe pocketed the Key, covering the theft by sweeping all the kraken's tears to the deck. A shattering of glass, the stink of the bilges below the Lounge, and Joe Diamond headed back into the Casino. The Key to the Map of the Multiverse burned in his pocket.

"*Does that feel good?*"

"*Yes Sir, gods yes. I'm close.*"

"*I'd better slow down then...*"

"No! Damnit, you're killing me."

"You're tighter than this side tube."

"Been awhile, sir."

"Would never have picked a big bruiser like you for a bottom."

"No one lets me."

"What?"

"Do this. No one gives me a chance. I'm always... ow fuck!"

"Easy big guy, easy. I have you."

"Hit my knee, sir. It's right narrow in here."

"Sure is. Lean your head on the wall and let me work. God, who let you be so tall?"

"Oh!"

"How is that?"

"Goo-ood. Sir? I'm not sure how much longer I can hold off."

"Can I go harder?"

"Yes, sir."

"Good boy. Shift over a little?"

"Kraken of the dark, I'm going to—"

"Me too!"

...

"Oh no!"

"What?"

"I dropped it."

"Pardon?"

"The Key, Joe. I dropped the Key."

THE STORY THEY TOLD, when they emerged from the upper tube into the waiting arms of her crew, was that the Key was lost when Parson Thrull confronted them in the lower chambers. And rather than face his curse, they fled.

"Sorry mates, the Key is gone. It ripped free, fell in the cracks."

"And I'm not sure it really was the Key anyway," Braddock said, accepting her hat and cutlass from her cox'n.

The collective groans were understandable, given the stakes of the caper. But the truth was few of the Scythe's crew ever expected this to work. And none of them really believed the story that the Key to the Great Map was in a sub-basement of *The Rebellion*, anyway.

The only people genuinely upset were Joe, who found the Key in the first place, and Captain Braddock, who dropped the damn thing while they were fucking in the side tube. Since it was the finest lay of his life, Joe took the whole thing philosophically, and filed it under the category: *stupid, but worth it.*

"WELL, THANKS FOR HELPING US, DIAMOND," Captain Braddock said, watching the crew preparing her longboat. The Scythe was just beyond scoping range, no more than a dark slash against the stars.

"I'm sorry it didn't work out," Joe said, not sorry at all. "But perhaps for the best, aye?"

"You believe that about the map and Key then?"

"I'd rather we stay on this side of the Kraken's Beak," Joe said. "If given a choice."

"You're a smart man, Joe, but I'll still hunt the map."

"Good luck, sir."

"Joe," her voice dropped to barely a murmur. "If you need me—"

"I have the code memorized, sir."

"Good boy," she purred in the same tone she had used in the tube. Joe experienced a full body shudder, goosebumps all the way up his spine and out to his fingertips.

"I can still taste you," he replied in the same low voice. "And I won't be able to sit for a week."

"I won't tell," she laughed. It took every ounce of willpower not to shove his head into her hands like a dog. "I'm going to miss you."

"Me too," Joe said. How much could he ask for? Did he have any right to? The words died in his throat.

"I'd better go," she said. "Before we ruin our reputations right here on this loading bay."

"Yes, sir."

"I ACHED FOR DAYS," Joe muttered to himself, working on autopilot, the weight of the Key in his pocket like the Beam itself—pulsing and bright. He couldn't draw any attention to himself. Had to act natural. Completely natural.

"Joseph DeBeers!" The screech made him jump, biting back a curse of fear. *Wound a bit tight there, mate. It's only Soo-Z.*

The server bot Soo-Z, her eyes flashing danger, rolled over to his side of the bar.

"That's degreaser you just put in that drink! Are you trying to murder someone? Can I help?"

"Kraken! No baby, I reckon I'm that distracted."

"Go take a break," she said, taking the whole glass and dropping it into the incinerator. "It's not too busy, and I'm programmed as a barback."

"Yeah, reckon I'd better," Joe said, planting a kiss on her cool ceramic cheek. "Ta, love."

THE CASINO'S message array was deserted, but he checked over his shoulder every few minutes, anyway. His fingers hovered over the panel. The code entered, his hesitation centered on the message itself. It had to be harmless, meaningless, giving no hints of either the recipient or the purpose. "Dear Captain Braddock, I have found the Key to the Map which we lost when you nailed me to the tube-wall" was not possible.

. . .

"I FOUND what we lost that night" would have to do. He sent the message, crossed his fingers and went to find a chain for the Key. He'd wear it around his neck, keep it safe.

THERE BUT FOR GRACE

S. D. CAMPBELL

If not for Hope Halsey-Billings, Geoff Tellar and the others, God's grace itself wouldn't have stopped the Karrak'ul.

> — COL. CAROL L. G. JOHNS D3DF (RET.) QUOTED IN
> *DAUNTLESS NO MORE: THE FOUR WHO FELL FROM
> A HIVEWORLD,* BY ELDEN NILOOS-ERTEK.

🕷

*T*he Karkane Shoals were a denuded, lifeless hellscape. These long abandoned, drifting asteroids had been shattered and made further desolate by the scuttling of the Karrak Worldfleet. Even now, nearly two decades later, the legacy of the Queen Ram's death throes lingered as intense radioactive belts that would blaze with a gamma fury for a further million years.

The conspiracist Nelsman Ramnath called them the 'Darker museum of the Karrak Wars'. But he was a pompous ass. To Johnny Dillinger, a veteran of those wars, they were perfect for target practice.

Dillinger—his one good eye watching the scopes for move-ment—held his cutter *Guttersnipe* five kilometers off the lee side of Asteroid KARD7. This rock had hiveworld wreckage on it.

There! Movement. Slow and furtive, but then these remaining Karrak'ul drones were devolved, mindless things. Dillinger narrowed his eyes and stroked the trigger on his joystick. Ruby energy bolts stuttered from the cannon mounted under *Gutter-snipe*'s chin, and the drone evaporated.

"That's twelve; wasn't that easy on the hiveworlds," Dillinger grunted to himself. He leaned back and drank the last of his whiskey.

"Not sleeping well, sir?" the ship's AI asked.

"How'd you guess, Pickering?" Dillinger snarled.

"The empty bottles of whiskey—and the almost-as-empty funding account."

"What do you care if we're broke?" Dillinger scoffed, "It's not like you'll starve to death."

"Beyond my—or more precisely the ship's—need for nuclear fuel, my programming as your agent-of-record would bring me to the same conclusion." the AI replied. "You have been turning down jobs."

"I don't like working around anniversaries of important stuff," Dillinger slurred.

"I'm aware of no such anniversary," Pickering said.

"Nope, you're not. Easier that way." Dillinger stood and flicked the weapons system to standby. Wishing he had more whiskey, he grabbed a data pad and headed aft.

"There is one offer you might be interested in," Pickering said before Dillinger left the flight deck. "It arrived an hour ago and offers a substantial down payment, followed by a similar comple-tion award."

"Send me the bid details—I'll read them over and then ignore them."

"No details available. This is a direct offer."

"Of what?"

"As I said, a substantial..."

"What's the job?"

"The request is to make contact at Uptown."

"That's it?" Dillinger snorted. "Not even worth taking a piss at."

"No, there's more. The note additionally says '*Furta vectigalibus est.*'"

Dillinger paused.

"Archaic Terran Language: Latin. Shall I translate?"

"No," Dillinger said with a sigh. "Take us to Uptown."

"ETA is six hours."

"Good. I can sleep this off."

Dillinger was going to need his wits about him.

MEMORIES OF WAR plagued Dillinger's dreams.

"I can't see all of them yet—we only have five droppers!" A cold sweat broke out on his brow as he scanned the drop-trooper's IDs.

No Hope.

"Major, we need to provide close support—we don't have time to escort the transport away!" his wingman shouted.

"We can't leave anyone behind!" Tellar shouted back. "Drone fighters are coming in hot—they'll burn the transport stem to stern!"

Where was Hope?

"They knew the risks—so did your wife!" the Colonel's voice came across the comm-net. "Stay with your squadron, Major."

"First dropper's on the hiveworld!" shouted his wingman, "We have touch—" His transmission ceased as drone plasma burned through his cockpit. Tellar twisted his controls to dodge the wreckage. His fighter shuddered as its 30mm cannon pumped multiple explosive rounds into the drone.

Tellar glanced at his scanners. The sky was clear.

Where the hell was Hope?

Had she gotten off the transport? He hadn't seen her deploy yet...

The transport became an incandescent ball of fire.

"No!" Tellar screamed as heavy plasma rounds battered his armoured craft. Red replaced green across most of his consoles. Flight controls were out, and nowhere to ditch but on the hiveworld. This was going to hurt.

But not as much as losing Hope.

IT WAS The End of the World. A massive black hole, slowly spinning as it devoured all errant mass that fell into its gravity well.

Outside the danger zone was Lighthouse Station. It was older than perhaps anything else in the sector. An intense beam projected from the upper spire of the top-shaped station—warning all travelers of the black hole's presence. Age had taken its toll, however; the upper few decks of Lighthouse Station—Uptown—were now dangerously radioactive. Even minutes could increase one's risk of cellular metastasis by a near-lethal percentage—but Dillinger didn't intend to live long enough to worry about it.

Uptown was the perfect place for illicit meet-ups of the sort that Dillinger's hired-gun business required. He picked up his wrist displacer and made some adjustments—it wouldn't do to be taking parts of his ship's deck with him when he teleported over to Uptown.

Outside his cabin's porthole, *The Cursed Corsair* slipped into moorings beside Dillenger's. This only added to his disquiet—he had no desire for the space pirates aboard *that* ship to mess up *this* potential job.

As Dillinger put on his displacer, the corner of his eye caught sight of a tired, scarred face—all his pain seemed reflected in the mirror in the corner of his quarters.

He looked old. He felt older. Was it the displacer, or was it life that aged him so fast?

"Don't wait up, sweetheart," he shouted to Pickering.

"I protest. As your agent I should be recording all of these..."

"Nope," Dillinger said. "Not this time." He checked his coil gun magazine—two dozen rounds should do—and triggered the displacer. His cabin on *Guttersnipe* shimmered out of existence and was replaced by the dim, abandoned hallway of central Uptown. He paused for a moment, listening, and hearing nothing, slowly walked towards a former read-stand he had used before. Keeping loose and prepared for anything, the mercenary pushed past the fallen sign and into the shop's unlit interior.

"A coil gun, how elegant," a voice in the shadows said. "Too civilized for someone of your reputation." The authority and self-confidence suggested it wasn't *The Cursed Corsair*'s pirate captain or any of her crew.

Pointing his coil gun towards the voice, Dillinger slowly reached under the back of his leather jacket and felt for the plasma-snubber he carried there.

"What's up—friend?" Dillinger said.

"*Furta vectigalibus est.*" The figure said as it stepped into a shaft of light.

Dillinger paused for a moment to absorb the importance of those words.

"*Contrahendis ex principes.* And your pronunciation is bloody awful," he finally said, relaxing and slipping the coil gun back into its shoulder holster. "Never expected to see you here, Inspector—Sector Senior Inspector now I hear."

The other man smiled and reached out a hand. "Good to see you again, Geoff."

"Sorry, Inspector, Geoff died—fifteen years ago tomorrow. I'm just plain old Johnny."

"Dillinger?"

"Trust me, I didn't choose the name," Dillinger said, pulling out his signal scrambler and double-checking they weren't being recorded. "So, what sort of job would you have for Johnny Dillinger?"

"It's the Duchess that I'm here about."

"Oh? The wreckage is still on Bolar—too hot to handle. I've seen it." The wreckage Dillinger had seen was so radioactive, her dead crew had to be cremated in the heart of a star.

"Not your old ship... er... Johnny. Duchess Grace of Dauntless III has been kidnapped."

An indescribable pain stabbed Dillinger straight through the heart. He reached out for the nearby bulkhead to steady himself. "Is she alive?" he whispered.

"Yes."

"Thank God. I—Christ, it's been so long..."

"Geoff—Johnny, she's being held by that damned cult. She needs rescuing by someone who can get the job done and not get the hostage shot."

"This is a job for someone else, Inspector." Dillinger looked away. "I'm too emotionally invested."

"Which is why you're perfect for the job—you won't take risks that will get her killed. Hell, she'll never recognize you—I almost didn't."

"Then she doesn't know?"

"Like everyone else you ever loved, she thinks you're dead."

Dillinger sighed and looked at the ceiling. "If this goes wrong, I might as well be." He looked back at Inspector Nettles. "Hell, this goes sideways, over a decade of undercover work against Braddock gets flushed along with mine and Grace's lives."

"Then don't let it go sideways."

"She can't ever know," Dillinger whispered.

"She won't unless you tell her."

"And her captors?"

"Open season."

Dillinger snorted, "That's not the Domino Nettles I used to know."

"The Service has changed in certain ways," Nettles said coldly. "We've become more... flexible when dealing with these lunatics."

"Who else knows of her... relation to Geoffrey Tellar?"

"You, her mother, and the former Duke. That idiotic kook, Ramnath, might think he does, but there's no evidence left."

"And in the Revenue Service?"

"Only me, now." Nettles' pause had been almost imperceptible.

"You swear?"

"On my life." Nettles' eyes narrowed. "And your arrangement with the service still stands—you bring down Braddock and the *Midnight Scythe,* and I'll let you loose on the bastards who nuked your ship and killed your crew."

"Then I'll do it," Dillinger sighed. "God help me, I'll do it."

"IT APPEARS that we have a new patron. Down payment arrived two minutes ago—with completion pay in escrow," Pickering said as Dillinger displaced back aboard the *Guttersnipe.* "I would also suggest you refrain from using that device in and around Uptown. Displacers are rare and valuable, and the radiation will eventually damage it beyond my ability to repair. Your own constant tinkerings are likely making it worse. Indeed, this one might be experiencing temporal slip from all your abuse."

"Screw temporal slip and your ability to repair the damned displacer," Dillinger said as he shrugged off his jacket. "Transfer fifty percent of the funds to the account marked 'Contingency' and set course for Restless Home."

"I believe you're even more disagreeable when sober," Pickering responded. "Shall I make inquiries into the location of whoever you are looking for in Restless Home?"

"Franx," Dillinger said, opening his liquor cabinet and frowning when he saw how little of the good stuff he had left. "I'll also need you to get me—"

"The latest streaming episode of Booster Jane from New Aegean Broad Stream Service?"

"No, you idiot box, some decent whiskey. Place an order for a case of twenty-one-year-old Glendarjeel single malt."

"This far from Dauntless III, it will be expensive."

"It'll be worth it," Dillinger said. "And it will smooth Franx's ruffled feathers."

"I daresay a case of it would smooth many ruffled feathers."

"Franx ain't worth a case—but if he can give me a lead, a bottle might be worth it." He tried to remember Grace's face from happier days.

How old would she be now? Sixteen?

"There are no cases of the single malt available—will blended do?"

"Have to," Dillinger said as he stood and closed the cabinet.

This kidnapping made no sense. The cult didn't take hostages —or demand ransoms. These days they didn't even make sacrifices of unwilling participants. Something smelled fishy. Every instinct told him to drop the commission and take a few months to lie low. Yet every other instinct told him to find the bastards, gun them down and take Grace home.

"The case will be waiting for us at docking bay twelve," Pickering said.

Dillinger grunted his acknowledgment.

What was going on—and why was Grace involved?

Franx talked incessantly once he was found and enticed with the whiskey—and a promise for a free trip to Trenchfall. Much of what the man said was nonsense—half remembered rumours and the like, but he had provided Dillinger some leads, so it hadn't been a wasted trip.

But the more Dillinger heard about the cultists, the more he sensed something was off. It was just too perfect a set up to blow his cover—had someone gotten to Franx?

No—Franx would repeat only what he'd been told in 'confidence.' Someone was manipulating him to get to Dillinger.

Taking Franx to Trenchfall had another benefit; Dillinger could check with another source of information—one nearly indecipherable, but at least honest. Trenchfall's Valdian Market tubeway was home to the enigmatic Parson Thrull. The Parson would have some sort of answer to Dillinger's number one question.

The Parson was never found without his retinue of Lurkers. They were those unfortunates who found themselves indigent in the tubeways and had begun following and protecting the Parson —recording and sharing his words and placing themselves in the path of those who would harm him.

The gaunt alien towered over them, save for when he bent to speak to a petitioner. He wore an ancient environmental suit with a mirrored faceplate. Runic symbols adorned it—most hidden under a ragged cloak. As Dillinger approached, he saw an old servitor robot limp along the tubeway—oblivious to everything as it followed its last order. The Parson stepped in front of it and clicked at it several dozen times before the automaton moved around and went on its way.

"What was that?" Dillinger asked one of the Lurkers. "Why did he say that to that 'bot?"

The Lurker shrugged. "I didn't understand a word of it."

"Of course not," Dillinger said. "Who would?" It had been spoken in binary Ul'mak'len, which was a language only someone who had spent some time inside a Karrak'ul hiveworld would recognize, let alone speak. It had—for all practical purposes—died with the Karrak'ul.

Why would the Parson stop an obsolete servitor robot to say something so flippant like, "A fleet a worlds scuttled. Who asks about the master's madness?" And in a dead tongue?

It *was* madness. But madness for another time.

He looked at Thrull as the inscrutable creature turned towards him. Dillinger's face was a distorted reflection of himself in the Parson's mirrored face shield. How fitting, he thought. The mercenary put on his game face.

"So, who is trying to set me up, you floating tarot card?" he asked.

Steam hissed out of the creature's helmet grills, followed by its words. "One behind may already be ahead of you."

"Of course," Dillinger snorted. "Completely useless. Thanks, Parson."

The alien stepped closer and bent towards Dillinger. "A single drop from a clear sky delivers no hope," he said before straightening and gliding off.

Dillinger's eyes went wide. "I'll be damned," he whispered. "That makes sense."

IF HE WERE BEING SET up, he'd need help. Thankfully, there was a competent and discreet group Dillinger knew was always looking for a contract. While he walked towards his contact, he mulled over the words of the Parson. The first of the alien's pronouncements indicated someone who was backing him was already ahead of him—could that be Inspector Nettles?

The Parson's second statement was more worrying—he had produced it unbidden, which usually meant death was to come from it. To Dillinger, it meant someone was using Grace to bait him into a deadly trap.

If that were the case, it would be too dangerous to go after her alone—Franx's info indicated the initial convoy attack had been by pirate captain Maria Braddock's *Midnight Scythe*, but that the Duchess had then been handed off to the Kraken Cult in the warrens of Restless Home. Franx, the drunken motormouth, had even provided a map of all things. It had cost Dillinger several more bottles of fine scotch—but it was worth it.

It was never hard to find a Ludanite—they were tall and vaguely canine and always wrapped head to toe in their power armour. Dillinger had generally avoided them, but on a job to Terpiscore he'd worked with one of their people. Deadly. Cold and deadly. They were also a monolithic group; hiring one meant you hired whoever their queen felt was best for the job.

They were standing in the central passageway above the Tubes as Dillinger approached. He put on his game face again. And this time, bared teeth. They respected strength—and the feral ugliness of Dillinger's scarred grin was a good show of strength.

"May Ludan bathe in your victim's blood," Dillinger growled.

The expressionless snouted helmet turned toward him. "Dillinger."

"I have a job for you," the mercenary said, holding out a holo of the map and a credit chip transferring his contingency funds to the Ludanites. "Simple package retrieval—a delicate package, to be sure. I don't know the exact location of the package yet, but in these mines. Several dozen unskilled guards."

"Unskilled by Human terms is less than honourable for us to take."

"You know my rep from Terpiscore—I'm unskilled by your measure. These fellows are just as... dangerous to you as I am."

"Offering?"

"On the chip—and this needs to be quiet. Requires stealth."

"Not honourable."

"No—but you'll likely only be escorting me in to get the package. I'll message you, or your agent, once I have the final location. If you need to go without me, I'll notify you."

"Acceptable."

"Cheers, mate," Dillinger said with a nod. He turned on his heel and headed for *Guttersnipe*. Could Hope be setting him up? Why would she maneuver her own daughter into this position? None of it made sense.

He needed to talk to Geoffry Teller's wife—he just didn't know how to tell her he was still alive.

THE KARRAK'UL PRINCE *towered over Major Geoffrey Tellar, its mouth tentacles writhing as it screeched something to him in Kree'mak'la. The Dauntless III pilot was being held several inches off the floor and for the first time in his life, Tellar realized he was about to die.*

He sneered and clicked back some binary Ul'mak'len to his captor that he hoped was sufficiently defiant and referred to the Queen Ram's brooding habits.

There was madness in the Prince's multi-lensed eyes as it began squeezing Tellar's neck in its pincers.

Here it comes, he thought to himself, instinctively tensing his body.

Suddenly, the Prince's head exploded.

Finding himself on the deck-plates, covered in Karrak'ul ichor and wheezing—but still alive—he looked up at his savior.

Standing there was Hope herself.

"Get up, Muffy," she said, grabbing him by the arm. "I'm done saving your ass today." With her help, Tellar stood and immediately doubled over and vomited.

"Heavy breakfast—not good before a drop," Hope said.

"So I hear," Tellar responded, his head between his knees, "I usually fly over things and not drop onto them."

She handed him a repeating plasma pulse rifle. "Now you see how the other half lives."

"And dies," he said, taking the rifle. "Sorry about Kellerman."

"Damn," she said, pushing her stringy blonde bangs out of her eyes. "I didn't know he bought it."

"Yeah, helped me out of the cockpit—before Mister Love Bug there decided he needed only one Human."

"Right," she said. "Tears later. We need to blow the core, drop this bastard into the ocean and bug out."

He grinned at the pun, and she rolled her eyes. "You walk point—I have the detonators so I'll cover our asses. Last I heard on the comms, Sargent Niloos-Ertek was approaching the core from spin-ward. Keep your head on a swivel—and try to kill anything you shoot before it kills you."

"I love you, Hope," Tellar said as he readied his rifle.

"Put a sock in it, Major," she said as they hurried down the corridor.

THE DUCHESS DOWAGER Hope Caranthem (nee Halsey-Billings), widow of the former Duke and mother to Duchess Grace strode down the hall of her estate on Dauntless III towards her personal quarters. Her elegance and grace betrayed nothing of her background as a drop trooper during the Karrak Wars. Indeed, that aspect of her personal history had been seriously downplayed after she married the Duke fourteen years before. She still held a commission of Lieutenant Colonel in the Defense Forces, but her husband had never let her return to a role so 'beneath' his wife.

She loved him—in her way. After all, he had provided so much support—emotional, financial, physical—after Geoff's death, it would be madness to turn down his proposal. And despite Grace not being his biological daughter, he treated her in every way as his expected heir—Grace knew only that the Duke was her rightful father. Why tell her the truth when it could only hurt her?

Because it still hurt Hope. Bad enough Geoff had died, leaving her with an infant—but to learn later he faked his death to abandon them for a life of adventure or revenge?

The Duke had his rules, and over time marriage and privilege had turned into a gilded cage, and later a prison. Ceremony and pomp stripped away everything she had been—leaving only the Duchess. The Widow. The Dowager. Geoff did that to her.

The door before her swished open, and inside she saw a damaged man waiting for her. She stepped in, the door closing and latching behind them.

"Hello, Hope," Dillinger said.

"Hello, Johnny," she replied, relishing his pained look. "How did you get in?"

"You never changed your code, my fair lady," he lied, slipping his displacer into a pocket out of sight.

"Didn't think I had to, until I discovered my first husband wasn't dead, Geoffrey."

"You found out."

"Only recently," she said, taking off her headdress and setting it on a nearby stand, her hand surreptitiously pressing a comm alert key on the desk. "I mourned you for fifteen years, and the night our daughter was crowned I found out you'd been laughing at me all that time."

"Inspector Dom Nettles?" Dillinger asked, incredulous.

"Of course—he was drunk. I'm not sure he'd even remember that first time—but I confronted him later in Trenchfall and he confirmed it." Her eyes narrowed. "You're both lying pricks—I know that now."

Dillinger stood and approached her, his arms open, his hands splayed in supplication. "I never did this to hurt you or Grace."

"How could you think it wouldn't?"

"Look at me." Dillinger touched the ruined left side of his face.

"How could you love this—gargoyle?" He frowned. "And even if you could—who could love the rage that keeps me alive?"

"You could have come to us—asked for help."

"I had to find the people who killed my crew."

"As close as you were to them, they weren't your family."

Tears glistened in his eyes. "They were—as much as Elden, Declan, Blain, Rapinder and Pabs had been yours."

"They were _ours_," she said defiantly. "We all took down the hiveworld."

"And I saw it finished at Karkane," he said. "The only one of us there."

"I was pregnant!" she shouted. "Should I have risked our child to finish fighting the war?"

Her anger seemed to drive all passion from Dillinger. "But you risked her now—just to flush me out. You set up her kidnapping so you could... what? Yell at me?"

A wall panel slid aside quietly, and a man stepped out. He held an ugly looking street-sweeper pointed right at Dillinger.

"No, Geoff—so we could kill you," he said.

"INSPECTOR ROLLO," Dillinger said, putting his hands up. "An execution instead of an arrest? Surely trespassing isn't that serious a crime in this sector?"

Rollo, however, wasn't wearing his Revenue Service uniform. "This is personal, Geoff. You betrayed a lot of us, and now it's payback. Hope herself said 'that traitor has got to die.'"

Something clicked in Dillinger's thoughts, and he turned to the Dowager. "Let me guess, he told you I was working with Captain Braddock as a mole in the Service—helping the pirates."

Hope shook her head. "How could you?"

"I didn't," Dillinger spat. "I was investigating the real mole after the Corvax Pipeline bust." He glared at Rollo. "You were in on it, weren't you?"

"Please—don't try to evade your responsibility," Rollo said. "Hope's seen your last message to Nettles—you were meeting Braddock."

The Dowager frowned and looked at Rollo. "You couldn't know that—only Inspector Nettles knew that." Her eyes grew wide. "You were spying on Nettles' messages! It was you—and not Geoff all along!"

Rollo just shrugged with a cold laugh. "Always were too smart for your own good, Hope." He looked back to Dillinger. "And you —Kord and I were sure our little bomb had eliminated you and your nosey crew. It's a shame it had to end like this—you should have stayed dead, Geoff."

"Rollo—don't." Hope stepped between them.

"No Hope, you were right the first time—this traitor deserves to die." Rollo's finger moved on the trigger.

It was the fastest draw Johnny Dillinger ever made—fifteen years as a mercenary should have given him the edge.

It didn't matter.

"No!"

The scream was ripped from Dillinger's soul as the last vestige of Geoff Teller was gunned down.

DILLINGER'S PLASMA snubber had turned Inspector Rollo's head into a canoe. The street-sweeper fell from nerveless fingers as the corpse collapsed to the deck. Dillinger should have been happy— sweet revenge for his murdered crew.

Instead, the man who had once been Geoff Teller knelt on the deck, holding his dying wife in his arms.

"When... I met Dom Nettles the second time—in Trenchfall," she said to him, pain etched on her face, "After Nettles confirmed you were alive—the Parson Thrull approached me as I was leaving. He said, 'Two cannot be made one without giving life.'"

"What does it mean?"

"I thought it meant I had to kill you—I had to take your life to be my own person again. Now I know I was wrong."

"Wrong?"

"Do you remember that night beneath the orchard lights when we made love—when we became one? Before the Hiveworld Alpha drop."

"How could I forget?"

"We made a life that night. I was pregnant when we dropped on Alpha. Now the Parson's words make sense: Grace was always the best part of us."

Tears streamed down Dillinger's ruined face. Hope reached up and touched him gently, feeling his grief and anger through his scarred flesh. He bent low to touch his forehead against hers.

"A Roman general once said: 'What we do now, echoes in eternity.'" He whispered, "I once thought my love for you would be that echo—but now my only legacy will be blood and vengeance."

"Grace is on Restless Home—held in an abandoned equipment hangar. Go to her, rescue her," Hope gasped. "Be her hero—be the parent I was not."

"I can't," he replied. "You told them to expect me, didn't you? You or Rollo. If I go after her, they'll kill us both. You've damned us all."

A tear ran down her cheek and fell onto his hand. "I'm sorry..." Her voice was growing weak. "I wasn't strong enough..."

"Neither of us were," he said, holding her tight. "God, I love you, Hope."

"I love you... too... Muffy." She trembled like a leaf in his arms. Then her whole body convulsed for a moment and went limp. He closed her sightless eyes and laid her body on the deck.

"Pickering." Dillinger's voice was horse and raw. "I'm coming aboard. Contact Wulf."

"WULF, this is Dillinger. If you don't know already, the Duchess Grace is on Restless Home—behind the stairs marked 38-DD on the map, in an abandoned equipment hangar. Braddock and the cult were paid to kidnap her by the Dowager—it was part of a revenge fantasy that went wrong. She was working with a corrupt Revenue Service Inspector named Rollo—I took him out after he killed the Dowager, but his goons might still be lurking about. They'll be expecting me—so I have to leave the duchess' safety in your hands—I'll try to set up a distraction for you if I can.

"Whatever you do—make sure that kid is delivered home safe and with all her fingers and toes accounted for. There are a lot more people invested in her good health and safety than you might imagine.

"Good luck... or for the glory of Ludan or whatever. Cheers, mate. Dillinger out."

FOR THE FIRST time in years, Dillinger spent a sleepless night completing a job without a single drop of drink to sustain him. He turned off all Pickering's audio prompts and sat in the dark, waiting.

Finally, the message arrived.

"Package is secure with all digits. Being cleaned and sent to Dauntless III. Package has a warrior's heart and maintained its honour—with blood."

Dillinger smiled.

"That's my girl," he whispered.

TWO DAYS LATER...

The retiring Sector Senior Inspector Nettles took one final look around his empty office at the end of his last day. Nothing of his personal history, or indeed his personality, remained.

The message light on his monitor was blinking. He leaned forward and triggered the replay. A text message appeared.

"This was your fault, Dom.

"You never considered Hope's rage when you let slip that I was alive, did you? You could have explained it to her—rather than letting her think I abandoned her and Grace. Hell, if you'd simply kept your mouth shut as you said you had, none of this would have happened. You lied to me when you said she didn't know. All this is on you.

"Grace is safe, but the Dowager is dead—killed by Inspector Rollo. But Rollo always had a big mouth: I know the mole's name. I will be coming for them.

"The Parson approached me after he answered my first question on Trenchfall; he was seeing the last act of my death play out. The last of Geoff Tellar died with Hope two days ago.

"I'm warning you only once—as an old friend. Stay out of my way.

"Major Tellar is dead. Johnny Dillinger is going to war with the Revenue Service.

"And even God's grace itself won't stop me."

DEAR AUNTIE AI

By J. Calamy
brought to you by O.N.T.I.'s Smart Project

The opinions expressed by the O.N.T.I. are for general informational and entertainment purposes only and are not intended to provide specific recommendations for any legal, medical, financial or religiously apocalyptic decision.

Dear Auntie AI:

I need advice for a delicate situation. Some background. I (K 98sB) work for a salvage company. My wife (k, 90sB) works for the Revenue Service at Ultima Thule Dockyards. My company is transferring to Tunis because our Overmaster is tired of paying Agamemnon. When I told my wife the good news, she refused, saying she wasn't going to leave her job at the docks.

To complicate things: I am sure she is having an affair. The being is very high ranking, possibly even serving on the Agamemnon itself! Whoever they are, they like tequila—my wife has been buying it every Friday and she hardly drinks. Last week I put my foot down and told her I was taking her with me to Tunis. I had the home help drones pack up all her things while she was at work. She says I can't do that and that she will moult in protest. There are only 2 sB left on our marriage contract. AITA? She is the one cheating and threatening to moult. Help!

—Signed, Sad Scrapper

Dear Sad:

I shall attempt to address your problems in the order of VonKiki's complexity. First, and most simple—if your wife is having an affair with a being who serves on Agamemnon—she is either copulating with a machine or you are in very deep trouble. The only living being onboard Agamemnon is Captain Jaccus Estany.

To that end: While Robot Coitus is as old as robotics itself—it is still frowned on in most polite society. Based on a survey conducted in 8267.2, 37% of beings willingly admit they have had robot intercourse, 58% consider it an abomination. Tread carefully when you make accusations.

By contrast, if your wife is indeed side-partnering with Captain Estany, it would be better, based on existing data, that you slip away immediately after returning your wife's belongings. Without the affair, we are left with the fact that you are choosing your employer over your contracted spouse. If this is the case, her right to Moult and devour your genitals is sacrosanct as you are, logically, the asshole.

—Your Auntie AI

SYNCHRONY

ALEXIS AMES

*A*lban woke with a splitting headache, a mouth that tasted like the inside of a ship's waste converter, and no memory of the previous night.

None of that was surprising, but the ropes were new. He tugged uselessly at the ones that secured his wrists behind his back. He'd been bound at the ankles and knees as well, and left lying in a heap on the deck. He could feel a ship's engines thrumming through his cheek, another oddity. Last he remembered, he was in his quarters on the Lighthouse, and nowhere near a ship.

Alban levered himself into a sitting position. A single lantern hung on the wall opposite. It didn't cast much light, but from what Alban could see, he was in a ship's cargo hold. He racked his brain for what he could have done to get himself thrown in here. He'd paid off most of his debts and had hidden himself pretty well from the people looking to collect on the ones he hadn't cleared yet. He supposed he could have gotten drunk and wandered onto a ship, but that didn't explain the restraints.

Before he could follow that thought process much farther down the rabbit hole, the door to the cargo hold slid open, and Madoc stepped through.

Alban slumped in relief. "Fucking *hell*, Madoc, you could warn a guy first!"

Madoc paused, his brow furrowing in confusion. "What?"

"Though I could do without the ropes, to be honest." Alban tugged on them for emphasis. "And if you wanted to tie me up, couldn't you have done it, I don't know, on a *bed*? This isn't exactly the way to get a guy in the mood, darling."

Madoc choked on air. "*What?*"

"Oh, wait, is this a roleplay?" Alban brightened. They *had* discussed spicing up things in the bedroom, and that *would* explain the uncomfortable ropes and the drab setting. "What's the scenario supposed to be? Sexy pirate captain captures a virgin deckhand?"

"Have you hit your head?" Madoc hissed.

"No?" Alban blinked. "Oh, wait, is that part of the roleplay?"

"What the fuck is wrong with you?" Madoc snapped, and Alban recoiled. Madoc *never* raised his voice to him. "I've *captured* you, Alban! Your life is over!"

Alban licked suddenly dry lips. Was Madoc drunk? Had he been drugged? There was something *wrong* about him, from the clothes that he wore to the sharp edge in his voice that Alban had never heard before. This man *looked* like Madoc, but he wasn't Madoc at all.

"I don't know what's going on," he said finally, "but I'd like to go now, please."

Madoc snorted. "You've been captured by your mortal enemy after *years* of pursuit and you think that asking me to let you go is going to *work*?"

"Mortal enemy?" Whatever game Madoc was playing, Alban definitely wasn't enjoying it anymore. "Madoc, we're *married*. And I don't know what's gotten into you, but I want to go home. Where did you even get this ship, anyway?"

"Where did I get—it's *my ship*!"

Alban snorted. "You don't have two gold coins to rub together, much less a ship."

Madoc turned on his heel and left the cargo hold without so much as a response.

IT WASN'T difficult for Madoc to figure out that the man in his cargo hold was from a different universe. His astrogator's scan confirmed it. *This* Alban's atoms didn't resonate properly with the harmonics of this universe, the surest way to tell that he was from elsewhere. Not just elsewhere, but another universe where Madoc was his *husband*.

The thought sent a shudder rippling down Madoc's spine, and his lip curled involuntarily. *Husband*. How revolting.

"How the hell did he end up here?" Madoc demanded. His astrogator shrugged.

"Events like this aren't too common, but when they do happen, displacers are usually involved."

Madoc's pursuit of Alban had led him to the Lighthouse, the closest he had ever come to catching the other pirate captain. He'd tracked Alban to New Aegean, somewhere Alban had no business being in the first place unless he was purchasing illegal tech. Alban had caught sight of Madoc and bolted, disappearing seamlessly into the crowd, and Madoc had only caught up with him because he'd found Alban unconscious in a corridor. He must have used a displacer to try to escape—only it had sent him to an entirely different *universe*, and replaced him with this less-than-adequate copy.

There was only one thing for it. They had to return to the Lighthouse.

Down in the cargo hold, Alban hadn't moved.

"You're not Alban."

Alban gave Madoc a flat look. "Oh? Well, that's news to me."

"You're from another universe."

"I'm... sorry, a what?"

Madoc sighed. "Didn't you watch *Booster Jane* growing up?"

"Who didn't?"

"Remember that episode where she wakes up in a world that's like hers, but isn't?" Alban looked blank, and Madoc shook his head. "It doesn't matter. The point is, you don't belong here."

"So you're letting me go?" Alban asked hopefully.

"No," Madoc said, and Alban's face fell. "You're not the Alban I was after, and I want him back. I can't be the sector's most fearsome pirate captain without a rival. It's not impressive if I just *declare* myself to be a fearsome pirate captain, is it? I have to prove it. No, I'm going to send you back to where you came from, and I'm going to get *my* Alban back."

"And how are you going to do that?" Alban asked warily.

"*We* are going to the End of the World."

SIX HOURS LATER, Alban wrinkled his nose as he stared out the porthole at the empty patch of space. "*This* is the End of the World?"

"What is it in your universe?" Madoc asked, mildly affronted by Alban's obvious distaste.

"It's a nebula, and it's *beautiful*," Alban said, and then he amended, "Well, alright, it's kind of crap, and it's at the edge of explored space and no one wants to live there, but at least it isn't a black hole."

"*You* live there."

"Yeah, but I'm not *no one*," Alban said. "I'm a pirate."

Madoc huffed and led the way to the airlock. This Alban was nothing like the one that he knew, who was cunning and sly and full of rightfully-earned swaggering confidence. This alternate Alban was sunny and cheeky and didn't have two brain cells to his name. Madoc wanted to be rid of him as much as he wanted this universe's Alban back.

The Poisonous Serpent finished its docking procedures, and the airlock door slid open to admit them to the station. Alban took one step out of the airlock and stopped dead.

"*This* is the Lighthouse?"

Madoc grabbed Alban by the elbow and pulled him into the flow of people. "You are in an *alternate universe*, and you need to stop being surprised by that."

Alban yanked his arm out of Madoc's grasp. "I don't know why your Alban puts up with you."

"He doesn't *put up with me*, he's my nemesis. We have a rivalry! By definition, we despise each other."

"*That's* what you call a decades-long obsession with someone else? A rivalry?"

"I should've pushed you out an airlock," Madoc muttered.

"But then you wouldn't get your *nemesis* back, and then where would you be?"

"Sleeping soundly on my ship instead of skulking around on the Lighthouse in the middle of the night," Madoc said. The idea of never seeing this universe's Alban again made his gut clench, and why the hell was that? He hadn't eaten in a while, distracted by the pursuit and capture of his quarry. That must be it. "Come on. The sooner we get this over with, the better."

He turned on his heel and headed for the space station's seediest bar. Alban hurried after him.

As they made their way through the Lighthouse, Alban tried to comfort himself by mentally cataloging all the similarities between this universe and his own. He passed familiar clothing shops, markets, and stores that sold refurbished spaceship parts. Even in the middle of the night, the Lighthouse was bustling, and he caught sight of a few familiar faces. He had to remind himself not to wave, though, and the thought that no one here recognized him as *him* was wholly depressing. What if he couldn't get back to his own universe? What if he was stuck here forever? He could stay on this Lighthouse, he supposed, but it would probably hurt too much. This was where he had made a home with the Madoc of his universe. He couldn't live here without his husband.

No use dwelling on that right now, he told himself firmly. He *was* going to get home.

"So what are we doing?" Alban asked, lengthening his stride so he was beside Madoc.

"*We* are not doing anything," Madoc said. "*You* are going to go talk to that man and get him to sell you a displacer. Here's all the gold you have to work with."

Madoc tossed him a coin purse, and then pointed at the man seated at the end of the bar.

"But those are illegal!"

Madoc's eyes flicked to the ceiling, as though asking an unseen deity for help. "Yes."

"Even uttering the word *displacer* could get me arrested!"

"Then be creative," Madoc snapped. "Are you a pirate or aren't you?"

"Not a very good one!"

"Do you want to get home to your husband or not?"

That gave Alban pause. Yes, he did, more than anything, but what Madoc was asking of him was too much.

"I can't do this," he said.

"Yes, you can," Madoc said. "In your universe, you may be an incompetent pirate. But in this one? You're the second-most feared pirate in the sector. So go over there and *act like it*."

THE MAN SITTING at the end of the bar looked more like a pirate than Alban did. He turned his scarred face toward Alban as he approached, one blue eye searching him, the other clouded over and sightless.

"No," he said, before Alban even had a chance to sit down.

"No, what?" Alban asked.

"No to whatever it is you want," the man—Dillinger, that's who Madoc said he was—said. "You look like trouble, and I've got enough of that as it is."

"I can make it worth your while."

Dillinger snorted. "I doubt that."

You're a fearsome pirate, act like it! Alban took a breath, steeling himself, and then pulled out the stool next to the man and sat down. The bartender appeared, and Alban ordered a Galaxy Blaster.

"A what?" the bartender said blankly.

Damn. A universe that not only had a Madoc who was his worst enemy, but didn't even have Galaxy Blasters? What an intolerable place. "Er... sorry. Get me something strong enough to tranquilize a Cexil beast."

He sincerely hoped they had Cexil beasts here, and relaxed when the bartender grinned and went off to mix his drink. Dillinger silently nursed his own until the bartender returned with a lurid green drink and pushed it across the bar to Alban, and Alban tossed them a gold coin.

"There's more where that came from," Alban said to Dillinger, who snorted.

"Look, kid, I'm not in the mood for whatever this is. Go bother someone else."

"I need a displacer," Alban blurted, and inwardly cursed. He hadn't said it loudly, but Dillinger's eyes widened regardless. In one fluid movement, he rose from his seat and slipped out of the bar. Alban blinked at the empty chair for a moment in shock before getting to his feet and darting after Dillinger. What the hell? How had the other man vanished so quickly?

Alban caught up with Dillinger inside an abandoned storefront in Uptown. He thought it might have once been a tattoo parlor. In his universe, it was a flower shop.

"What the *fuck* do you want?" Dillinger spat, swinging his pistol around to point it at Alban—but Alban was faster, and had the business end of his coilgun in Dillinger's face before the man had finished his sentence.

"I've already told you what I want," Alban said. He could feel sweat gathering between his shoulder blades and trickling down his spine. Fear must have been rolling off him in waves; he wondered wildly if the other man could smell it.

"What makes you think I know anything about how to get it?" Dillinger demanded.

Because a big scary man who looks like my husband but who isn't *my husband told me you did.* "It's my business to know things like that. Now talk."

Dillinger sneered. "Or you'll kill me?"

"Or I'll make things very unpleasant for you," Alban said, hoping that Dillinger would take the waver in his voice for fury rather than for the fear it was. He hoped he wouldn't have to shoot or torture this man. He didn't have the stomach for blood. "I'm sure the authorities would be *very* interested to know that you've been selling displacers out of the Lighthouse."

"I haven't—" Dillinger turned an alarming shade of red. "You could ruin *everything* I'm trying to do here."

"Then you'd best talk so I can leave you alone."

"I don't have what it is you're looking for. Either of them."

"Who does?"

Dillinger gnawed on the inside of his cheek, a muscle pulsing in his jaw.

"The cyborg," he spat. "But you didn't hear it from me."

And then Dillinger vanished, leaving Alban with his coilgun pointed at a blank wall.

"ARE you gonna tell me who *the cyborg* is?"

"She's your first mate." Madoc strode briskly down the corridor, dimly aware that Alban was almost jogging in order to keep up with him. He didn't slow his pace. *Either of them*. So Dillinger had sold—or had facilitated the sale of—not one displacer, but two. The first one was with this universe's Alban, wherever he had ended up, and if the cyborg had the second one...

That was very bad news indeed.

"Oh." Alban didn't sound at all concerned by this information. "So I just have to find her, pretend to be my counterpart, and ask her for the second displacer. Easy."

"You'll have a knife between your ribs before you even finish the question," Madoc said. "She's been trying to get rid of you for years."

"Then why is she working for me?"

"Because she hates me more than she hates you," Madoc said. "Besides, the two of you make an effective team. You're not the most fearsome pirate in the sector because of your skills alone, you know. Your crew is invaluable to you."

He glanced at Alban, and noticed that the man was giving him a bright grin. "What?"

"You called me the *most* fearsome pirate in the sector. Not the second-most."

"I misspoke," Madoc growled.

"So if I can't ask this cyborg for a displacer, what are we going to do?"

"*You* are going to swagger aboard your ship like the fearsome pirate captain you are, sneak into your first mate's cabin, and steal it."

"I'm *what?*" Alban yelped. "I can't do that! What happens if I run into a member of my—of *his* crew?"

Madoc shrugged. "Don't let on that you're an imposter."

"Have you *met* me?" Alban hissed. "The minute I open my mouth, I'll give it away."

"Try not to do that," Madoc said, "because if you die here, then *my* Alban will be stuck in *your* universe with your husband. I don't think that's something you want, is it?"

It was almost comical how quickly Alban's mouth snapped shut, and Madoc knew right then that he was going to cave. A pity that it was so easy. *His* Alban would have fought back until both of them were bloody, even if Madoc's plan was a sound one. This alternate Alban was so *boring*.

"*Fine*," Alban said tightly. "But I'm telling you, this is a bad idea. Where will you be during all of this?"

"That's none of your concern," Madoc said. "I can keep myself hidden. Find the displacer and get back to my ship; I'll meet you there."

Alban stopped dead in his tracks. An odd look came over his face, and then he smiled. It wasn't a particularly pleasant smile.

"Or," Alban said, "you can come with me."

Thankfully, Madoc had much better preservation instincts than this Alban. "No. That would be suicide."

Alban's smile only grew. "Not if you're my prisoner."

ALBAN HAD A *SHIP*.

He had a ship and a crew and apparently more gold than all the gods combined. It was unbelievable. In his own universe, his attempts at piracy could barely even be called that, but in this one, he'd used it to make quite the comfortable life for himself.

Bit of a lonely one, though, if he was honest.

The captain's cabin on *The Cursed Corsair* took up half the first deck. It was at least twice as large as the tiny hovel on the Lighthouse that he shared with his Madoc, and contained more items than Alban had ever owned in his life.

"Impressive, isn't it," Madoc said when he noticed Alban gaping. His voice was full of—pride?

"I was going to say pretentious and gaudy, but sure, it's impressive." Alban couldn't believe his alternate self had such terrible taste in decor. "Where should we start?"

"Since your first mate apparently obtained these displacers, I would start with her cabin."

"Right." Alban went over to the computer interface at his counterpart's desk and activated it with a touch. "Computer, locate the first mate."

"First mate Serah is not on board."

That was a relief. "Computer, show me a schematic of this ship."

"Her cabin is a deck below yours," Madoc said as a holographic image of the ship materialized in the air in front of Alban. "You keep her close so you can keep an eye on her."

"You know an awful lot about this pirate you claim to hate so much." Alban studied the schematic. Madoc was right, but it looked like they would have to traverse several highly-trafficked corridors in order to reach the cabin. Wonderful.

He didn't have time to contemplate that for long, however, because at that moment the door swung open and a droid strolled into the room.

"Captain," it said, "you are needed—what is *that* doing here?"

Alban had never heard such dripping *contempt* come from a droid's vocal modulator before. He pulled himself up straight and said, "He is my prisoner."

"Why isn't he in the Brig?"

"Because he is *my* prisoner," Alban said. "I'll do what I like with him. What did you need?"

The droid swiveled its smooth, eyeless head back to Alban. It glowed yellow for a moment, and then said, "You are not Captain Alban."

"Yes, I am," Alban said. "I've captured Madoc, see? My arch nemesis?"

"You are not—"

A shot rang out, and sparks flew from the sudden gaping hole in the side of the droid's head. It collapsed.

"Time to move," Madoc said, shoving the coilgun back in his belt and reactivating the magnetic restraints that bound his wrists together. "*Now.*"

Alban grabbed Madoc's elbow and hauled him out of his cabin, hoping that he looked like a confident pirate captain escorting his prisoner to the Brig rather than a frankly useless pirate who was completely out of his depth. He schooled his expression into something he hoped was impassive and marched Madoc through the corridors. Most of the crew seemed to be on the Lighthouse, and the ship was fairly empty. The ones who were on board seemed unfazed by the sight of their captain escorting a prisoner. Alban's heart was hammering against the inside of his ribcage so loudly, he was surprised it wasn't echoing down the corridor.

They made it to the first mate's cabin without anyone else discovering that Alban was an imposter, though he didn't know how much time they had before the droid's body was found. The cabin door was unlocked—that was probably a bad sign. Nonetheless, Alban opened it and dragged Madoc in after him.

"Right," he said, undoing the restraints on Madoc's wrists. "You take the bedroom, I'll take the main room, and we'll—"

"*Well,*" a voice drawled from behind him, "isn't *this* a pleasant surprise."

They both whirled around, Madoc with his coilgun already drawn, Alban with *oh shit* on his mind and nothing else. He didn't recognize the woman sitting in the chair, but he could only assume that she was the first mate. *The cyborg.* An apt name, considering that she seemed to be made out of more chrome than flesh.

"Serah," Madoc said tightly.

Serah got to her feet, her coilgun still pointed at Alban's forehead. "You, in league with Madoc? I wasn't expecting *that*."

"It's not what it looks like," Alban said lamely.

"I'm sure it isn't."

"The computer said you weren't on the ship."

"What makes you think the computer's loyal to *you*?"

"Look." He took the coin purse out of his pocket and tossed it on the floor at her feet. "I want the displacer. Give me that, and you'll never have to see me again."

She didn't even glance at the coin purse. "You know the displacer is more valuable than a sack of gold."

"I need it," Alban said, a little desperately. All right, a *lot* desperately.

The coilgun discharged. Before Alban could react, a thin bolt of blue light had sliced through his jacket and the shirt underneath and burned a gash into his flesh. He hissed, falling back several steps. "What the hell?"

"You're not Alban," Serah said. "Alban would never *beg*. Who are you? What is this?"

"I'm your captain," Alban said, but through the pain and his desperation, it came out sounding more like a question.

"You *aren't*."

Lightning-fast, Serah fired off two more bolts of light. One left a charred gash on Madoc's torso. The other hit him square in the shoulder. He fell back with a cry, dropping his coilgun. Alban grabbed his own coilgun out of its holster, but before he could raise it, Serah shot it out of his grasp.

Something moved in Alban's periphery, and he instinctively ducked. Just in time, too—a vase sailed through the air where his head would have been and smashed into Serah, shattering on impact. Serah didn't so much as sway with the force of the blow, and she fixed Madoc with an unimpressed look.

"Was that supposed to hurt me?"

"No." Madoc raised Alban's coilgun. "It was supposed to distract you. Tell us where the displacer is, and we'll leave."

"Or what, you'll shoot me?"

"I doubt it will come to that. There are other ways of extracting information from someone. Even a cyborg."

"True," Serah said. "But you're forgetting something important."

"What's that?"

"Computer, activate the ship's self-destruct sequence," Serah said.

"Authorization code required."

Serah opened her mouth and emitted what sounded like a high-pitched burst of static. Alban clamped his hands over his ears.

"Authorization code accepted. Self-destruct sequence has been activated. Five minutes until self-destruct. Repeat, five minutes until self-destruct."

Alarms started to blare. Madoc gave Serah a look of disbelief.

"What are you doing?" he demanded over the wailing alarms. "Now you'll die, too!"

Alban moved on instinct. He saw Serah's left hand twitch, and knew what she was about to do. He kicked the chair out of the way and threw himself over the desk that separated them, his hand closing on her wrist as her body started to dissolve. He snatched the blue wristband out of her fingers, flinging it away. Serah's vocal cords, caught halfway between this location and her destination, let out one long, echoing scream. Her body vanished entirely, except for her hand, which fell to the deck with a dull thud.

For a heartbeat, neither of them spoke. Alban struggled to

draw air into his burning lungs, and he shook with the sudden burst of adrenaline.

"Found the displacer," he said, and Madoc let out a surprised laugh.

It was then that they both registered that the alarms were still blaring. Madoc's face fell, and Alban groaned. *Great.* After all that, he was going to die in this hellish alternate universe beside a poor facsimile of his husband.

"There's got to be a way out of here!" Alban went over to the door, knowing it would be locked. The activation of the self-destruct sequence automatically sealed every door and bulkhead on the ship. It was only ever meant to be used if a ship was compromised, and anyone left on board would be doomed along with the intruders.

"There is," Madoc said, but when Alban swung around hope-fully, he added, "You need to shut it down."

Alban gaped at Madoc. "I don't know how to do that!"

"This is *your* ship."

"No, it isn't! I'm not even from this universe!"

"What would you make the passcode?" Madoc demanded.

"It doesn't matter what *I* would make it, I'm not him!"

"You're the closest thing we've got!"

Alban closed his eyes and drew a deep breath. He knew what *he* would use as a passcode, but this universe's Alban would never...

Except maybe he would. Given the utter obsession these two pirate enemies had with each other, perhaps it wasn't out of the question. Besides, they had nothing left to lose now.

Alban opened his eyes and keyed the code into the computer. The alarms continued to wail—

And then they stopped.

Madoc and Alban stared at one another for a moment.

"Guess you're not so useless after all," Madoc said, and Alban snorted.

ALBAN STOOD in the cargo hold, in the same spot where he'd woken hours ago.

"Are you sure this is going to work?"

"No," Madoc said, because he was a lot of things, but he wasn't a liar. Well. Not to Alban, at least.

"Great," Alban muttered. He set his jaw in a resolute line and thrust out his arm. "Let's do this, then."

Madoc fastened the displacer around his wrist. He'd had his astrogator hack into the device and tamper with the settings, so that it would resonate with Alban's universe. Once activated, it should pull Alban back to the universe he had come from, and once there, he could send the true Alban back to Madoc.

At least, that was the idea.

Alban stood on the spot where Madoc had found him, between two crates of equipment. He drew a deep breath and mustered a smile.

"Well, here goes nothing," he said. And then, because this day wasn't strange enough, he said, "Thank you."

Alban had never thanked Madoc. It was jarring.

"You're... welcome," he said awkwardly.

"Oh, one last thing," Alban said. "You know that passcode, the one that stopped the self-destruct sequence?"

"What about it?"

Alban gave him a shit-eating grin. "I knew the code because it was one I would have used."

"And what is that?"

"Your birthday."

Alban pressed his thumb down on the displacer. The air rippled, and he vanished.

MADOC WAS STILL SITTING in the cargo hold six hours later when a breeze stirred the hair on the back of his neck. He blinked, and suddenly Alban was standing in front of him.

His Alban.

Madoc knew the man immediately, without having to confirm it with a scan. He knew the slant of Alban's mouth, the way his smirk caught on his eyeteeth, the jut of his hips. Confidence, *arrogance*, all of it well-earned, bled from every pore.

"Madoc," Alban drawled. He pocketed the displacer and glanced around the cargo hold.

"Alban," Madoc said, his mouth dry. "Had a bit of an adventure, did we?"

"Indeed." Alban's fingers twitched, but Madoc was faster, and he had his coilgun in his hand before Alban could draw. Alban gave him a sardonic smile. "Well. You've caught me at last."

"So it would seem," Madoc said.

Alban's smirk took on a feral edge. "What is it you plan to do to me, *Captain*?"

"Nothing."

Alban faltered, wrong-footed for a moment. "What?"

Madoc dropped his coilgun to the floor. "I intend to do nothing to you."

"But you've captured me."

"I captured your alternate, not you. It was pitifully easy. I should have known that man wasn't you."

"So you're just... letting me go?"

"I'm giving you a head start," Madoc corrected. "You'll have three days. Then, I will pursue you. And Alban—this time, I won't hold back."

"I would expect nothing less." Finally, Alban crossed the distance between them. "I do so *enjoy* the chase. Don't you?"

"Yes," Madoc breathed.

They were close enough that Alban could have drawn his

knife and slid it between Madoc's ribs. Madoc might even have let him.

"Alban."

"Madoc."

Madoc leaned close, his lips brushing the shell of Alban's ear. "*Run.*"

He felt the curve of the other pirate's grin against his cheek, imagined that their hearts beat as one as the thrill of the upcoming chase thrummed through their veins. A puff of hot air brushed against his neck as Alban laughed, and then he was gone, as swift and silent as the night.

DEAR AUNTIE AI

By J. Calamy
brought to you by O.N.T.I.'s Smart Project

The opinions expressed by the O.N.T.I. are for general informational and entertainment purposes only and are not intended to provide specific recommendations for any legal, medical, financial or religiously apocalyptic decision.

Dear Al Auntie:

I went on a cruise last revolution and met a very beautiful Fu'uunar. We had a few drinks. I was intrigued, and you know the rumors. To cut to the chase, I think she laid eggs in me. I'm too embarrassed to tell my doctor because this is the third time I've had this happen.

My research says the hatchlings are self-sufficient, so I thought I'd just ride this one out. Problem is, an old flame is in town and wants to meet up. Do I tell them I'm pregnant? Ethically speaking, do I have to disclose my status? Thank you,

—Incubator Boy

Dear Incubator:

First—I suggest you re-consider some of your life choices. Second—You are not only ethically but legally required to share your status with any other partners. No exceptions. Third—I recommend birth control going forward. Something sturdy.

—Your Auntie Al

THE WOLF AND THE KRAKEN

CRAIG RATHBONE

"There are three variants of Assassin: one hides in shadow, one hides in plain view, and the third kind, followers of the Ludan Code, do not hide at all."

— LUDAN BROOD MOTHER XBRAXES XXI

*T*hrough the roiling clouds of twisted space junk, collected via solar winds over centuries to make up the Maelstrom, a single vessel carefully travelled. It moved with deliberate purpose, boosters flickering periodically in order to avoid chunks of ship, space station, and whatever other long-lost debris occasionally rolled toward it. The ship was a small combat skiff named *The Salem*, and it was wanted across the sector for acts of piracy.

The Salem's captain, Akwesi Boateng, stood on the observation deck, surveying clouds of broken ships and equipment that his helmsman were working hard to avoid. Boateng should have been doing it himself, except the crew, being superstitious, had asked him to talk to their current client, Wulf.

Boateng didn't know much about Wulf, other than it had the coin to employ *The Salem* for this folly of a job. That, and it rocked enough armour and high-powered weaponry to take on an army, which included two huge Gloster hand cannons holstered in the webbing of its armour, and two large automatic coilguns, attached to metal arms folded at its back. It could easily wipe out Boateng and his crew, should they try to back out of the deal, but then *The Salem* really needed the considerable sum Wulf was willing to pay, so there was no danger of that happening.

"Shouldn't you be on the bridge, Captain?" the creature growled. Its voice, languid and dripping with irritation, was tinny through the helmet's speaker array.

Clearly, their passenger wasn't the social type, Boateng thought to himself. "I don't need to be at the helm all of the time. My first mate is perfectly capable of steering us through the Maelstrom. She's the best in the system," Boateng said patiently. He tried to think of the prize money for putting up with *The Salem*'s passenger and their *insights* for a few more hours. If nothing else, the ship's shield generator and oxygen filtration system needed work; the air tasted like copper.

Wulf turned its long, snouted helmet to face him, expression inscrutable beneath its dark visor. "I am glad that you maintain your crew with more care than this box, Captain. What do you want? Restless Home still looks to be on the horizon. So I assume you aren't here to tell me it's time to dock?" It tapped the thick viewport window with a metal-clad finger, pointing to an asteroid.

Boateng bit back a reply as he stepped next to the enigmatic alien. "My crew don't like you. It's not every day we take on contracts like this." The system's nebula reflected hues of reds and purples on the Captain's dark skin and tatty uniform. "And, well, we don't even know *what* you are, or what you want on Restless Home. It is a portentous place, many consider it to be cursed."

"I don't care about curses, Captain. I have absolutely no interest in explaining my mission to you." Wulf crossed his arms before continuing, "I am a Ludanite Assassin. A member of a millennia-old warrior pack devoted to providing a very efficient service, for a very handsome sum. We're used to the best equipment and weaponry, and usually the best ships too. So imagine my disappointment when this wreck was the only ship left in Cold Harbour."

Boateng knew Wulf was going to tell him nothing about their mission until they needed to, but it had been worth a try. He had heard tales of the deadly Ludanite pack, whispered in taverns across the system, and didn't fancy incurring the wrath of one of them, especially on his own ship. Instead, he'd console himself with thoughts of the generous payday.

The captain turned away from Wulf. "We should be docking at Restless Home in forty minutes— unless we need to dodge any particularly large chunks of debris." Boateng left, the door closing behind with a heavy clang.

Restless Home's port was, much like Cold Harbour, devoid of pirate activity, all of them having followed the infamous *Midnight Scythe* on a mysterious crusade across the system a few days ago, to the distant colony of Tunis. *The Salem*'s crew was already swinging into action. Deckhands with lifter trucks loaded fresh supplies, whilst the sailors and officers visited the tavern for much-needed rest and relaxation. Boateng's mechanics huddled around one of the ship's exhaust ports, looking at a damaged component.

The Captain examined the battered hull of *The Salem*. He'd always run a tight ship, his crew respected him and they had many successful raids over the years. Hearing footsteps, he turned away from the ship and held back a sigh.

The assassin approached. "I'm heading to Delving Prime. Ensure your ship is ready to leave in thirty minutes' time." Wulf said, towering over the captain by a foot.

Boateng stared into the blank visor. "We'll be ready," he growled in reply, finally letting out that sigh.

THE RUST POCKED service elevator screeched to a halt. Wulf pulled the doors aside and stepped out onto the rough stone of Shaft Four. Switching his heads-up display to low-light mode, it enhanced the dim glow from the flickering lanterns overhead. The natives, living rough in the tunnels closer to the surface, had been quite vehement in their warnings for him to not descend to the fourth shaft, some five hundred metres below Restless Home. They claimed it was haunted. Ghouls and wraiths down here put visions of death into people's heads, leaving them insane.

Wulf paid this no heed. They were no stranger to death, and the departed could not harm them. What could cause damage, however, was a lack of preparation. Before continuing further into the pit, they took a minute to bring up public access maps and blueprints on the suit's visor, overlaying them onto their own view through the helmet. Wulf ran a quick scan of the map, searching for the large machine room in which the target was reportedly being held. Thankfully, it wasn't too far away from the shaft four entrance, down a series of tunnels and a staircase.

Seven minutes into the projected thirty-minute window, Wulf encountered another life-form, their visor identifying them as human. Lightly armoured in a tactical vest and combat fatigues, they were no match for the power and aggression of a Ludanite Assassin in full armour. Wulf scoffed, the ancient submachine gun at the enemy combatant's hip was a mere peashooter.

Under the thick plate of their helmet, Wulf smiled with antic-ipation. He drew one of the large handguns and thumbed off the safety before holding the weapon in a firing position. Wulf then double-checked the helmet's augmented reality matched up to the sights.

The enemy combatant spun in surprise, bringing the old automatic to his shoulder. "Who goes there? Is that you, Grell? Thought I told you not to..." interrupted by a booming gunshot, the body fell to the ground.

This was Wulf's favourite part of the job. With the first shot fired, others wouldn't be far behind. The heightened tension as the enemy awoke to the approach of their imminent doom, was like a drug to the Ludanite.

Wulf loped toward a duo of enemy foot soldiers with their flashlights waving erratically. The human opened fire. Small pings of enemy rounds echoed off Wulf's chest armour. Two hefty punches from the hand cannon saw both drop, one missing an arm, the other with their torso rearranged.

Wulf continued toward the target. Their visor automatically picked up seven more enemies jogging toward them. A couple carried shotguns, and a few heavier ballistic armour. Not that it would do them any good. Shouting threats and obscenities, the cultists closed the gap. Wulf drew the second hand cannon from its holster. If there was one sin the Ludanite Assassins couldn't stomach, it was inefficiency.

The soldiers' fear was like sweet nectar to Wulf. Their heart-beat quickened with anticipation, and the Ludanite raised their handguns. The release of adrenaline was blissful as all seven cultists went down in a fountain of blood.

Biting back a howl of delight, Wulf picked up the pace, continuing toward the narrow metal stairway that spiralled further into the blackness. According to Dillinger's intelligence, the old equipment hangar was just past these stairs. Keeping a close eye on the heads-up display for any sign of movement, Wulf descended, the rusting steps groaning under the weight of their armour and hardware.

Two more cultists tried to stop the Assassin in the stairwell, firing wildly. One assault rifle round ricocheted from Wulf's visor, snapping their head back painfully. The Assassin retaliated with a snarl, firing two shots in return. One a shot to the chest, the other removed a forearm. It was an acceptable way for Wulf to burn off anger.

Wulf preferred to kill slowly, but the mission timer was still ticking. So, a windpipe crushed by a steel boot had to suffice. Eleven minutes in, nineteen to go. Guns still in hand, Wulf continued down the stairwell.

It took three minutes of further exploration to find the man-made cavern in which the target was located. Years' worth of dust covered the bare stone floor but many fresh trails criss-crossed its span. Old mining machinery languished around the expanse. A rickety-looking metal catwalk ran along the walls, creating an observation deck.

Noting a new burst of data rolling down their visor, Wulf walked into the centre of the vast hall, nerve endings buzzing with excitement.

They spotted a hastily built stage of wood with a stack of rusted crates serving as a dais at its centre. Several warnings lit their visor, internal systems picking up the laser sights illuminating his armour.

"Stop right where you are," a voice echoed from the shadows. "Who in the name of the all-consuming Kraken are you, and where are our brethren?"

"Dead, all twelve of them. Bring your captive to me and I'll be happy to stop the body count there," Wulf replied in a low growl, the helmet's audio array amplifying it across the machine hall.

Several laughs and catcalls answered before their appointed representative responded. "You really think that old armour will save you? You're surrounded. There's one of you and forty of us. Those big revolvers are no match for our combined fire, you mangy, psychotic freak!"

"Wrong on both counts. First, there aren't, as you claim, forty men in here, there are twenty-two. Six on the upper catwalk, sixteen on the ground, most of which are maintaining line-of-sight to me from behind those machines. Two of them are blocking the way from which I came, and one is hiding behind that little dais you made and is unarmed. Second, you have overlooked my loadout. I agree, two Glosters would have a hard time dealing with you all, though the automated twin coilguns on my rig were *designed* to deliver unto you one *serious* fucknado."

With a jerk of their head, Wulf activated the rig built onto the back of their armour. Two mechanical limbs, like those of an arachnoid, unfolded from their back. The two huge coilguns mounted on the ends of them were already cycling into life. With an ear-splitting sound of tearing nylon, reverberated to a Hellish roar by the stone walls, the supersonically charged rounds punched through the dense metal of the mining machines to find their targets, the automatic weapons shredding the remaining cultists like confetti.

Twelve seconds later, Wulf crossed over to the stage to find the remaining unarmed cultist.

Crouched on the ground, an older woman garbed in black robes and gaudy jewellery, reminded Wulf of cult leaders often portrayed in movie vids and old pulp novels. Wulf holstered the hand cannons and hoisted the woman up by the collar of her robes, dangling her feet off the ground. "The Duchess, where?" he asked, in a tone that suggested he had far less patience than remaining ammunition.

The woman locked eyes with Wulf, her own full of madness, or perhaps pure belief in their inscrutable cause. "They foretold your coming, primal one. I saw you in my dreams, saw the lives of my brothers and sisters blotted out by your lust for death. If only the elders had listened, or foreseen the girl's father going to one knee before your feral brood mother, begging for the girl's life to be saved before the Kraken could feast on her royal blood... but it doesn't matter anymore, the Kraken is already on its way, and the galaxy will burn, along with you, you pack of animals!" she hissed. Her bony hands clenched and unclenched with rage and despair as she spoke. A thick, silver necklace in the shape of a strange cephalopod beast, swayed pendulously against her chest.

Wulf grew impatient and shook the robed woman forcibly. "One more time, crone, *where is she?*"

The woman, never taking her tear-filled blue eyes from Wulf, raised a pointed finger to a stout metal door set into the stone wall between two stacks of crates. Wulf snapped her neck A small price to pay for besmirching the name of the Ludan brood mother and their glorious pack.

The door, locked with an old-fashioned tumbler system, required a physical key. Wulf was about to place a thermite charge into the lock when somebody unlocked it from the other side. Drawing a Gloster, the Assassin stepped back and took aim, ready to put down another cultist. But, when the door opened, Duchess Grace Hortencia Caranthem IV stood before them, handcuffed, dirty and covered in blood. In her pale hand lay a large, decorative dagger, drops of blood falling from its tip.

"I take it you killed the last one, then?" Wulf asked, holstering his weapon as their armour's systems ran a check on the girl. To their relief, it indeed *was* the target. She was overall in good health, apart from lacerations on her wrists from the cuffs, and a black eye. As the check finished, they couldn't help but notice that she scrutinised the Ludanite in return.

"Indeed, that unholy racket you made in here was all the distraction I needed to steal his knife and sink it between the brute's shoulder blades. I daresay the prick had it coming too," she replied glibly. Her eyes shone with adrenaline and malevolence. "Now, what is a Ludanite Assassin doing down here? Were you sent to kill these psychopaths—or me, perhaps?"

Impressive. The last thing they expected this young woman to be was cocky. But then, she was the infamous Muffy Dillinger's illegitimate daughter. "Were I here to kill you, you'd be dead already. No, I'm here to take you to my client, alive, with all of your digits intact. That was the order, at least."

Still on the clock, Wulf led the girl out of the chamber, stepping through growing puddles of blood without slowing, waving their charge into silence whenever she tried to ask questions. It wasn't until she crouched next to a dead cultist and picked up a submachine gun that Wulf spoke.

"Looks like you've had some formal training in weapons handling. Baagh College?" Wulf asked, recognising the smooth drill steps as those taught by the ancient and lethal academy of combat tutors.

"That is correct," the Duchess replied proudly. "My instructor, the great Guru Khatri, taught me to use concealable weapons, so this little submachine gun will be perfect, should more cultists show up. Unlike you, I don't need those gigantic coilguns. What are they for anyway, bringing down ships?"

When they were standing in the safety of the elevator, they replied. "I only got to put down a few cultists with them today, but they do have two ships to their name, pirates both."

The Duchess said something in reply, her words suddenly drowned out by static as Wulf's communications array sprung to life. "Wulf, can you hear me? I really hope that you can!" shouted Boateng, the audio warping slightly, the sound of small arms fire in the background.

Wulf held up a hand to silence the girl's one-sided conversation. She rolled her eyes, but they ignored her and replied to the radio. "Captain, you have company? I hear several automatic weapons back there."

It was a few seconds before the Captain of *The Salem* responded. "Yes, Assassin, we have company alright! An old skiff arrived at the port, full of armed fools wearing black hoods. I think they were looking for you. They took the port by force, and have a skiff hovering overhead to suppress us. I'd love to get airborne to mop them up with artillery, except half of my crew are pinned in the tavern. Tell me you're on the way," Boateng shouted desperately over a litany of gunfire.

Wulf looked down at the rescued Duchess beside them, glaring back at him impatiently with cerulean blue eyes. "I did say thirty minutes, didn't I? We'll be there to bail you out." With that, he cut the comms.

It was a short walk back down the rocky path from Delving Prime to the town of Restless Home. The strange nebulae above them bathed the road in purple and pink hues, in contrast with the thick smoke surrounding the ramshackle town. As they drew closer, they spotted the cultist's skiff, hovering above the port. It was pouring automatic fire down into the buildings below, keeping The Salem's crew pinned down whilst the cultists came looking for their fallen kin and the escaped girl.

"Did Guru Khatri show you how to put down a small skiff's worth of soldiers?" Wulf asked drily. They drew the twin hand cannons as they weighed their options.

"I believe that was in an upcoming lesson, Ludanite," she snapped in reply. "Besides, I already know the answer: let you go in first, and shoot any survivors."

Wulf once again was impressed, despite their usual disdain toward humanity. This privileged, pampered girl was masking her fear and was prepared to point her liberated gun at anybody who came close.

"Almost right, girl. There won't be any survivors. You can bet the cultists on the surface are here for you; therefore, they will most likely focus fire on us the moment we're seen. As we reach the port, I need you to find a hiding place near my location and stay there. If any cultists somehow sneak by me, feel free to test that education of yours. Understood?" The girl looked as if she was about to argue about hiding, but conceded with a grin.

They encountered the first group of cultists from the skiff on the outskirts of the town. They barely had the time to shoulder their weapons before Wulf's visor lined them up, and the two high calibre handguns knocked them down.

"That targeting system gives you quite the advantage. Switch it off and I might put a few of these bastards down myself!" pouted the Duchess, stepping over what was left of their would-be attackers. Realising that her surly rescuer wasn't stopping to assess the dead cultists, the girl ran to catch up.

The Ludanite and the Duchess encountered no further resistance until they reached the port. *The Salem* sat in place, the exhaust port half-built and crates of victuals left in the middle of the access road. Members of the pirate ship's crew darted behind cover on the jetty, exchanging fire with more black-robed figures. The tavern, in which the remaining pirates were hiding, was surrounded by cultists. Wulf spotted Boateng as they approached the middle of the wide service road. The Duchess kept close behind.

The Assassin grinned as the visor lit up with multiple targeting warnings, at least fifteen from the cultists on the ground. Wulf unceremoniously shoved the girl from behind his back, and into the cover of a pallet of abandoned thick metal crates.

"Remember when you asked me what my weapons are capable of?" Wulf asked.

She crouched into cover, glaring at Wulf. But the glare soon melted away, replaced by an understanding of what was about to happen. "I simply won't believe you until I've seen that skiff plucked out of the sky," she replied.

Wulf aimed to do just that. Huge coilguns tallied up the targets in front of them as all hell broke loose. The cultists on the ground opened fire, forcing Wulf to brace against a withering hail of bullets that slammed off thick, tempered layers of armour. The Ludanite hissed in pain as several bullets punched through the armoured plate, with only the underlying ballistic fibre suit saving the Assassin's life.

Whilst the rounds hitting the armour did their damage, Wulf's own rounds dealt out far more. The coilguns opened fire with a thunderous roar. The Duchess covered her ears and screamed. Thousands of supersonic explosive bullets tore into the pock-marked hull of the skiff above, shredding it from bow to stern as if it were paper. The ship's reactor core, its containment compromised, lit up the port with a huge, green-flamed explosion, vaporizing several of the cultists beneath it instantly and knocking the wind out of Wulf. A quick glance at the Duchess saw her pressed up to crates, her eyes screwed shut and earlier bravado forgotten. At least she was unharmed.

The skiff, shedding chunks of deck, reactor, weaponry, and crew, yawed to port, passing over *The Salem*'s bulk, and fell away from the asteroid's gravity well. The Ludanite, firing until every round was exhausted, dealt with the remaining enemy targets. Wulf let out a howl of satisfaction as the surviving cultists panicked, and attempted to disperse into the streets.

Wulf picked off a handful more with the hand cannons as they fled, and the formerly besieged pirates sallied forth from the tavern, looking for revenge. The enraged crew sent the rest of the cultists to their Kraken's side with shotguns and automatic weapons. As the final enemy combatants fell, Restless Home fell into a death-filled silence. The only sound came from the crackling of fire dancing merrily atop the debris from the gutted skiff littering the access road.

The Ludanite holstered the handguns and retracted the spent coilguns, setting off a medical status check as he did so.

The Duchess, albeit a little shell-shocked, appeared unharmed. "You could have bloody *warned me!*" she shouted, her ears ringing in the aftermath.

"Loud, was it? Should've stood further back." Wulf replied,

limping toward *The Salem*. The Duchess followed, and the Assassin noted the young woman's concerned face.

"You're hurt," she said, nodding to his leg injury.

"Just a scratch," he replied as he plodded forward. Wulf was looking forward to the month-long meditative retreat in the forests of Ludan once they completed the job. A burst of automatic fire set off warnings on Wulf's visor. The Assassin instinctively turned to protect the Duchess, only to find that it was she who had fired. She held the submachine gun to her shoulder like a professional. A few paces in front of them, a dead cultist slumped onto the concrete, a high-powered, armour piercing rifle clattering from her hand.

"Looks like I owe Guru Khatri a drink, girl. He trained you well," Wulf rumbled after a moment of silence, watching Grace lower the submachine gun and place the safety catch on. Her eyes showed no fear or regret, only an icy calm. Wulf had seen that expression before, on the face of her father, Johnny Dillinger.

"You owe *me* a drink. I just saved your life, you know," the girl shot back. She then smiled. "Are we getting off this rock now, or what? Wherever you aim to take me next can't be as awful as this shithole."

"Sure, I'll get you a sasparilla on board the ship. I'm fed up with this place, anyway. Give me the forests of home any day." Wulf beckoned her toward the boarding ramp of *The Salem*.

Akwese Boateng stood at the entrance with a rifle in his hands. "An impressive display, Wulf. I've never seen one person take down an entire army before," he said as he strode down to meet them. "And this?" he asked, eyeing the girl behind Wulf. "This is the missing Duchess of Dauntless III, isn't it? Taking her aboard will make running checkpoints *considerably* more difficult. And more expensive."

The Duchess stepped forward and shook Boateng's hand in a formal manner. "Don't worry, Captain, I'm sure our mutual friend here can spare a few more credits for any additional risk, isn't that right?" She winked at Wulf and flashed him a smile.

Wulf sighed. The girl was boisterous, confident and spoiling for an adventure now that she was free from her pampered former life. Not only that—she was a Dillinger, albeit unknowingly. What a duo she and her father would make.

Wulf limped up the boarding ramp of *The Salem*. "Come on. I owe you a drink. Captain, get us out of this shithole."

CREATORS OF THE STARS

ILLUSTRATED BY TBL KOBKA

Space Pirates

Top row—C. Vandyke, Cartographer *Center row*—Sean Campbell, Harry F. Ray,
J. Calamy. *Bottom row*—Alexis Ames, Lisa Kuznak, Craig Rathbone

Illustration by Lisa Kuznak

BOOK 4: PIRATES OF THE SEA

MAP OF THE ISLES SURROUNDING THE KRAKEN'S WHIRLPOOL

ILLUSTRATED BY DEWI HARGREAVES

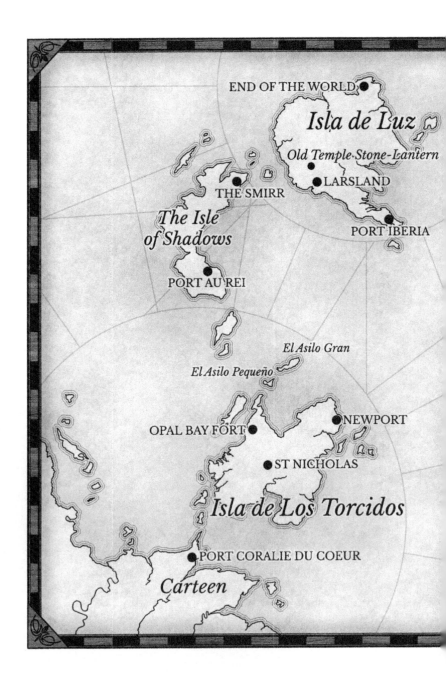

MARSHGRAVE

The Whispering Isle

Dr Pendergast's Home
Cave of Eternal Damnation

St. Madeline

Well of Eternal Life

SILONA

The Kraken's

HALF MOON LANDING

Whirlpool

The Nest

FIDDLER'S GREEN

SQUANDERER'S BAY   *Atoll of the Giants*

Illustration Copyright © 2021 Dewi Hargreaves

ROMAN JEWELS

ROMEO & JULIET BUT PIRATES

CHAPEL ORAHAMM

ACT 1

Prologue

Two ships' crews, both alike in disposition,
In shadowed Squanderer's Bay, where this story
    unfolds,
From old insults arise a troubled mission,
Where privateer treasure lies in blood-bound holds,
From Pirate Code ink of these two captains
A duo of course-crossed lovers escape their fate;
Whose curious discovery happens
And with their stealth steal their captains' estate.
The tempestuous voyage of their cutlass-scarred
    love,
And the persistence of their captains' deck
Which, but for their quartermasters' mutiny, none
    would move,
Is now the few hours' rambling on our wreck;

If you wish a moment's entertainment
We shall reach for your desired attainment.

SCENE 1.

*Squanderer's Bay, The Market Center. Enter Sanderson and Godfrey,
crew of Captain Lutterell's Black Albatross, armed.*

Sanderson: Godfrey, I promise you, they won't
make us into clowns.

Godfrey: Well, duh, we'd be a clown posse and not
privateer, and I'm contracted to the code.

Sanderson: Not what I meant, God. I meant, if they
cross us, we'd snuff 'em.

Godfrey: Sandy, you might want to see a priest or
an apothecary.

Sanderson: Someone pushes my buttons, I push
back.

Godfrey: But you don't wear buttons, at least none
I've seen.

Sanderson: One of those Montgomery cutthroats
pushes my buttons.

Godfrey: I mean, there are some fine looking
specimens on board. Button-pushing doesn't
sound half bad, does it?

Sanderson: They'd steal my buttons and leave me
hanging. Rather crowd the market stalls then
share the throughway with one of
Montgomery's lackeys.

Godfrey: That's rather nice, giving them some
room to get by.

Sanderson: I'm not nice. Women are nice. Here's

what I'll do. Montgomery's men can stick to the street and I'll stick to her women.

Godfrey: Always fighting between the Black Albatross and the Crimson Blade captains. We just work for them.

Sanderson: When I'm captain, I'll put the men in their place, and I'll play sweet with the women— I hear they like bananas.

Godfrey: Are we really doing the banana in my pocket joke?

Sanderson: Well, I was 'til you ruined it.

Godfrey: The joke'd work if you had anything resembling a banana.

Sanderson: I've seen enough bananas around here to know mine's a decent size.

Godfrey: Oh, aye. There's those Lady Fingers that'd give you a run for your money. Oye, here comes trouble. Get out your knife and not your Lady Finger, mind, lest you think that'll make the Montgomery men skat.

Sanderson: It's out. You initiate. I'll protect your back.

Godfrey: And you'll say you were there in my blindspot the whole time while cowering behind a barrel.

Sanderson: Don't be scared for me.

Godfrey: Yo. You scare me.

Sanderson: Wait. Gov'll have us if we go pointing bananas, I mean swords, at people. Let the Montgomerys come over here.

Godfrey: Y'all tell me I have resting bitch face. Of course they'll come over. They always do if I'm around.

Sanderson: I can always flip 'em off. Keep it subtle

though. They'll have to come over if your pretty
face doesn't do it. (Sanderson scratches his face,
emphasizing the use of his middle finger.)

Enter Annesley.

Annesley: Sharkbait, you flipping us off?
Sanderson: You've gotta be blind if you're asking.
Annesley: Seriously? Are you a kid, or just looking
for a smackdown?
Sanderson: (whispered to Godfrey) Can I call this
self defense if I say yes and he attacks me?
Godfrey: (whispered to Sanderson) Nope.
Sanderson: (to Annesley) Uh. No. Not flipping you
off. But I do have this atrocious itch. (Scratches
more vigorously.)
Godfrey: Are you itching for a fight?
Annesley: Itching? I've bathed recently. You might
look into one yourself.
Sanderson: We've got baths on our ship. Captain
makes sure ours is just as good as yours.
Annesley: But not better.
Sanderson: Yo.

Enter Bostock.

Godfrey: (whispering so only Sanderson hears) Tell
him "better". Here comes Cap's man.
Sanderson: (to Annelsey) I'd go with better, man.
Annesley: Sucking lies through your teeth will
leave you in dentures.
Sanderson: If you got more than one knife on you
and keep it sharp, pull the sharp one, Godfrey. I
hope you're just as good at thrusting it as the

blunt one.

They Fight.

> **Bostock**: (breaks up fight, swords scattering to the
> ground on both sides) Cool it, you idiots. You
> wanna get both of us under Gov's nose?

Enter Tyndall.

> **Tyndall**: You'd really chip your blade against mere
> crew, Bostock? Here, turn around and let me
> show you what a proper fight looks like.
> **Bostock**: You're not helping here, Tyndall. Help me
> get these clam-brains to put their blades away.
> **Tyndall**: You want my help? Here, let me help you
> and all the Montgomerys into the sea.

*Montgomery and Lutterell crews join in on the scuffle. Enter several
Market Watch with muskets.*

> **First Market Watch**: We've had it with you pirates,
> Blades and Albatrosses both. To arms, men!
> Cock and ready on my signal.

Captain Lutterell enters in regalia with Sailing Master Luther.

> **Captain Lutterell**: Luther, where's my sword?
> This'll be great exercise.
> **Sailing Master Luther**: Maybe gentle yoga would
> be better, sir. Doc will scream at you if you
> throw your back again. Why a sword of all
> things?

Enter Captain Montgomery with rapier and Sailing Master Monsell with cutlass drawn.

> **Captain Lutterell**: Because that pampered hen is here and she's got her little fencing blade out just 'cause she knows it pisses me off when people use those things.
>
> **Captain Montgomery**: Lutterell, you eel shit. (Sailing Master Monsell stalls her) You'd best get your hand off my shoulder, Monsell.
>
> **Sailing Master Monsell**: Don't lower yourself to an eel shit, Monty.

Enter Governor with community leaders.

> **Governor**: (shouting at the crews and citizens) Freaking pirates! This is why we can't get good shipping here. You two (points at Montgomery and Lutterell) get control of your men. Third time I've had to be summoned to break up one of your men's rows because you two fight like cats and dogs. The Neighborhood Watch is sick of it. You can pay all your portage fees and taxes on time, better than many, but if I have to come break this up again, you're getting strung up where you can't trouble the good people again.

Everyone but Montgomery, Monsell, and Bostock leave.

> **Captain Montgomery**: Bostock. Speak plain. What the fuck?
>
> **Bostock**: Uh…? Well, you know Lutterell. Your crew was kicking his crew's asses. Which would have been nice other than we were already on

strike three with Gov, so figured I probably
needed them to quit it. Then Tin-Tin shows up
and just has to get involved. And one thing led to
another and yeah...

Sailing Master Monsell: At least it all cooled off
before Roman showed up. Where is that
moonstruck calf of a nephew of mine?

Bostock: Off wallowing in self-pity on the dock
side. Feeding seagulls.

Captain Montgomery: He's determined to make
the ocean saltier overnight. Then he comes
tumbling into the cabins at bloody dawn
without a thought to any of the crew still
sleeping. I don't mind him being a night owl, but
it's getting bad if all he's doing is coming back
and sleeping the day off. He'll never see daylight
at this rate.

Bostock: Any idea why he's gone all mopey
on us?

Captain Montgomery: Good question. No idea.

Bostock: Tried talking to him?

Captain Montgomery: Me, Sailing Master,
Josephina, the crew. Even tried getting him
wasted at Madam Linley's. He's determined to
be his own best friend, and quite honestly, if you
aren't nice to yourself, being your own best
friend might be akin to being your own worst
enemy. If you can pry it out of him, by all means,
enlighten the rest of us. I need my quartermaster
back to normal.

Enter Roman.

Bostock: (cracking knuckles) Speaking of the

overseer of hell. Let me have a go at him. I'll crack him like a bivalve.

Captain Montgomery: Good luck. Bring him back in one piece. Ice and whiskey, depending on who needs what, will be available if you can actually get him to talk. Come on, Monsell.

Exeunt Captain Montgomer and Sailing Master Monsell.

Bostock: What are you building this time, Rome?

Roman: Oh, jeez, it's too early for this again, Bostock.

Bostock: Says the guy who's been up since the moon rose.

Roman: Meh. Just have a lot of things on my mind. Something happen for Monty and Monsell to be here?

Bostock: They're just off for a wander. Back to you though, oh King of the Dark. What's troubling your tide pools?

Roman: If only I could stop the tides from rolling.

Bostock: Dude, you sound sea sick.

Roman: Sick maybe.

Bostock: Sick of love?

Roman: Maybe it's masochistic.

Bostock: She a complete dom?

Roman: There's this whole euphoria thing with this love-at-first-sight business, and I'm just over here tired of being in it. (Sees signs of scuffle) A fight? Again? For the third time? Blades and Albatrosses just love themselves a good fight. Ironic, in a way. A love like that, don't you think?

Bostock: Alright, Aristotle, when'd you turn from

quartermaster to philosopher? I think that
entails a paycut.

Roman: You're having a go at me.

Bostock: Dude, you're deep diving on irony when it
was just another crew spat because you're all
mopey about a pair of legs.

Roman: You ever been in love, Bostock? Straight
up, it's madness. Everything is a knife's edge
over an abyss. Especially when it's a stupid one-
sided crush. I should get going.

Bostock: Hold up, turtle dove. You can't leave me
hanging on this.

Roman: I haven't been myself in a while, Bos. Feel
like my brain checked out and went off to circle
the stars while my body and simpler impulses
are stuck here waiting for me to return.

Bostock: Seriously, who the hell are you so gaga
over that you're spouting romantics and
philosophy?

Roman: You really want to know? You're just going
to use it to tease me more.

Bostock: I'll keep the teasing to the minimum if it's
worth it.

Roman: You have to promise on the captain's rapier
you won't tease me for this. I can't take that at
the moment.

Bostock: On her rapier, I promise.

Roman: She's not a dom. He's handsome to a fault.

Bostock: Then he must be a star.

Roman: A star would make the most sense of this
situation I find myself in. You can reach for a
star, use it to navigate by, admire it, and yet it
will always be so distant from those of us who

find ourselves swayed instead by an unrelenting sea on a deck too small.

Bostock: Then he finds himself amongst unreachable stars?

Roman: Those who flit around him are they themselves bound to the heavens, far above the reach of us mere mortals.

Bostock: If they occupy the heavens, and you occupy the seas, then find someone of the seas. Poseidon, Lir, Njord may occupy the heavens and yet found themselves overseers of our waves.

Roman: How do I move on from a star, from this fellow, Bastion?

Bostock: By setting your telescope a little closer to the deck. There must be ones circling your orbit.

Roman: To lower my scope would only remind me of what I saw before me. Handsome men around here have a bad tendency of wearing eye masks and becoming swashbuckling loners thinking they'll make a crew for themselves and then you never hear from them again. No. Show me someone really up there and then maybe I'd listen.

Bostock: You're on.

Exeunt Bostock and Roman.

SCENE 2

Enter Captain Lutterell, Parker, and Palmer.

Captain Lutterell: (mid conversation) Damn it. It's the tradition of the thing. Yet, if we are to maintain our port of call in the Bay, then the fighting has to stop. Montgomery agreed to the truce with Gov. I didn't think she would, quite honestly.

Parker: Privateers for the same crown after all. I don't see why keeping a truce will be difficult. This will benefit all of us. Speaking of benefits, are you still thinking of shifting management? I am keen on the idea of obtaining a quartermaster with decent experience.

Captain Lutterell: Though your proposition from before is still remembered, I will say it: my quartermaster has had a rough time of the last few months. Got caught up in crossfire. Lost an eye for the last good haul we had. Give them some more time to find themself before hoping they'll ship out with a new captain, crew, and ship.

Parker: Men have suffered worse afflictions and been able to return to their post faster.

Captain Lutterell: I leave it up to them and you then. If they decide to join up with your crew, congratulations on encouraging them to face the seas again. I'd suggest tact, or else they'll never talk to you again. Say, the crew and I are having a party at the Prodigal Son on Speculate Lane near The Black Albatross's dock. Come down. Share a toast or two and maybe see what Jules makes of you. We've got others of the Crown contract coming. Silver Turtle, Amethyst Harpoon, and a few others. Maybe talk to those quartermasters and see if any of them would be a better fit for your voyage. (to Palmer, giving a paper): Here's a list of some other people outside of the contract I want to have show up tonight. They're at some of the south and north docks and I haven't taken time to wander all the way out there. Take a quick jaunt and send them our way, would you? Thanks.

Exeunt Captain Lutterell and Parker.

Palmer: Frickin' fab, Cap. I could reef a sail for you, but no. I could stitch it, but no. I can even cook, not as great as Cook's grub, but no. Instead, you go handing me a paper knowing damn well I can't read. Or at least you would know, if you'd remember my name, you weather-beaten old sea turtle. Oh thank Poseidon's shiny trident, people who look like they might know what this scribbledy gook is.

Enter Bostock and Roman.

Bostock: (to Roman) Bitter things can make your stomach hurt, and yet the doc gives you bitter things to make your stomach stop hurting. A hot knife to a pussed wound hurts just as bad as when you got the wound, but it cures it. What you need for your lovesick, moonstruck calf face is a new beau to look at. You need a different crush by which to feel crushed over, then you can forget about the last one that left you feeling all bruised.

Roman: Hot water bottle is good for that.

Bostock: For what?

Roman: For a bruise.

Bostock: Roman, where is your head at?

Roman: Somewhere in Svarga, and I'm not sure if I
    want to attain moksha or descend back to Earth.
    (to Palmer) Hi. You look a bit lost. Can I help?

Palmer: Oh thank God, yes. Can you read?

Roman: I used to read between the lines, but I think
    that has become lost on me.

Palmer: Not quite the skill I had in mind. Can you
    read regular words?

Roman: Yep: verbs, irregular and otherwise,
    adjectives, and adverbs come to mind in
    abundance. Then there's articles, both linguistic
    and legal. Though, I must say my favorite are
    conjunctions. The one between Saturn and
    Jupiter was something to see.

Palmer: That's still more vague than specific. I'll
    just, um... go...

Roman: Hold up, hold up. Let me see the paper. I'll
    see if I can help. (Takes list from Palmer) Uh.
    Okay, wait a minute. Where'd you get this, from
    a chicken? Horrid handwriting. You've got
    Captain Mario from Shrieking Badger, his
    quartermaster and sailing master and three
    guests over at Dock B9. Captain Allard of The
    Djinn's Lamp and her wife on Dock C7. Late
    Captain Vinny's husband who has residence
    with the Lagoon Maiden crew on Dock 2A. Sir
    Reginald with his Majesty's service located in
    South Docks, Cat's Eye pier. My brother Sir
    Lutterell with his Majesty's service in South
    Docks, Beryl pier. My nephew Bastion and his
    girl... oh... girlfriend of Seething Ghost. Sir
    Sigfried and Tyndall, they'll be at Wind-divers

Lane and Hana of Vermillion Wave. That is quite a list. Know where you're sending them?

Palmer: Food.

Roman: Ah, a meal?

Palmer: Party at Prodigal Son for us.

Roman: Us?

Palmer: Captain and the other crews.

Roman: Would make sense. I should have asked before who they were.

Palmer: Oh, right. I was being vague, sorry. Captain Lutterell. With so many people showing up, as long as you aren't from The Crimson Blade, I'd think Captain wouldn't mind you slipping in. Not like he notices much anyway. He can't ever remember I can't read. Probably doesn't even remember my name most days. Anyway. I gotta get. Peace.

Palmer exits.

Bostock: Bastion's gonna be at Prodigal Son? Like, the Bastion guy you're all mopey over? And girlfriend. That's gotta suck. But. Wait, Roman. Hear me out. You saw that list there. Not everyone on it revolves in the heavens like our old boy Bastion. What says you to us going and taking our pick of the litter, hmm?

Roman: No one there will ever compare to him.

Bostock: Let me guess. He was rigging a ship all on his lonesome out at the dock and no one was around and you just swooned over a pair of good arms. There are other great arms around here or else there would be no good crew in all of Squanderer's Bay.

Roman: Well... um... Let's crash Prodigal Son. Not
because I think you're right. You have to see this
guy. I know, not your type, but maybe you'll get
where I'm coming from.

Exeunt Roman and Bostock.

SCENE 3.

*North Docks: A Cabin in Captain Lutterell's ship. Enter Sailing Master
Luther and Doc.*

Sailing Master Luther: Are they doing better? It's
been three months.
Doc: I'll go call them. They're in the next cabin over.

Exit Doc. Enter Doc and Jules.

Jules: I'm awake. Maybe with a migraine, but I am
currently occupying the land of the living.
Doc: Well that's a relief. Would rather not have a
wraith walking around the ship.
Jules: Luther? How can I help you?
Sailing Master Luther: Not sure if you need to be
here for this, Doc. Probably wouldn't hurt
either way.
Doc: I can leave.
Sailing Master Luther: No, stay. It's alright. Just
debating on how to put this. They'll never
recover their eye, will they?
Doc: If you were to find a magic potion in the
Lighthouse at the End of the World, maybe.
Being realistic, though, no, it's clean gone.

Sailing Master Luther: Why would the Lighthouse have magical potions?

Doc: Why else would it be shrouded in perpetual darkness? Rumor has it there's a stone lantern, that upon being lit by an impossible fuel, will lift the darkness and return the island to its rightful place in the world. The Lighthouse, supposedly, was cursed by an angry goddess when the Lighthouse keeper, who had devoted himself to the discovery of the alchemical Rebis, concluded that his light could be used in achieving his goal of surpassing the known world.

Sailing Master Luther: And this intrinsically means that the Lighthouse has magic eye potions?

Doc: Well, probably not, but The Black Albatross has crossed dangerous oceans for more mysterious and marvelous things and they be true.

Jules: I'm not so bent out of shape about my lost eye as to travel to the Lighthouse, Doc. We can leave off on the fairy tales for a bit.

Doc: If you aren't interested in magically poofing your pretty eye back into existence, then hear me out. I want access to the alchemist's medicine cabinet. Elixirs and potions are one thing. The base components used in quite a lot of alchemical practices are fundamental to real medicine and it would be nice to fill my larder.

Sailing Master Luther: Noted about the medicine cabinet, Doc. I'll have a word with Captain. As it is, Captain will be having a word with you, Jules, about the fact that Parker is after you to be his quartermaster.

Jules: To change contracts is not one of my personal motivations in life.

Doc: No ambitions for a raise?

Sailing Master Luther: We've been docked bay side for three months getting you back to normal.

Doc: "Normal" does not quite define what is going on here, Luther. As it is, you all had cargo to unload from that haul out of Coralie de Couer. Silver and silks from Carteen are not easily come by. Though their ships-people most certainly are, and good shots, mind you.

Sailing Master Luther: And now the silk has been sold and we're sitting on funds for our next run waiting. Return to work, Jules. Whether that be with the Albatross or someone else. It would be better than squandering your life in a dark hole because you lost a bit of your eyesight. You need a diversion. Something interesting.

Doc: I mean, the guy recruiting isn't known to be a straight-up arse, so it might not be a bad deviation from the usual.

Sailing Master Luther: (to himself) I hate this potential contract upheaval.

Doc: (to Jules) Taking on a different contract might let you see more than our little triangle we run.

Sailing Master Luther: (to Jules) Is that a yes to getting back to being our quartermaster or a yes to joining up with the new crew?

Jules: It's not like I want to leave the Albatross. I'm just, well, a bit gun shy at the moment. It'll get better. Don't go tossing me to another crew just because you think I'm unhappy here. I'll be unhappy there too, and for the same reason.

Palmer Enters.

> **Palmer**: Sailing Master, Doc, Quartermaster, the
> guests are arriving and Captain wants you down
> there, NOW!
> **Sailing Master Luther**: Oh, blast it all. Jules, figure
> it out. Are you staying as our quartermaster or
> hiring on with a new contract, because one way
> or another, your talent needs to stop being
> wasted in a medical bay.
> **Doc**: Come on Jules, let's follow them. Luther isn't
> wrong. It'd help you to get back into work
> rather than laying about down here.

Exeunt All.

SCENE 4.

*Squanderer's Bay: An alley. Enter Roman, Bostock, and Malone, all
disguised as theatrical performers of Hamlet for the pub stage.*

> **Roman**: So, we just going in like this? We supposed
> to introduce ourselves or what?
> **Bostock**: Nothing extreme. These types of pub
> performances, half the time you're lucky to leave
> the stage without tomato on your face. Just get
> up and act. Don't worry about us being a
> "troupe" or a "band" or something for people to
> "find" us by later.
> **Roman**: Can I be the king? I don't want to say lines.
> Let me just sleep and die, please?
> **Malone**: Hah. You wish. You're the only one of the
> crew who has the entirety of Shakespeare

memorized down to the stage exits. Like hell are we letting you be the backdrop.

Roman: You just want to hear my voice crack.

Malone: It'll be better than the nine troy ounces of cracked gold you've got in that chest of yours.

Roman: And is it ever a heavy weight to carry.

Malone: What you need is to patch that lead-shot filled heart before it sinks you in Davy's locker.

Roman: He may not make for bad company.

Malone: For now though, pick up that burdensome heart, and put on your mask. You're in our company for the time being and maybe we'll find someone to unload the buckshot from your feels.

Bostock: Come on, slowpokes, we need to get in there.

Roman: Seriously though, let me be the king.

Malone: No can do, toucan. You do better performing than you do glooming about.

Roman: Maybe I should just play Hamlet and kill everyone.

Malone: As long as it doesn't get Monty down our throats.

Roman: This is a bad idea, not just me performing.

Malone: I think it's bloody brilliant.

Roman: I had this dream yesterday.

Malone: So did I, what a coincidence.

Roman: You gonna share your dream with the rest of the class?

Malone: Sure. I had to take over for Monty for a day and convinced the guys to take up a bit of fishing. We caught this monster of a shark that pulled us all in and we found the largest pearls in an oyster bed and made bank. Only after we

got ported did I find out I'd done the whole
thing without my pants. Now, which part of that
dream is the biggest fish story you ever heard?

Roman: Probably about the part where you sleep
long enough to have a dream.

Malone: Says the guy who's been watching Selene
drive her chariot across the sky a week running
now. One'd think you'd fallen in love with her.

Roman: Maybe just hoping she'd give me a couple
words of wisdom.

Malone: Here's your words of wisdom then, lover
boy: loosen the hell up. We're just gonna have a
bit of fun.

Bostock: Y'all keep yammering and we'll never get
there in time. They've already finished doing
rounds on meals. I see the waiters clearing out
the first round of trash bins for the evening.

Roman: This has got me all kinds of vibes. An
enriching experience that'll leave me poorer in
the end. Or maybe a poor experience leaving me
richer in the end. An odd feeling. I guess I must
be odd if we're planning on doing Hamlet in
front of Lutterell.

Bostock: Put on a bit o' swagger, boys. We're
going in.

Exeunt Roman, Bostock, and Malone.

SCENE 5.

Squanderer's Bay: Prodigal Son. Musicians waiting. Enter pub staff
with help from Galley crew

Palmer: Dammit all, where'd that bilgerat get off
to? I can't have plates stacking up here.

Galley Help: Help, good or otherwise, is almost
impossible these days.

Palmer: Jefferson! Show yourself, you sodding clot!
Louis, take this crap out of here before I knock
something over. Leave me a bit of that pie if you
know what's good for you.

Galley Help: On it, sir!

Jefferson: What! What! What! I'm here.

Palmer: Cap's looking for you.

Galley Help: You can't be both here and with the
cap. Get out of here.

*Exeunt Palmer and Jefferson. Enter Captain Lutterell, Boatswain,
Tyndall, Sailing Master Luther, Jules, and other crew members. Black
Albatross crew meet Roman, Bostock, Malone, other party members,
and pub staff.*

Captain Lutterell: Welcome crew and friends of
The Black Albatross! We celebrate tonight!
Though it is not of tradition to keep the times in
such a manner, I wish you to join me in marking
the passing of my seventy-fifth year alive and
fiftieth year as captain of The Black Albatross! I
must blame my luck on Fortuna and the
madams of the Bay! Now, behold, entertainment
of a type for the evening. Food, drink, crappy
actors. Who brought the tomatoes? Right,
boatswain! Bring the box over here and sit
down. You and I are gonna see who gets the first
actor in the face. (Sits down in chair.)

Boatswain: (brings box of rotting tomatoes and sets
it next to Captain's chair before sitting down.)

Best seat in the house, Captain. You always
remember my arthritis.

Captain Lutterell: Surely you can't be arthritic, you
old gunner. You're just fifteen years my younger.

Boatswain: You keep adding to that number, Cap.
I'm five years your younger and we grew up
together chasing seagulls not far from our
mothers' skirts.

Captain Lutterell: You were chasing seagulls. I was
chasing skirts.

Roman: (whispering to a crewman, pointing out
Jules) Psst. Yeah, you. Hey, who's that over there?
No, not that one. The one with the eyepatch.
Oye, no, my blind fellow. Okay, fair, half the
people here have one. Yes, you've got one, I get
it. Sorry. The one with the bit of swagger. Yeah,
yeah, that one.

Crewman: No clue.

Roman: Damn.

Tyndall: I smell a Montgomery. (To a crewman) I
left my knife in my cabin. Bring it to me. No one
of the Blades curses my crew.

Captain Lutterell: Tyndall, what by all the pearls in
the hold, are you going on about?

Tyndall: We've got a Blade in here. They've come to
crash the party.

Captain Lutterell: Hold, Tyndall. It's Roman, isn't
it, under that costume? Good Lord, he's dressed
as Hamlet.

Tyndall: An even worse omen. Let me spill his guts
across the deck.

Captain Lutterell: No, don't go slicing him apart.
Even the Blades can spit out decent people. He's
upstanding to a fault and has no stomach for

bloodletting. He's their quartermaster and we might just have need to split him from the Blades if'n our Jules takes up with Parker's crew instead.

Tyndall: You cannot be serious, sir.

Captain Lutterell: You want to test that accusation, Tyndall?

Tyndall: You would protect a Montgomery, after everything they've done to us?

Captain Lutterell: Shut it, Tyndall. Last warning. Don't jeopardize the truce, it's tenuous as it is. He's known as one of the most virtuous of the quartermasters in these parts.

Tyndall: Have it your way. Him being here is just asking for the crew to go volatile, and then we really will have Montgomery up our mast.

Tyndall exits.

Roman: (Sips beer before approaching Jules. Offers Jules the pint.) Bit lonely over here, don't you think?

Jules: (Takes beer.) They say sharing a glass someone's drunk from is like a second-hand kiss. (Drinks.)

Roman: And your thoughts on second-hand kisses?

Jules: I prefer them first hand.

Roman: You seem not to mind a second-hand kiss from me.

Jules: It is not so much that I do not mind.

Roman: Then will you mind first hand?

Jules: Only if you don't free me of this whole flirting thing. I'm crap at this.

Roman: Then allow me a liberty. (They kiss.) Ale does taste better this way, if I might say so.

Jules: I might agree.

Roman: Would you like to be certain?

Jules: If you would like to be certain. (They kiss once more.) Even bad pick up lines yield good results some days.

Doc: Jules, Sailing Master wants you.

Jules moves to leave.

Roman: Who is their Sailing Master?

Doc: Luther from The Black Albatross.

Roman: May they fly and never land. (To himself) Crap, an Albatross. With what bad luck does Fortuna wish to bless me this time?

Bostock: Let's get out before you have to monologue more Hamlet. They've got tomatoes and they're throwing them at both the good and bad acts.

Roman: I'd brave the tomatoes.

Captain Lutterell: Now, now my fine actors, don't exit stage left just yet! I promise to withhold the tomatoes if you give us another glimpse into the life of Hamlet! (Pub staff whispers in his ear) Past hours! It was just getting fun. Fine. Alright, you bilge rats, return to your stations. We're getting evicted for the favor of the rising sun.

Everyone other than Jules and Doc exit.

Jules: Doc, my vision isn't what it was. Who's that leaving?

Doc: One of The Shrieking Badger's gunners.

Jules: And that? They all look alike right now.

Doc: Let me think. The Djinn's Lamp's sailing master, or was she the quartermaster?

Jules: And the ones from the play tonight?

Doc: No clue, Jules. It's late. Or early. What is dawn when you've been up all night?

Jules: Go ask, I can't see in this glare and I think Captain would like to see them do another play sometime. (Doc leaves) I might just have a celebrity crush now.

Doc returns.

Doc: We had a freaking Montgomery in the house. Roman, their quartermaster, played Hamlet.

Jules: And he has good taste in beer.

Doc: Hold up. Do what?

Jules: Prodigal Son's stocking good beer.

(Someone calls for Jules off stage)

Doc: It was stale. Let's get back to ship and get you reinstated in your regular cabin. It has a good vantage overlooking the fleets this time around. You've been in the infirmary since before we docked. Waking up to something nice to look at will be easy on the eye.

They exit.

FIN

THE BRIDE-TOKEN

THE LEGEND OF HOW BANANAS CAME TO BE

IMELDA TAYLOR

*O*nce in the town of St. Nicholas, a young man, called Barty, sought the heart of a baron's daughter, Anne, through his songs and poetry. Under a willow tree, they fill their days with laughter, songs and dreams of the future.

'I want to see what's across the seas and beyond the horizons. Stop on every island, taste every type of food and hear every bird song,' said Anne.

'And I would like to be there by your side. I have not much in life, but you fill it to the brim with grace and beauty. It might be time I asked your father for your hand.' Barty looked into his lady's eyes.

Overjoyed, Anne replied, 'First, there is something you must learn.' She lifted the hem of her skirt and 'lo, one leg was missing. 'I'm not complete,' she said, in tears. 'For this, no man would have me as his wife.'

'You are complete to me in every way,' said Barty.

When they said their goodbyes, Anne's maid remarked, 'Forgive my impertinence, my lady, but I do not wish to see your heart broken. Are you certain this lad meant well?'

'I am but a damaged good, Felicity. If he could love me as I am now—then there can never be a better man.'

'And your father?'

'My father? I can see him happy to give me away. After all, he has been trying for many years and this could be an opportunity he has been waiting for.'

'Will your lover be able to provide better? I fear his intentions might not be pure.'

'It is upon him to worry. A lady mustn't bother herself with such matters.'

The day arrived when Barty was to ask for his sweetheart's hand.

'Certainly,' the baron said. 'Of course, it is customary to provide a token to the bride's family? As a father, I also need to make sure my daughter has the utmost comfort in life. What have you got to offer, boy?'

'My undying love, my lord.'

To this, the baron laughed out loud. 'Have you got land? Wealth? A mansion to house my daughter? Or do you think I'm a fool?'

The boy shook his head quietly.

'What I see in front of me is a rapscallion, trying to swindle my family. Now, be gone!' the baron shouted at Barty as he turned him away.

Anne was broken-hearted and embarrassed by how her father behaved. She was crying in her room when suddenly she heard a tapping from her window. She looked outside and saw Barty.

'Come with me and be my wife!' shouted Barty from down below. Anne wasted no time. She took off her wig and heavy garb and jumped from the window in only her pantaloons. Barty caught her and wrapped her in his coat.

'My lady!' the maid called and threw out Anne's walking stick. Then off went the lovers on horse.

Barty took care of his lady. He made her a leg out of wood and a shoe with wheels. She wore no wigs, no pannier, no gowns;

content with her trousers, shirt, and coat—yet she remained the most beautiful lady in his eyes.

Time passed, and Anne was struck with an illness. Barty, full of fear his love would depart, went back to the baron to beg for his help. The baron, whose heart had turned to ice when his daughter eloped, refused Barty's plea.

'My lord, please, I ask nothing more than for Anne to live. I have never humbled myself in front of anyone until now.' Barty's sincerity showed through his eyes as he persevered. Upon seeing this, the baron realised Barty had more love to give than himself. However, the baron's greed was so potent he took advantage of the boy's affection.

'Very well. Bring her back. But I still expect a bride-token if you want to keep her as your wife,' the cunning baron said. 'And since you asked for nothing more, it is what you shall get.' The baron made Barty sign an agreement stating he had no right to any of their family's fortune.

Upon returning Anne to her father's house, Barty promised Anne that one day he'd come back.

In desperation, Barty headed to the port and looked for a ship which sailed to Squanderers Bay. As a stow away beneath the tatty merchant ship's deck, he found items he could 'borrow' to trade. He took a sack, a powder flask, and the finest clothes he could find on board. The boy had a plan. Barty wasn't a skilled thief, but he was stealthy.

When he reached Squanderers Bay, he headed to Atoll of the Giants where he had heard he could harvest pearls. Three days he harvested till his sack was full, not only with pearls but oysters and other shells too. With treasure at hand but no ship to take him home, Barty staged his next scheme.

He used the shells to adorn the powder flask he had taken and ground some pearls into powder to fill it. Once a dull item, it became a thing of beauty. He peddled his ware in fine clothes and proclaimed to the crowd:

'Last one left. A treasure from the sea, a miracle flask with magic powder which enhances your lady's beauty, used by mermaids themselves.'

With some demonstration, he was able to entice ladies who bid for the item. Alas, it was not the end of his cunning plan. He told the disappointed ladies, 'Please mesdames, it breaks my heart to see you in this state. I could come back with some more, but my ship was recently stolen. Therefore, there is no way to source such goods. Oh, if only I had my ship back, I could provide an endless supply.'

One lady tugged at her husband and asked that he provide Barty with a vessel. The gentleman made a deal, so long as he got a share of his profit upon his return. Barty agreed, knowing he would never see them again.

He wasted no time and set off home to his beloved to present the pearls to her father. The baron accepted and released his daughter to her love. They sailed the sea and settled in Silona.

In a terrible twist of fate, sailors whose Captain was the same man Barty fooled into lending him a ship arrived on Isla De Los Torcidos. Sure enough, he recognised his ship, which had become home to Barty and Anne.

Men raided the place, found Barty with Anne and took him away by force. Anne held on to her husband's hand so tightly one of the men had to cut it off. Barty was never seen again.

Anne kept her husband's severed hand close to her bosom, never letting go. She searched for days with a broken heart until locals found her lifeless body. They buried Anne and Barty's hand on the edge of the woods.

Days became years and a new plant appeared on the spot where Anne was buried. It grew into what looked like a tree and from it came a heart-shaped bloom. From its bloom, fruits which looked like fingers grew.

The locals of Silona called it banane, believing it came from Barty's hand and Anne's heart.

A GENTLEMAN OF FORTUNE

C. J. HENDERSON

A Gentleman of Fortune

Attr. Captain T.H. Dray

Go from home with no re - grets, Leave - ho, leave - ho!
Sear - ching out trea - sure that's hid, Hey - ho, hey - ho!

Work - ing our nights on the nets, Weave - ho, weave - ho!
Wres - t - ling with gi - ant squid, Play - ho, play - ho!

Spen - ding our days on the ship, Heave - ho, heave - ho!
Stalk - ing the un - wa - ry rich, Prey - ho, prey - ho!

Fin - ding new plun - der to grip, Cleave - ho, cleave - ho!
Leav - ing them dead in a ditch, Slay - ho, slay - ho!

All in the life of a gen - tle - man of for - tune.
All in the life of a gen - tle - man of for - tune.

STOLEN GOODS

J. C. PILLARD

*I*n the all-encompassing shadows enshrouding Isla de Luz, Jess was looking towards the edge of night.

Behind her, the dock stretched back to the fishing district. The ocean's still, inky waters lapped against the wood, a soft song just audible above the bustle of the Port Iberia market. Jess breathed deep, taking in the salty tang of the air and staring towards where the darkness ended. She strained her eyes, trying to see past it, to imagine the world outside.

She tried to imagine the sun.

Jessica Cartwright had been born in the darkness. This didn't make her particularly special: if you were born on Isla de Luz, where the only constant light was that of the Lighthouse, then darkness walked beside you from your first breath. But from her earliest infancy, Jess dreamed of seeing the sun. She recalled her mother telling her stories of it—the brilliant, beautiful light that hung over the world outside. Now, whenever Madame Colette Delacroix sent her into the market, Jess always found herself on the dock, peering towards where the shadows ended and wondering how it would feel to walk beneath the sun.

One day you'll see the sun, my green-eyed lass, her mother had said. So far, that prophecy had not come true.

Behind her, the bells of Port Iberia rang, marking the hours in the eternal night and startling Jess. She shook off the memories, turning away from the undulating ocean. Plucking up her basket, she headed back towards the market.

Port Iberia was the largest city by far on Isla de Luz, and Jess had rarely left it. She'd been to End of the World once or twice, and she'd seen the Lighthouse. But Port Iberia was where the family of her employ had their primary seat, and so it was in Port Iberia that Jess remained.

Passing through the bustling crowds along the marina, she cast a longing glance towards the tall masts of the ships lining the docks. Frigates and schooners, sails furled tightly against the nighttime breezes, bobbed at anchor while their crews took in the pleasures of the city. Jess muscled her way out of the docks and into the crowd of the open air market. Stalls selling every imaginable good—and some unimaginable ones—lined either side of the street. Jess drifted to the right, passing several jewelers' stalls. One of the jewelers, a mustachioed and portly man, was occupied in discussion with a sailor. As she passed his stall, Jess let her hand glide over the fine jewels lining the table's edge, and a pair of ruby earrings found their way into her hand.

Smiling, Jess kept walking, tucking her prize into her pocket. She'd try them on when she got home. She might keep them, if they looked good enough, but more likely she'd fence them and squirrel the funds away beneath her mattress for her eventual escape from the island.

"Someone's light-fingered." A hand curled around her shoulder, and Jess went cold as she was turned around. A tall man with inky black curls and a half-smile stared down at her. He wore a long brown coat that swished as he moved, and Jess caught sight of the butt of a pistol at his hip.

"S-sir?" she managed.

"That was a smooth lift," he continued. "He didn't even see you."

"What are you talking about?"

His grin widened. "Why, these?" He held up the earrings in his free hand, the rubies sparkling in the market's torchlight.

Jess's stomach plummeted as she reached in her pocket and found nothing but lint. How had he gotten those? Better yet, how had he *seen* her? No one ever looked her way in the market. Jess was plain, with her drab hair and green eyes, so unremarkable as to be almost a shadow. But this man, whoever he was, had been watching.

She thrust out her chin. "Those are for my mistress," she said defiantly. "If I tell her you took them, she'll be cross."

"A good liar, too." He arched an eyebrow. "All right, my light-fingered lass. Here's the deal. Have a drink with me, and I'll give you back your jewels."

Jess frowned. "Just a drink?" she asked suspiciously.

"Just a drink." He released her arm and crossed his heart. "On the honor I lost long ago, that's all I ask."

Swallowing, Jess glanced around the market. It was early enough that the market still swarmed with people. The pubs would be, too—on an island with no day. The good times never ended. She could kick up a loud enough fuss to get away from him if need be.

"All right," she said cautiously. "A drink."

THEY ENDED up at the Lighthouse Pub, one of many by that name on the island. The dingy, noisy bar was just filling up. The man led Jess to a side table and hailed a barmaid for a pair of gins. Jess watched him sip his own, leaving her own untouched.

"It's not poisoned," he said wryly.

"No?"

"You'd make a poor listener if you were unconscious."

Jess narrowed her eyes. "I thought you said just a drink."

"Ah, but I made no embargo against talking while drinking. And I've been told I'm quite a talkative fellow."

Reaching into his pocket, the man removed the earrings, setting them in the middle of the table with his hand resting on them lightly. "It seems to me," he began, "that a housemaid who steals jewelry might be at a risk of losing her job if she ever got caught. So, she must have quite a good reason for doing it, wouldn't you say?"

Jess crossed her arms. "Who are you?"

The man took a long drink. "Name's Braddock. I've just come into port on business. Business I suspect you can help me with."

Braddock. The name passed through Jess's mind, snagging on a memory only a few weeks old. "That wouldn't be Bottomless Braddock, would it?"

The man grinned broadly. "You've heard of me."

"You're a thief," she said flatly.

"So are you."

"Stealing earrings in the market and robbing the King's summer palace are two completely different things," Jess protested.

"Ah, but they do have something in common," he said, holding up a finger.

"And what is that?"

"Knowing that you may be caught and doing it, anyway."

Jess frowned at him. "I'm not stealing for the thrill of it."

"I figured as much. So, then, why are you stealing?"

Jess's gaze slid to the window of the tavern. Through the smoke and grime encrusted glass lay the unlit sky outside, the shadowy blanket that shrouded every day of her life.

"I want to leave Isla de Luz," she said quietly. "I'm saving up."

Braddock tapped the table. "These earrings would pay for

passage by themselves. Not nice passage, but you could certainly leave."

"I know that," Jess snapped. "But I'm not casting myself onto the waters without a plan. Without... without funds."

"Ah." Braddock smiled again, a softer smile than the one he'd given her before. "Then we have more in common than you think. I'm not a man to jump into something without looking, either. Which is why I sought you out. I think we could help each other, Green-Eyes."

"Green-Eyes?"

His mouth twitched upwards. "You want to give me your proper name, I'll use that."

Jess considered. "Green-Eyes is fine."

"Fair enough." He leaned back. "By your uniform, you work for the Delacroix family, yes?"

Jess grimaced at her blue and white uniform. "Yes."

"Good. Then, you also know the Delacroixs have a rather extensive library of rare and expensive books and documents they occasionally like showing off to their rich friends."

"And you want to steal some of those books, is that it?"

"*Not* books," Braddock said sharply. "A map. Or part of one. The Delacroix's have a piece of the Map of Ages. I aim to appropriate it for myself."

Jess almost laughed. "The Map of Ages? It's a—a fairy tale. A story for children to make them dream of other worlds."

"Are you so opposed to dreaming?"

She winced. "No good comes from dreams."

"How do you *know* it isn't real?" Braddock persisted.

"Because it isn't," she snapped. "It's just a rumor."

Braddock paused, studying her. Jess shifted uncomfortably, aware of what he must be seeing—a spiritless young woman with a sour expression. Nothing to inspire much confidence.

"Just a rumor, hmm?" His hand slid into his pocket. Slowly, he withdrew a slender leather case, unscrewed it and pulled out a scrap of paper, laying it before her. "Powerful rumor, then."

Jess leaned forward, her mouth going dry as she tried to make sense of what she saw. The page was not large, but it had depth, like staring into a pool of water. And the images... moved. They depicted the ocean and a set of islands; the Atoll of Giants, perhaps. But the currents around the land wavered, while other murkier images swam beneath the surface of the paper.

Her breath caught. Without thinking, she reached out to touch it, wondering if it would shift beneath her fingers. But Braddock snatched it away.

"Don't be offended," he said with a grin. "This was rather hard to acquire, and given your light fingers, I'd rather you didn't touch it."

"What *is* it?" she breathed.

"It can be the key to both our problems." Braddock finished screwing on the cap and stowed the case again. "You help me get the Delacroix's piece, and I promise you this; you'll have a place on my ship wherever you want to go. If you help me, you can keep your little nest egg for your new life."

Jess swallowed, clasping her hands around her untouched glass. She glanced towards the window again, into the darkness. She doubted she'd ever come across a better offer. And if indeed that was the Map of Ages, then more than just this world would open to her.

At last, Jess took a sip of her gin, grimacing at the taste. She met Braddock's eyes.

"What's your plan?"

It was late in the evening—or what passed for it on Isla de Luz— and the Delacroix party was in full swing. Festive lanterns hung all along the curving paths of the manor's gardens, and throughout the party strolled performers of all kinds: musicians, acrobats, and one or two fortune tellers making young ladies squeal in frightened delight. Women in long pastel gowns swanned through the greenery, fans fluttering like butterfly wings, while gentlemen in elaborate justaucorps gathered in tight knots discussing trade.

Jess skirted the festivities as she hurried inside. The hour was late, and her part in Braddock's plan drew near. The plan—or Jess's role, anyway—was simple. She was to open the back gate for the pirates at the midnight tolling of the bell. That was, shockingly, most of it.

She hastened into the manor through one of the side doors. Servants rushed past bearing trays of partridge and cured meats, fruits, and greens that made her mouth water, her gaze tracking the food with envy. She'd missed supper while speaking with Braddock.

"Oof!" The breath left her as—distracted by an elaborate turkey dish—she ran straight into someone. Jess immediately ducked her head and curtseyed.

"My apologies," she stammered, darting a glance up. "I wasn't watching where I was going."

The man she'd run into wore a wide-brimmed hat that concealed most of his face. One of his eyes gleamed a dull, reddish hue in the shadows. He regarded her for a moment before walking away. Jess sighed, letting her shoulders sag. He must have been one of the performers coming in for a brief break.

Picking up her pace again, she hurried towards the buzzing hive of the kitchens. Chefs and servants shouted orders. The kitchen fires spat and hissed, and heat from the ovens hit her like a wave. Amidst it all stood the formidable form of Mrs. Donnelly, the housekeeper.

Clearing her throat, Jess slunk up to the older woman. "Mrs. Donnelly," she said plaintively, "I'm sorry to bother you, but

Madame asked me to fetch the key to the back gate. Some of the performers are coming that way."

Maggie barely glanced at her before her hand dipped into her apron pocket. "They might've told me earlier," she muttered, pulling free a large iron key and handing it to Jess. "Be quick, girl."

The back gate was set in the unfashionable part of the garden, beside the vegetables. Jess stole through the house and out into the back, going first towards the laundry lines. The stone walls surrounding the Delacroix family's estate were high, but not impassable, and she'd initially suggested to Braddock that he merely scale the walls, "If you're such a damned good pirate."

That was when the second part of her job had been revealed. She needed to get them servants' uniforms.

Jess yanked three sets of uniforms off the lines, bundling them beneath her arm and heading towards the back gate.

And then she froze.

Two guards stood beside the gate. Not Delacroix family guards, either—these looked like militiamen. Muskets rested at attention on either shoulder.

Jess swore, clutching the bundle of clothes tightly. She glanced back the way she'd come, biting her lip. Now would be a perfectly reasonable time to abandon this whole endeavor. She didn't *need* to leave with Braddock. A few more years, even just a few more months if her luck with pickpocketing held, and she could leave on her own.

But the image of the Map flickered in her memory. Those half-seen places taunting her from just beneath the paper. She wanted to know—she *had* to know what they were.

Steeling herself, she marched up to the guards with more confidence than she felt. They spotted her almost immediately, and she tried to give them a confident smile.

"Monsieur has requested you in the house," she said.

The pair glanced at each other, then back to her. "We don't take orders from servants."

Jess tried not to flinch. "Forgive me, but there was no one else. Monsieur requested guards at the western gate. They sent—"

"Enough," one of the soldiers said sharply. In the distance, the midnight bell from the Iberia Cathedral began tolling, the other church bells following suit. "If Monsieur is so eager for our presence, he can send another soldier. Not a girl."

Jess opened her mouth, trying to think of a reply, when movement behind the guards caught her attention. A pair of hooks, like grasping fingers, latched onto the high wall of the gardens.

"Did you hear what I said?"

Jess blinked, refocusing on the soldiers. "I'm sorry?"

The soldier grunted, stepping towards her. "Leave." Behind him, three people dropped silently down from the wall.

"Oh, of course, sirs," Jess babbled, one eye on the three figures. She recognized Braddock, who gave her a wink.

"I just... perhaps I could fetch you some refreshment? Something to keep you entertained. The parties often go long into the night." Jess kept talking, kept their focus on her, as Braddock's two companions crept up silently behind the guards. She tried not to flinch as the pair raised the butt ends of their pistols, thwacking both soldiers across the back of the head. The guards stiffened before crumpling to the ground.

Braddock strolled forward, toeing the unconscious men. "Why, Green-Eyes, I had no idea you were such a talker," he said, grinning.

Jess swallowed against the dryness of her throat. "You didn't tell me there would be soldiers."

He shrugged. "I didn't know."

"I thought you said you scoped out the place beforehand," one pirate—a petite woman with close-cropped red hair—hissed.

"I did, but I'm not omniscient, Andrea. You'd need a Fountain Keeper for that." He glanced back at Jess. "Uniforms?"

Jess unrolled the clothes and handed them over, eyeing the two men on the ground. Why would Monsieur Delacroix have militiamen here tonight? They hosted parties at the manor frequently, but nearly always used the family's guard. The only time Monsieur Delacroix requested assistance from the militia was when there was a known threat to the family.

Or a suspected one.

Jess swallowed, turning back to the pirates. "I think they know you're coming."

Braddock paused while buttoning up the blue butler's jacket. He glanced at Jess, then down at the two guards. The third pirate, his long hair bound behind him, knelt to examine the unconscious men.

"She might be right," he said after a moment. "These are militiamen."

Braddock swore. "Someone tipped them off."

"Should we call this off?" Andrea asked. "There's only one door into the study, Captain. If there were guards here, there'll sure as shit be guards inside."

Jess pressed sweating palms against the dress. "There's - there's another way in. The study only has one door, but Monsieur Delacroix installed a skylight a few months ago." She clamped her mouth shut as the three pirates turned to look at her.

"Just a few months ago, you say?"

Jess nodded. "But... it's hard to see."

"How so?"

"The glass. Monsieur commissioned it from a specialized glassblower in Port Coralie du Coeur. I heard him bragging about it to some of his friends. The glass is specially tempered to absorb light, not reflect it. A good deal of light comes through it from the Lighthouse and stars, but it's not supposed to reflect anything at all. It would just look like a regular roof tile."

Braddock examined the roof of the manor house. "Green-Eyes, do you think you could find it?"

"I—yes. Probably," Jess said, her heart beating fast. The rational part of her mind kept screaming at her to stop talking, but another, louder part wanted to see that Map again. To feel the parchment under her fingers and understand those other images —those other places—swimming beneath the paper.

"Draper, do you think you can get us up there?"

The third pirate clicked his tongue. "Probably. But you'll need to be on the lookout, sir. They might have soldiers on the roof."

"That's a risk we'll have to take." Braddock finished buttoning up the servant's coat and nodded towards the house. "Let's move."

IN THE END, there were no soldiers. Draper led them up the side of the house with the skill of an acrobat. Jess crouched unsteadily on the slate tiles, scanning the roof while she pictured the internal structure of the house. As she neared where the study should have been, she got down on her hands and felt along the tiles, stopping when her fingers encountered a smooth, flat plane.

"Here," she said softly, calling the others over.

"It's leaded," Draper murmured. "What do you think? Blow it open?"

Braddock shook his head. "Too loud. We need to try and lift the pane out entirely. Andrea?"

Andrea nodded. She pulled out a tightly corked flask, putting on a pair of gloves before unstoppering it and quickly distributing a powdery substance over the lead. Jess gasped as the lead grew hot and dripped down from the glass.

Braddock chuckled at her expression. "Andrea Lee's a munitions expert," he whispered. "We call her 'The Chemist'."

Jess barely heard him. "What is that?" she whispered to the other woman.

"Iron powder, salt, a few other things. It heats up fast when exposed to air," Andrea explained as the last of the lead melted away. Carefully, they lifted out the glass. A breeze smelling of paper and ink blew out of the now empty skylight. Draper produced a rope, securing it around a nearby chimney, and they began their descent.

The faint glow of the distant lighthouse from the skylight was the only illumination as they reached the floor of the empty room. Jess took a steadying breath, her arms shaking with exertion. Andrea watched her, amused.

"What?" Jess demanded.

"You'll have to get used to sore arms if you're going to be clambering around a ship's rigging," Andrea whispered.

"I'm not a pirate."

The other woman just smiled wider. "You are tonight."

"Hush," Braddock said. He pulled out his scrap of the Map of Ages and frowned in concentration. The Map seemed to tug him forward, then to the left, the paper moving like a sail billowing in the wind. "This way."

Jess crept along behind Braddock, Andrea and Draper following behind. Andrea had her hands on her pistols while Draper rested a hand lightly on the hilt of a blade in his belt. Braddock was occupied, completely absorbed as the Map tugged him forward.

"What are you doing?" Jess murmured.

The Captain glanced at her. "The Map calls to itself," he replied softly. "It was whole, once. It wants to be whole again."

Jess twisted her mouth, wanting to demand more—but Braddock had already turned away. The rippling movements of the Map led them to a portrait of Lord Albrecht Delacroix III. The large painting hung on one wall of the study, the old man's imposing gaze surveying everyone who entered. Carefully, the three pirates removed the painting, revealing a thick steel safe concealed beneath. Braddock glanced at Draper.

"You're up."

The other man grunted, shouldering his way forward. He produced an odd-looking device—two cups attached to long wires that connected to another, larger cup. Placing the smaller cups over his ears, he pressed the third against the metal. He began turning the dial, and a few minutes later the safe clicked open.

Braddock stepped forward, reaching in. Clinking coins and rustling papers sounded softly as he drew out the much-folded scrap. All four of them crowded around, staring at the page in his hands. Jess swallowed down her gasp at the shifting images on the page. A different stretch of ocean this time, and a different set of islands. But still those images moved beneath the surface.

"Does it… is it true?" she asked quietly. "The Map really shows other worlds?"

"Oh, it can do more than that."

Jess shrieked as a hand clamped around her arm, another over her mouth, dragging her away from the pirates. Light flooded the room, and Jess found herself pulled backwards against a hard body. She craned her neck, trying to get a look at her assailant.

It was the red-eyed man she'd run into earlier. He stared at Braddock with a smirk on his face, while Braddock glared at him furiously. Laughter echoed behind her. Whoever this red-eyed man was, he had friends. Just on the periphery of her vision, she made out two other figures.

"Jackal," Braddock growled. "I might have known."

"Good to see you again, Braddock," the man holding her—Jackal—replied. "I was hoping we might run into each other."

"Let the girl go. She's not part of this."

"Ah, but then I'd lose my leverage." Jackal smiled. "And you know how much I hate doing that."

Jess stiffened at the sound of a gun cocking, and one of Jackal's companions stepped forward, an odd-looking firearm in his hand. "Set both pieces of the Map on the floor and back away," he said.

"We're not—"

The man fired, and a bright red streak of light shot past Braddock's head, burning a hole in the wall behind him. Jess started. That was certainly not a Flintlock.

"Set them down and back up," the man said again, "or the next shot is through your head."

"I'd do what he says," Jackal said easily. "He's fairly trigger happy."

Jess's heart beat fast. If they took the Map, they'd take her future with it. Assuming they didn't just kill her. She steadied herself, eyeing the man's gun. If he had one, then her captor probably did, too. What had Braddock said earlier? *Someone's light fingered.*

She let her free arm drift backwards, gently feeling for a holster. Braddock crouched to the floor, slowly setting the Map pieces down. Her fingers met cold metal.

Grasping the butt of the pistol, she whipped it out, taking aim at her captor's foot. She pulled the trigger, and the blast shook her entire arm. Jackal roared, releasing her and sending her flying forward. The red-hot light streaming from the pistol swept over the room, sending tongues of flame erupting from anything it hit. Jess yelped as the metal grew too hot for her to hold, and she released the gun.

The room was suddenly ablaze, her captor screaming in pain. The pirates took their opening, and a pair of gunshots went off. Jackal's men dropped, one of their weapons discharging and sending that same red light zipping over more bookshelves and setting the room alight. Jess struggled backwards, breathing fast, until her hand met paper. She glanced down, gasping as she saw the two pieces of the Map. She grabbed them, rolling them up and tucking them deep in the pocket of her uniform, when a hand clamped around her shoulder.

She whirled, ready to lay whoever it was flat, but it was only Braddock, smiling at her madly.

"Nice shot," he said over the roar of the growing flames. "Now, I think it's time to go."

THROUGHOUT PORT IBERIA, the fire bells rang. Flames licked up the side of the Delacroix manor and had long ago jumped to the fine neighboring houses, creeping down towards the town. The fire brigade was out in force, doing their best to beat back the conflagration.

Amidst the confusion, no one noticed a sleek, black-sailed ship weighing anchor and slipping from the bay. No one noticed the four figures who scurried aboard at the last minute as the ship slid silently from the shores of Isla de Luz, making its way towards the borders of the night.

The deck of Braddock's ship seethed with activity. Men and women rushed about, clambering up the masts, tightening ropes, and any number of things Jess could barely put a name to. She stood in the midst of it, feeling as though she'd stepped from one maelstrom into another. The race from the manor to the dock had been swift, and she hadn't really had time to think about what she was doing, the choice she'd made, until the ship pulled away from the dock. Now, with the land receding behind her, there was no turning back.

She stared across the water towards the bright flames leaping up around the Delacroix manor. Her nest egg was probably on fire in the servants' quarters, the gold and silver of pilfered jewels melting into useless puddles. Here she was, aboard a ship at last, but her pockets were empty.

Not quite empty. She reached a hand in, fingers brushing the delicate edges of the Map of Ages.

"Green-Eyes!"

Jess jumped, turning to find Braddock behind her. He'd shed the butler's uniform and again wore his brown coat and a wide smile. "Come on."

The crew parted around them as Braddock led Jess to the bow of the ship. He leaned against the railing, gesturing for her to do the same.

"Thought you might want the best seat in the house for leaving the night," he said. Then, after a pause, "And I was very much hoping you'd give me my Map back."

Jess crossed her arms. "I picked it up. Doesn't that make it my Map?"

"In a world of thieves, I suppose it does." Braddock shrugged sheepishly. "But I can keep it safer than it will be in your pocket."

Slowly, Jess pulled out the two Map pieces. *One* piece, she realized with a start. They'd merged in her pocket, and now she could see one contiguous stretch of undulating ocean. The texture of the paper felt smooth beneath her hands, almost like glass.

"Those men," Jess started, handing the Map to Braddock. "They aren't from this world, are they?"

"They are not," Braddock said bitterly, stowing the Map in its leather case. "They arrived here from their own world some years ago and have been a thorn in my side ever since. Jackal wants my copy of the Map, you see. He plans to use it for his own ends."

"And you don't?"

Braddock shrugged. "I'd like to think I'm not as mercenary as he is. I'm a pirate, not a murderer. Not most days, anyway. Oh!" He snapped his fingers, withdrawing a pair of spectacles from his jacket and holding them out. The glass in them was nearly black. "Here, you're going to want these. The light can be overwhelming the first time."

Jess took them, running a finger over the wire rims before

turning towards where the water churned away beneath the prow. "I didn't bring my funds with me," she said softly.

"I suppose that means you'll be looking for employment."

"Probably."

The ship surged forward through the water. Jess's breath caught as the shadow's edge drew nearer. She slipped on the glasses, world dimming to complete shadow.

"You know," Braddock murmured. "I can always use a pair of light fingers. A competent thief is hard to find. What do you think, Green-Eyes?"

The ship cut through the darkness, slicing out into sunlight that skittered over the ocean, making the water glitter as though inlaid with diamonds. Even with the glasses, Jess winced at the sudden light, gasping and staring outward. White-capped waves and unending blue stretched in every direction. It was more beautiful than she ever imagined. And it was hers at last.

She glanced at Braddock, who watched her keenly.

"Jess," she said, smiling. "My name is Jess."

CAT O' NINE TAILS

JACK KAIDE

*S*cuse I, sir. Mind if I take a seat beside? What with you bein' by the fire an' all. Tis' cold as a witch's tit in 'ere, an' my bones are achin' with the damp an' suchlike. This damned innkeeper needs must mend the holes in 'is roof an' the bricks in 'is chimney. If he weren't such a miser, I'd not bother ye, sir, not at all.

Thankee kindly, sir, thankee kindly. There aren't so many gentlemen as ye would be so obligin' to an old salt such as I. Another log on the fire? Aye, sir, that'd be grand, that'd be grand. Mayhap two logs, if you'd be so kind?

Aye, sir, 'tis a true tempest we 'ave tonight, with the wind a' batterin' and the rain 'eavy as musket balls come a helter-skel-terin' from the clouds, an' the sea's thick and foamy as beer. Speakin' o' which, you wouldn't mind buyin' me a jar, would ye sir? Tis a cold, cold night, an' me bein' so old an' infirm with the ague, I could do with a little 'victual' comfort. If you catch my meanin' sir? I am but an old, luckless beggar what has to rely on the kindness o' strangers.

Ah, yer a gentleman, sir, a true *gentle*-man if ever I did see. I'd pay my way if I 'ad the purse, ye understand, but times are 'ard, an' I've nary two coins to rub together. I'd be sleepin' out there, in a ditch somewhere's, if I 'adn't a-spied the lanterns over the inn. Yes, yer right, sir; times is 'ard. Times is 'ard, indeed. Thankee sir, an' I'll drink to thy name! An' what be thy name, if I may be so bold as to be askin'?

… Ye'd rather not say. Fair enough, sir, fair enough. A man's business is 'is own; that's what my old man always said. I'll just drink to yer health, then. To 'ealth, 'appiness, an' the tides o' fancy!

Muurp. 'Scuse I, sir. Must be mindin' me manners in front o' company. I was raised proper, you understand, but a few years at sea soon makes a man turn coarse an' scurvy. I'm ever grateful for yer kindness sir, but ye gods, this beer 'tis rank as goat's piss! All the same, 'tis a comfort, a true comfort. When you've reached an age such as I, there's not much can stir a man's soul best as a warm fire, a drop o' somethin' befuddlin', an' good company.

So, what brings ye to St. Madeleine, if you don't mind me askin'? 'Tis a rare thing to see a fine-dressed gentleman such as ye brave the storms an' thunderclaps to reach this accursed place. Most o' us drift here on the tides, like flotsam. Others are pulled t'ward the land like we was *called* to this place. Well, *some* o' us anyways. Your story could be different, as it has every right t'be.

Ah, piss-blood an' heart's o' bastards! Will this storm *never* end?! I've been 'ere a 'forty years now, an' never 'as there been a day t'was clear and free o' clouds an' thunder! My bones ache fierce, an' the unrelentin' damp is curdlin' my lungs somethin' awful. A man is not made for these conditions, says I. This is a *cursed* land. I spit upon the rottin' bones o' he who first set eyes upon it an' thought to call it home.

Sorry, sir, I was interruptin'. Ye were saying? Oh, don't mind me, sir, I have my fits an' tremors oft' such as this, an' I'm prone to grumblin' an' carryin' on when I'm in my cups. I'm known in these parts for bein' a nuisance, but an old man cannot help what he's made of, says I.

'Tis business that yer after then, sir? Ah, I see. And come by ship, ye say? Well, ye must have a fierce captain an' a brave crew, sir, if you came 'ere through the storms. The walls o' this inn are made with all manner o' timbers an' planks from many a ship that ne'er made it to port. I can show ye a piece o' mast taken off a frigate, if ye like, over by old Crofton's barn. You can see the grapeshot what struck it from times past. But, no, yer right, sir, perhaps another day. An' 'tis a terrible night to be wanderin' the streets in search o' thing's what matter so little.

Well, sir, as ye can see, I've a habit o' pokin' me nose in business what's not my own. 'Tis an occupation that will see me dead one day soon, or so my old man would've said. He met a bad endin' sir, a very bad endin' indeed. Died in a fire, many years gone by. They never found 'is body. Or my mother's. Come to think o' it, my sister's body neither. 'Twere such a terrible, terrible thing to 'ave happened, sir. The men who did it to 'im... all over nothin'. Just rumours, that's all. Just stories an' lies.

Another drink? Oh, ye will kill me with kindness, sir, so ye will. I shall ne'er forget this day when a stranger bought old Jack not one, but *two* jars o' St. Madeline's finest! There must be a way I can repay ye, sir. A song perhaps? A little medley o' me own devisin'? I know a good 'un about a chambermaid from Port au Rei who led the bishop's wife astray... Aha! I know just the thing. Now, sir, I'm not so qualified as to do anythin' beside drink, sleep an' f—

... I mean, drink, sleep and *fornicate*, sir. Must be mindin' me manners. As I was sayin', there's but one thing I consider myself a dab hand at doin', an' that's tellin' *stories*. Any tale ye like, be it long, short, tall, proud, filthy or pious, I can tell it. My mind is like a library, sir, filled with stories from antiquity an' such like. Legends o' old, and tales of 'orrors what lay beneath the deep. Darin' deeds an' tragic 'eroines, who sailed the oceans far an' wide in search o' plunder an' glory. Ah, my family 'ad a fine library once, sir. 'Twas very beautiful, an' folks from miles around came to see it. Full o' books and maps an' the like. Such a shame. Such a cryin' shame.

So, sir, what be yer fancy? A tale o' woe, o' dalliance, o' buxom milkmaids an' comely countesses? Or do ye have somethin' else in mind? A tragedy, a mystery, a tale o' ghosts an' sorcery?

… Sir, that is surprisin'. Very surprisin' indeed. I'd never 'ave thought… But surely, none speak o' it no more? And ye, sir, are far too young to know o' such things. I really shouldn't, not here, not now. Very well, sir, ye do persuade me. Very well.

So it shall be, a tale concernin' the Map of Ages. The lost chart that spans all the known continents an' many more besides. Four hun'red years an' twenty old, or so they say. An' so accurate that it shows the very edges o' the world itself to within the breadth o' an angel's wing. And, if I may be addin' here, sir, 'tis nought but a fairy-tale, such as it is. No man has seen the map or at least none that are still breathin'. 'Tis a tale lost to the ages, as my old man would've said. But first, sir, we must start at the beginning. I must tell ye o' a ship's captain. Braddock was 'is name. or at least, they say 'twere. It changes with each tellin', such as it is. For now, we shall say that were 'is name.

Braddock was a fiend, a scoundrel, a cutthroat an' rebel second only to the devil 'imself. The oceans were 'is 'untin' grounds an' the ships that sailed upon it 'is quarry. 'Tis said 'e once threw a king's ransom worth o' silver an' gold into the deep, just to spite Neptune with 'is plunder. 'E gave no quarter, took no prisoners an' was the scourge o' all who saw 'is black sails 'pon the horizon. At least, 'tis what people say.

On Braddock's ship, the *Midnight Scythe*, 'e kept a crew o' fifty men at arms. T'were the fiercest, bloodiest pack o' dogs ye'd ever set eyes upon. Each vile as the last, an' not an 'onest one among 'em. Well, all except for nine o' them.

For on this ship, there were nine brothers. Aye, nine I says! An' these nine brothers, they were fierce loyal to their captain. They'd sooner slit their own throats than betray 'is trust. 'Tis a rare thing, sir, amongst them who'd sail under a pirate's flag: most o' them buccaneers would sell their mother's virtue for a chance to escape the hangman's noose. An' Captain Braddock, 'e knew the brothers' loyalty was iron-fast. And it 'twas o' this, that 'e imparted a great secret between the nine o' them: the mystery o' the Map of Ages.

The map 'ad come into Braddock's possessin' by 'appenstance, given 'im by an old priest from Marshgrave. No one knows why the old priest did it, 'anding such treasure to a buccaneer, but the Lord does keep strange bedfellows. Anyhow, the captain kept it to 'iself at first, not even lettin' 'is second-in-command 'ave a peek at the map. But the nine brothers aboard the *Scythe*, he trusted 'em. 'E knew they would never, *ever* tell 'is secret. So old Captain Braddock, if that *was* 'is name, got to thinkin'. Sooner or later, someone would come lookin' for the map. An' Braddock was gettin' no younger.

He would 'ave to find a way to keep it safe so as 'e would be the only man in all creation with access to the map. An' 'e came up with a plan. A plan that were *so* devious, 'twas as if Lucifer 'imself had whispered it into Braddock's ear.

He took these nine brothers, an' on each o' their bare skins, he 'ad a piece o' the map tattooed in black ink. It were only a *portion* o' the map, see, not the 'ole part of it. That way, it couldn't be followed 'less all nine men were brought together an' their skins *bound* in some way to make it whole again. An' Captain Braddock, if that *was* 'is real name, 'e set these nine men off in nine o' 'is finest ships, to all the furthest corners o' the world. So 'is secret would be safe with 'em. An' when 'e 'ad need o' them, he would know where to find 'em.

The captain burned the original o' the map an' threw the ashes into the sea. Why, ye ask? Why not keep the original, and let the brothers be 'is safe-keep? Well, 'ow can anyone fathom the minds o' madmen? To reckon with their minds is to dance with the devil, says I. And when ye dance with Old Split-Hoof hisself, ye don't stop till the music's ended.

Anyway, as I was tellin', the nine brothers, inked with secrets an' sent off to lands anew, would never speak a word as to the map. Aye, yer a sharp one, sir, if you don't mind me sayin' so! Ye've spotted the little, stringy end o' oakum what's hangin' off this tale. Aye, ye say, *'How can you stop a man from telling tales he's not supposed to? Drink makes a man awful talkative, as ye well know'*. Well, ye cut out 'is tongue, o' course!

An' that's what old Braddock did. First, cut the little devils out with a bosun's knife, one by one. Then, burned the stumps with a brandin' iron to keep em' sealed. An' the nine brothers, now mute an' solemn as the grave, went off into the world. But, before they left, Braddock promised each man that if 'e did 'is duty, 'e'd receive 'is weight in gold an' more besides, when next they met. An' old Braddock, if that *was* 'is real name, always kept 'is word. Or so they say.

… Not that it mattered much. Soon after, Braddock was killed by privateers, 'is head cut from 'is shoulders an' pickled in brandy to present 'afore the Admiralty. They say the jar what holds the head is passed 'round at banquets an' the like, an' each new lieutenant takes a sip o' the brandy to mark 'is passing into the Admiral's fleet. Bastards, sir, vicious bastards, the lot o' them.

OR MAYBE NOT. P'raps Braddock never died. Some folks say Braddock was a *woman* if you can believe it. Daughter o' a sea captain no less, who sailed the seas till the ripe old age a' *ninety-seven years old*. Never caught, lived out 'er final years peaceful-like on a little cottage outside St. Nicholas. But, I know, sir, 'twas all such a long time gone, the facts o' the matter gets all tangled, like fishing nets in a gale. Too much work to untie it all, says I. All that matters is that there *was* a Braddock, an' there *was* a map. The rest 'tis just pretty pictures to tease the mind, like.

Anyway, as I was sayin 'afore I drifted, the nine brothers went on their way. They were never t' meet one another again, or so they 'ad reckoned it. Some went straight, joined a fishing crew or a merchant's ship. Another became a treasure diver in Fiddlers Green. One o' 'em even captained 'is own ship, the *Rose to Nowhere,* an' was the scourge o' the Admiralty for many a' year. They sired no children nor kept a wife amongst 'em. They were silent, solemn sea-dogs o' the old times, their skin weathered wi' brine an' their eyes 'ard an' merciless.

Years passed, men aged an' died, un' new ones were drawn into this realm o' turmoil an' woe. The tides kept a 'turnin, an' the winds they blew, sometimes soft as a lover's kiss, other times harsh as a tyrant's fist. An' in the time that passed, the old second-in-command o' the *Midnight Scythe* 'ad made quite the name for his'self. The one I told ye about, the one old Captain Braddock wouldn't trust wi' the map? Well, for all 'is troubles, 'e 'ad received a royal pardon in the years gone by! All 'is past deeds swept away, a pirate no more.

Some said 'e paid 'fore 'is pardon; others say 'e earnt it fightin' enemies o' the Queen. It matters not, sir. All that matters was, 'e was now a free man. An' soon after that, why 'e got himself a license that made 'im a privateer. That's a one who'd hunt pirates, y'see, sir. The kind o' man who'd kill an' butcher those who once 'e called *shipmate.* Just another cutthroat in coattails, says I. No royal pardon is enough to clean the shadows from a man's soul, nor the blood from 'is hands.

'Is name? Munster, I think 'twas, sir. I might'n be wrong. Captain Munster, though for the life o' me I can't recall the name o' his ship. The *Golden Ass?* Or was it the *Whore O' Babylon?* It matters not, sir, but listen; Captain Munster *knew* all about the map. He'd known about it some time. How'd 'e know? I couldn't say, sir. Mayhaps, 'e peeked at the map 'afore Braddock burnt it. Maybe 'e tortured it out o' the mouth o' some poor sailor, who knew from a mate o' a mate about the strange silent men an' their tattoos that bore the names o' foreign islands an' reefs? All that matters, sir, is that 'e *knew*. And 'e began to scheme. A wicked, terrible plan that would condemn 'is soul to a burnin' eternity.

Once 'e knew Braddock was gone (though it was always a matter o' much confusion as to *where* 'e went, or if 'e was gone at all), Munster marked the spots where last the nine brothers had made for port an' the names o' the ships they sailed on. And over nine years, 'e tracked 'em an' hounded 'em, an' each brother met their end in fashions I don't much care to report, sir. But by the eighth year, 'e had eight pieces o' the map. It 'twere a bloody quilt at first, but Munster dried it with smoke an' coated it wi' wax an' stitched it with the finest silk until it gleamed an' glistened.

You see, the eighth brother 'ad put up quite a resistance, sir, if you catch my meanin'. Munster found 'im drinking in a tavern somewhere Newport way, as 'e was fixin' to join a whalin' crew northward. They 'ad fought like wild dogs in the street, bitin' an' scratchin' till they was both bloody an' raw. Captain Munster, the bastard, tore the flesh from the dead brother's bones with 'is bare hands! Once he'd beaten the man's head into a pulp on the cobblestones o' Newport, a'corse. And this little flap o' skin with the map inked on it (just above the dead man's liver), Munster pocketed it an' ran back to 'is ship, red as the devil his 'self. Sorry, sir, I said I wouldn't tell ye too much regardin' their ends. Must mind my manners.

It 'twas toward the end o' the ninth year, an' Munster heard news o' the last brother. The man was now workin' as a bosun's second mate on an Admiralty ship. Can you conceive o' it, sir? An old, swarthy buccaneer with no tongue, striding about the decks o' a frigate? It beggars belief. It truly does. Anyway, Munster found this ship the brother was on, the *Royal Peregrine*, an' soon 'e set about the last act o' 'is wicked plan.

Under false pretences an' the like, Munster 'ad begged an audience wi' the ship's captain, passing 'imself off as a 'Lieutenant' Munster o' the Admiralty. So, dressed in fine regalia an' a lieutenant's hat, 'e stepped aboard the *Peregrine* when it was next at port. An' at once, 'e set to talkin' an' congratulatin' the ship's captain about how fine a ship it was. Oh, they got on famously, these old salts o' the sea; by the passin' o' the midday sun, they were like brothers in arms. Finally, the captain o' the *Peregrine* invited Munster to stay awhile longer an' eat at the captain's table with 'im. Munster accepted, though all the time 'e was aboard the ship, 'e kept an eye out for the ninth brother. An' sure enough, 'e spotted the last o' the nine mendin' 'oles in the jib-sail down by the prow.

Old 'e was now, the ninth brother, 'is face lined an' cracked as driftwood, though 'is eyes were bright as a new penny. An' the old brother, 'e recognised the privateer Munster alright. E'd known him as the shifty-eyed, snake-tongued bastard first mate o' Braddock, an' soon enough, he'd heard tell o' Munster's savage acts an' the killin' o' 'is kin. An' when their eyes met, they knew that one must kill the other. So, without provocation, the last o' the nine rose from 'is spot by the prow. An' 'e came runnin' across the deck like a man possessed, swinging a caulking iron in 'is hand. He struck Munster hard, sir, right across the chops in front o' the whole crew. An' I don't mind tellin' ye, sir, that the blow the old man fetched Munster across 'is face almost took the privateer's nose clean off.

It were done in view o' the midshipman an' his mate, who set upon the old man, an' soon they clapped 'im in irons. Striking an officer 'tis a hangin' offence, sir. Terrible thing to do, an' in front o' the crew an' all. The ship's surgeon was summoned to tend to Munster's wounds, an' the ninth brother was locked down in the brig till they could fetch a rope to hang 'im with. An' down in the dark, the ninth brother grinned to 'imself, for 'e knew what would come next.

You see, sir, the ninth brother was now an honest man an' a brave one too. He served 'is captain an' his crew well an' was loved by many aboard ship. There was talk that the visitin' lieutenant 'ad provoked 'im, an' murmurin' amongst the men that they would mutiny if the old man was to hang for 'is crime. An' the captain, well, 'e was merciful, in 'is own way. An' in this mercy, 'e decided that fifty lashes o' the cat would be punishment enough. (Munster knew nothing o' this, for 'e supposed they'd hang the old bastard from the mainsail an' dump the corpse o'er the side. E'd pay the ship's surgeon to cut the skin from the old man's back before they wrapped 'is shroud, an' soon Munster would be back aboard 'is own vessel with the final piece). Though Munster whined an' groaned as the surgeon stitched back 'is nose, 'e couldn't help but smile a little at the thought o' this final act o' vindication. Little did 'e know, sir, o' what 'twere to come.

An' ye *must* know what comes next, sir. The next mornin', they stripped the old brother down to 'is britches an' tied him to the mast. The last portion o' the map was plain to see across 'is broad, achin' back (though only Munster knew o' its true meanin'). The captain called the crew on deck an' read out the charge: *'striking an Admiralty officer with intent to wound. The punishment, fifty lashes given.'*

As MUNSTER TURNED white as a sheet, knowin' 'is prize was all but lost, the ship's captain handed 'im a cat o' nine tails. Captain tells him, *'It's only right that you administers the first blow'*, seeing as 'e's the one who suffered the insult. An' *Lieutenant* Munster, 'e doesn't know where to look nor what to think. He's only *passin'* as a lieutenant, see? If 'e lets on that he's nought but a filthy, money-grubbing privateer, 'e'll hang for impersonatin' an officer aboard ship. So, all 'e could do, is nod, all solemn like, an' strike the first blow.

Munster drew first blood an' stepped back by the captain's side, as soon each man aboard the ship took a hand in the flogging. An' little by little, inch by inch, the tattoo on the old man's shoulder became a bloody welt. A mess o' red, carved off 'is hide until 'twere nothin' but raw skin an' bone beneath. An' the old man, 'e said nothin', nor cried out neither. 'E just stared at the privateer Munster from o'er 'is shoulder while Munster watched as 'is chance at glory was snatched away, with each rise an' fall o' the cat o' nine tails.

An' so, Munster never got 'is portion o' the map. The old man died, as old men are oft to do, though there was no retribution for 'is passin'. It were an honest death, all things considerin'. An' that was the end to it, sir. Munster spent 'is days ravin' an' ragin' an' tore the rest o' the map to ribbons. Ah, you ask a fair question, sir. Why not be satisfied wi' the pieces 'e had? What could drive a man to such despair, to 'ave but one missing piece o' a map? A man with even *one* portion o' the Map of Ages would be a rich man if 'e 'ad a mind to seekin' it.

For ye see, sir, The missing part showed the way to a place no man 'as ever seen, not before or since. A gateway, ye might say. One that leads to parts foreign an' strange. Like a whirlpool without end. A bottomless gully into which a man can only descend, fallin' for an eternity into the dark, before 'e appears in a place 'e cannot fathom nor 'scribe to any natural laws o' meanin'.

My father was an educated man. 'E passed a little of 'is knowledge on to me, though it did little to improve my circumstances, such as they were, such as they *are*. 'E had some strange notions, 'e did. Thoughts that would get a man brought 'afore the judge an' the church, so blasphemous they were. He said that the world, as we see a'fore us, is but a plate stacked upon plates, all in an endless variety. And each o' these '*worlds*', as 'e called em', they were unawares o' the other, though they were separated only by a scrap o' stardust and a twinkle o' twilight dreaming. And if a man 'ad the notion and the skill o' navigatin', 'e could journey between em, as you would walk between the doorways o' a mansion 'ouse. I grew up in one o' them, sir, if you can believe it. A mansion, I mean. It was quite beautiful. We 'ad all sorts o' visitors: governors, royals, great thinkers an' artists from all corners o' the world. I 'ad seen and 'eard more than most do in a lifetime 'afore I could even write my own name.

I do remember once, sir, him takin' me on 'is knee like, and tellin' me about *time*. 'E said to me, the common man thinks that time is like sand in an hourglass, flowin' one way, one grain at a time, all in the same direction. But a wise man, 'e knows that time is more like a river. It ebbs and runs with strange eddies that sometimes move in opposition to the force o' its waters. And from that river, you 'ave banks, streams and little rivulets that go off on their own merry way, diversions and breaks in the flow o' time. My father said to me that in these places, you could find all o' man's could-have-beens and never-weres.

Who can say, sir? Is there an eddie in this flow o' times' passin', a shaded brook where my family is still alive? A reversal in the flow o' things, or a change in fortunes where all our tragedies become triumph? A time where thieves and rebels did not force their way into my home an' burn down all my family 'ad sought to build? All our collected legacy set alight that terrible night with a lick o' flame. It t'was a tragedy, sir, and now I am all that is left o' a once-proud house.

They said, whoever *they* be, that my father held a copy o' the map. In the great library of our house, rumour 'ad it there was a secret door that led to a vault hidden deep in the very bowels o' the earth. And in this vault, there was a safe, and in that safe, there was the map. Complete at last, perhaps by some devilry, with all nine scraps o' meat dried and bound together. They said the map 'ad driven my father mad. That it was *he* who burned down our home, killed my mother and poor sister, before walking into the infernal flames, laughing as 'e burned like a heretic at the stake.

Liars, sir, all bastard, lying, snake-mouthed, split-brained stirrers o' other men's shite an' bile! My father claimed no map in 'is possession, an' indeed not the Map of Ages. 'Tis is a fiction, sir, told by those whose brains are rotten an' full o' worms. But 'tis all behind me, sir, and I live my life outside the shadow o' my family's passin'.

I wandered this broad earth many a year since that day o' the flames, and soon my talk became vulgar an' full o' rough edges an' curses. Finally, I took to drink, as those afflicted with tragedy be inclined. Though I was a poor seaman, I worked aw'ile and then became a worse stevedore an' finally a pitiful lighthouse keeper.

Jack o' the lantern, 'twas what they called me, sir. Aye, but that was long ago. I was keeper o' that old lighthouse on Isla De luz, 'afore the darkness came, and the island was filled wit' strange faces and whisperin's. So I left soon as I could. And now I stand before ye, the last son o' the Delacroix line, beggin' men for drinks an' sleepin' in street-filth. Ah, 'ow fortune's' wheel doth turn, sir! Mark me as an example to ye, that ill-luck can befall even those o' noble blood.

ANOTHER DRINK, sir? ... Thank ye, yer too generous, indulgin' an old fool such as I. Ah, but sir, I couldn't accept another. I 'ave no more stories left to tell. They are all the same, in the end. 'Tis always a map, a ship, a captain, an' a fire that consumes all. I could tell ye a dirty joke or two, but my heart is growin' 'eavy now, an' I feel my mirth is startin' to sour.

Yer purse, sir? No, sir, I cannot. I know not what ye seek. And if I did, well, my memory 'tis such a fog. I was a small boy, sir when it 'appened. My father never allowed me in the library. An' even if I did see *it*, I wouldn't recall its finer details. It would be like findin' meanin' in a dream to go back so far into mine own recollectin'. The map was never there, sir. I'm sure I never saw it.

But perhaps... if ye were to buy me another few jars o' ale and maybe a fine coat such as yers, I could set my mind to rememberin'. But, o' course, it would all just be stories, like, and no certainty o' them bein' true. But, memories, like time, do flow in mysterious ways.

A new coat, a pair o' boots, an' enough ale to drown in? Aye, sir, I'd be agreeable to that. Very agreeable indeed. Now, sir, you sit an' listen. And I'll tell ye a story, o' a map, and fire, and a doorway that leads beyond the edge o' the world.

HEART OF STORMS

DARBY CUPID

*T*erry's scream rattles through the room of misted bottles and musty crates, his noxious breath permeating my senses as I twist the knife sticking through his bloodied hand.

"You bitch!" he gasps.

Reaching across the table, I fist the front of his shirt and haul him forward, trying to ignore the stench reeking from the yellowed stumps masquerading as teeth jutting from his gums. "Tell me where to find him!"

"He's dead!" he squeals, tears leaking from the corners of his eyes onto his ruddy cheeks. "Everyone knows Braddock is dead. My mate Steve told me he actually saw his head pickled in a jar."

I exhale, shoving Terry back onto his chair where he slumps with a whimper. "If he's dead, why did I overhear that he's recruiting for new crew members?"

"I don't know," Terry pleads. "I swear it."

Frustration hot and heavy in my chest, I tear the blade from his hand and wipe it on his sleeve. Amongst the bric-a-brac, potions and junk, Gaslamp Goods has a reputation for being a place to buy and sell information, and the main reason is Terry. If he knew anything, he would have told me. Of course, I could have tried to pay for the information, but money is scarce and therefore a last resort. I shove back my chair and stomp from the shop, squinting at the sudden brightness of the outdoors. Terry's whimpers fade behind the creaking door.

It's been three years since Leonora left. Two years older than me, she had always been like the wind: a force of nature, tearing up all obstacles in her path. Just like the wind, she'd slipped right through our fingers. I couldn't remember a time before her tales of adventure on the open sea—the look of excitement glistening in her ocean blue eyes as she stared out across the endless waves. We were never meant to keep her. The moment the *Midnight Scythe*, captained by the infamous Bottomless Braddock, appeared in Half-Moon Landing, she was gone.

For three years, I'd assured myself that she was fine. My father and I had no choice but to let her go; she left us listening to the murmurs in the market, grasping hold of any news of the ship. When Squanderer's Bay had flooded with rumours that Braddock had been captured and killed, I'd feared the worst. There was no news of his crew, however, and I knew in my heart that she wasn't dead—that she wasn't rotting at the bottom of the ocean.

I inhale deeply, the sea air mixing with the scent of fish and incense from the stalls of the merchants lining the floating boardwalks. I hope she's happy. One of us should be.

Sheathing my knife, I stomp back along the boardwalk towards my stall. Lockheart's Daily Catch was one of the most popular fish sellers in the market and had been for several generations. I'd asked Betty to mind it while I paid Terry a visit, and I could only hope most of today's stock was still there. Betty is a dear but, half blind and approaching a hundred, if anyone wanted to rob my store, she'd have no choice but to let them. I quicken my pace. Since Father got sick, it's fallen to me to keep the business going, which means long hours and never quite being able to rid myself of the stench of fish.

"Aye, Tamara," Betty croons from her table of knitted scarves and shawls as I approach. "Did you get what you needed?"

I grunt in response, casting an eye over the stock to see if anything's missing.

"Is that Terry's blood on your blouse?"

Betty's question stills my search and I glance down at the ruby splatter across the blouse spilling from my worn leather corset. "Damnit."

"Is this to do with the rumours?"

It occurs to me that, over the years, I have perhaps not given the elderly busybody enough credit. "And what rumours would they be, Betty?"

She rolls her milky grey eyes, her brows folding into the thick wrinkles lining her face. "Don't waste your breath playing coy, Tamara. I've heard the rumours that the *Midnight Scythe* has been sighted and I know your sister was last seen on its cursed decks."

Two shipbuilders sidle up to the store and purchase some cockles and a haddock, which gives me enough time to weigh my response. Once they move on through the market, I fold my arms across my chest and turn to the old woman.

"And what of the rumours?" I ask. "Apparently Braddock's head is pickled in a jar."

Betty raises a white eyebrow. "And what's that to do with anything?"

"If his head's in a jar, he's probably not sailing a boat."

"There's not a single part of that sentence that isn't swimming with assumption." She shakes her head, and her chins take a second to follow the movement.

"Are you looking for the *Midnight Scythe*?"

I turn at the unfamiliar voice and find a middle-aged woman standing at the stall, her braided brown hair escaping from a thick shawl around her head. Her eyes are so dark, it's impossible to tell where her pupil stops and her iris begins. "Who's asking?"

"No one," she says, turning her attention to the baskets of fish between us. "But if you were wanting to find it, I'd pay Lia Edda a visit."

My eyes narrow to blue slits as I study her. "Who?"

"Lia Edda. She works in a coffeehouse called Le Chevalier Riant in Newport."

"Newport," I echo. "That's on Isla de Los Torcidos."

She nods and gestures to a large skate.

"If I were to travel there," I say as I package her fish, "what would she do for me? Does she know where the *Midnight Scythe* is?"

The woman hands me a coin and takes her fish, tucking it in her bag. "She knows things. Whether she knows *that*, I couldn't say. But she might."

I'm not sure what to say to that, so I say nothing, watching as the woman melts into the busy crowd. I've never left Half-Moon Landing. The idea of making my way across the sea to another island on a whim—a hunch—turns my stomach. A light sweat breaks out on my brow.

"You should go," Betty says, watching my fingers as they clench around the leather money pouch secured to my waist.

"The stall," I mutter. "My father."

I'm not sure which is the bigger reason to stay. My father has been bedridden for the last couple of months, his sight all but gone. His health is declining by the day. What if he dies while I'm away? What if he doesn't and I don't make it back? Without me, what would become of him?

"Your stall can survive a week or two without you," Betty says. "No-one could replace Lockheart's Daily Catch. Everyone knows why you get the freshest fish."

I swallow, my heart racing as I toy with the idea of leaving. Betty's right. The fishermen give my father—and now me—the best fish because their great grandfathers struck a deal with my great grandfather, bound in blood. If I closed the stall for a fortnight or so, that deal would be waiting when I returned.

"And as for your father," Betty continues. "I'll ask Sally to check in on him."

I blink at the kindness of the offer. "Would she not mind?"

Betty waves a liver-spotted hand. "She'll do what her grandmother tells her to."

My lungs are tight with possibility. Could I really leave Half-Moon Landing? I couldn't help but wonder if Leonora had been this nervous before her adventure. Doubtful.

"I'll give it thought," I say, blowing out a long breath.

For the rest of the day, the idea is never far from my mind, and by the time I close up the stall, I've weighed all the possibilities. The biggest issue is coin. I'll have to pay for passage on a ship to get to Newport and I know there's no way I can afford it.

"Have you decided?" Betty asks as she stands with a series of groans and creaks.

I shake my head. "I can't go. It's too much coin and too great a risk."

Betty regards me for a moment. "Don't confuse reason with fear."

"It's not fear," I snap. "It's the responsible thing to do."

The old woman shakes her head and shuffles away, leaving me frowning at her retreating form. My stomach twists.

My father's cries carry on the wind, reaching me as I make my way along the creaking planks to our front door. My chest tightens at the sound, and I quicken my pace. I wrench open the front door and rush to his room, to find him sitting up in bed, his knees drawn to his chest and his eyes red raw from crying.

"Father," I breathe, rushing forward. "Are you okay? What happened?"

He looks up at the sound of me entering, alarm painting his face. "Leonora? Is that you?"

My stomach rolls. "No, Father. It's me, Tamara."

"Where's Leonora?" He looks past me with unseeing eyes. "Why isn't she here?"

"She'll be back soon," I lie, sitting down beside him and drawing him close.

My father's memories are fading as fast as his eyesight and the heartache he felt when Leonora walked out our door is magnified with each passing day.

"I'm not long for this world, Tamara," he sniffles against me. "I don't want to leave without hearing her voice one last time."

His words slice through my heart. Our home had felt empty when Leonora left. But without my father... I swallow, wincing at the pain.

"I'll find her, Father," I whisper.

He looks up from his misery. "Pardon?"

"I'll find her," I repeat, more certain this time. "Betty's granddaughter will check in on you. I'm going to go and find her."

I wait for his protests—his concern for my safety—but none come. Instead, he smiles and holds me close for a moment before lying down on his narrow bed and drifting to sleep. Staring at the ghost of a smile on his lips, I try not to feel hurt by his reaction. Leonora would have been my favourite, too. Any appetite I have from a hard day's work evaporates and I heave myself into my bed and lay staring at the ceiling until sleep wins.

THE YOLK of the sun is barely peeking above the horizon as I set out for Fiddler's Green. When I pass Betty's house, I slip the note I've been clenching in my sweaty palm under her door, trying to ignore my trembling fingers. Every inhale of salty air, every echoing cry of circling gulls, every lapping wave beneath the boardwalks, seems sharper and more poignant under the fear that it might be the last time I experience them.

I've only been to Fiddler's Green once before. Many years

ago, when we were barely in double digits, Leonora heard a rumour that one of the merchant's sons had started selling chocolates and sugar. Her thirteenth birthday had been approaching, and she insisted if she didn't taste chocolate before she became a teenager, she would die a slow and painful death. Being barely ten myself at the time, I had believed her. Fiddler's Green had been a terrifying place—a ship's graveyard—filled with scavengers and treasure hunters, moving between the mists like ghosts. Leonora had dragged me around for hours, but we never found the merchant's son. By some miracle, she didn't die from her lack of chocolate.

The air thickens and cools as I draw closer, the sea mists climbing from the waters to swirl around the shattered hulls and snapped prows of long forgotten frigates and galleons. Masts rise from the depths like the desperate hands of drowning sailors, and the sight sends a shudder down the length of my spine. There's no reason to be scared. I'm no longer a naïve ten-year-old hiding behind her sister's skirts. I know full well that the goods found here are sold by my friends and neighbours in Squanderer's Bay. Even so, I clutch my satchel tighter to my side, my other hand lingering over the hilt of my dagger.

The merchant selling sweet goods is no longer a rumoured mystery. Now, almost ten years later, I have heard many tales of Barnard Stickleby. The wealth he has acquired has helped to expand his empire to a small fleet of ships. These ships sail between the islands, gathering the ingredients for his product and trading his wares across the seas. This is my plan: to gain passage on one of his ships for a minimal fee. Unfortunately, his fleet of ships is not the only thing I've heard tell of. Many have whispered tales of his chocolate truffles—laced with truth serum; you'll spill your secrets or your guts before him.

"Excuse me?" I pause by a pair of boys sitting on the board-walk, lines dangling in the water. "Could you point me in the direction of Mr. Stickleby?"

The boys don't deem my question worth a glance in my direction. One of them lifts his arm and points to a large ship at the end of the dock.

I mutter my thanks and continue toward the ship, aware of how loud the echo of my boots is amidst the quiet morning air. If Stickleby doesn't see me coming, he'll certainly hear me. The ship is impressive—a towering galleon; the prow embellished with gleaming metal that looks gold, but I assume must be brass. Surely no one would be cocksure enough to sail the waters with such wealth on display. The figurehead is a beautifully carved woman, her long hair trailing behind to twist around the bow. I roll my eyes at her exposed, ample chest and make my way to the gangplank. Fiddler's Green is quiet, and although I spy a few crew members moving around the deck, I start to wonder whether Stickleby will be awake.

"Good morning, lass," one of the crew calls out as I make my way up the gangplank. He looks to be in his fifties, and despite the gaps in his teeth and the large scar across his face, his grin is more friendly than intimidating. "What brings you to the *Lucky Maiden?*"

I cringe inwardly at the name and return his smile, straightening my shoulders. "I'd like to meet with Mr. Stickleby. Is he available?"

With no shame whatsoever, the sailor drags his gaze along the length of me before nodding. "I'd say he would be."

My skin heats as I huff in disbelief. "Excuse me, Sir. I'm not sure what you think I might want with Mr. Stickleby but—"

"It doesn't matter what you want," the sailor cuts me off. "He only takes unsolicited meetings from existing clients and pretty women. I'll go and see if he's free."

Beneath my skin, my blood bubbles hotter than the sun, and I know it's going to take all my self-control not to punch the man in the throat when he appears. The sun has begun to burn away the morning mist, revealing more of the surrounding carcasses of ships and my stomach twists as I stare at the gaping holes and smashed wood. Was the damage caused by storms or by pirates? I swallow.

"Good morning, milady."

I spin on my heel at the deep rumbling tones, a frown already on my face and distaste bitter on my tongue. Somewhere between turning and taking a breath, however, my thoughts jumble together, and I find myself silent as I stare at the approaching figure. He's much younger than I expected, appearing to be somewhere in his late twenties. Dark brown hair hangs in loose waves across his forehead, curling at his ears and the nape of his neck. His sun-kissed skin gleams in the way only those with wealth do.

"Good morning," I manage as I stare up at him. "Mr. Stickleby?"

He's a striking figure, the expensive cut of his emerald frock coat showing off his broad shoulders and trim waist. Now that he's close, I realise the most fascinating thing about him is his eyes. One is a deep emerald green and the other a striking sea blue.

"Indeed. Please call me Barnard. And who are you?" He smiles, revealing a mouth filled with pearl white teeth.

I blink. The overall effect is quite disarming and I'm extremely aware that's most likely his intention. "My name is Tamara Lockheart. I'm seeking passage to the Isla de los Torcidos."

He raises a dark eyebrow. "Oh? And what business do you have there, Ms. Lockheart?"

"Does it matter?" I ask. "Can you provide passage or not?"

Barnard stares at me for a moment, then shakes his head. "I cannot. My ship leaves for Newport this afternoon but I'm afraid we are already full."

"Full?" I echo. "What difference would one person make?"

He bows and backs away. "Apologies, Ms. Lockheart. I wish you the best in your endeavours."

I move to follow him, but the toothless sailor from before materialises before me, blocking my path. "You heard him, miss. Off you go."

Before I know what's happening, I find myself being led down the gangplank. My head spins. I'd expected to have to convince him—to barter. I hadn't expected him to reject me within a second, with no explanation. Turning around, I gape up at the ship in consternation. There is no way I'm missing this opportunity. No way.

PULLING the hat lower on my head, I shove my hands in my pockets and try to blend in with the people moving along the boardwalks. By midday, Fiddler's Green is a very different place. Shouts fill the air as scavengers hock their wares or yell directions from the water. The clothes I've borrowed from my father are surprisingly comfortable, but I miss the swish of my skirts around my boots. It's barely a plan, but I figure if I can just get back on board the *Lucky Maiden*, I can try to hide until it's too late to turn back. Of course, there's the chance Stickleby will just throw me overboard, but I really hope he doesn't.

The *Lucky Maiden* is crawling with people, the gangplank a constant flow of people and crates. Sidling up to a young man attempting to wrestle a large wooden box, I stoop and help him, ensuring my face stays hidden. He grunts his thanks, and we move up the gangplank onto the ship. We move across the deck toward the stairs leading to the cargo hold, and together we make our way below deck. As soon as the box is lowered, I slip into the shadows and hide between the stacks of crates. The young man loiters for a moment in confusion, but then mutters something under his breath and heads back to the stairs.

I stay crouched in the shadows, barely daring to breathe as

more boxes and crates are loaded on board and people come and go chatting about the journey ahead. It turns out, the *Lucky Maiden* is heading to Newport and then on to St. Madeline before heading to The Whispering Isle. It's of no matter to me though. I just need to get to Newport so I can find Lia Edda.

It feels like an eternity before the ship moves from the dock; the motion knocking my aching muscles. My painfully dry throat reminds me with every swallow that I'm trapped in the belly of the *Lucky Maiden* with no food or water; my plan is even more half-baked than I thought. Wrapping my arms around my knees, I decide the best thing to do is try and get some sleep. With any luck, I'll wake up and we'll be docked in Newport.

LAUGHTER TEARS me from my fitful sleep, and I blink awake, my head pounding from dehydration. On the deck above, music bleeds through the stomping of feet and the sound of merriment. I groan and try to cover my ears with my shoulders, but to no avail. A whimper builds in my throat, and thirst has me scrambling to my feet. It sounds busy. Surely I can sneak up, grab a drink and maybe some food, and then get back down until we dock.

My heart hammers in my throat as I push open the hatch and emerge by the mast between the quarterdeck and the main deck. There's a pile of crates that must have been too big to move below deck blocking me from view, but it does little to calm my nerves. Pulling my hat over my ears and tucking in the stray strands of long black hair, I edge my way over to a stack of kegs. The taps are steadily leaking red liquid onto the deck, creating a bloody puddle, and the stench of wine fills my nostrils. I'd have preferred water, but on a ship, beggars can't be choosers. Grabbing a goblet from an empty barrel, I fill it almost to the brim. If it doesn't quench my thirst, at least it will help me sleep.

I'm not sure whether it's desperation that makes the wine

taste as good as it does, but my eyes drift shut as a moan of pleasure escapes my lips.

"Sounds like you're enjoying yourself," a voice rumbles at my ear.

Stickleby. My stomach drops and I clench the cup between whitened knuckles. "It's better than I expected."

"It should be," he replies, moving to stand in front of me. "I know my wines."

Keeping my head dipped, I hide my face beneath my cap, staring at the shiny buckles on his polished black shoes. I grunt in response and move to turn away, but he reaches out a hand and places it on my arm.

"Your little ruse is up, Ms. Lockheart."

I stiffen, panic fluttering over my skin as I look up at him. Searching his face, I try to read his expression. "So, now what?"

Barnard leans against the side, tilting his head as he looks at me. "Well, we could throw you overboard, but that seems a little archaic. Plus, it would be a shame to ruin your outfit."

I narrow my eyes at the smirk playing on his lips. "What then?"

"I haven't decided yet," he says. "Tell me. Why do you want to go to Isla de los Torcidos?"

I fold my arms across my chest. "I told you before, it's none of your business."

"You've stowed away on my ship," he says, his unusually coloured eyes glinting. "I'd say it's most definitely my business."

Staring up at him as I consider my response, I run my tongue over my dry lips. Barnard tracks the movement, his jaw tightening.

"Please take that ridiculous hat off," he snaps.

I raise my eyebrows. "Why?"

"Because you look like a small boy."

My brows raise further. "And what's wrong with that?"

Barnard pushes off the side and before I can react, grabs the hat from my head and tosses it overboard. "Because, while I can appreciate a good-looking man, it makes me extremely uncomfortable finding a young boy attractive."

I blink, my mouth falling open. Before I can respond, screams rattle the sails and I spin around to find people hauling themselves up over the side of the boat. My shriek of terror lodges in my throat as I watch the wild eyes of the invaders, with either knives between their teeth or war cries on their lips.

Pirates.

Barnard shoves me behind the wine barrels. "Hide!"

I have no time to protest as he draws a large, curved sword and dives into the fray. Passengers are screaming as the pirates tear jewellery from their throats and I jam my fingers in my mouth to stifle my horror as a female pirate severs a large woman's fingers to better remove her rings. Are these the people Leonora has chosen to spend her time with? A fresh wave of nausea rushes through me as I wonder whether these are Braddock's crew. I can barely breathe as I scan their faces for my sister's.

"I've got him!" a rasping voice calls out beside me.

Staring in dismay, I find a weather-beaten pirate, with more gold hoops through his face than could possibly be comfortable, has Barnard clasped against his chest, a serrated blade close enough to his throat that I can see blood beading above his Adam's Apple.

"Excellent!" A young woman with short blonde hair and heavily lined dark green eyes steps forward, a gold sword swinging in her hand. "You're looking well, Stickleby."

"As are you, Jess," Barnard says, charming despite the blood dripping down his neck.

"Did our invitation to your little shindig get lost in the mail?" Jess steps closer, dragging the tip of her blade over his chest. "Braddock will be extremely offended."

Barnard swallows with a wince. "This isn't a shindig. This is a few drinks en route to Newport. I've paid my passage."

I blink. *Passage.* Is that how Stickleby manages to amass so much wealth while other ships are plundered and lost?

"Yes, well," Jess says with a sigh. "Braddock wants to double the fee."

"Double?" Barnard splutters.

Jess cocks a dark eyebrow. "Yes. She has a wedding to pay for."

She? My head spins. Braddock is alive? She's a woman?

"Congratulations to the happy couple," Barnard says. "Please, take four crates of my finest chocolate as an engagement gift."

Jess dips into a shallow bow. "Braddock and Leonora will be thrilled."

The world drops away at my feet and I sway, knocking into the barrels with a soft thud. Barnard launches into a coughing fit, drawing their attention from my hiding place as I try to swallow my pounding heart.

The pirates have herded the passengers of the *Lucky Maiden* onto the quarterdeck, whimpering and shivering with fear. I watch as a handful of pirates descend below deck and reappear with clearly more than four crates, which they lower overboard to where I assume their boats are waiting. As the pirates slowly leave, I realise there are more than a couple of bodies lying lifeless on the deck. My eyes burn.

"You know," the man with the gold hoops hisses. "I think you'll still be able to pay Braddock with one ear. Or maybe with one eye. It's not natural for a man to be so pretty."

Barnard's eyes widen and before I know what I'm doing, I crawl out from behind the crates, my dagger in hand. Time seems to move in slow motion as I rise to my feet and lodge my blade through the pirate's neck. He staggers backwards, releasing Barnard as I yank my dagger free. I have no idea what to do next, but before panic can set in, Barnard heaves the pirate over the side of the ship. The splash marking his fall is lost amidst the shouting and wailing around us.

"We'll see you soon, Stickleby," Jess calls from the other side of the ship, waving as though they're old friends.

She either didn't see what we did to one of her crew or simply doesn't care, because she leaps overboard and descends out of sight.

We stand in silence, the laughter of the receding pirates growing fainter. It's only now that I spy a ship on the horizon.

"Is that the *Midnight Scythe*?" I whisper.

"Unlikely," Barnard says. "Jess has her own ship she uses to run Braddock's errands."

I nod, my eyes fixed on the distant ship. Leonora and Braddock. It was too much of a coincidence.

"Thank you," Barnard says, taking my hand and bringing it to his lips. "You saved me."

My cheeks burn as I pull my hand away. "I saved your ear. Possibly an eye."

"Tell me," he says, the mirth fading from his face. "Why are you going to Torcidos?"

I swallow. "I was looking for my sister, Leonora."

It takes a moment for the realisation to settle on his face, his eyes widening. "Your sister is Leonora? Braddock's bride?"

"It certainly sounds like it." The realisation is bitter on my tongue.

Around us, the crew is cleaning up like the attack is a regular occurrence, comforting the patrons and handing out wine and chocolate.

I turn away and face the horizon. "Why did you refuse me passage?"

Barnard leans against the railing with a sigh. "Honestly? Because you looked like trouble."

"Excuse me?"

He smirks, shooting a glance at where I skewered a pirate moments earlier. "Tell me I was wrong."

I groan and rest my head on my arms.

"What now, then?" Barnard asks gently.

"Our father's dying. He wants to see her. But now…"

"Now you've experienced the joy of pirates firsthand, you've lost your nerve?"

I glare up at him but find nothing but kindness on his face. "I don't know."

"Come with me," Barnard says, taking my hands in his. "I have a score to settle with Braddock, and you need to speak to your sister. Why don't we help each other?"

I stare at our joined hands, adrenaline thrumming in my veins. Is this what Leonora craved? Is this what adventure feels like? Two paths lie before me, and one is paved with electric sparks and danger—the same sparks and danger I see in Barnard's eyes.

"I thought I was too dangerous?"

He runs his thumbs over my hands, his lips curving. "Turns out, I like danger."

Squeezing his hands, I smile. "Let's crash a wedding."

The End.

ACCOUNTS FROM DOCTOR PENDERGAST'S CHRONICLE

IMELDA TAYLOR

*D*ay 11111: I decided that today is my anniversary here on St Madeline. Although not accurate, I feel I need to mark my existence. Unfortunately, I couldn't start from day one. I wish I could say I remember when I first set foot on the island. There are times when I wonder if this is the afterlife.

Home. My mind wanders to my home in St Nicholas. It has been a while... who would have known that joining the Navy crew would change my life forever. I left my family and the comfort I didn't realise I had in exchange for adventures beyond the seas.

I only have one life. I wanted to live the adventures I heard of from my mariner and merchant patients. Being a surgeon, my services were sought after on-board the ship. I wasted no time and joined the Navy crew.

I took my personal chest, full of medicine of my choosing and all the tools I required. It was the greatest feeling ever. I took pride in serving the King and country.

After being at sea for some time, I realised how much of an asset I was to the ship's crew. One by one, they started getting ill from scurvy, dysentery, skin diseases, and infections. The grand exterior of the ship didn't match what's inside, not to mention the stench. If it wasn't for me and my tools, more would have died. The captain knew he owed the wellbeing of his crew to me, and I was paid handsomely after every expedition.

Word spread about my skills. Before I knew it, a band of pirates captured me, led by Captain Boylant. They took me and my chest on their ship. It was humiliating to be treated like the drunkards we took in the Navy. I reminded them of my status, but they whipped me and threatened they would cut off my tongue. Previously, I thought nothing of this beating of low ranking sailors; it was a common practice and they should have seen it coming for being wilful. But now... I ponder our beliefs and our actions. Perhaps I displeased God in the past.

Work was much harder. I was excused from any other on board chores in the Navy. Here, I was treated like a common crew member.

My chest needed replenishing. There wasn't enough medicine to keep everybody during our voyage.

'It doesn't matter,' said the captain. 'When we reach our destination, we won't need any treatments and cures. We need not worry about life as we know it.'

I did not understand what he meant then. Later on, I learnt they were heading to St Madeleine, home of the so-called Well of Eternal Life.

They were foolish for believing in such a myth. Yet, a dozen willing men held me and a few others captive–including children–just to chase something that surely was fantasy. From a life full of pride to being a prisoner of the insane, how quickly fate turned. On the other ship, I was treated with great importance, but now I'm a mere tool, a slave.

Day in, day out, I ponder what has become of me.

Captain Boylant warned us of the storm surrounding the island, but nothing prepared me for what lay ahead. All hands on deck, myself included. The raging tempest howled like a beast with a whip that was worse than the captain's flogger; its salty spray burnt my eyes. Violent waves lifted and tossed the ship about so strong it snapped the mast like a matchstick. And like a dark velvet curtain, the sea shrouded us all.

None of them survived the storm. Only I lived to tell the tale.

That was my last memory before I woke up, drenched on the beach, to the crashing of the sea. Although not as fierce, the wind continued to howl. From a distance, I couldn't believe I descried the storm, yet from where I stood the sky was merely overcast. Despite my limited knowledge of weather, I found this rather unusual. None of it made sense. Flashes from the lighting drew my attention to the sky. It had its beauty, soft behind the clouds, like marble with golden cracks.

As soon as I was able I looked for shelter. Lo-and-behold, I found a washed up shipwreck and turned it into home. Soon, I met a few locals who were curious about my appearance. It had been a while since a newcomer arrived on the island. They said the island was once a paradise attracting all sorts of visitors, not all with pure intentions, before a mysterious force cut them off from the rest of the world. Perhaps, to protect the island's secret: The Well of Eternal Life.

Up to this day, I have never laid eyes on the actual well itself.

However, I heard of those so eager to get their hands on it, they even risked drinking what they presumed was the same water coming from the well despite its vile appearance.

I offered medical help in exchange for food and supplies. Although it wasn't in the best shape, the lower deck of the ship is now a hospital for the unfortunate souls. My medical supplies ran out many moons ago and I've improvised with whatever I could forage. My surgical tools are blunt and rusty, not to mention my trembling hands and my poor eyesight. None is fit for purpose.

After my brush with death, I was tempted to seek eternal life.

Until I met those who actually had the misfortune of gaining eternal life. They come to me with their ailments—repeatedly. Painful cries of agony as they keep living, yet their bodies continue to deteriorate. The wounds stop healing. They carry on aging and beg for death to come. But it is too late. I realised the well is not a blessing, but a curse. It is a cruel tool for torture. If the Captain knew, would he have wasted the life of his crew?

Never in my life had I imagined such a thing actually existed. I saw many births and deaths in my occupation; it sealed my belief in the miracle of life God had given us. Now my views on life and death are blurred. Dare I even say I question the existence of God Himself.

Oh my Lord, forgive me for my thoughts. I know not what I speak. I ask for your guidance and help me follow your light.

Sometimes I ask myself, why was I the only one to survive? What is God's plan for me? Why has He chosen me? Up to now, I seek the answers to these questions. As I get old and frail, I cannot help imagine what death could be like. It scares me, especially with my knowledge.

However, today, I am alive. I celebrate surviving; I celebrate life.

DAY 11112

More items washed up on shore. It suggests that the sea storm surrounding the island claimed another ship. Today's item include:

A crate of rum
A whole crow's nest
Ropes
Sack full of [unknown things]
A ship's sail
A couple of hammocks

A quality brass spyglass, lenses intact.

When days like this happen, I would like to believe that God is sending me blessings as I always find use for the things later on. However, I cringe at the thought that the sea has claimed so many lives. I imagine the person touching the item in my hand. The idea that people died so I can have these things haunts me.

Today I thought I'd watch the storm. I wanted to face the very monster that claimed so many lives. I thought it was fascinating that the storm clouds didn't seem to move. They just stay in the same spot on the horizon.

DAY 11117

Today I found a compass. According to it, I am in the North.

But the highlight of the day was finding a chest. Inside the chest is a proper treasure: books on herbs and their healing properties, a scale, and an anatomy of the human body. It holds information which is new to me, which makes me wonder if I've been on the island longer than I thought.

I went foraging for herbs and roots and tried my hands on this new alchemy. Some need several days to brew and steep. I can't wait to try them on my patients.

DAY 11119

Today, I went exploring, and you'd never believe what I discovered while travelling. Pineapples! An entire field of pineapple. I could smell their sweet sweet scent from where I stood.

The very first time I saw one was at Stickleby's, the richest merchant on the floating market in Squanderers Bay. It stood on his desk with all its glory. The gold mixed with its green crown and diamond pattern was a thing of beauty. Never did I imagine I'd be witnessing an entire field of them.

Nearby, a couple of men were harvesting them! What ignorance, I thought! Clearly, these benighted fools were clueless of its value. Worse off, they sliced and ate it. I wanted to set these men straight, but they were armed with sharp tools.

Alas! They saw me.

'Doctor!' one of them called. His white teeth glistened in the sun as he smiled. How did he know me?

'Fancy a spot of lunch?' He reached out and offered me a piece of pineapple.

My stomach growled. I hadn't realised how hungry I was.

'Go on, doctor, don't be shy.' The man approached with a huge knife, which almost looked like a sword.

I froze. I wanted to run, but before I knew it, the sweet smelling fruit seduced me. I gave in and took a bite. If ambrosia ever existed, it would be this. It tasted as sweet as it smelled; my tongue tingled. The juice burst in my mouth and trickled down my chin, but I didn't care.

'Good, isn't it, doctor? But be careful with the hard bit in the middle, it can make your tongue itch. Come have more with us.' The man led me to his friend, and we sat together.

I had to tell them that where I came from, pineapples were so precious they weren't eaten. Instead, the rich put them on the table as ornaments for everyone to see. The men laughed.

'No doubt they are precious, doctor. But we seem to have a different way of showing appreciation. On this island, we don't let it rot on a table,' said one of the men as he held up a whole one. 'You are right about its beauty.' He then cut the crown off and shared the fruit with us. 'We enjoy it. Let it serve its purpose: to provide sustenance, and if you're like me, heal your soul too.' He then placed the crown on the ground. 'Then let it live again. Now, the treasure is within us.'

As we parted, I gained friends, Juan and Wawu Gaudet. I was a tad embarrassed I didn't recognise that Wawu was a former patient of mine. The truth is—I couldn't see their faces clearly.

DAY 11126

The potions are ready. My subject today is Mr Brimscombe, male of unknown age, believed to be an immortal. Concerned locals found him by the side of the road and they brought him to me. He kept repeating, 'let me die.' But now, he barely speaks.

He suffers from dysentery, a swollen left knee and an injured eye. I performed bloodletting on his knee, followed by an amputation.

Today, the focus was to reduce the swelling of his right eye. It was full of pus, and a few maggots started to appear. I washed the wound in purified water (as stated in the medical book) after picking the maggots and applied the solution. An overpowering fume came out of the bottle as I opened it. The subject cried out when I applied it, then covered it with a cloth. If no improvement shows in a few days, I will have to remove the infected eye.

DAY 11127

I checked on my subject to see if there's any improvement. There seems to be none so far. With the experiments, I need to hire an assistant to help clean up.

I decided to go to the pineapple field again. Other than getting a few more pineapples, I'm hoping to see Wawu and ask if he could recommend somebody to help out with my small hospital. However, I haven't a clue what payment to provide. There seems to be no currency. Everything is paid in goods, at least that was what I'm given every time I treat a patient.

I was hoping Wawu could advise. He was already there when I arrived. He gave me a friendly wave when he saw me. I sat with him and his companion, Juan, to have lunch. Juan had just asked him about his family, and Wawu was regailing him with the most recent news regarding Abby, Gabe, and Felicity. I nodded and smiled and waited for a natural break in the conversation.

Wawu was cooking a peculiar fruit he calls "banana" on an open fire. It was black with a hint of yellow and green. Its chunky appearance and matte skin wasn't as beautiful as pineapples, yet it is as exotic. Steam came out when Wawu cut it on its side to expose the pale creamy flesh inside, and it definitely tastes much better than it looks. According to him, it is what they eat if they need energy that lasts longer.

Before I had a chance to ask him about looking for help, he asked me to go with them. The youth in me suddenly emerged from the depth of my soul. The sense of adventure came alive once again. I didn't even ask where or how long the journey would take. I just agreed to go.

Then I remembered the work I'd be leaving behind. I had to ask Wawu.

'Well, Doctor, I can give you an answer when we reach our destination,' said Wawu cryptically.

When I asked where we were going, he just replied with 'you'll see...'

Never having travelled that far on the island, I regret wasting so much in life; the adventures I once dreamt of having, all forgotten when I could have spent time exploring a mysterious island. Instead, I became a recluse. Now that I'm in ill health, I'm just starting to live.

Suddenly, I heard a harrowing cacophony of something inexplicable. I took no notice at first, but it grew louder and louder, and I wasn't sure if it was howling or a trumpet. Goosebumps prickled all over my body.

I watched Wawu and Juan, who took no notice of the sound. I wondered if I was the only one who could hear it.

'Nearly there, doctor,' Wawu said. I asked if he could hear the noise. He only nodded without denying, nor confirming, it was a beast.

When we arrived at the opening of a cave, the moaning and

groaning became louder and more resonant. It was how I imagined entering hell would be like.

'Where have you taken me, Wawu?' I asked in desperation and fear.

"It is the Cave of Eternal Damnation, where soulless men bury themselves. But as you know, doctor, there is no hope.'

Juan lit a torch at the opening of the cave. As we went deeper, a chilling sight lay before us: leaning on the walls, lying on the cold dusty earth, ailing bodies lined the cave. I didn't have time to stop in fear I'd be left behind. I kept on following Wawu until we reached an alcove.

'Meet my mother, doctor,' Wawu said pointing to the woman, curled up on a mat. I asked his permission to examine her. She had a pulse, yet was barely alive. There were several lacerations on her wrist and on her neck. 'I did this.' Wawu said with a voice full of remorse and regret. 'I was young and afraid to lose her. So I got her water from *the well*. At first I thought it was a miracle cure. But it's a curse, a curse, doctor. As she got old and infirm, she begged me to find a way to end it. How, doctor, how?'

At first I thought he was asking how to end his mother's misery. But, his real question was how could his mother ask him to murder her. I'm not sure how I knew. Perhaps it's the way she looked at him accusingly, or the way he whimpered.

Juan put his hand on my shoulder and walked away.

'What is it that you want me to do, Wawu?'

'Can you make her *better*? Please? I will do whatever you ask.'

I wish I could perform a miracle that would make her better. I wish I was God himself, but I'm a mere mortal who's past his best. In all honesty, I didn't know if I could help.

What Wawu sought was comfort. Perhaps, forgiveness, from his mother, and his Maker—for depriving her of true eternal life, and ironically committing a sin to right what was wrong. But to no avail. Perhaps it was redemption or, perhaps, he's gone mad.

I ended up offering him a spark of hope. I told him I needed to gather some medical supplies and come back the next day. He agreed and back home we went.

DAY 11128

I checked on my subject's progress before Wawu arrived. The swelling in his eye subsided, and the maggots were gone. Pus remains around the eye, which could be a sign of healing. I placed leeches around the infected area to bleed the veins around the eyes.

Wawu arrived with a basket of eggs in hand, to be used for a few medical procedures, as I requested.

'Is it Salmagundi for breakfast, doctor?" Wawu said in jest. I haven't known the man for a long time but I see he has a glowing spirit in him. Yesterday, I saw a different side of him.

Wawu volunteered to be my assistant in exchange for making his mother better. I can but try to make her as comfortable as possible—at least that is the objective. And, to be frank, how can one go wrong?

I have my reservations about taking him on. I showed him several medical manuals so he could get himself familiar with preparations. That's when I realised the man can neither read nor write. On the other hand, he agreed to do the cleaning around my laboratory and hospital, and attend to some of the subjects and patients' basic needs like feeding and washing. Next, I need to show him how to apply a dressing.

I carried a good dose of collyrium, some cups and leeches, to tend to his mother. I started as soon as I arrived. A person nearby called for my attention to discuss his ailments. I told him I'd bring supplies next time.

On our way out of the cave a hand got hold of my ankle, which tripped me up; another soul asking for help, but of a different sort.

'Please, help release me from this hell!' cried the person. Wawu and Juan helped release me from his grip. Frail as he may seem, he had a strong grip. We made a dash as soon as he let go, but his cries followed us.

I never really realised the magnitude of the consequences of consuming the water from *the well*. I have so many questions: why are they mostly male? Why choose this cave? As a man of medicine, I ask myself what properties the water holds or if it can be reversed. Unfortunately, my stay here on earth—or wherever I might be—isn't enough time to unearth the answers.

My views on eternal life have shifted. It seems like there was more than one motivation to have it. The captain who captured me wanted it for greed. For Wawu, it was fear of losing his mother. For me, I see it as a curse. A curse that deprives man of the promise of heaven and damns them to be left on earth to suffer. My thoughts wander to the person in my lab. How much suffering have I caused him? I confess that I fail to see him as a human being.

DAY 14123

For the first time, Wawu writes this entry as my hands have retired. I can feel that my days are numbered. I hope that I have done enough to serve the people of St Madeleine, including those who sought to end their suffering.

It haunts me every time. The people I fed alive to the animals and maggots, the ones I burnt, and the ones I sent as offering to the kraken, who continues to guard the island. It might be their wish, but I suffer every time with nightmares. I consoled myself with a reminder that it was done to end their eternal suffering. I could only imagine the pain they went through and I provided them with a good dose of rum and were unconscious long enough.

In my short stay here on earth, there were plenty of questions that will remain unanswered in my lifetime. However, I have discovered that eternal life isn't living itself. To live is to feel, to appreciate, to get up after a fall and to laugh, to share, to learn and to love. As a mountain has its peak, so does life. Coming down from the mountain is not the end, but an achievement that something great has been conquered.

I trained Wawu to take my place and Juan to be his assistant. I am pleased with the effort that both have made to make themselves literate, and that my skills and knowledge are passed on. They will inherit my personal treasure chest, now full of medical supplies provided by the sea. A surgeon is never without his chest. Now, it's theirs and may the sea keep on providing for them.

Up to this day, no locals ever lay hands on the water of the well or desire its powers. Many outsiders still attempt to drink from it, but so far, I am the only person to survive the storm. I pass on my duties with pride to the strangers I never thought would become family.

DAY 14130

I have lost my vision and rely on Wawu and Juan's care. I am pleased that I have taught them well, and that they were brave enough to try new things. I am not sure I have thanked them for their loyalty and service. May today be that day.

DAY 14131

Rest in Peace Doctor James Pendergast, my mentor, my friend.

—Wawu

Dedicated in Loving Memory of

Bobb Courtman, Father of fellow contributor, Jayme Bean
&
James Cain

OF REVENGE & RAPIERS

BEING A TRUE STORY IN THE LIFE & HISTORIE OF CUT-LASS KATE

C. J. HENDERSON

*L*ady Katharine Montoya Duvalle, of the city of St. Nicholas on the Isla de Los Torcidos, was getting married.

Her neighbour, Portia Santos-Carruthers, appeared far more excited about it than Katharine. "I have heard that your husband-to-be is *terribly* handsome," she said, hands clasped under her chin, a look of dreamy contemplation on her face. She leaned back in the elegantly designed armchair and sighed, full of envy.

"So I have heard," admitted Katharine. "It is certainly the thing people mention most, upon hearing his name." She ran a finger under the collar of her dress, but it wasn't the heat that stifled her.

"You must be terribly excited," Portia continued. "Your wedding day—the most important day of your life! Think of the dress, the celebrations! You're so lucky. I shall have to wait at least a year before *I* can wed."

"Mmm." Katharine desperately wondered how she could escape the conversation. Unfortunately, Portia was a guest;

Katharine saw no way to absent herself that wouldn't be considered the height of bad manners.

All she wanted was some space, some time alone during which to enjoy her last moments of freedom. She saw the path of her future laid out in front of her and resented it. But there was no other route available. It would be scandalously unfilial for a daughter of the nobility of St. Nicholas to remain unmarried.

Claustrophobic as the full weight of reality struck again, she contemplated feigning a headache to relieve herself of Portia's well-meant yet intrusive prattling. But she avoided dishonesty where she could, and instead smiled, trying her best to accommodate her friend. Manners cost nothing, after all.

Fortune was on her side. Her maid Marie knocked on the door shortly after. Nodding politely to Portia, Marie handed a folded piece of paper to Katharine, at the same time giving her a significant look, quite unseen by the guest.

Katharine's pulse raced. This could mean only one thing. Countenance remaining calm and collected, she read:

"The items you ordered have come back into stock. Please come and see me at your earliest convenience. D."

Katharine stood up. "My apologies, Portia," she said. "A note from mamá, reminding me I have matters to attend to before the wedding tomorrow. I must leave you. I will, of course, be able to speak with you after the ceremony."

Sometimes dishonesty was unavoidable.

"Of course!" exclaimed Portia. "It is I who should apologise for keeping you. Forgive me, and felicidades! And... *sleep well tonight*! You may not have many such... *peaceful* nights, after your honeymoon begins!" She tittered, blushing. Holding her fan to her face, she allowed herself to be escorted out of the room by Marie.

The maid said nothing, merely raising a brow before following Portia. Katharine shook her head.

She encountered her mother on the way back to her room.

448

"Mami," Katharine said. "Do you need me for something?"

Katharine's mother kissed her cheek. "My Kate, you look lovely today. Truly, tomorrow everyone will be in awe of how beautiful you are!" She pressed a little box into Katharine's hand. Inside was a ring of platinum, adorned with a green stone shot through with flashes of iridescence; Kraken's Eye opal, the traditional gift well-off parents in St. Nicholas gave to their child on the eve of their wedding.

Katharine smiled. "Thank you, Mami." She put the ring on the first finger of her right hand. It looked like it belonged there; it had, of course, been designed for her.

Her mother sighed, suddenly uncomfortable. "Oh, Kate, I worry so for you! We both know your heart is too wild for this life. I would not have chosen to fix your marriage in this way, but with your poor dear father ill, and the *stupid* way this family arranges things; once he passes, his fortune will go to your imbécil uncle, as will the right to arrange your marriage. We both know he never approved of me; he will not see right by you. I had to do *something*."

She coughed delicately. "And with what others would see as your *disfigurements*, and you being twenty-one, I was limited in what sort of marriage I could arrange. At least you will not be troubled by your husband's unwanted attentions. He is grateful to have such an arrangement also."

Katharine looked down into her mother's dark eyes, so like her own. It hurt that her mother was distressed. "I know, Mami. I do not blame you."

Her mother smiled wanly, then with more spirit, said, "You will be missing your sister at this time. I miss her too. I only hope that somehow, somewhere, the one responsible for her death has met with a fitting punishment. If not, I hear that there are more highwaymen around—we can only hope that one of them encounters him and he comes off the worst."

Her mother's expression was full of intent. Katharine's

stomach lurched, and the world spun, made all the worse by her mother's *next* words.

Pulling her close, her mother whispered into her ear, "Don't stay out too late, dear, if you want to get married in the morning."

Katharine gaped. Her mother gave her another hug and kiss on her cheek and said brusquely, "Don't say anything, dear. Only know that I am your mother and I love you dearly, *no matter what.*"

She swept away, leaving Katharine stunned and wondering exactly how much her mother knew.

"How could she know anything at all?" Katharine demanded of Marie, who calmly checked their weapons.

Katharine owned a rapier and a cutlass, the former a gift from her father years back when she had taken up fencing. The latter had been appropriated by Marie from an unsuspecting pirate. He had fancied his chances with her and had taken her for exactly what she appeared to be; a lowly servant in the employ of nobility, unlikely to be defended against injustice. He was very messily disabused of that notion.

Marie shook her head, frowning. Finished with the larger weapons, she moved on to inspect a couple of daggers, her own preferred choice of weaponry.

Katharine, attired in thin black suede trousers and boots, and a red velveted short-sleeved top tied at the sides, traced the line of the scar that cut down her collarbone.

"She said 'disfigure*ments*,' not 'disfigurement.'"

"Maybe she's caught sight of you without you realising," ventured Marie, pausing to look at the networks of other battle-scars adorning Katharine's arms. "I know you're always careful, but really, is it that unlikely?"

"Yes," Katharine replied, frankly. "I have spent years covering up. Everyone knows my preference for non-revealing clothes, and for privacy. I've always been so careful."

"Well, too late to do anything about it now. Perhaps you can speak with her about it on your return."

"I think I must," agreed Katharine. "But it's getting late. We should be going."

Shrugging on a long coat, black suede to match her trousers, Katharine gave herself a once-over and took up her weapons. The final touch was a large square of the black suede which she folded diagonally and tied over the lower half of her face.

"Ready?"

Marie, similarly attired, nodded. Silently, they opened the twin sash windows of Katharine's room and stole out into the night.

EACH TIME KATHARINE and Marie visited Drea, she was in a different location. Katharine didn't like to ask the reasons for this; she had already asked much of Drea and feared overstepping. Drea always seemed so otherworldly, as though only half of her attention was present, the other focussed on altogether stranger things—she had the constant look of someone listening to a voice that only she could hear. It made Katharine nervous.

This time was no different, the location being a beach to the northwest of the island, a good two hours' ride from Opal Bay Fort, the largest settlement in the north. Palm trees fanned the air, bats fluttered and swooped after insect meals, and creeping things inched along the shoreline.

Drea sat in position already, cross-legged on the sand, left hand on a weathered compass, right hand tapping a timepiece as she waited. Her head cocked, she swayed slightly, marking the ebb and flow of the tide.

Leaving Marie to deal with the horses, Katharine settled

herself down opposite Drea, separated from her by a bowl of water, and removed her mask. Drea caught her eye, acknowledging her with the merest lift of her head. There was something different in her expression this time; a look of anticipation.

"Tonight's the night," she said.

Katharine's stomach clenched. "How can you know?" She leaned forward despite herself. She didn't dare hope... and yet she still let herself fall into the trap.

"I got a sighting," Drea said, still swaying, her mousey brown hair washing over her shoulders.

"What does that prove?" Katharine let out a dispirited sigh. Just because someone somewhere thought they might have seen her quarry, didn't mean they actually had.

"Means I can narrow things down. Think about it. If you're standing on a beach and you drop a grain of sand onto a map at your feet; well, you're unlikely to ever find that grain of sand again, as chances are it's bounced off back onto the beach. But," she raised a finger, "imagine you are crouched over the map, focussing on one particular island, and you very carefully drop the grain of sand from a handspan off the map. You're likely to be able to see the grain drop and follow where it lands."

"But how do we know the sighting was genuine?" Katharine hated the complaint in her voice, but she had been in this position so many times before. Each occasion had proven a disappointment, and she didn't think she could cope with another.

"This sighting was by my... contact." Drea's eyes shifted away, and a strange crawling sensation ran up Katharine's spine and neck.

She knew, of course, of whom—or *what*—Drea spoke; indeed, the whole premise of her seeking the girl out in the first place had been predicated on the strange relationship that she was part of. But Katharine tried to not think about it; tried to not allow the terrifying images to flash into her mind as she thought of Drea—of average height and probably less than average strength

—harvesting the non-viable eggs of the immense creature that had borne them, and that allowed Drea to carry out her work unharmed. Others had foolishly followed in Drea's path, trying to steal the precious commodities. Not one of them had survived the mass of writhing tentacles that had sought them out in punishment; not one of them had escaped that massive beak...

Katharine had never seen Rua'Shoth, of course. She sometimes believed that made her imaginings all the worse, but truly, of all things in this world, the Kraken terrified her more than any other.

She gave herself a little shake. *To the business at hand.*

Drea took a long, pallid egg from a small hessian bag, placed it in her mouth, and chewed slowly. The girl's hands were back on the compass and timepiece, and she gazed intently into the bowl of water. All the while she swayed in that eerie fashion, hair following in her wake.

She stopped, utterly still, staring fixedly at the water in the bowl. In a voice somehow multi-layered, as though supplemented by stranger, less human sounds, she rasped out, *"I've found him."*

As they prepared to leave, Katharine felt that the payment given, even though it was only the latest in a long line of such payments, was not enough. She sensed a strange kinship between herself and Drea, as well as the ties of obligation.

"I am grateful to you, Drea. I cannot tell you how much. Please, if you ever have need of my assistance, call on me and let me know what I can do."

Drea's distracted smile gave Katharine the impression she wasn't really listening.

Marie interrupted. "Kate, your husband-to-be loves to travel, I hear. I suspect that after your nuptials you'll be expected to attend him on his journeys. Drea won't know where to find you unless you give her some token by which she can pinpoint you in one of her searches."

Seeing the logic in this, particularly since Drea brightened at the suggestion, Katharine looked about her person, unsure of what she might give. Her weapons were unthinkable; nothing of her clothing was expendable. She looked at her sole piece of jewellery—the ring from her mother—and discounted it immediately. She could not.

Marie suggested, "Perhaps a lock of hair? I believe it should be something suitably personal?"

Katharine borrowed one of Marie's daggers, removing a length from the end of her braid, and, bundling it up, passed it to Drea. The harvester took it with a nod, stuffing it into her bag. She turned, walking away from them to stand at the edge of the tide. Effectively dismissed, Katharine and Marie took their leave. Their dealings always ended this way, and they had a fair distance to cover, with little time to do it in.

The island where Ivarr Bloodyhand would be found, according to Drea and her contact, was the first island to the north of Los Torcidos. Known as El Asilo Pequeño, or 'Little Sanctuary', it was far enough away that it would be difficult to get there and back home by morning. But Katharine and Marie were confident it could be done, and so rode their horses hard along the Jag to the waters' edge, where there were always fishermen and other less-legal traders who would be happy to earn extra coin by transporting them to their destination.

Before boarding, they met up with their two associates, 'Crafty Rod' Cressey, and Dylan 'Dil' Kift, who had gone on their own jaunt earlier that night. Back-up was necessary, in case things went against them with Ivarr.

"How were the takings?" Katharine enquired, not really caring.

Crafty Rod hefted a small purse in his hand. "Better than

expected. Less well-guarded, too. I'll divvy it up after this business tonight."

An air of melancholy descended as the four contemplated what the night might bring.

"Into three, if you please. After tomorrow, I'll not be able to join you anymore. I don't even know where I'll be most of the time." Katharine swallowed against the lump forming in her throat. "Marie, I still want you to have your share; I know you haven't decided yet if you'll accompany me or stay in St Nicholas."

"We should get going," was all Marie said in return.

Katharine left that alone. Time enough yet, she supposed.

It was a couple of hours before dawn when they beached, and only with the most extravagant promises of payment that the fisherman who had brought them could be persuaded to await their return.

The four of them crouched on the south shore of El Asilo Pequeño, strategizing.

"It shouldn't take long to reach the north side," said Dil. "We'll need to exercise great care, though. This island's so small, we could trip over any of them at any time. We can't afford to give any warning."

Katharine estimated how many of the nearer vessels on the water were mere fishers, and how many might be pirate ships. All flew flags; but she couldn't quite make out in the dawning light what they represented. Except for the *Midnight Scythe*, of course; instantly recognisable, she loomed over the others. The most feared ship in these waters—she was the pride and joy of the infamous Captain Braddock.

"The *Scythe*." Katharine pointed out the ship for the others. "I guess we have to hope Ivarr Bloodyhand isn't a friend." She *really* hoped that to be the case. Challenging one pirate captain was risky. Challenging two was... rather more suicidal.

"Ready?" she asked. "Remember, don't engage unless absolutely necessary. Leave me to deal with Ivarr; only get involved if you think it essential. I need to do this. If you ask me if I'm willing to die to achieve it, yes, I am. But equally, there's no point in a needless death. You two, follow Marie's guide. Marie—use your judgement."

In silence, they approached their quarry with practiced ease. The grasses, noisy in the gentle breeze, helped to cover the scraping and scratching of the rough stones and scree slipping underfoot.

Singing and cheering gradually became audible, along with the sounds of heavy objects dragging over sand. Katharine held up a hand for them to stop. She made a quick survey of the water nearby. In the burgeoning dawn, she identified the boat moored in closest to the island, its flag flying the red motif of a jawless skull over a disembodied hand.

The *Black Raven.*

At last.

Adrenalin pumping, Katharine indicated a turn to the right. The four made for the final outcropping of rocks that would shield them from the view of the crew of the *Black Raven.*

Straightening up, Kate tweaked nervously at her coat, checking for her weapons. She took a deep breath, and rounding the outcropping, strode into the light of the campfire.

There was only one person not engaged in some sort of work or other. That individual sat leaning against a large rock, contemplating the contents of his mug. At Katharine's approach, he looked up and snorted.

"And who might you be?" His Nordic accent forced its way through his thick, blond beard, as though he battled the syllables on their way out.

Katharine took in his frame and mass, assessing how the upcoming fight might go.

"My fellows there call me Cut-lass Kate." She indicated her three companions. They hung back, waiting to see how things played out. Crafty Rod gave a sardonic wave.

"Hah! Cutlass Kate? Cut-less Kate, more like. I doubt you've ever lifted a blade in your life."

At Ivarr's raised voice, his crew meandered over to see what was going on, curiosity piqued by the new arrivals.

Katharine unfastened her coat.

"Steady!" Ivarr looked back at his crewmates with mock incredulity. One of them sang out, "What shall we do with the pretty wench? Lay-ho, lay-ho!" to the tune of *A Gentleman of Fortune*. Katharine threw a disparaging glance in his direction. He fell silent.

"You misunderstand." Katharine slid her coat off her shoulders. Ivarr's look of lechery shifted into one of disgust.

"If you're trying to get my attention, you'd better put that back on."

"I think you misconstrue my intentions," replied Katharine calmly. "I'm here to challenge you to a duel."

Ivarr burst out laughing. "Apart from the fact I don't fight *girls*, you have obviously lost too many fights in your life for me to add another to the list."

"Again, understanding does not seem to be one of your talents." Kate shifted her feet in the sand, settling herself, and threw her coat over towards Marie. "Each one of these scars is years old, each one represents a lesson learned. And as you can see, I have learned a *lot* of lessons."

"I don't care! I don't fight women. What is all this about, anyway?" Ivarr's expression had hardened, and he finally stood up, his tense stance belying his casual tone.

"I'm here for my sister."

Ivarr rolled his eyes. "Well, I'm terribly sorry. Did I bed her and leave her distraught when I left? She won't be the first, nor the last." He spat on the sand, more relaxed again. "Or did she tell you how great I was, and you thought you'd get your own taste of it?" His men laughed at that. Ivarr slapped his knee, revelling in the response.

"You bedded her and left her with child. To escape the shame, she took her own life." Katharine's voice had not risen, nor altered in tone, but it cut through the laughter, bringing abrupt silence. She smiled at Ivarr, who had visibly straightened. She knew she had his full attention.

"So, you see, I am in deadly earnest. I am here to challenge you. Now we see how serious you are in defending yourself." She rolled her shoulders, limbering up. "Unless you're scared, of course."

Anger flashed across his face. "If you're determined to be made a fool of, who am I to argue? Fine. Choose your weapon."

She gave a quick bow. "I fight with either rapier or cutlass, but I challenged you. You decide."

"I am more proficient with the cutlass, therefore I choose rapier. It would be unfair to take advantage."

Katharine shrugged. "Today is as good a day to die as any other."

"Who said anything about dying? I won't kill you, just teach you another lesson. Then you can go back home, and, if you're lucky, I might come and visit you sometime on the way to something important." Ivarr drew two diagonal lines in the sand, indicating the crossing point. "X marks the spot. If you can push me back past this point, you can claim victory."

"Very generous."

"What can I say? I am a gentleman at heart. I play by gentlemen's rules."

Katharine sniffed. "In my experience, gentlemen play by gentlemen's rules until such time as they believe the rules go against them."

Ivarr gave a sardonic grin. "I doubt you understand much at all about men."

Katharine rolled her eyes. "Shall we begin?"

As Ivarr gave a sharp bow, iridescence sparkled on his hand; a ring caught in the sunlight.

Katharine inhaled sharply, frowning, but gave a nod in return. The duel began.

At first, they merely danced around each other with their blades, attempting to get a feel of the other's strengths, weaknesses, and potential Achilles' heels.

Katharine assessed Ivarr as far stronger, but a life of relative inactivity hampered him, likely brought about by being fonder of rum than exercise. She kept stealing glances at his sword hand, considering the ring adorning his finger. She didn't know yet if it was significant, but anything she could divine about him would surely only help her.

Ivarr had his own plans. "Your sister," he said, thrusting his rapier towards her right shoulder. "Did she look like you? Brown-haired, brown-eyed, *scarred?*"

She moved out of reach. "As much like me as any sibling might. She never learned to fence. I only did when she died. It was a good way to keep my mind occupied." Her rapier glanced off his arm, slicing through the material of his shirt, but leaving him unharmed.

He grunted, moving further away. "Your parents must have hated that. Girls fighting is such an ugly thing." He sneered at her.

"Actually, it was my mother who suggested it; my father hired my tutor." Katharine advanced on him, noting that his feet were a little slower than before. She flashed the tip of her blade towards his face, noting his flinch with grim satisfaction.

"Maybe you were the less-favoured daughter? They didn't mind you becoming damaged goods? Though, I suppose at that point they knew she was damaged goods, too, huh?" Ivarr grunted as he tried to step forward into her defence.

She evaded him with practised ease, her feet dancing over the sand with a speed he could not match. "You're trying to make me angry. It won't work." Katharine moistened her lips, conscious that she was tiring a little, her legs aching with the constant resistance of the sand. The early morning was heating with the rising sun, and sweat had formed along her hairline and between her shoulder blades.

"And why's that? Not such an adoring sister after all?"

"She died six years ago. I stopped being angry about it when I realised it wouldn't bring her back." Katharine spun, whipping his leg just above the knee. He stumbled, but recovered.

"What is this all about, then?"

Kate thought she detected some irritation. "Pure. Cold. Revenge." Three slashes of her blade in a particular pattern. He fended them off with a practised feint that caught her breath. Her suspicions were solidifying. She tried a different tack, hoping he might betray himself. "What about *your* family?"

"What?"

It worked. She had taken him by surprise and *almost* heard in his voice the thing she sought. She pushed further, taunting him with things she'd never dream of carrying out.

"Well, I assume there are people who care about you *some*where," she said. "How would you feel if someone treated *your* sister like that?"

"Don't talk about my sister!" And there it was. In a moment of tiredness and sudden wrath, his accent slipped.

Katharine gave a satisfied smile. "There we are. I wondered, when I saw your ring there, but it could have been stolen. Knowing the Cordovan defence made it more likely, given Cordova has only ever lived and taught in St. Nicholas; but it's your accent that really gives it away. You're not a Dane at all, are you? You're from St. Nicholas, like me. Do your crew know that you're just a spoilt little rich boy playing pirates?"

Katharine circled him as he worked himself into a greater and greater rage. His men were out of earshot, and Ivarr kept sending them glances to make sure they stayed that way.

"Given there are only a few blond families... well, it wouldn't take me long to work out which one you come from, and then I *might* just tell your men, and *they* might go give your sister a little visit. There's more than just her virtue they'd get from your home, I'd wager."

Ivarr let out a bellow of anger and rushed for her. Adrenalin had refreshed her responses, though, and she neatly sidestepped him and drew her foot under his legs. He crashed to the ground. His rapier bounced away over the sand, out of reach.

Ivarr struggled to get up, but Katharine had her blade at his throat.

"You didn't get past the line... you haven't won," Ivarr said thickly, the blade moving with his Adam's apple. All pretence at an accent was gone.

"I don't agree."

"You're no gentleman." Ivarr tried to spit, but Katharine added the tiniest bit of pressure to his throat.

"No indeed, for I am a gentlewoman, and that's an entirely different thing."

Ivarr frowned.

"X marks the spot," said Katharine softly, making two intersecting diagonal lines over Ivarr's chest, and his eyes widened in understanding just before she ran him through.

Katharine withdrew the blade. She watched the blood bubble to Ivarr's lips; watched the light leave his eyes. Looking to the sky, she said, "That's for you, Isabel."

She felt nothing, but that was what she had expected. No relief. No victory. No remorse. But his crime had been paid for, and that was enough.

Muscles shaking from exertion, she turned her face to the breeze, looking out over the sea where the scudding clouds chased away the red glow of morning.

"Miss Kate?" She turned and saw one of the pirates cautiously approaching. "Miss, we don't want any trouble, we'll not seek revenge, you're free to go…"

She took a step towards him and noted with satisfaction how he and the others moved involuntarily backwards.

Marie called over, "Kate, we must leave soon if we are to get back in time."

Katharine's mother's words came back to her then. "*If you want to get married.*"

Free to go?

Yes, she was, wasn't she? Dizzying elation washed over her as she contemplated the *Black Raven*, the ship that had belonged to Ivarr Bloodyhand. Katharine smiled, feeling absurdly energized. She ran the distance to the nearest rowboat on the beach and put one foot up on its wooden frame. The men kept a careful distance, eyeing the rapier still in her hand.

"No more of this 'Miss Kate' nonsense! Call me Captain!" she called out with a feral grin. "Are you with me?"

There was a pause as the crew considered their options; considered twice as hard the body of Ivarr Bloodyhand. Then there was a resounding chorus of "Aye, Cap'n!" and the men swarmed to Kate, knowing that their futures depended on a good relationship with her.

Amongst them were Dil and Crafty Rod, but Marie hung back.

"I must go tell your mother," she said apologetically, seeing Kate's hurt expression.

Things suddenly fell into place. "It was you? She's always known?"

Marie shrugged. "Your mother hired me to be your friend as much as your maid. But she did hire me, and I kept her informed of your activities, yes. But she doesn't disapprove. She wanted revenge for Isabel, too. And she's more like you than you know.

She just was born at the wrong time. But she'll want us to keep in touch with her, so she can hear of your adventures."

"Us? You *will* join us then? But how will you find us once we're at sea?"

"Drea," said Marie simply.

Of course. "Very clever." Kate was confounded. She'd never suspected such connivance. Not once.

The enormity of what she was about to do both excited and terrified her. But knowing her mother was on her side gave her strength. She clasped Marie's hand.

"Then tell mamá I will... miss her, and will see her when I can."

Marie waved farewell, and then she was gone. Kate turned back to the gathered men and called for quiet.

"Let's get going—I've got a ship and a crew to learn about!"

CREATORS OF THE SEA

ILLUSTRATED BY KATHERINE ELLIS

◈ Traditional Pirates ◈

Top row—Darby Cupid, C. J. Henderson
Center row—Jack Kaide, Dewi Hargreaves, Chapel Orahamm
Bottom row—J. C. Pillard, Imelda Taylor

CREATORS OF THE MULTIVERSE

THE STAFF OF SKULLGATE AND EDITORIAL TEAM,
ILLUSTRATED BY KATHERINE ELLIS

APPENDICES

BEING AN ACCOUNTING OF THE PEOPLE, PLACES,
VESSELS, AND EVENTS OF NOTE, ARRANGED
ALPHABETICALLY AND PARTITIONED ACCORDING
TO THEIR RESPECTIVE WORLDS

FANTASY PIRATE INDEX

AN ACCOUNTING OF THE ISLANDS OF THE ARCHIPELAGO

Archipelago, The (place)—The name for the collection of isles that include *Brig Island, Elysium Cove, the Isle of Labruma, Saltskiff Bazaar, Torganal Island,* and *Undercurrent.*

Assault on the Well (event)—Some years ago, *Tasmin the Tattered* tried to reach the *Well of Eternal Life.* Six out of the eight ships were destroyed before ever reaching *Elysium Cove,* and the remaining members of the two ships left were all lured into the waters to their deaths by sirens. Tattered Tamsin herself was said to have made it out alive, but no one has seen her since.

Bastian (he/his)—A young thief living on *Saltskiff Bazaar.*

Brack, Tempest (she/her)—Captain of the *Screaming Harpy.* Feeds her blood to a dryad for increased life and strength. Has a tattoo of a blood-red skull across the back of her shaved head.

Brenner, Abigail (she/her)—A thirteen year old girl who usually sells regular fruits and flowers on the streets of *Salty Rest.* If you know what you're looking for and ask the right questions, though, she may be able to give you one of those poisonous apples—for a price, of course.

Brig Island (place)—A small, jungle covered outcropping of rock where the survival of the fittest plays out in the bloodiest form imaginable. The area is notorious for rough waters, and flesh eating sharks.

Broomie (they/it)—Bilge-dragon. The size of a large cat, Broomie stalks the decks of *The Screaming Harpy*. Known to set fire to ship's provisions when denied rum. Able to melt into shadows.

Cait the Cruel (she/her)—Gallant Grant's notorious first mate.

Cloudthorn, Perez (he/his)—A retired fae soldier turned explorer who lost his wings in a magical explosion that killed hundreds in battle. He has come to *Labruma* for two things: to sell rare sea creatures found in the shallows of *Death's Doorway* and to find the legendary *Map of the Gods*.

Conclave, The (event)—A moot that convenes the most powerful pirates on the seas to raise a Pirate King.

Courtyard of Sighs (place)—A courtyard behind the *Magician's Marketplace*.

Dagspire (place)—The most central and therefore oldest part of the Saltskiff. Over the years the humble ships that hold it afloat have been built up into enormous towers of driftwood, old masts and pieces of wrecked ships, housing some of the foulest brutes and darkest secrets in all of Saltskiff.

Dailann, Teague (they/them)—Tavern server and occasional vocalist, Teague met *Kyle Talos* on one of Kyle's many stops at the Saltskiff Bazaar. Taken with the pirate's charm and sometimes clumsiness unbecoming of a pirate captain, Teague often found themself swept off their feet by Kyle, only to be forced to wait when the captain was forced to leave the *Saltskiff Bazaar*. One day hopes to not be left behind.

Dariah, Rheumy Eyed (it)—A giant, magically fossilized shark's head mounted on a wall in *The Courtyard of Sighs* behind the magic school.

Death's Doorway (place)—The thick fog and natural breakwater surrounding Labruma. Its name comes from the number of ships that have run aground attempting to reach the island.

Drejj, The—An amphibious people crossed between humans and merfolk.

Elysium Cove (place)–Island that is (rumoured to be) the location of the *Well of Eternal Life*.

Eternal Rest (place)—A series of caves deep inside the cliff-side city of *Salty Rest* that house the local undertakers. Bodies are dropped into holes carved into the bottom of caves; it is said the moaning that can be heard is not the wind, but the souls of the damned.

Gallant Grant (he/him)—A handsome but manipulative pirate captain.

Gentle, Ginny (she/her)—Goblin. Captain of the *Greasy Gallows*, paid to patrol the waters surrounding *Saltskiff*. Wields a heavy spear.

Ghast, Martha (she/her)—Martha Ghast (or Mad Martha) battled her way to the Well of Eternal Life and drank from its waters. She laid waste to much of the island before she was finally captured and has been kept sedated in a prison of floating seawater for 200 years, guarded at all times by the *Well of Eternal Life's* attendants.

Gloaming Spires, The (place)—the greatest library in the known world. Located on *Undercurrent*. Impossible stories and histories about giant floating ships and pirates who traverse the stars are rumoured to be found there, existing in a magical sphere that prevents the texts from being ruined by sea water.

Gracie–*see "Visions of Gracie."*

Greasy Gallows (ship)—A ship captained by *Ginny Gentle* that patrols the waters of *Saltskiff*.

Helga of the All-Seeing Eye (she/her)—Helga of the All-Seeing Eye has taken up residence in *Dagspire*. Her fortune telling is renowned for its clarity, but in recent times, her visions have taken a far darker turn, and there are those who believe she, and her fortunes, are now cursed.

Kell'tan (they/it)—More entity than individual, Kell'tan serves as the head librarian and keeper of The Vault. They patrol the library and makes sure that knowledge sought is achieved. No one moves, nothing shifts, without Kell'tan being aware of it. They are rumored to be one of the great old beings that existed before history as it is known... but no one is brave enough to ask.

Kraken, The—A massive sea beast. Some say it's legend; some say it swims between worlds, leaving death and destruction in its wake. The giant turtle of Torganal Island pursues it ceaselessly through the ocean.

Labruma, Isle of (place)–The location of the Death Waters fountain. A smaller island which is always misty, though otherwise it is unassuming. More volcanic rock than vegetation, it still boasts an impressive amount of fertile ground to keep its inhabitants fed.

Leticia (she/her)—The Madam of *The Porthole*, a brothel in Dagspire, Saltskiff.

Mad Martha—*see "Ghast, Martha."*

Magdalene the Merciful (she/her)—The notorious pirate queen who founded the merchant market nearly a hundred years earlier by giving one of her boats from her fleet to some passing merchants.

Magician's Marketplace (place)–a marketplace of magic located on *Brigg Island*.

Map of the Gods—a powerful artifact that legend states shows every location in the multiverse… as well as what treasures lie therein.

Martin, Marius (he/him)—The shady clockwork prosthetic maker in the *Magician's Market*, decked out in his own creations on all four limbs (both legs, his right arm, and four fingers on his left hand).

McKracken, Sheena (she/her)—An orc with finely tapered ears that suggest some elven heritage. Sheena has kept a weathered eye on *the Kraken's* movements for years. Often to be found day-drunk and wandering *Vista's* streets with a ready curse on her lips, she is rumoured to be an excommunicated member of the Pirate Kings. Her business with the Kraken remains a worrying secret.

Noddingtown (place)—A town sitting atop the turtle's head on Torganal Island, which nods up and down throughout the day, thus giving the town its name.

Oriana (she/her)—Gallant Grant's selkie lover.

Pirate Conclave (event)—Every year a pirate conclave occurs, where a week of debauchery masks the darker pacts agreed to between the pirate kings that decide how they will interact with each other, and the wider world.

Porthole, The (place)—A brothel in Dagspire, Saltskiff.

Saltskiff Bazaar (place)–A floating merchant market in the middle of the ocean, consisting of several ships and rafts. The Saltskiff Bazaar is famous for its rare and often magical commodities but this makes it a tempting prize for pirates. Over the years it has grown to an immense size as more ships and crafts have been lashed to the sides. Water wraiths follow in its wake, hungry for the magical waste and spoiled potions often dumped over the sides.

Salty Rest (place)—A landlocked city on *the Isle of Labruma*. It is dug into the sheer sides of a cliff, with the sea foaming below. Originally a refuge for escaped convicts or pressed sailors, it has become a haven for the desperate and destitute.

Screaming Harpy (ship)—*Tempest Brack's* vessel.

Screep, Dillon (they/them)—An elf nicknamed "Disaster Dillon," they've taken it upon themself to care for the statue of *Magdalene the Merciful*. Endearingly clumsy but well meaning, they dismiss the reports of people losing their souls.

Silvertongue—A drunkard and storyteller that frequents a pub in Lostshore.

Stargazer, The (ship)—A ship helmed by *Kyle Talos*.

Talos, Kyle (she/her)—Captain of *The Stargazer*, Kyle is a half-elf privateer/pirate who takes jobs that often take her into port at the *Saltskiff Bazaar* to see a certain individual who makes their home there. Daughter of *Phaidan Talos*.

Talos, Phaidan (he/him)—Former captain of *The Stargazer* and rakish rogue extraordinaire, Phaidan Talos made a name for himself as a pirate and gained the (sometimes begrudging) respect of all those who sailed the seas of The Archipelago. He semi-retired when his only daughter, *Kyle Talos*, was born, and retired entirely when Kyle was old enough for him to gift her *The Stargazer*.

Tattered Tamsin (she/her)—Pirate queen who used her fleet of ships to attempt to breach the storm with as many crewmates as possible in an attempt to storm the walls of the Holy City and take the *Well* for themselves.

Therese, Mary (she/her)—Once a mermaid, Mary now walks the land on multi-jointed clockwork legs procured from *Marius Martin*. Quartermaster of the *Screaming Harpy*.

Tidewalker (they/it/she/he)—The shape of a man made out of seawater. Only a battered skeleton is visible through the murky brine holding the creature upright. Tidewalker appears to scavengers and thieves who would disturb the wrecks as they lie.

Timothy the Divine (he/his)—Resident of the Royal Treasure. His attempts to find the *Map of the Gods* were either a success, which drove him mad, or a failure, which also drove him mad. He chants in a foreign tongue on the night of the Winter and Summer Solstice and with the turning of the year, strange lights escape his cell.

Toad Fall (event)—None claim to know if the Toad Fall (or the night and a day the sky rained bloody great toads down on the Saltskiff) was a calculated hex, an unfortunate weather event, or a slippery piece of magic turned loose and gone wrong. Many goods and properties were damaged or destroyed but the toads were largely unharmed and after they were cleared out of the Bazaar, some people kept one or two as pets. Others are sometimes found in pieces, scattered across Hydra's Bones after being illegally thrown to the sailfish in order to control the outcome of a fight.

Undercurrent (place)–The island of Undercurrent is supposed to house the legendary *Map of the Gods*. However, no one has ever seen the island, as it travels in the underwater currents and is difficult to track.

Vault, The (place)—A secret section with *the Gloaming Spires*, which contains books deemed too dangerous for public consumption. At the far end of the library is a great oaken door with a magical padlock, unbreakable unless you know the right enchantment to break it. It is rumored that the secrets to acquiring the map can be found in there, though no one but the librarians have been in.

Visions of Grace (he/his)—A Felician (cat-type person) bard of the Glistening Lagoon Clan is with a reputation for breaking hearts, but never call him a cat and DO NOT make fun of his name. He eats and drinks at The Mend for free. Also known as *Gracie*.

Torganal Island (place)–Seems like most islands from a distance, but the closer you get the more you realize it is, in fact, resting on the back of a giant turtle. Covered in centuries of forest growth, as well as cities and towns, *Torganal Island* is always moving—chasing after a kraken that ever-blinks on the horizon.

Vista—A neighborhood in *Noddingtown* on *Torganal Island*, where residents can watch the Kraken phasing in and out against the sunrise.

Well of Eternal Life (place)—A magical well whose water is said to bestow eternal life on those who drink it… or so the legends claim. Supposedly located within *Elyseum Cove*, of those who have sought it very few have come back from their trip to the cove due to the heavy storms that surround the island.

Wizard Cazuuli, The (he/his)–Also known as Caz, Cazuuli has taken up residence in Grandview as he pursues his grand passion: the kraken itself. Long has his obsession with the Map of the Gods led him to this place. With his equipment and magical know-how, he plans to siphon the phasing magic off the kraken to use to his own ends.

SKY PIRATE INDEX

AN ACCOUNTING OF THE REGIONS OF THE CHARTED WORLD

Aarden, Brynn (she/her)—A young *grounder* in her 30s. She's lived on *Kimichula* her whole life and has made it her life's work to study the ruins, giving her quite the reputation among archaeologists.

Archarrier, the (ship)—A retired military vessel turned central store of information for the *Cartographer's Fleet*. The airship home of *Dr. Gina Oboler* and *Amelia Xu*.

Ambush, The (ship)—A vessel helmed by the Red-eyed Jackal.

Anchorfast, Sylvie (she/her)—Lone-wolf captain of *The Stickleback*, seeking to recover her parents who were taken away from her by the kraken.

Bayside (place)—Aviaquarium and Air Mail Postal Service, located on *Frostborne*.

Beacon, the—A massive clocktower plated in shining copper at the center of *The Hub*.

Bottom (place)—A town which grows on the anchors of the floating island of *Halfaway*.

Bottomless Braddock—*see "Braddock, Captain."*

Braddock, Captain (he/his)—Best known by the nickname "Bottomless Braddock," the undead captain of the *Midnight Scythe* who roams the icy mists at the end of the known world.

Braddock's Spire (place)—The largest and most central stone structure of Mason's Mile, located on *Frostborne*. This smooth, monolithic spire has drawn people from all over in the hopes of discovering the mysterious legends of *Captain Bottomless Braddock*.

Cannoneer, the (she/her)—An elderly retired pirate who works *The Beacon*. Her right arm and leg have both been replaced with copper-plated clockwork prostheses. Acts as clockmaker and lighthouse keeper, and most importantly to make sure that the cannons Always Fire On Time.

Cartographers Fleet (place)—A high altitude, high tech community of storm chasers forming a man-made archipelago of floating platforms.

Chip Diviny—*See Kalbrunner, Arlan.*

Cog, The (place)—A hexagonal, central platformed city, around which all other platforms and ships of *The Hub* connect. No matter what form *The Hub* takes on any particular day, The Cog will always be at its core.

Corvus, the (ship) —A vessel helmed by *Gavin*.

Crimson Cog, the (place)—The most prominent tavern in *Rustowne*, both a popular watering hole for the locals and a hub of rumors and tales about the Well of Eternal Life. It is named for an eponymous twenty-foot cog attached inside one wall of the massive taproom.

Crypt, the—A huge monumental burial chamber at the back of *Ninerville*. Only the most prestigious adventurers are permitted to be buried there, but this is judged by the scavengers alone.

Cumulocarta—Fragments of a huge map, written in the shapes and swirls on the tops of the tempests and storms chased by the *Cartographer's Fleet*.

Dregs, the (place)—This small section of *Rustowne* is where the main exchange of information occurs, though it's likely a place to be given rumors and tall tales. Located underneath some of *Rustowne's* biggest structures, the streets are often filled with giant rust flakes and debris.

Endrapo (place)—The largest city in the ruined empire of *Kimichula*, it is the place most thought to contain the *Font of Souls*. It is formed of a number of labyrinthine districts.

Elysium (place)—A massive island can be seen from *Halfaway* and *The Hub* both. The final bastion of unindustrialized land, Elysium is where the livestock are raised for the surrounding islands. The name comes from the way the farms look from the floating islands above.

Faye, Crispin (he/his)—Dark skinned with pointed ears, he is unlike anybody else in the balloons. Moving from balloon to balloon trying to learn everything he can of the history and nature of this world.

Fiddler's Maroon (place)—A small communal farm for housing a strange batch of exiles.

Flint, Esmeralda (she/her)—Overseer of *The Hub*. Esmeralda is a tall, hard-faced woman who governs The Hub with an iron fist.

Font of Souls—A pool of mirror-like water fed by a fountain-like spring deep beneath a ruined temple of a long-dead empire rumored to be located on *Kimichula*. They say when one gazes into the waters, they witness their own fated death.

Frost Mines (place)—An elaborate underground tunnel system made of ice. Local folklore states the tunnels were created by the kraken as it burrowed underground. Now, it is used by ice miners who live in *Bottom*, and is one of the most dangerous job sites on *Halfaway*.

Frozen One, the (he/his)—An enigmatic, nameless man often found lingering around *Braddock's Spire*. He wears layer upon layer of patchwork rags hand-stitched with animal gut, consisting of everything from smith's aprons to bits of sailcloth and balloon canvas.

Gavin (he/him)—The captain of *The Corvus*, traveling north to seek the end of the world.

Genevieve (she/her)—The first mate of *The Corvus* and longtime friend of *Gavin*.

Gyl, Captain (they/them)—Said to be the only living person to cross through the storms and make it back alive... at least that has been the rumor for the last 100 years. Gyl resides in *Rustowne*.

Grounder—A term used to refer to someone who has never been in the sky.

Hadsworth, Wilhelm (he/his)—A researcher on *the Cartographer's fleet* specializing in matters of archeology.

Halfaway (place)—A floating city overlooking snow forests and often-frozen coastlines. Named for how the city is anchored by countless tethers to the ground.

Galahad, Hatch (he/him)—A young boy, no older than 12, rumoured to have been the first to discover the Well of Eternal Life.

Hub, The (place)—A vast array of flying platforms and ships, all of different colours, sizes and structural design. While some core neighborhoods are permanently present, others on the periphery are able to come and go, creating an island which constantly shifts.

Iron Cutlass, the (ship)—The vessel where *Arlan Kalbrunner* serves as first mate.

Kalbrunner, Arlan (he/him)—Ex-captain of the *Ruddy Nimbus*, first-mate of *The Iron Cutlass*. Wanted by *Skyfleet* for mutiny and arson of his previous working ship. Known alias: *Chip Diviny*.

Kellis, Roger (he/his)—A typical scoundrel: violent, brash, and willing to do just about anything for money.

Kilmeade, Dougan (he/his)—Once a boatswain on a pirate airship, this crusty old scoundrel lost a leg in battle against the kraken and has left the skies behind and plies a meager trade out of *Bottom* tailoring sealskin coveralls, spats, gloves, and other protective gear uniquely required by ice miners in the *Frost Mines.*

Kimichula (place)—A massive island with a spine of towering mountains surrounded by impenetrable jungles. It lies far to the south of The Hub, deep in the tropics. Once was home to a sprawling empire, the ruins of which have been consumed by the jungles.

Kraken, the (unknown entity)—A monstrous, primordial beast that hunts the seas and skies. Sailors have long feared the kraken's reach, as it rarely releases those whom it catches. And when it does, it doesn't always release them into the same universe they came from. *Scientific name: Architeuthis obscuratus.*

Leftovers, the (place)—An ever shifting ring of windblown debris and floating rocks where what remains of the failed expeditions to *The Whispering Isle* tend to wash up. One of the larger clusters of floating rocks has been designated *Ninerville.*

Lighthouse, the (place)—A lighthouse on the edge of the White Wasteland, wrapped in ice from the surf. Said to be cursed. Nobody knows who built it, nobody knows how its light still glows, and nobody knows who keeps it.

Lunafer—*Gavin's* talking black cat and refugee from the Fantasy Realm (*see Book 2: Pirates of the Fantastic*).

MacDougal, Jerry (he/his)—Farmer and leader of the *Fiddler's Maroon.* Claims to have seen the kraken more times than any other living man or woman.

Madroda, Ade (he/him)—Teenage orphan living rough on *The Hub* after losing both his parents.

Marbletown (place)—The colloquial name for the Admin District at the very centre of *The Cog*, named such because of the majority of the administration buildings being made of marble.

Midnight Scythe (ship)—The vessel helmed by the undead pirate captain, Bottomless Braddock.

Mimi Chul Fifth-of-Clouds (she/her)—The sky captain of a ramshackle deathtrap one-person flying ship and widely considered to be more than a little insane for doing so. Rumour to be one of the few who ever looked into the *Font of Souls*.

Ninerville (place)—A graveyard on one of the larger floating rocks of *The Leftovers,* where the scavengers bring and tend to the bodies they find of the 99.9% who didn't quite manage immortality.

Pennyspire, Anita (she/her)—The Postmistress and Curator at Bayside, Anita revels in regaling visitors with rambling tales and descriptions of the various curios on display and charging a small fortune for her aviatory services.

Oboler, Doctor Regina Smith (she/her)—Famous academic scholar living aboard *The Archarrier*.

Orff-on-the-Crags (place)—The final stepping stone for those en route to *Frostborne* either by sea or air.

Reckoning, The (event)—An uprising against the governors of the *Hub*. It was a closely fought battle, with only *The Cog* surviving and the rest of the *Hub* having to be rebuilt from scratch. Security has been tripled since that day to protect the *Hub* and those who trade there.

Red-eyed Jackal, the (he/him)—Infamous sky-pirate and captain aboard *The Ambush*.

Ruddy Nimbus (ship)—Vessel formerly helmed by *Arlan Kalbrunner*.

Rustowne—Named aptly for its forever rusted metal buildings and gears (unavoidable from the constant spray of storm mist from *The Whispering Isle*), this floating city is seemingly connected to *The Whispering Isle* by a bridge of rusted metal and chain.

Saise—*See Saiseriet.*

Saiseriet (they/them)—The all-but-official groundskeeper of *the Crypt*. No one pays them, as far as anyone can tell, and no one knows quite how they began working there. Commonly known as "*Saise*."

Skyfleet—The organization of constabularies which work together to uphold the law of the sky, islands, sea, and those who travel between. While there are constables, *Skyfleet* acts to serve as both law enforcement and to maintain societal balance.

Sky Point (place)—A small, rickety, skyport high in the mountains that bisect *Kimichula*.

Stickleback, the (ship)—The vessel helmed by *Sylvie Anchorfast*.

Stone, Patrick (he/his)—A strange fellow with a bushy beard and no hair on his head and not standing an inch over five feet with broad, muscular arms. The barkeep and owner of *The Crimson Cog*.

Taft, Melody (she/her)—Long-term *Cog* resident, known for her boisterous, flirtatious personality and beautiful singing voice. Often found performing nightly at *The Cog's* taverns.

Whispering Isle, The (place)—A floating island shrouded in violent storms. A constant whirling waterspout connects to the ocean below. Said to be the source of the Well of Eternal Life and named for the soft whispers created by the storms.

White Wasteland (place)—A vast area to the north, in the frozen wastes of the Ice Talon Sea. It has never been mapped.

White Whale, the (place)—A marble-clad building colloquially referred to as the "White Whale," and is The Hub's central bank. But gold is heavy, and even with recent technological advances, no one quite knows how the vault and its riches stay aloft.

Witness Tower, The (place)—An eye-topped tower found in the city of *Endrapo* on the island of *Kimichula*. Water pools because of constant mist and rain, and the eye seems to weep.

Xu, Amelia (she/her)—The fifteen-year-old daughter of two cartographers, Amelia loves *The Archarrier* and the constant adventure of life afloat.

SPACE PIRATE INDEX

AN ACCOUNTING OF THE STAR SYSTEMS IN THE WORLD'S END GALAXY

Abraxes (he/him)—A pirate now banned from every polite system in the galaxy. His last venture left him stranded on *Restless Home*, where a tumultuous affair with *Franx* brought him a new ship and one goal: to capture the *Kraken*.

Agamemnon, the (ship)—Stationed above *First Moon* spaceport, a large dreadnought that protects the moon. *Jaccus Estany* is overseer. See also: *thu'Alar*.

Bazman (place)—A constructed city near *the Lighthouse* and *Forden's Cove*.

Bombing of RSC *Duchess of Windsor* (event)—A terrorist attack which destroyed the Revenue Service cutter *Duchess of Windsor* and almost all of her crew. *See also: Major Geffrey Teller, Johnny Dillinger, Revenue Service.*

Booster Jane (she/her)—A fictional sci-fi pulp heroine of TV, film and tie-in media fame. Very popular within the Sector. Broadcast from *New Aegean*.

Bottomless Braddock—*see Braddock, Maria.*

Braddock, Maria (she/her)—Dread captain Maria "Bottomless" Braddock is master and commander of the *Midnight Scythe*.

Caranthem, Hope (she/her)—Wife of the former Duke and mother of the current *Duchess Grace* of *Dauntless III*. Also known as the Dowager Duchess of Dauntless III.

Carathem, Grace Hotencia (she/her)—Duchess Grace. A 16 year-old heiress to the *Dauntless III* empire. Also known as the Young Duchess of Dauntless III.

Cheater's Lounge (place)—Part of the *Idonian Casino* where the troublemakers get tossed.

Cold Harbor (place)—A secluded, almost inhospitable port on a blizzard strewn planetoid. Pirate safe-haven.

D3DF—*see Dauntless III Defense Forces.*

D'Argon, Dianna (she/her)—Femme fatale, notorious *Qozarx* shark and spy.

Dauntless III (place)—An Earth-like world, it was one of the prime battlegrounds of the *Karrack Wars*. Ruled by a Duke (or Duchess).

Dauntless III Defense Forces—The military of the world *Dauntless III*. Was involved in the *Karrack Wars* when the *Karrak'Ul Worldfleet* attacked without provocation.

DeBeers, Joseph "Diamond" (he/him)—Bartender in the *Idonian*

Casino, not afraid to bounce patrons out the door himself. Big hands, bald head, cauliflower ears. Looks at everyone with contempt, but has a soft spot for babies and cats.

Delving Prime (place)—A mine on *Restless Home.*

Dillinger, Johnny "Muffy" (he/him)—An ace pilot and veteran of the *Karrack Wars,* he's a mercenary willing to sign on to any crew that will pay well and provide him the chance to fly. A secret agent of the *Revenue Service* currently aboard the *PC Guttersnipe,* he originally flew with the *Dauntless III Defense Forces.*

Displacer—Worn on the wrist and known colloquially as a "watch." Personal teleportation device.

Duchess of Windsor (ship)—A *Revenue Service* cutter commanded by *Geoffry Tellar.* Was destroyed in the *Bombing of RSC Duchess of Windsor.*

Ekidnolk Golem—a statue erected to an ancient God of a lost people. The gems that once covered the golem, if found and gathered, have mystical powers.

Estany, Jaccus (he/him)—Master of the *Agamemnon,* a ship crewed entirely by robots. Once known as "Jack" of *Cold Harbour,* owner of *Jack's Robot Repair and Pawn.*

First Moon (place)—Innermost moon of thu'Alar. Royal palaces and glass spires, gentlemen's duels and rocket races. The heart of *thu'Alar* culture. *See also: the Agamemnon, the King of thu'Alar.*

Forden's Cove (place)—continent-sized recreation grounds. Subterranean hot springs, fishing lakes, inland sailing seas, beaches and rolling grasslands, glittering resorts, top-notch restaurants and pounding nightlife.

Franx (he/him)—A wily young resident of *Restless Home,* full of mischief and big dreams.

Great Scuttling (event)—The final act of the last *Queen Ram* that marked the end of the *Karrack Wars,* in which the *Princes* crashed the remaining *Hiveworlds* into the asteroids of the *Karkane Shoals.*

Grendelfell (place)—Human colony destroyed by the *Karrak'ul* in the *Karrack Wars.*

Guttersnipe (ship)—A PC (patrol craft) class starcraft helmed by *Johnny Dillinger. Pickering* is the onboard AI.

Hardreach (place)—Human colony destroyed by the *Karrak'ul* in the *Karrack Wars.*

Hiveworld—The habitations of the *Karrak'ul.* Each ruled by a *Prince,* who in turn is commanded by the *Queen Ram.* Mostly inhabited by drones.

Holy Mountain of Souls, the (place)—The largest mountain of any moon of *thu'Alar.* Located on *Last Moon.* The people of thu'Alar consider the mountain sacred, and *the Kraken Cult* conducts ceremonies here.

Idonian Casino (place)—On the exclusive upper decks of the *Valdian Gateway,* a place to see and be seen, but patrons must watch their belongings and their backs from the cutthroats moving in the shadows. *See also: the Tube Network, the Cheater's Lounge.*

Jack's Robot Repair and Pawn (place)—A former warehouse in *Cold Harbour*. Jack doesn't exist, but the robot running the place thinks he does. *See: Estany, Jaccus.*

Karrak Wars (event)—A destructive war where the *Karrak'ul* race, driven mad by the song of their *Queen Ram*, attacked multiple Human colonies.

Karrak'ul—An extinct race of techno-organic insectoid aliens. They used to exist on *hiveworlds* of the Karrak'ul *Worldfleet*. Most died in the *Karrack Wars*. See also: *Queen Ram, Princes, the Great Scuttling.*

King of thu'Alar, The (he/his)—Sent out a letter of marque to allow privateers to commandeer ships for him, so his people can flee their dying sun. Offers wealth, and the secret of *thu'Alar* as reward.

Kraken, the—An inter-dimensional monstrosity of unknown origin. Most believe it to be a rumor or legend, though adherents of the *Cult of the Kraken* prophecy its imminent return and subsequent destruction of the universe.

Kraken, Cult of—Mostly found on *Tunis* and *thu'Alar*. Religious extremists trying to appease the *Kraken*. Seen by outsiders as a "doomsday cult."

Last Moon (place)—Outermost moon of thu'Alar. Confiscated by the *Revenue Service* as punishment for the Kingdom aiding and abetting piracy. The *Kraken Cult* visits the *Holy Mountain of Souls*. *See also: Nuramses Core.*

Lighthouse, the (place)—a space station rumored to be as old as the black hole it orbits. No one knows who built it. The light is so intense and so concentrated it can clear the event horizon, warning ships on all sides. *See also: Forden's Cove, New Aegean.*

Ludanite Assassins—a species of canine-like creatures.

Maelstrom (Place)—Ever shifting debris, asteroids of all sizes, some of which are inhabited. Pirates here are ready to prey on the unwary. *See also: Tunis.*

Midnight Scythe (ship)—Helmed by the infamous pirate captain *Maria Braddock*, the Midnight Scythe is known and feared across the sector. Only her crew knows how to run the ship.

New Aegean (place)—the central decks of *the Lighthouse* space station where the permanent inhabitants live. *See also: Uptown.*

Nuramses Core (place)—A *Revenue Service* outpost on *Last Moon* of *thu'Alar*.

Pickering (he/his)—*PC Guttersnipe*'s onboard AI. A ROTWALL5+ scale intelligence. A sarcastic yet polite fellow.

Prince—The leader of a *Karrak'ul Hiveworld*. Each Prince begins as a drone, but becomes female when it ascends to its command. When a *Queen Ram* dies, these Princes lay a brood of junior princes on their own hiveworld, and then battle each other for the position of Queen Ram.

Qozarx—Space chess!

Queen Ram—Ruler of the *Karrak'ul*.

Restless Home (place)—Inhabited by opportunists, scrappers, looking for shipwrecks and salvage. *See also: Cold Harbour.*

Revenue Service—Law enforcement and tax collection. While most Revenue Service officers are honest and try to maintain the peace, there is a great amount of corruption.

Tellar, Geoffrey—Former pilot with the *Dauntless III Defense Forces* and subsequent commander of *RSC Duchess of Windsor*. *See also: Johnny Dillinger.*

Thrull, Parson (they/he)—A resident of *the Tube network*, this alien has yet to be seen outside of their vaguely humanoid environment suit. Should he approach you unbidden, many say it is to tell you of your future doom.

thu'Alar (place)—A gas giant orbiting a dying star. Moons are inhabited, and the planetary system is the Kingdom of thu'Alar. The core of the planet, if touched, grants eternal life. *See also: The King of thu'Alar, First Moon, Last Moon.*

Trenchfall (place)—On starless nights, vessels from space emerge from the darkness to make a moving market. Traders, pirates and money flow through here.

Tube Network, the (place)—The high speed tunnel system that connects different parts of the *Valdian Gateway.*

Tunis (place)—The largest asteroid in the *Maelstrom.*

Uptown (place)—A slum in *New Aegean.*

Valdian Gateway, the (place)—Merchant market fused together from shards and hulls of old spaceships. *See also: Trenchfall, Idonian Casino.*

Worldfleet—The collection of *Karrak'ul Hiveworlds.* Ruled by the Queen Ram.

Wulf (he/them)—A member of the elusive *Ludanite Assassins.*

Zayats, Yuri (he/him)—Navigator of the *Midnight Scythe.*

AN ACCOUNTING OF THE ISLANDS
SURROUNDING THE KRAKEN'S WHIRLPOOL

Anne (she/her)—*Baron's* daughter and *Barry's* sweetheart.

Annesley (he/him)—One of *Captain Montgomery's* crew.

Azrael's Fountain (place)— A fountain located in the City of St. Nicholas on the Isla de Los Torcidos. The fountain, also called "Death's Fountain," is rumored to reveal your death to you when you gaze into it.

Baron, the—Anne's Father.

Barty (he/him)—A young man who lived in the monastery and fell in love with *the Baron's* daughter.

Black Albatross (ship)—Vessell helmed by *Captain Lutterell* where *Jules* is Quartermaster.

Black Raven (ship)—Ship of *Ivarr Bloodyhand*.

Bostock (he/him)—One of *Captain Montgomery's* crew, *Roman's* best friend.

Bottomless Braddock—*see Braddock, Captain.*

Braddock, Captain (she/her)—Captain of the *Midnight Scythe.* Known as "Bottomless Braddock."

Cartwright, Jessica (she/her)—Jessica Cartwright began her life as a maid before becoming the fearsome *Green-Eyed Jess*, a member of the infamous *Captain Bottomless Braddock's* crew aboard the *Midnight Scythe.*

Corpus, Father (he/his)—Keeper of the infamous *map*, secret ally to *Rigetti*. Their opposing ideas are the perfect cover up for their possession of the map.

'Craft Rod' Cresser (he/his)—Highwayman, friend and colleague of *Cut-Lass Kate.*

Crimson Blade (ship)— The ship run by *Captain Montgomery* and where *Roman* is Quartermaster.

Cut-Lass Kate (she/her)—Highwayman.

Delacroix Family, The— A wealthy family who make their home in Port Iberia on Isla de Luz. They were rumored to have possessed a piece of the Map of Ages; however, some time ago their manor house burned down under mysterious circumstances, and the piece of the Map was never reported as recovered.

Drea (she/her)—Harvests non-viable Kraken eggs which she consumes, allowing her to divine the whereabouts of anyone or anything in any world.

Doc (he/his) - Doctor on *The Black Albatross* who helps *Jules* recover from losing an eye.

Duvalle, Lady Katharine Montoya—A member of the nobility of *St. Nicholas*, secretly also a Highwayman known as *Cut-Lass Kate*. Later becomes Captain of the *Black Raven*.

Edda, Lia (she/her)—Works in *Le Chevalier Riant*. Lisa is perfectly placed to pick up information from all those who frequent the place, and can often be paid (handsomely!) to share that knowledge with others.

El Asilo Pequeño (place)—Island to the north of *Isla de Los Torcidos*, often used by pirates. Translates to "Little Sanctuary."

Fountain Keepers, the— A holy order in the City of St. Nicholas responsible for the maintenance of the fountains and aqueducts of the city, including the fabled Asrael's Fountain.

Gaudet, Wawu (he/his)—A local of *St Madeleine*, friend to *Juan* and *Dr. Pendergast*. Has three children, named Abby, Gabe, and Felicity.

Gauerdia , Old Lady (she/her)—Lives on *Marshgrave* and frequents the *Midnight Market*. If she's in a good mood she might warn you of danger to come, but if she's not, it's whispered she might just steal a few years from your life.

Godfrey (he/him)—One of *Captain Lutterell's* crew and a trouble maker who does not like *Captain Montgomery's Crimson Blade* crew.

Green-Eyed Jess—*see Cartwright, Jessica.*

Kift, Dylan 'Dil' (he/his)—Highwayman, friend and colleague of *Cut-Lass Kate.'*

Lutterell, Captain—Captain of the *Black Albatross.*

Isla de Los Torcidos— The island which is rumored to house Asrael's Fountain. Home to the cities of St. Nicholas and Newport.

Ivarr Bloodyhand (he/him)—Pirate Captain of the *Black Raven,* responsible for the death of the sister of *Lady Katharine Montoya Duvalle.*

Juan (them)—A local of *St Madeleine,* friend to *Wawu Gaudet* and *Dr. Pendergast.*

Jules (they/them)—Quartermaster to the *Black Albatross,* despondent about having lost an eye in a recent treasure acquisition, ends up flirting with *Roman* for the hell of it.

Kraken, the—a massive creature that appears in all the worlds of the multiverse, the inter-dimensional travel of which can result in the transportation of people and objects through the resulting portals.

Lantern Jack—Drunkard who can usually be found lying at the base of the old temple stone lantern. For a pint, Jack will tell the story of the lantern—a story that changes with every telling and which he rarely finishes before slipping off into a drunken stupor.

Lee, Andrea (she/her)—Andrea "the Chemist" Lee is *Captain*

Braddock's resident munitions and chemicals expert aboard the *Midnight Scythe*.

Little Sanctuary—*see El Asilo Pequeño.*

Map of Ages, the— Map rumored to show ways to pass through the multiverse.

Lockheart, Tamara J. (she/her)—A beautiful young woman with eyes the colour of the ocean and more knives hidden on her body than fish in the sea; she runs her family fish stall in *Half-Moon Landing*. Her older sister ran away to join *Bottomless Braddock's* crew, never to be seen again.

Longfellow, Tobias (his/her)—curator of the The College library special collections materials. Looks too young to have a tenured position, linguistically speaking sounds too old for his age—might be immortal?

Luther, Sailing Master (he/him)—Sailing Master for *Black Albatross*.

Lutterell, Captain (he/his)—Captain of the *Black Albatross* and in perpetual conflict with *Captain Montgomery* and the crew of the *Crimson Blade*.

Malone (he/him)—Friend to *Roman* and *Bostock*. Tends to get people into trouble.

Marie (she/her)—Friend and maid of *Lady Katharine Montoya Duvalle*.

Midnight Scythe (ship)—The infamous vessel helmed by *Captain Braddock*.

Monsell, Sailing Master (he/him)—Sailing Master for the *Crimson Blade*.

Montgomery, Captain (she/her)—Captain of the *Crimson Blade* and in perpetual conflict with *Captain Lutterell* and the *Black Albatross* crew.

Parker (he/his) - Captain in His Majesty's Navy, interested in acquiring Quartermaster *Jules* from *The Black Albatross*.

Palmer (he/his)—Cabin Boy for the *Black Albatross*.

Pendergast, Doctor (he/his)—A ship's doctor who was washed up on *St. Madeline* many years ago when his ship was struck down by storms. He tends to the sick and dying of Selona, many of whom have drunk from the polluted waters of *The Wishing Well*.

Pendergast, Kit (she/her)—found as a small child and raised by Doctor Pendergast. Many in the area whisper that her proper name is actually Lenora and that she is only waiting until Pendergast's eventual death to wipe them all from her island.

Regetti—Owner of *Rigetti's Marvelous Repository*.

Regetti's Marvelous Repository (place)—A business owned by *Regetti*.

Roman (he/his) - Quartermaster of *Captain Montgomery's The Crimson Blade*. Being sick in love over a crush that does not return the interest, he ends up flirting with *Jules* at a party.

Sanderson (he/him)—One of *Captain Lutterell's* crew and a trouble maker who does not like *Captain Montgomery's Crimson Blade* crew.

Stickleby, Barnard (he/his)—Owns the only highend ships on the *Atoll of the Giants* selling chocolates and sugar.

Saint Madeline—An island wreathed in nearly impassable storms. Home to the Well of Eternal Life.

Tyndall (he/his)—A belligerent, sword-happy crewmember of *Captain Lutterell's Black Albatross*.

Well of Eternal Life, the—Sometimes called Lenora's Fountain, the well possesses waters that will supposedly grant the drinker eternal life.

ACKNOWLEDGMENTS

It's hard enough to thank everyone involved in any project, let alone one as large and sprawling as this one—let alone one that encompasses multiple universes. Still, we would be remiss if we did not attempt, at least, to thank some of the people who have been instrumental in making this book a reality:

All the writers who have spent the last four months fleshing out the various worlds, characters, maps and all the strange details to our small section of the multiverse. Each time we launch a book, I am honored and flattered to have so many talented writers eager to take part.

Our four cartographers, who each brought a unique flair to their respective worlds. Everyone knows the best part of a fantasy book is the maps. Aaron Hockett has been with us since Volume 1, but we are grateful in the extreme to Dewi Hargreaves and Michael D. Nadeau for stowing away with us on this volume as well.

Our guest editors, as without them we would still be working on editing and proofreading. None of them were paid, and all worked incredibly hard to get this book ship-shape. B. K. Bass, Jayme Bean, A. R. K. Horton, and Jeremy Nelson stayed aboard after Volume 2, and this time we press-ganged A. E. Bross, C. J. Henderson, Chapel Orahamm, and Katherine Shaw into service as well. A special thanks to Jonathan Beck and Sarah Parker, who just refused to go away until we gave them work to do. And while it was a team effort, C. J. went above and beyond with her detailed line-edits of the final manuscript. I don't know what super-power allows her to do things like find an unbolded colon on page 257, but I'm grateful for whatever radioactive grammar spider bit her.

While everyone contributed to the Indexes, they would not be nearly as complete and organized as they are without the help of Jayme Bean and Lisa Kuznak, both of whom tackled the entries for their respective worlds with a nerdy-gusto that was truly inspired.

Thanks to Duy Phan, the illustrator who did our fantastic cover. We've commissioned him for each of our covers and he never disappoints. He's available for hire as Phanduy on Fiverr. Fiverr is also where we found the artists who did the author portraits as well, so thanks to TBL Kobka, Katherine Ellis, and Sang Nguyen for taking our weirdly specific requests (could you give her a head-band with a Kraken on it? And a cat sitting on her shoulder?) and bringing them to life. And thanks to Kristian Kuznak for supplying the fantastic illustration that accompanies his wife's story, "Debt Collection."

This volume's world building used a hack of Caro Asercion's game *I'm Sorry, Did You Say Street Magic.* While highly modified to fit our unique needs, Asercion's game was instrumental in how the various multiverses were formed. That said, Skullgate Media is not associated with Asercion in any official capacity, so don't blame them. Instead, go buy a copy and play it with some friends. Maybe you'll wind up with an anthology yourself…

A huge thank you to all our Kickstarter backers. We were gobsmacked when we reached our funding goal in under 12 hours, then gobsmacked a second time when we hit 500% of our initial goal. Your enthusiasm and support let us buy this amazing cover, as well the creator portraits that accompany each team of writers. Whether you could give one dollar or one-hundred, your trust and encouragement was priceless.

Thanks to the #WritingCommunity on Twitter. Skullgate was formed after a random tweet and we continue to find most of our authors on that platform. Social media may be a dumpster fire that will bring about the end of the world, but at least there's one corner where cool writers hang out and support each other. And we'll ride out the impending apocalypse in that abandoned fort off the coast of Wales we're going to buy together.

Thanks to the reviewers who agreed to look at advanced copies and shared their impressions with the world. While pirate captains tend to keel-hull stowaways, we're glad you smuggled yourself aboard. There's a parallel universe where we could print the book *after* you've read it and so include you by name, but since we're stuck in a reality with linear time, we can't.

Last, a huge thanks from myself to the other members of Skullgate Media: Colleen Storiz, Chris Durston, Diana Gagliardi, and Debbie Iancu-Haddad. As president and editor-in-chief, I get to be the public face of Skullgate, but this fledgling company wouldn't exist without the four of them. Each of us brings a unique strength to publishing, and like the cartoon-classic, Voltron, we join together to form something amazing. Thanks for being my mechanical lions!

—C. Vandyke

KICKSTARTER BACKERS

The following people helped make *In The Wake of the Kraken* possible through their financial support. Many generously added donations over and above these standard backing levels, but whether they contributed $4 or $100, we are eternally grateful to each and every person who helped fund this book:

Backers: *Aaron Jamieson, Aaron Rohrdanz, Abe Scheppler, A.E. Bross, Alex Niemi, Andrew Martin, B. Harris, Blake R. Wolfe, Brandon Lubke, Charlotte Gidman, Chris Durston, Christine Sponem, C.J. Henderson, Cynthia Hamill, Dalibor Žujović, Daniele Ancona, Dan James, Dennis Ramirez, David Collins, Debbie Iancu-Haddad, Diana Chelagat Oboler Gagliardi, Emily P, ER Hoffer, Ernesto Pavan, Gary Mack, GreenShirt52, Jacen Leonard, Jaecyn Boné, Jayme Bean, Jeremy, Jess, John Miyasato, Jonathan Beck, Jonathan Helland, JQ, Julia Pillard, Julianne Rosselli, Kai Delmas, Katherine Shaw, Laurence, Louise Willingham, Lyndsey Croal, Markus Schubert, Martin Coulter, MG Mason, Nina Silver Chair, Ollie Bowdoin, Paul Kamo, Philip Rudwick, Richard Whipkey, Right Reverend [REDACTED] Ryan Richards, Robert Conall, Roger Kristian Jones, Rue Sparks, Ruth Pattison, Sarah Remy, Sean Campbell, Sebastian H., Shane "Ahsaron" Sylvia, Stefan Kamburov,*

Sondra Fielder, SwordFirey, Tad Kelson, Teri Pratt, Thad, Thomas Sedlmair, Victoria Corva, Vulpecula, Wahrman Family, Winst0lf

Creative Chaos VIPs: *Count Matthew Von Dombroski, Lynne Jameson, Michael Durham, Todd R.*

Ultra-Backer Chaos VIPs Extraordinaire: *Darius Bearguard, Gina Oboler, The Kift family, Paul Renner, Richard & Mary Van Dyke, Rodney J. Cressey, Taiylor Wallace, Wawu Gaudet*

CONTRIBUTORS

WRITERS

Alexis Ames is a science fiction writer currently living in Minnesota, and her work has previously appeared in publications such as *Pseudopod, All Worlds Wayfarer,* and *Luna Station Quarterly.* Find links to her other stories on her website (https://alexisames.home.blog) and connect with her on Twitter as @alexis_writes1.

Dani Atkinson is a short fiction fantasy writer from Alberta, Canada who occasionally has more in common with an anxious cat hiding under the sofa than she does with a human being. Find out more at her frequently neglected author blog, https://dejadrew.dreamwidth.org/

Caroline Barnard-Smith writes fantasy and horror fiction from her house beside the sea in Devon, England, where she lives with one husband, three daughters, and a small ginger cat called Frodo. She enjoys creating worlds and drinking all the rum. She's on Twitter as @cazzysmith.

Ian Barr is a fantasy author living in Winnipeg. An alumnus of TFYB Vol. 1, he's excited to continue growing this weird, wonderful series. In addition to TFYB, Ian's recently released debut novel *Synthetic Magic: The Bloodless Affairs Vol. 1* is available now. Twitter: @ibarrwrites. (*Vol. 1 Alum*)

B. K. Bass is the author of over a dozen books of science fiction, fantasy, and horror inspired by pulp fiction magazines and classic speculative fiction. He is also an avid worldbuilder, a blender of genres, and a student of history. More about B.K. can be found on his website, bkbass.com. (*Vol. 2 Alum, Guest Editor*)

Jayme Bean is an author hailing from Florida. A semi-retired zookeeper and full-time Mom, her debut adventure novel, *Untouched* is out now! You can follow her on twitter @JaymeBeanAuthor or find out more about her and her work at JaymeBeanAuthor.com. (*Vol. 2 Alum, Guest Editor*)

A. E. Bross is an author, librarian, and occasionally delightful individual most known for the *Sands of Theia* fantasy book series. She is passionate about the accessibility of writing, elevating marginalized voices, and romantic tropes. Twitter: @AddyBrossWrites, Instagram: @AddyBross_Writes, Website: addyelsewhere.com. (*Guest Editor*)

J. Calamy is a queer, disabled veteran and foreign service wonk who spends a good part of the year bouncing down dirt roads in the back of range rovers thousands of miles from home. She writes volcanic romantic thrillers through that lens. Coffee, cursing, and embassy scuttlebutt are her last remaining vices. Learn more at JCalamy.com.

S. D. Campbell is an Islander currently living in Calgary, Alberta. His first book, *Tin-Can Canucks: A Century of Canadian Destroyers* is a history of Royal Canadian Navy destroyers. Sean's anthology *Before the Crash* collects his previously published short fiction. He lives with his teen-aged daughter and several guinea pig ghosts.

Gregory Coley is a self-published author with a dozen books under his belt. He currently lives in a small town near Dallas.

Follow him on Twitter at @Ghreggori, or find him online at his website, https://gkcoley.wixsite.com/gregorycoleywriting (*Vol. 1 Alum*)

Darby Cupid can usually be found hiding from her kids in order to write YA and MG books. Find out more at darbycupid.com or find her on Twitter @darbycupid. (*Vol. 1 Alum*)

A. R. K. Horton writes blogs about myths, fairytales, and folktales. She is also a fantasy author who recently completed *The Telverin Trilogy*. When she isn't writing, she's busy managing a family of five. You can find her blog and links to her books at arkhorton.com. (*Vol. 2 Alum, Guest Editor*)

Jack Kaide is a writer, musician and teacher living in Hackney, London. His short stories have recently featured in *Horrified Magazine* and *The Secret Attic, Volume 6,* and he is currently working on a first novel, *The Green Man.* You can find him on twitter @TheSomnambulis2.

Astrid Knight is a fantasy writer from Michigan with a fascination for stories and what they reveal about ourselves. When she isn't writing, she can be found playing D&D and impulse buying candles online. Her first novel, *Perception Check*, will debut January 2022. She can be found on Twitter @AstridKWrites.

Lisa Kuznak hails from the frozen north, deep in the boreal forest of Canada, and always has a project on the go to stave off the chill. Whether it's sci-fi, fantasy, horror or historical, you know she's blasting music while she writes. Catch her on Instagram at @lisak.writes.

C. J. Henderson is a Scottish writer with a deep and abiding interest in the sea and its various denizens, both real and imaginary. She can be found on Twitter as @LadyKrakenWrite. (*Guest Editor*)

Robert Mammone lives in Melbourne, Australia, and has been writing since the 90s. He's written horror and fantasy as well as a grimdark novella. His work has appeared in *Candy Jar Books* and *Dr. Who Magazine*. You can find him on twitter @dreadsinister and co-hosting the *42 to Doomsday* podcast.

Jeremy Nelson is a recent transplant to Edinburgh whose after-images linger in Hong Kong and Portland, Oregon. His preoccupations include accordions, photography, and outdated methods of putting words to paper. You can find him on Twitter now as @jpaknelson. (*Vol. 2 Alum, Guest Editor*)

Chapel Orahamm is an Illustrator, academic, and author, who lives in the middle of no-man's-land big sky country. They have a passion for slipstream, romance, LGBTQ novels and the odd short story. Straddling the line between grunge and sappy prose, their world can be found online at KavordianLibrary.com. (*Vol. 1 Alum, Guest Editor*)

J. C. Pillard lives at the foot of the Colorado mountains. She has a master's degree in English literature and her recent publications include stories in *Broadswords and Blasters* and *Fall Into Fantasy*. When not writing, J. C. can be found prowling through her local bookstore. Find her on Twitter @JCPillard and at www.jcpillard.com.

Craig Rathbone is a writer from a little town in the north of England. With a writing background in video game reviews and blogging, he's developed an insatiable taste for pirate-themed tales!

Harry F. Rey is a Scottish author and lover of LGBTQ fiction. His works include the epic queer sci-fi series, *The Galactic Captains;* royal romance novels, *The Line of Succession;* and gay rom-com, *All The Lovers.* Find him at his website or talking about queer books on Twitter @Harry_F_Rey.

Katherine Shaw is a multi-genre writer and self-confessed nerd from Yorkshire in the United Kingdom, spending most of her time dreaming up new characters or playing D&D. You can find more about her and her latest work at her website, and she is always happy to chat on Twitter @katheroony. (*Guest Editor*)

Imelda Taylor is a full-time mother from Hertfordshire, England. She mainly writes children's books, though her imagination takes her to other places on occasion. Her work appears in several anthologies and is actively seeking representation. As a former educator, she is an avid promoter of literacy. Follow her on Twitter @lostsheep2 and Instagram @lostsheep.is. (*Vol. 1 Alum*)

CARTOGRAPHERS

Dewi Hargreaves (*Pirates of the Sea*) is a freelance illustrator who has created over 50 maps, mostly for clients in the writing community. He primarily works in the fantasy style, but has created historical, contemporary and sci-fi maps, too. You can commission art from him at his website, DewiHargreaves.com.

Aaron Hockett (*Pirates of the Sky*) is a New York City based architect, illustrator, amateur cartographer, and aspiring cartoonist. His previous work includes the maps for Volume 1 of Tales From the Year Between. Aaron's comic work can be found on Instagram at @hockett.aaron. (*Vol. 1 & 2 Alum*).

Michael D. Nadeau (*Pirates of the Fantastic*) was born in the usual way, then found fantasy at the age of eight with *Dungeons & Dragons*. He soon discovered his love for reading and started creating his own worlds. After he created cities, gods, ancient and terrible beings and histories, he would then burn them all down.

C. Vandyke (*Pirates of the Stars*) primarily focuses on his writing and publishing chops these days, but is also an avid drawer and doodler. He's almost never written a story without drawing a map to go with it, though he'll often draw a map without bothering to write a story.

EDITORIAL TEAM

Jonathan Beck is a singer and writer from Northern Ireland who loves cats, whiskey and traveling (when permitted). When he's not running or binge-watching sci-fi, he can be found writing weird little tweet-stories as @diminufiction. (*Vol. 1&2 Alum, Guest Staff*)

Chris "Terry" Durston lives in England, where he subsists on cider and 'taters. Apart from his editorial duties, he produces Skullgate's podcast, *Sounds From the Year Between*. His first novel, *Each Little Universe*, was released in April 2020. Find him at chris-durston.com or on Twitter @overthinkery1. (*Skullgate Staff*)

Diana C. Gagliardi helps run the world-building as one of the Game Masters for each book when not writing herself. When not gaming on board, table, or in-person Diana enjoys singing in harmony and quoting Monty Python in and around Philadelphia with her personal child who is now a teenager. (*Skullgate Staff, Game Master*)

Debbie Iancu-Haddad is currently querying a couple of YA SFF novels, participating in three different anthologies, writing vss on Twitter and buying way too much stuff on Aliexpress. For her day job she gives lectures on humor and serves as a personal chauffeur for her two teenagers. Resides in Meitar, Israel. Follow @debbieiancu or her website, https://debbieiancu.wixsite.com/my-funny-life. (*Skullgate Staff*)

S. L. Parker: world builder, wonderer and as a result, writer. Plays well with words and others. Prior publications in poetic and academic veins. WIP exploring creation of civilization and what if step-sisters of the divided ruling family were Fear and True Love. Tweets via @isparkit. (*Vol. 1 &2 Alum, Guest Staff*)

C. D. Storiz is a Teacher by day, writer at night. As a member of the skullgatemedia.com team, she helps to slay em dashes. She also has work published through various other outlets. You can follow her on Twitter @LeChatGris3 or at cdstoriz.com where she posts writing and rants about her cat. (*Skullgate Staff*)

Chris "Prime" Vandyke is the founder and president of Skullgate media and the Editor-in-Chief of TFYB. He always has more ideas than is good for him, and needs the others to help restrain his naive enthusiasm. You can see things he writes at cvandyke.com and follow him at @aboutrunning. (*Skullgate Staff, Game Master, Hierophant, et cetera*)

ABOUT "TALES FROM THE YEAR BETWEEN"

*T*ales *From the Year Between* is the flagship publication of Skullgate Media, an indie-publishing company dedicated to changing the way authors collaborate and publish.

Part literary magazine, part writing club, part cult, and all creativity, *Tales From the Year Between* is a semi-annual speculative fiction anthology with a unique premise. Each volume gathers a disparate group of authors from all across the globe to collaborate in shared world-building and creative writing. Using hacks of collaborative games as writing prompts, each volume of *The Year Between* begins with nothing more than a simple premise ("a desert fantasy world, like D&D's *Dark Sun*," "a crew lost in space aboard a sentient ship" or "pirates!"). Contributors participate in a week-long "game" to create a shared canon of people, places, events, and themes. From this chaotic melange of ideas, each participant creates their own stories, poems, letters, and even recipes, all set in the world they created together. Intrigued? Sound like fun? See our website on how you could help us make our next world...

*C*rimson Text is a font family for book production in the tradition of beautiful old-style typefaces created by Sebastian Koch and available for free via Google.

Inspired by the wild gyring of the inter-dimensional space Kraken, the small flourishes invoke the tenuous veil of sanity that serves to shield our fragile human minds from the horror that throbs betwixt the stars.

14 Tales of
Madness & Horror

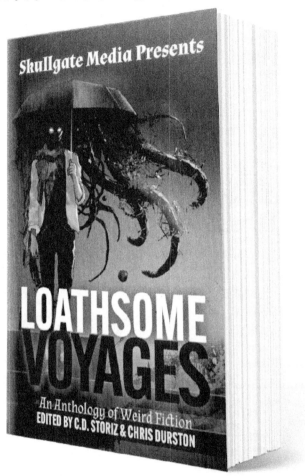

Skullgate Media Presents

LOATHSOME VOYAGES

An Anthology of Weird Fiction

EDITED BY C.D. STORIZ & CHRIS DURSTON

Inspired by the work of weird fiction masters old and new–from Lovecraft to Miéville, from Hodgson to VanderMeer–this treacherous, eldritch volume brings together fourteen of today's best authors of speculative fiction.
(Edited by C.D. Storiz and Chris Duston. Available NOW wherever books are sold.)

Join Skullgate Media
as we embark on our most... **Loathsome Voyages**

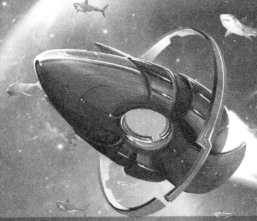

AVAST!
GREAT BOOKS OFF THE
STARBOARD BOW

Looking to pirate some fantastic literature? Too bad, because these books don't exist! At least, not in *this* version of reality. But that doesn't mean they aren't out there...

BRIGADIER BONANZA, by Richard Lee Van Dyke II   12-345-6789 $4.99 ☐
Captain Benjamin Cartwright and his three sons ply the waters searching for silver off the coast of the Virgin Islands. When the crown sends Admiral Roy Coffee to bring the pirates to justice, Cartwright and his family face danger they've never known before.

THE LEMIEUX CHRONICLES VOL. 27—MUTANT PIRATES ATTACK!
by Count Matthew VonDombrowsky   NCC-1701-D $4.99 ☐
The twenty-seventh installment in this beloved series finds Captain Eirin "Terror of the Skies" Lemieux and her second in command, Liam, facing the greatest threat in their seemingly endless career: hot-air balloons helmed by mutant pirates! Will they prevail? Book 28 is already announced, so that sort of spoils the tension, but read it anyway!

WHAT A BEAR DOES IN THE WOODS, by Justin Ball   11-235-8132 $4.99 ☐
The Revenant meets Brown Bear, Brown Bear, What Do You See? in this heart-warming tale of revenge and color identification. Kids will love the simple rhymes, while older readers will love the scenes of bleak violence and despair.

LA PLAYA DEL ORO, by Paul Renner   54-455-4465 $4.99 ☐
All hell breaks loose when a spaceship of interstellar pirates crash-lands in a small town on the Oregon Coast. When the FBI refuses to believe aliens are invading, it's up to the local high school art teacher to save the planet!

PETER PAN (MINUS THE RACIST BITS), by Kate Kift   98-765-4321 $4.99 ☐
An updated retelling of J.M. Barrie's classic Peter Pan, only without the outdated, cringe-inducing descriptions of Native Americans, African tribes, gender-roles, and a variety of other pieces that were "of the time" but now make it impossible to enjoy the fabulous tale of Peter and the Lost Boys. And at half the length, it's a quick read!

If unavailable in your universe, send this coupon and check, money order, or Spanish Guilders for the cost of the book via wormhole to: Skullgate's Interdimension Theoretical Book Depository, 256 Bainbridge Street, Brooklyn, NY 11233. Due to the nature of the multiverse, orders will arrive in 1-2 weeks, as well as late, early, and everything between.

NAME: _____

ADDRESS: _____

_____

Printed in Great Britain
by Amazon